FAR TURN
IN A DEADLY RACE . . .

Up ahead Alex saw the partially open door that led to the several rooms occupied by his old friend and his staff. Pushing through into the outer office, he called out, "Paul, it's me, Alex." The door to the general's inner office stood closed. Alex rapped sharply and opened it. "You ready to . . ."

The room lay dark, silent.

"Paul?" His eyes tried to pierce the darkness.

With his left hand, Alex groped for the light switch. The floor and table lamps about the traditionally decorated room blinked on. Alex's attention was immediately drawn to the colorful American and Air Force Academy flags flanking the general's desk across the room. And then his eyes lowered to . . . what was it? Alexander Kidd's normally strong stomach suddenly wrenched tight as he realized exactly what that disgusting, slimy pile of gore on the desk before him was. "Oh, God," he gasped, trying to swallow the wave of nausea surging up from within him. Turning away, he fell to his knees, forcing his handkerchief over his mouth.

THE THIRD FURY

RUSSELL RHODES

PINNACLE BOOKS   NEW YORK

THE THIRD FURY

Copyright © 1985 by Russell Rhodes

An original Pinnacle Books edition, published for the first time anywhere.

First printing/May 1985

ISBN: 0-523-42525-2
Can. ISBN: 0-523-43476-6

Printed in the United States of America

PINNACLE BOOKS, INC.
1430 Broadway
New York, New York 10018

9   8   7   6   5   4   3   2   1

to Mary Shirley Rhodes
who drove ponies with sleighs down from the
Hill to school in New Hampshire winters,
who cringed as lightning danced over telephone
wires newly strung across the dining room,
who danced to the thing called radio, and then
laughed when television came with Lucy.
And now satellites and shuttles to the moon.
She remains the new generation
and very much loved.

THE THIRD FURY

CHAPTER 1

Howling wind and the crash of waves battering against their small boat drowned the sound of the thunderous blast. Only a brief orange flash gave witness to the explosion off the rugged Albanian coast.

"Enver! Look! Look there!" Beqir Drin shouted into the gale. "What was it?"

"Where?" the other fisherman called. Enver Shkumbi held fast to the swaying mast as he rose unsteadily to squint through the darkness.

"Over there. A great light."

Enver shook his head in disgust and eased himself back down into the boat. "Your Christ walks on water again?" he called back sarcastically.

The other said nothing. He stared westward through the rain toward the detested, capitalist island of Corfu only two kilometers off the Albanian mainland. Enver Shkumbi followed his gaze. A powerful burst of wind momentarily cleared the night air; he saw a red glow in the distance.

"A boat? On fire?" he shouted, knowing the answer. The ancient motor laboriously swung the small boat away from their homeland toward it. His stomach knotted. One of the few things Enver really feared was fire at sea. And in a fierce storm like this one could anyone have survived? But the glow ahead drew them onward.

The violent storm slammed a loose shutter noisily back and forth against the rough stone wall of the old villa. A thick grove of stunted trees screened the house of "The

1

Greek," as the villagers called its foreign inhabitant, from all prying eyes save those from the sea. Below, waves crashed upon the rocks and coarse pebbles of the cove and broiled up toward the beached fishing boats.

In a plain whitewashed room in the villa Shura Butov nagged, "Must I listen to that racket all night? Are you just going to sit there and do nothing?"

The heavyset man seated across the room said nothing. His eyes were riveted to the dials of the radio transmitter before him.

"Anatoli?" she called. "Are you listening to me?"

He looked up scowling and stared at the faded blond woman. Her once beautiful skin hung slack and creased around a too large mouth. *"Never,"* he said slowly, his voice even and stern, *"never* again use that name here. Do you understand?"

She stared back, mocking him with her eyes.

"I am Demetrias Bralo. You are Helene Bralo. I am a doctor, a retired doctor."

"More butcher than doctor."

"And you are my wife, my *Greek* wife," he said.

"And we were married in Athens," Shura Butov continued sarcastically. "Who the hell cares in this forsaken place? We might just as well be on the moon. What have we done since they sent us here? Nothing! What is there to report? Nothing! When last were you contacted by the Resident in Tirane? Six months? Seven? How important does that make you feel, eh?"

"It is only temporary," he countered.

"Temporary?" she shrieked. "Eleven years? Eleven years is temporary?" Tossing aside her well-worn magazine, Shura stood up and strode toward the bedroom. She could have married Gershuni or Veklenko; they had moved up within the organization. Turning back toward Anatoli Butov, she hurled her frustration at him. "You are a failure. Admit it. You have been passed over. You will never . . ."

A loud banging on the villa's door cut her off. They looked questioningly at each other. Butov quickly snapped shut the book-covered doors in the bookcase to conceal the radio, and rose. "Stay back," he cautioned.

As soon as the door was opened, the fisherman Enver Shkumbi staggered into the narrow hall, carrying his sodden burden. Beqir Drin helped his comrade ease the limp, unconscious man from his shoulders down onto the tile floor. "He's alive," the old fisherman said to the doctor, "but not other one."

"Where did you find him?" Anatoli Butov asked as he knelt to begin a rough examination of the large man.

"In the channel. His boat blow up in storm. We bring him to you."

"To me," Butov mumbled. To me, he thought, after you stripped him of every piece of jewelry. He noted the white band of skin on the left wrist of the well-tanned arm.

"You think will be reward?" Enver Shkumbi asked, wiping his wet hair from his eyes. "For saving life?"

"Perhaps," Butov replied. The man should be fine in a few hours; he seemed to be suffering only from exhaustion. The Russian rose and went into his small office. Returning with a hypodermic, he raised the unconscious man's arm and inserted the needle deep into the artery. "Were there any others?" he asked, looking up at Drin.

"One—dead, God take his soul."

Enver Shkumbi cuffed the old man protectively. "Is dead. No breathe."

"Show me," Butov ordered. "Maybe there will be two rewards."

The fishermen looked at each other. Shkumbi smiled.

The trip down the face of the cliff to the cove below was normally treacherous, but the storm made it even more dangerous.

"There," Shkumbi shouted against the wind, pointing toward the dark form sprawled facedown on the pebbles. The man's nautical jacket and white trousers were in shreds, his left shoe missing.

Butov put down his lantern and, kneeling, turned the

body over. Looking back up at the fishermen, he asked, "Does Scutari know about this?"

The two men shook their heads. Sometimes it was best not to let Mehmit Scutari, headman of the village, know about things. He always demanded his share.

"Do you know who this is?"

Again they shook their heads.

The wind and rain forgotten, Butov heard again the words of his wife. "Failure. Passed over." How wrong she was. This was just the beginning for him. In the dim glow of his lantern, the KGB agent smiled as he looked down into the face of the former President of the United States. His hand felt the faint beat of the man's pulse. "Hello, hello," he urged in English.

His eyes still closed, the American's lips tried to form words. Butov leaned low, putting his ear to those lips.

"Yes?" he asked eagerly. "Yes?"

The voice was ragged, barely discernible. "Acheron."

CHAPTER 2

Nearly seven years later, Baron Miklos Androssy stepped from his elegant Sutton Place mansion. Glancing at his watch and waving aside the umbrella his chauffeur held, he sprinted to the open door of the black Rolls-Royce. Resplendent in a dark pin-striped suit and appropriately somber tie, the titan of international finance settled back into the soft leather and ran both hands over his ears to smooth the distinguished streaks of gray hair flowing over his temples. The baron's six-foot-two frame and face looked far younger than his sixty-three years, and he was well aware of it.

As the limousine wound slowly through the Saturday afternoon traffic toward St. Bartholomew's Church on Park Avenue, Androssy stared blankly out through the rain at the smart Manhattan shops and his mind traveled back to the stormy beach in Albania. It was a long distance from there to the Park Avenue church where former President John James Warren lay with the flag of the United States draped over his casket. It would be a simple ceremony befitting a man who had taken pride in his humble origins and befitting an unpopular President who had been secluded from the public eye for seven years. Few people of great importance would be present, only their representatives and those with close personal ties to the late head of state. But among those few might lie the clue to the riddle of Acheron.

He had planned to arrive early to carefully scrutinize those who had come to pay their last respects, but the rain had halted the procession of official limousines and taxis and Androssy found himself trapped within his Rolls. Tapping his fingers impatiently, he allowed his eyes to play over the architectural details of the beautiful Romanesque church up ahead.

He loved beautiful things, had a passion for them. It was a passion that had been nurtured by generations of Androssy scholars and collectors in his native Hungary. He had been born into a pampered life and was surrounded by paintings, porcelain, and sculptured gardens until his world had come crashing down around him with the German invasion in 1939. The family bank collapsed and their fortune evaporated. By the time the Russians occupied Hungary in 1945 he was twenty-four years old and hard—hardened by six years of fighting with the Hungarian underground, by the massacre of his highborn family, and by killing Nazis in personal retaliation for that massacre. Then as now, what drove him on was his ruthless determination to regain the beauty of what he had lost. It had taken years, and he had been forced into strange alliances, but Androssy now stood at the top of a mammoth banking empire of his own creation.

His eyes came to rest on the iron cross atop the great dome of St. Bartholomew's. Supported by stone arches, the dome's elaborate pattern of marble tiles glistened in the rain. He studied it and smiled grimly. He had regained his world of paintings and porcelain; he would keep that world no matter the price.

Finally reaching the entrance, Baron Androssy waited for the chauffeur to open the door and strode briskly up the broad steps of the church. As he walked, his eyes scanned the faces of cameramen and curiosity seekers jamming the pavement on either side of him. He made a mental note of the few people he recognized.

Shaking off the attentions of an usher, Androssy crossed the vestibule. He was so intent on his purpose that he was only barely aware of the marble columns beside him and the brilliant gilt mosaic in the vaulted ceiling overhead. He entered the church by the smaller side aisle. As he moved forward, the soft, somber organ music engulfed him, one subtle chord slowly dissolving into another, one tone into the next flowing smoothly from the nine thousand pipes behind, before, and above him. Although the seating capacity of the church was well over a thousand, less than a hundred mourners now sat on the hard wooden pews. There would be more, he thought, but not many.

The great mosaic figure of Christ, arms outstretched, hovered ominously above him. He took a seat facing north across the pews in the main body of the church. From there he had an unobstructed view not only of the pulpit and lectern, but of all those who had come and would come to mourn the late President.

Israel as well as the moderate Arab states were well represented by ambassadors and top officials who were seated in places of honor. He smiled wryly. John James Warren's administration had not only been characterized by its indecisive and vacillating foreign policy, but by its obsession with the Middle East and the stability of the area. Under his leadership, the United States had poured billions of dollars of military arms, planes, tanks, and guns into Israel, Jordan, Egypt, Saudi Arabia, and the Gulf states—a rash move, most thought. With Warren's death, only three Americans remained who knew the reason and the secret behind it. Those three *and* Miklos Androssy.

The baron looked from one face to the next. Most were personally known to him. His position with the International Bank for Reconstruction and Development had enabled him to make many useful contacts within both the poor and wealthy nations, personal contacts that had proved indispensable to the rapid growth of his financial empire. His eyes moved on.

General Paul George Carmody and his wife were seated in the fourth-row pew directly behind those reserved for the widow and her family. Androssy was well aware of the special relationship that had existed between the general and John Warren. Looking at his blunt, open face, the baron wondered why Carmody had not used that friendship to

advance himself further within the Air Force. But perhaps it
was no surprise. Carmody was a straight shooter and a man
of principle. Warren had chosen well in putting his trust in
the general. Androssy's gaze continued to move down the
pews, stopping, studying each face, and then going on to
the next.

Across Manhattan Alexander Kidd ducked under a
camera boom as he walked across the movie set.

"*Chéri,*" Minon Serron called from the dressing room,
"where have you been all day?" The French star brushed
aside her makeup man and offered both cheeks for Kidd's
kiss.

Instead he slapped her on the backside. "Tied up at the
network. How's it going?"

"*Terrible,*" she pouted. "That director of Oscar's is a
madman, *complètement fou.* He has no soul. He is . . . he
is . . ."

"Not French?" Alex offered.

"Exactly, *chéri,*" she smiled. "You know me so well.
Tonight? My suite?"

"Tomorrow."

The pout returned to her face. "*Bête!* Who is she? Which
one?"

"You know I love only you," he laughed. "Have to
run."

"*Cochon,*" she called after Kidd as he picked his way
back through the maze of electric cables and arc lights.

Outside, he jumped into his Mercedes convertible, taking
the wheel from one of his company's drivers. Ten minutes
later Alexander Kidd leaped out and started for the steps of
St. Bartholomew's but changed course toward a group of
cameramen on his left. The tall, dynamic owner of one of
the most successful satellite television news and international sports networks raised his hand in greeting. Considered a
rogue by the entertainment industry for his willingness to
take business risks of frightening magnitude, Alex Kidd
ruled both his network and his life with hardheaded and

stubborn determination. His risk ventures had made him a wealthy man and enabled him to indulge himself in his passion for sailing. He had just entered his sleek new racing yacht, the *Privateer*, in the Whitbread round-the-world race. It would be Alexander Kidd's first attempt at an international trophy. He was an odds-on favorite. To date, Captain Kidd, as he was often called by the press, had never failed to prove himself, had never lost a major battle.

"Frank?" he inquired of the small man with the camera resting on his shoulder.

"Hi, boss."

"Getting good footage?"

The comely blond woman standing next to the cameraman answered his question. She held a microphone bearing the letters of KWEN in her hand. "No, there's no one of any real interest. I want the Kissingers of the world, at least an astronaut or two. It's a bore out here, Alex." She paused. "And I'm wet." Sandra Bannister pulled the belt of her trenchcoat more tightly, unconsciously emphasizing the curve of her body beneath.

Kidd smiled into her deep blue eyes. "Just one of the many benefits of being a glamorous star reporter for the Kidd Worldwide Entertainment Network," he replied lightly.

She returned his smile. "I can think of things far more glamorous and entertaining to do."

"When the ceremony starts, join me. I've cleared you with Sheila."

"Right."

Giving her arm a nearly imperceptible touch, he turned to mount the broad steps where Page Shepard, executive vice president of KWEN, waited. The two men entered the church together and, as Baron Androssy had done earlier, shunned the attentions of an eager usher as they slipped into a pew to the rear of the rest of the congregation.

"A pretty poor turnout," Shepard commented as he looked about them.

"It's understandable; he was underestimated," Alexander

Kidd replied softly. "We'll see what the historians have to say."

"Oh, come on, Alex, you're fooling yourself and you know it. He was . . ."

"He was my *friend*," Kidd interrupted.

Page Shepard sighed. He knew better than to argue with his old college classmate. When Kidd was a scholarship student at Yale, the Shepard family had tried unsuccessfully to teach the roughcut newcomer the polish and manners of Boston society, but as a man, Kidd had opened their eyes to the weapons of the street and the power they could bring. Try as he could, Alex was always too outspoken for good manners, and the elegant Shepards could never bring themselves to use his street weapons. But they both agreed firmly on one thing—loyalty.

In his rise in the telecommunications world, Kidd had carried Page Shepard with him. In return, Page had always defended him against his detractors and smoothed the controversial waters through which Kidd set the course of his growing network. Like Cain and Abel, they were brothers. But unlike Cain and Abel, they felt no jealousy for the talents and successes of the other.

"How are Mary and the boys?"

"Mary's spending the summer at the Fishers Island house," Page whispered. "Quin's working in the city. He has another year at law school."

"And John?"

"Sailing with his grandfather in Maine."

Alexander Kidd's heart warmed at the thought of Page's father, Quincy Shepard. The stern old disciplinarian had first taken him as a novice aboard his boat and taught him to love the sea. Under his approving eye, Alex had learned well the skills of the sport and revered his mentor as if he had been his own father.

"Where's Mark now?" Page inquired of his friend's twenty-three-year-old son.

"Switzerland, Tangier, who knows?" the other replied sarcastically. "Ask his mother, not me." Alex glanced up as

Sandra Bannister entered the pew and slipped across Page to sit between the men. She pulled the wet Hermes scarf from around her neck and stuffed it into her trenchcoat pocket. The three sat in silence for some minutes.

The organ music stopped abruptly. In the stillness of the great church, sharp footsteps on the tile floor could be heard clearly as Sheila Warren, widow of John James Warren, and her daughter crossed from the side door to take their places in the front pew. Simultaneously, a simply dressed, statuesque woman with coal-black hair wound in a loose bun at the nape of her neck entered Alex's pew from the side aisle and sat beside him. He looked at her in surprise.

"What the hell are you doing here?" he growled.

"Come to pay my last respects to John along with my husband," she replied coolly.

"Judith, I . . ."

"Later." Leaning forward, Judith Kidd smiled and nodded at Page and Sandra Bannister. The somber ceremony began.

The rector's voice droned on as Miklos Androssy studied Sheila Warren's pale, drawn face.

". . . Lord, let me know mine end, and the number of my days; that I may . . ."

How much, if anything, did she know about Acheron? Had her husband confided in her before or after the yachting accident off the Albanian coast? Did she know the names of his co-conspirators?

". . . for man walketh in a vain shadow, and disquiet himself in vain;"

Androssy's patience had worn thin.

". . . he heapeth up riches, and cannot tell who shall gather them."

As the baron tried to penetrate her thoughts, Sheila Warren sat upright and proud, staring straight ahead, her eyes not seeing the flag-draped coffin resting in the chancel before her. Instead they saw the raging gale in the Strait of Otranto and seven years of pain.

". . . O spare me a little, that I may recover my strength, before I go hence, and be no more seen."

That day had started so perfectly—hot, a rippling crystal sea, blue sky, cloudless—ideal for JJ's fishing trip with their English host and his son. It had been John Warren's first real vacation since his reelection defeat. A trip to Greece. Far away from the poison of the gutter press, away from the political knives of Washington.

She would have gone with them that morning had she been feeling better. Instead she had stood on the balcony of the villa and waved to the men as they sailed out of the little harbor below. A chill ran through Sheila Warren now as she once again felt the cold Adriatic wind gusting through the open window that had later awakened her from her afternoon nap. The mosquito netting hanging from the ceiling flapped over her bed. The sun had disappeared, hidden by tumbling black clouds. Sheila recalled Angela's tense voice as she phoned the harbor. The boat had radioed high seas; it was coming in. But it had been so terribly far away.

And then the rain. That horrible, horrible rain. Dark sheets of water that blotted out everything. She and Angela had stood all night staring across the black harbor looking for a light.

In the morning peasants along the north shore of the island had found pieces of the boat washed up on the beach, found the bodies. Poor Angela. Hugh, little Tommy, the captain, they were all there. But not JJ and not Steve, the security man who had been with the President for years.

Helicopters soon found the rest of the shattered and charred boat floating half submerged in the strait, but no more bodies. They had appealed to the Albanian government through French, Turkish, and Greek diplomatic channels, the only ones open to that isolated Communist country. For days she had stood agonizing on that balcony, looking across the water to that mysterious coast only a little over a mile away. It was four days before word finally came. JJ was alive. Barely. The bodyguard had drowned, apparently exhausting his strength in the attempt to save her husband.

JJ lay paralyzed from the waist down, his mind confused. It never cleared. The doctors could not explain what had happened to him. Shock, brain damage from a blow, the drugs used by the primitive doctor to keep him alive—his body had been filled with them. From that day on, Sheila Warren and her husband secluded themselves from the world. She endured the private agony of watching the slow degeneration of the man she loved and honored. She had forced herself to bear it, but she could not bear to have his memory destroyed. Sheila Warren wanted the country to remember John James Warren as a vital, active man, a man of peace. Not even his closest friends were permitted to see him. Only the family. Perhaps she had been wrong, but she had done what she felt best.

During the first year, he had seemed to be trying to tell her things, terribly important things, but then he would drift off into wild worlds of fantasy, worlds of mythology, worlds of space. Or were they? His ramblings had been so persistent. She felt he had given her the clues to some strange puzzle, one that she could not put together.

There had to be answers to JJ's wild ravings, there had to be. Glancing quickly at those seated in the church behind her, Sheila opened the black purse on the pew beside her and withdrew a small pad of paper and gold pen. She began to write.

". . . Unto God's gracious mercy and protection we commit you. The Lord bless and keep you. The Lord make His face to shine upon you, and be gracious unto you. The Lord lift up His countenance upon you, and give you peace, both now and evermore. Amen."

CHAPTER 3

Alex and Page followed Judith Kidd and Sandra Bannister down the aisle after the ceremony.

"You didn't know Judith was coming?" Page asked quietly.

"No," the other mumbled under his breath. "She's full of little surprises these days. Look, will you drop Sandy off at the airport?"

"I take it your plans for the weekend have just come a cropper." Page smiled at his friend's dirty look; Alex's sexual meanderings and exploits had never failed to fascinate and amuse him. Although approaching forty-five, his friend's well-toned, athletic build, his square jaw and rugged features topped by wavy dark blond hair made him a not unprotesting magnet to women of all ages.

As they joined the others at the top of the church steps, Judith took her husband's arm with casual possessiveness while continuing her conversation with Sandra Bannister. Kidd looked down the steps at the diplomats standing stiffly in tight small knots waiting for their drivers. The rain had stopped. Crowds began to form once again behind the news- and cameramen. They craned their necks in hopes of seeing and recognizing some real celebrity.

"Alexander." General Carmody's gruff, low voice reached Alex at the same time as the powerful grip on his shoulder. He turned. Joan Carmody came forward and was introduced to Alex and Judith by her husband. The two men drifted slightly apart from the group and spoke in hushed tones.

"The end of an era, Alex," the general said. "And of a great responsibility."

The other nodded.

"Thank God we never had to use the boatman."

Again Alex nodded, both men skirting around the subject thay had not mentioned in years. "I thought Simon might be here. Have you heard from him?"

"After the first years, we agreed never to talk except in an emergency. Safer. And you?"

"No. I assume you know his company was taken over. Apparently he came out with a fat consultancy contract and all the cash he'll ever need. He's probably back climbing mountains."

"Not Simon," the general smiled. "He's probably busy inventing some new electronic miracle. He is the most . . ." Paul Carmody was interrupted by the surprise arrival of Sheila Warren's daughter. "Why Beth, hello," he said. "What are you—"

"General Carmody, Mother asked me to give you this." The young woman pressed a scrap of paper into his hand and then turned to the others. "Mr. Kidd, Mrs. Kidd."

"Darling," Joan Carmody said softly, hugging the girl to her. "How sorry we are. Is there anything Paul or I can do? Just ask, you know."

"I know, and thank you," Beth Warren replied, smoothly extricating herself from the older woman's embrace. "I'm so glad you all came. It meant a lot to Mother."

"How is she, dear?" Joan asked gently.

"She's taking it very well, but she's tired. The last months were exhausting for her."

Joan Carmody nodded sympathetically. Her eyes were misted over.

"I'd better get back to her."

"Certainly. Give your mother our love."

"I will," Beth Warren promised. Turning, she reentered the church.

Joan shook her head sadly and returned her attention to Judith Kidd.

"What is it?" Alex asked Paul Carmody.

The general unfolded the small piece of paper and read the precise handwritten message. "Sheila wants me to have supper with her this evening."

"Where, darling?" Joan Carmody asked.

"In her suite at the Waldorf." He frowned. "Alone."

"Do you know what it's about?" Alex held out his hand for the paper. Carmody did not extend it to him.

"No."

"Then you must dine with us," Judith said to Joan. She looked at Sandra Bannister. "And you and Page, if you're free."

"I'm dropping Sandy at the airport," Page replied quickly.

"I really should be dashing right now," the beautiful reporter added, catching Alex's quick glance. "Washington waits for no man."

"Or woman," Judith corrected lightly. "I understand you're terribly successful, one of Alex's best."

"That's very kind of you," Sandra smiled, extending her hand. "Nice to have seen you again." Her comment was directed to the entire group. "Come on, Page." She took his arm and the two moved into the crowd at the foot of the steps, bumping into one of the German cameramen. Offering apologies to the smiling young man, Page pulled Sandra through the onlookers, fending off the autograph books of those who recognized the KWEN anchorwoman.

"Hey, that's my public back there," she protested.

"Move it, you swollen-headed egomaniac," Page retorted. "We don't have much time."

"I have."

"Well, I don't." Waving his arm, he hailed a cab and jumped in behind Sandra. "La Guardia," he told the driver. "Eastern Airlines shuttle terminal."

"What's your rush?" she asked. "I thought Mary was at Fishers."

"She is."

"Well?"

"I have plans, that's all," Page said shortly, ending the subject.

Sandra Bannister looked at him curiously. She and Page Shepard had been good friends, almost like brother and sister, ever since Alexander Kidd had discovered the talented young woman in his newsroom and encouraged her rise within the network. They could speak openly to each other—and always off the record. This was not like him. She changed the subject. "Did you know she was in town? Did Alex?"

"By 'she' I take it you mean Judith. No. I'm sure Alex was taken completely by surprise."

"How long have they been separated?"

"It's hard to say. They've been drifting apart and back together again for years. Judith's been pretty much living abroad in Europe and Tangier for the last three or four years."

"Why, what went wrong?"

"I don't really know." Page looked wistfully at the gray East River as the cab sped up the Drive. "I guess different interests, different values. After the success of the network, their lives seemed to go in opposite directions. His to business, show business, to building his empire. Hers . . ." he hesitated, trying to put his thoughts into the right words, "hers into holding together traditions, dignity, caring about life values, people. Judith's no shrinking violet little housewife, you know. She's got brains—and wit."

"You like her."

"Very much."

"I do too, damn it." They sat in silence for a minute. "She still loves him," Sandra said softly.

Page kept his eyes on the river. "So do you."

"Where are you staying?" Alex asked as his driver relinquished the wheel to him and walked around the sports car to assist Judith in.

"At our apartment, of course," she replied smoothly. "I

see you've made some changes." Finding lingerie that was not her own had hurt.

He said nothing.

"I like the new Rauschenberg oil in the bedroom. Very trendy. Your taste? Or . . ." Judith paused for effect, "or the gallery's? I assume you're still on Castelli's patron list."

"Mine."

"Good."

Alex gripped the wheel tightly to control himself. His knuckles were white. Shifting gears, he headed north up Park Avenue. The simple, diverting action served to relieve some of the tension he felt. Behind the wheel of the powerful car, he was once again in command. "When did you fly in?" His voice was flat, emotionless. "I assume you flew in."

"This morning. You weren't at home when I called from the airport." Judith added with a trace of mischief, "Sorry if I inconvenienced you. Only heard about the memorial service at the last minute and couldn't get through on the phone from London before I left."

Alexander Kidd said nothing. He turned left on Seventy-second Street and headed for Central Park and their sprawling apartment in the venerable Dakota whose leaded turrets and peaked roofs dominated the west side of the park. "How's your refugee organization going?"

"Fine," she answered, and then upon a sudden impulse grabbed his arm. "Alex, put down the top."

"You'll get wet," he replied irritably.

"Don't be silly, it's not raining. Please."

With a reluctant sigh, Alexander Kidd pulled the car to the side of the street and lowered the top of the Mercedes as Judith reached behind her neck to remove the pins holding her hair. Shaking her head, the long black hair that had first attracted Alex to her on campus years ago fell about her shoulders. She looked over at him and smiled.

"Thanks. I just wanted to smell the wet grass and trees. I've always loved it."

Tearing his eyes away, Alex put the car into gear and

moved down Seventy-second Street into the park. "How are your parents?"

"Still in Israel and still working."

"Give them my best when you see them next."

"I always do."

They lapsed into silence. Finally he asked, "And your precious son? Where is he these days?" Why, he chided himself, did you have to say it that way? Too late, the wound was open.

"*Our* son is spending the summer painting at the Castle in Tangier and in London. And, since you ask," Judith's voice became icy for the first time, "he has just turned twenty-three, a fact apparently gone unnoticed by his father." She glared at Alexander Kidd. "You haven't seen him for nearly four years."

"We have nothing to say to each other, not since . . ."

"His studies at the Sorbonne are going very well," Judith interrupted, not wanting to recall the final confrontation that had estranged father and son. "Most of us who have taken the time to know him are very proud of his talent and accomplishments."

"He could have had it all and the fuckin' kid throws it away," Kidd mumbled audibly. "Mommy's boy."

"Everyone has his own life to lead, and if it's the macho image you're worried about, my dear," Judith retorted sarcastically, "your son, by all accounts, is one up on his old dad in the area of sexual prowess." She was about to say more, something about the clothing she'd found at the apartment earlier that morning and the cosmetics, the eye shadow matching that of Sandra Bannister's, but bit her lip.

Feeling the verbal slap, Alex gripped the wheel of the Mercedes more tightly and swung the car into a sharp turn, taking pleasure in the squeal of its tires on the road beneath. "What did you really come for? You're going to give me the divorce?"

"You really don't want it; our vows keep you safe, my darling, in all your little affairs." Judith ran her hand over her hair as it blew in the rush of air. "And I don't want it.

Not yet. If your friends are willing to tangle publicly in bed with the famous Alexander Kidd of KWEN and put up with whatever little embarrassment comes from that today, well then, so am I." Judith looked over at his face. The muscles of his jaw bulged as he clenched his teeth. She laughed. "Oh, come on. Now that we've got Mark and our marital status out of the way, we've got nothing left to fight about— really fight about, that is. Relax. You know you don't hate me all that much. Life does go on."

He glanced over at her, still soft, desirable, yet beautifully dignified, superior.

"What if I say I'll only be here a short time?"

He looked away, then back into her dark, teasing eyes.

"A very, *very* short time. You can even lock your bedroom door."

"You fuckin' bitch," he laughed, looking back to the road and, jerked to attention, swerving the car abruptly and sharply into another turn. "You're going to kill us both, you know that," Alex Kidd said, his voice nearly drowned by the shriek of tires.

"I'll leave that honor to you, darling."

Less than an hour later, Page Shepard pushed through the revolving doors of the Waldorf-Astoria. He forced himself to a casual walk as he nervously approached the cluster of small tables and banquettes of Peacock Alley, the Waldorf's chic cocktail lounge. The tables of the Alley were crowded with late afternoon guests, some talking business, some there for fun, some just to be seen. Being seen worried Page.

Taking a deep breath, he crossed the lobby and moved between the tables to one set against the back wall far from the shiny black grand piano. The young cameraman he had bumped into earlier that afternoon looked up. His lips parted in a dazzling smile. "You're late."

"Sorry," Page Shepard apologized as he slipped into the chair opposite him, "I had to take Sandy to La Guardia and I—"

"Hey, it's all right," Helmut Bruck interrupted softly, gently pressing his knee against the other's under the table. Page jerked his quickly away. "I was late too. Had to get my film to the agency." He raised his hand to attract the attention of a nearby waiter. "Your usual?"

Nodding, Page Shepard relaxed back in his chair, his eyes moving over the features of the strikingly handsome twenty-nine-year-old. His face was finely crafted, with a sensual, well-defined mouth and high cheekbones. It had been Helmut's intense green eyes that had first attracted Page's attention at the international news conference in Hamburg several years ago. His voice had a gentle, low tone that seemed to come from deep within his body, a body that Page knew was crafted as well as the face. He slowly moved his leg back to touch the young man's. A smile flickered across Helmut's face, and his eyes glanced quickly at him and then back to the waiter as he finished giving the order.

"Why, for God's sake, did you have to pick this place?" Page asked. "It's not exactly private."

"I wanted to show you off," Helmut teased, knowing exactly how nervous Page felt. And then he sobered. "Besides, it is exactly one block from St. Bartholomew's so you wouldn't have to go running across town in the rain. Relax, it's also the last place anyone would ever think Page Shepard would take a . . ." he lowered his voice, "a lover." Page glanced uncomfortably at the couples seated on either side of them. "Seeing us here, your pals will think we are just talking business, that you are interviewing an extraordinarily talented cameraman for your precious KWEN." He smiled and, leaning back, asked casually, "What was the ceremony like?"

Page described the funeral service briefly.

"And the general you and Kidd were talking to on the steps outside? Who was he?"

"Paul Carmody."

"You know him?"

"No, met him for the first time today. Apparently he's an

old friend of Alex's, although he's never mentioned him before. Probably afraid we'd sic our Washington news desk on him."

The waiter returned with Page's gin martini straight up and a glass of ice on the side. Helmut accepted another beer. They chatted easily about their dinner plans for the evening, selecting and then rejecting one East Side restaurant after the next until Helmut finally put an end to the discussion by insisting on a small place he knew in the Village. "It is completely straight, Page, I swear. We will be the only . . ." Seeing the beginning of Page's frown, he amended his statement, "*I* will be the only gay in the place." The banter went out of his voice, and he pressed the older man's knee firmly while looking deep into his eyes. "I love you, Page," he whispered. "Love you more than I can believe."

Page Shepard looked back at him, mesmerized by the green eyes. He felt like a small, helpless animal staring up in fascination at the swaying eyes of a cobra. "And I you," he replied softly.

Helmut broke the intimacy of the moment with another dazzling smile. "How about another round?" he asked, raising his hand once again for the waiter. "By the way, who was the girl with the general—his daughter? She gave him something."

"Beth Warren. Had a note from her mother, an invitation for supper tonight." He took a handful of salted almonds from the glass dish before him. "Seemed more of a command performance."

"She is staying here, you know, in this hotel."

"So I understand. Hey, where are you going?"

"Got to take a piss," Bruck replied as he rose. "Order me another beer, will you?"

Page watched him leave and then stared down at the remains of his first martini. What was he doing? he asked himself for the hundredth time. A happily married man—he *was* happily married, he knew it—with two sons of whom he was very proud. And here he was having an affair with another man, a man only seven years older than his son, Quin. No, he corrected himself, it was more than an affair. He loved Helmut, was genuinely and deeply in love with him. He had never felt this way about a man before, never had a homosexual urge, had never even slept with another woman, only his wife, Mary. His life had always been so structured, so correct in every sense of the word until this young Teutonic god came along. Then, blam! Suddenly Page Shepard, good old straight-arrow Page Shepard, boring old Ivy League Page Shepard with his receding, short hair, his fading classic WASP good looks and his dated Brooks Brothers suits found himself not torn between, but accepting and living two lives. One open and social, the other in shadows and intimate. What was it? The flattery of a younger man's attention and devotion? Middle-age crisis? Had a homosexual inclination always been there but never recognized? Analyzing his feelings as much as he had during the last two years, Page always came back to one certainty. He did not know the reason, and he didn't have to know it. He loved the young German, loved his vitality, his assuredness, loved everything about him. And he needed him.

Swinging back the glass door, Helmut Bruck stepped out from one of the long lines of telephone booths and headed back toward Peacock Alley. "I've reserved a table for two at eight," he informed Page as he eased himself onto the banquette across from the KWEN executive. "Hope that is all right."

"It's fine," Page replied, smiling. "Everything's just fine."

Far above Peacock Alley in the Presidential Suite of the Waldorf, Sheila Warren paced restlessly back and forth across her bedroom. Beth was napping in her room on the other side of the living room. Wine and a cold light supper had been ordered, and Paul Carmody would soon join her. Now that it was all over, she had to confide in someone she could trust, someone that JJ had trusted.

The first light knock went unnoticed. The second penetrated her exhausted mind and, without thinking it strange that room service should be delivering supper to her bedroom door instead of to the living room, Sheila Warren unbolted the door and opened it. A large uniformed chambermaid holding a pile of neatly folded towels stood before her in the hall.

"May I turn down the bed now?" she inquired. Without waiting for her reply, the woman pushed past the late President's wife into the room.

"But it's far too early for that," Sheila protested. "It's not even six and . . ." Further words froze in her throat as she felt the powerful grasp of the maid's hand on her wrist slowly pulling the doorknob from her hold. With her free hand, the woman closed and bolted the door behind them. "What are you . . . ?"

"I think we should have a little chat, Mrs. Warren," the heavyset maid interrupted. She drew Sheila firmly away from the door and forced her down on the edge of the bed. The woman towered above her.

"You . . . you're not a woman, you're . . ."

"Yes, Mrs. Warren, I am a man. Tell me about Acheron," he ordered without pausing.

Sheila's initial surprise and shock turned to cold terror.

"Acheron, Mrs. Warren. We don't have much time."

Sheila looked wildly about her for escape; she leaped suddenly from the bed, trying to rush past him. A rough hand clamped firmly over her face from behind and muffled all sound as she was lifted like a doll and carried struggling to the window. Holding Sheila Warren against his body with one powerful hand, he reached forward with the other, unlocked and quickly pulled up the window. Sheila felt the cool, moist air against her face. As the net curtains billowed back into the room around them, she went limp.

"That is right, Mrs. Warren. It would not do for the wife of the President to accidentally fall out, fall all the way down there, now would it? People might think you were so upset that you committed suicide. You would not like that, would you, Mrs. Warren?"

Still pressed back against his chest by the hand over her mouth, Sheila tried to shake her head. He felt the slight movement. "Good. Now I am going to take my hand away and you will behave, eh?" Again he felt the nod of her head against his chest. He removed his hand and stood holding her from behind so that she could see the small cars and antlike people moving along Park Avenue far below. "Who is Alecto?"

Alecto, Acheron—those were among the names JJ had spoken in his ravings. Sheila remembered others: Tisiphone, Megaera, Charon. He had mixed them up with names of jet planes and tanks, with spaceships. None of it had made sense to her.

"I don't know." Her answer was barely audible.

"Think again, Mrs. Warren, think again." He moved her closer to the window.

She *tried* to think. She had looked up the names in dictionaries and reference books over and over. They were all from mythology. Acheron: a river in hell over which the boatman called Charon ferried the souls of the dead. But what did that mean? And the other names? Alecto, Tisiphone, Megaera: the avenging Furies, the three daughters of Acheron. Sheila saw the pictures of them in her mind, serpents in their hair, flailing those before them with whips made of scorpions.

"You are almost out of time, Mrs. Warren." His voice was hard, its tone final. "Who is Alecto?"

"Alecto is a Fury, she's a Fury," Sheila cried desperately. "She doesn't exist."

"Your last chance, Mrs. Warren."

"I don't know what you want," she sobbed. "I . . ."

Scooping her quickly up in his powerful arms, he threw the surprised woman out through the open window. For an instant Sheila Warren seemed to hang in midair, her horrified eyes looking back at him. Reaching out in space for the drapery that had been swept out with her, Sheila's long fingernails tore against the heavy fabric. Her shrill death scream followed her frail body as it turned over and over, fading as she plummeted down to smash on the sidewalk below.

"You ran out of time, Mrs. Warren," he said coldly. Crossing the room, the intruder silently opened the bedroom door and, picking up the folded towels, lost himself in the long corridor.

CHAPTER 4

"It's so terrible, Papa," Katherina Androssy wailed, as she stood in the doorway of her father's elegant paneled library in the house on Sutton Place. "It's all on the news."

The baron looked up from his desk at his favorite daughter. "What is on the news, Katty?"

"The President's wife . . . she committed suicide just a few minutes ago. She jumped out the window. Oh, Papa, she jumped." Her large black eyes filled with tears.

Opening his arms to her, Miklos Androssy embraced the child who ran to him and caressed her long dark hair in an effort to comfort her. Katherina was the youngest of the five Androssy children, a beautiful, fragile child born for his love. She was nearly eighteen, eight years younger than Andras, his namesake, and she was the pet of the entire family.

"Mama's crying."

"Where is she?" he asked softly.

"In her room."

"Then we had better go and cheer her up, had we not?"

The young girl nodded against his shoulder and stepped back as he stood. "Why would she do it?" Katherina asked her father, looking up at him and taking his hand in hers.

"She must have been very unhappy," he replied, walking to the door with his daughter. They crossed the hall and mounted the wide, curving staircase to the third floor of the mansion. The baron tapped lightly on the door to his right and then opened it. Edith Androssy lay propped up by lacy pillows on her large bed, watching the television screen set into the far wall of the room.

"Oh, Mickey," she said, pressing a handkerchief to her eyes and shaking her head mournfully, "can you imagine anything so awful? I just . . . I . . ."

Dismissing the detested nickname, Miklos Androssy crossed the room to her and sat on the edge of the bed, putting his arm around her shoulders to press her gently to him. "Edith, Edith, Edith," he said softly. "Yes, it is sad, but you must not take it so personally. You cannot take all the cares of the world as your own, my darling." Androssy kissed her forehead and then leaned back to look at his wife of thirty-two years.

Edith had never been a beautiful woman. In her debutante days, the social columns had avoided the subject of her plainness by referring to her as "handsome" or "distinguished." Now, at the age of fifty-two, her face was plump and a bit jowled, her ample figure a testament to her enjoyment of cocktails and the lavish dinner parties she threw with great regularity at Sutton Place. Even though her makeup was flawless and her hair kept a youthful blond and carefully arranged in the most current fashion, Edith Androssy looked older than her husband instead of eleven years his junior.

Her vast inheritance and social position had first attracted the debonair Androssy upon his arrival in America and had certainly been major factors in supporting his financial enterprises and giving them legitimacy after their marriage. The dashing foreigner had made good use of his title and flattery to win her. But over the years he had developed a genuine affection for his wife. She was the adoring mother of his children, warm and loving in everything she did. And he enjoyed spoiling her, pampering and caring for her as he would a prized possession. Edith was always there, loyal, pleasing, and, above all, unquestioning.

The distraught face of Beth Warren appeared on the television screen, capturing his attention. Surrounded by pushing, shouting reporters as she tried to leave the

Waldorf, the bereft young woman could only repeat over and over, "Leave me alone, please leave me alone." A flashbulb exploded in her face. Staggering back, she cried out, "Mother!" in anguish. Baron Androssy reached across his wife and pressed the button on the remote control to switch off the set. His eyes lingered on the family photograph framed in silver on the bedside table: Stephen, now aged thirty, an investment banker married with two children of his own; Bela, twenty-nine, a fine equestrian, one child; Tibor, twenty-seven, the radical of the family, producing films on the West Coast; Andras, twenty-five, in medical school; and, of course, little Katty sitting on his lap while holding her mother's hand. It looked like a fine family, a stable and well-publicized family, a perfect frontispiece for Miklos Androssy.

"Who will be here for dinner?" he asked, trying to distract Edith from Beth Warren's emotional outcry.

Edith began to count on her fingers. "Stephen and his family, Tibor and . . ." she paused, looking up at her husband, "and his . . ."

"Mistress?" the baron finished.

"Oh, Mickey, you mustn't be upset. Ann is a very fine actress and I'm sure she's genuinely fond of—"

"I am sure she is," he interrupted, "as well as of Tibor's production company and my money."

"Don't be upset, dear, please."

Androssy smiled at his wife. "She does not upset me in the least. It is *you* she upsets. All the more power to her if she can pull something off. Tibor is asking for it; it will be a good lesson for him."

"Mickey, what a terrible thing to say, and in front of Katty."

Winking at his youngest daughter, Androssy rose from the bed. "I have things I must finish before dinner." As he crossed the room, he glanced at the dark television screen and turned back to his wife. "And do not turn that damn thing on again tonight. I forbid it."

Edith Androssy smiled and nodded acceptance of her husband's order as the door closed behind him.

* * *

At precisely 10:20 that evening, Miklos Androssy bid farewell to his family and left the house on Sutton Place. Walking a block to First Avenue, he stood on the corner, his right hand raised to hail an approaching taxi. As it pulled to the curb, the baron opened the rear door and slid in. He nodded to the driver, who curiously did not have to be told where his passenger wished to go. But it was not odd at all. The driver, dressed in a wild-patterned Hawaiian sport shirt and jeans, was Victor Kamera, the Androssy family chauffeur. Turning left on Fifty-seventh Street, the taxi took the next right up onto the ramp leading to the Queens-borough Bridge.

Across the East River, a short, thin, innocuous-looking man dressed in a nondescript suit left the elevated subway station of the BMT line at Astoria Boulevard and began walking west. Under normal circumstances it would be unusual to find the fifty-year-old director of external relations in the United Nations Public Information Office walking in this neighborhood at this hour of the night. But these were not normal circumstances. Vladimir Savich was, in reality, the KGB Resident in New York and, as such, responsible for all Russian undercover operations in the area. All but one. His ferretlike face screwed up in anger as he thought of his exclusion from what he suspected to be the most important operation his country had ever mounted. Pausing, he watched a taxi stop a few yards ahead of him and studied the passenger who got out. The two men walked slowly toward each other, both sets of eyes probing the darkness on either side.

Meeting, Miklos Androssy nodded silently and turned. Vladimir Savich fell in beside him and, hands in pockets, the two walked back toward the river under the thick abutments supporting the Triborough Bridge.

"Thank you for the information on the Warren-Carmody meeting," Androssy said.

The other nodded.

"What was its source?"

Instead of answering, Savich asked, "Your man?"

"A chambermaid."

"Who?"

"My man, that is all." He repeated his question. "Who informed you of Carmody and the Warren woman?"

"My source, that is all."

The two stopped and turned to face each other. Androssy was the first to speak. "Vladimir Savich, you do not like me. I detest you. Let us both get that out of the way. However we must work together. This operation has been put completely in my hands and all the resources of your agents can be sequestered should I deem that necessary. Must I make this clear to you again?"

Savich glared at him, then turned and began to walk forward.

"Comrade." Savich stopped at the command and waited for Androssy to join him. They proceeded toward the river. "Here are the names of those attending the funeral service today," the baron said, handing the other an envelope. "I need a complete history and all the facts, no matter how minute, on all of them by Monday morning. Those underlined are of prime importance." Vladimir Savich silently placed the envelope in his pocket. To be treated as a mere errand boy was more than the resident could stomach. "Pay particular attention to Baily Oliver, Stanton Thomas, Alexander Kidd." Androssy noted the slight rise in Savich's eyebrows at the mention of the last name and continued, "Taylor James and Ramsey Williams. They appear to be acquaintances of General Carmody."

They walked on in silence for a minute or two. Androssy spoke. "You have something to tell me about Mr. Kidd?"

"The information concerning the Warren-Carmody meeting came from an associate of Kidd's."

"His name?"

"Shepard. A Mr. Page Shepard."

Baron Androssy nodded, recognizing the name as one on his list. "And how did you obtain this information from Mr. Shepard?"

"One of our agents in the news section, a 'raven.'"

The baron nodded again, understanding the KGB term for men skillfully trained in the art of sexual entrapment.

"He has been in close contact with Shepard for nearly two years. A German boy."

The two men walked slowly on into the darkness beneath the bridge.

The tops of the skyscrapers in the Rockefeller Center complex in mid-Manhattan were among the first to catch the rays of the rising sun Monday morning. They glowed golden in the cloudless blue atmosphere.

In a darkened room on the twelfth floor of number 19 Rockefeller Plaza, Alexander Kidd, his shirt-sleeves rolled up, pushed his feet against the top edge of the control console before him and tilted back in his viewing chair. His eyes moved over the stacks of television monitors flickering with the jumble of news and sporting events as he absently held out his coffee mug to be refilled. On either side of him, editors made notes and consulted over which of the taped events would be cut together and beamed up for transmission to the KWEN satellite that floated in stationary orbit over twenty-two thousand miles above the surface of the earth. Through the satellite transponders, the network electronically relayed its twenty-four-hour news and sports programs back down to the polished, dish-shaped earth-station receivers of hundreds of television cable systems scattered throughout the United States.

"Shit," Kidd mumbled, shaking his head in disgust, "where's the excitement, the interest? This is nothing but a lot of boring crap. Who's going to pay to look at this junk?"

"News is news," an editor to his right commented wryly. "We can't make it happen, you know."

"At least you can make it more interesting," the head of the network fired back. "That missile launch, why just run a long shot for three minutes? Give me rapid cuts between the faces watching, technicians, the first flash of the lift rockets, faces, long shots, close-ups. Make it exciting, damn it, dramatic. The world is tired of seeing some fucking missile sitting on a pad, a lot of smoke and steam roaring around its base, and then the damn thing going straight up into the sky. It's old hat. Boring. And that Middle East stuff. It could be war soon; they're shooting over borders again. Let's see some blood and guts, not a lot of houses with holes in them. Make it real. Let's *feel* it. Make it human. Use some imagination."

"Look, Alex, you know we're limited on the number of cameras we can assign to any one event. We're spread too thin. You've got us strung out around the world like . . . like . . ."

"Grab some of the syndicated service stuff then." Alexander Kidd's voice was loud and angry.

"You sign the contract and we will." The editor's voice too was heated.

"So I'll sign it. Does that make you happy?"

"You know damn well it doesn't. Whatever happened to the 'exclusive' that used to be attached to our name. Whatever happened to the Kidd integrity? Give me more men, that's all I ask. More men."

"I'll give you more men *after* you give me some creativity. You're an editor, goddamn it, so edit!"

"Then give me a free hand."

"You've got a free hand."

"I do, do I? Okay, Alex, then we'll push the follow-up material on the Warren suicide."

"No!" Kidd shouted. Slamming his coffee mug down on the console, he stormed out of the room.

Shrugging his shoulders, the senior news editor slumped back into his chair. "Roll 'em again, Eddie," he called to some faceless technician.

Raging down the corridor, Alex nearly bumped head-on into Tom Petterson, the gruff head engineer of KWEN. The two had worked side by side since the day Alex had been hired as a space salesman by an Indiana radio station in 1962. Within three years Kidd had become marketing manager, begged, borrowed, and stolen enough money to

merge three stations and assume the leadership of the group.
Soon after that he had added his first television station.

From that point on, the career of Alexander Kidd soared.
In 1970 he served as adviser to the Federal Communications
Commission where he began to earn his reputation as the
industry's dissident radical. In 1972, among his other
public-service pursuits, he became adviser to the National
Foundation on the Arts and Humanities and used his
position skillfully to move within the corridors of power in
Washington. By 1974 Kidd was in a position to begin his
own television programming company, and the following
year, much to the surprise and rancor of the major networks,
the Kidd Worldwide Entertainment Network satellite was
launched with government approval.

Tom Petterson had been instrumental in much of the early
design of the transponders, working in close harmony with
Simon Felton, a young electronics genius brought in by
Alexander Kidd. Petterson considered the satellite his baby,
lavishing attention on its every need, personally monitoring
its position each day.

"Morning, Cap," the head engineer said, using the
diminutive of captain, the nickname that had been attached
to Kidd as much for his pirating business activities as for his
obsession with sailing. "See you've got the wind up as
usual."

"Those fucking boy geniuses," Kidd mumbled, indicating the editing room from which he had just come. "They
want everything on a silver platter, no imagination. 'Give
me this, give me that.' Won't move their asses to do
anything for themselves. Sometimes I yearn for the good
old Indiana days, Tom."

The older man smiled. "And that boring little radio
station? You're talking to Tom, Alex. A day without discord
would be a day without Alexander Kidd. You love it."

Alex returned his smile. "You're fucking right I do.
How's the boatman this morning?" he asked of the KWEN
satellite. "Hanging in there?"

"Right on course, Captain."

"Have you ever had the urge to send her whirling around the world, Tom? Just once?"

"My fingers get pretty itchy at the controls every once in a while."

"You're the only one who knows how to do it."

"You and me." He paused, thinking. "And that Simon feller."

"Not even him, Tom." Alexander clapped Petterson on the shoulder and started down the corridor for the stairs. "You'd better keep healthy."

The other waved and turned as Kidd pulled open the door to the stairwell and mounted the steps two at a time, an exercise he did whenever possible to keep his body in fighting trim.

By eight o'clock, when Page Shepard entered his office, Alex was buried deep in balance-sheet and cash-flow statements. He looked up at his friend and gave a nervous smile. "Page, old buddy, how would you like to take a little risk?"

That look of Alex's was all too familiar to Page. Sinking into a chair across the desk from him, he groaned. "What is it now?"

Kidd sobered. "We're in trouble. We either make a move now or we go slowly down the drain."

"What in the hell are you talking about?"

"They're squeezing us, Page. ABC, NBC, CBS, they want the cable TV pie all for themselves."

"That's nothing new. The big three have been after you and Turner for years." Page paused and studied the expression on the face of his old friend. "Okay, let's have it. What have you heard?"

"They're going after the twenty-four-hour world news slot again."

"How do you know?"

"Marty leaked it this weekend."

Page Shepard sat up. "Which one?"

"All three. They're throwing in together to get us."

"That's illegal. The FCC will never allow it, you know that," he protested.

"One network will front the operation, the other two will sell 'for a nominal fee,'" he sneered at the phrase, "access to material from their international newsrooms on a one-day-delay basis. That means the new channel will be able to cover any event in far greater depth than we can and at far less cost."

"Jesus," Page cursed, shaking his head. "When? Did Marty give you an idea of the start-up date?"

"Soon. They've already felt out several of the major metro cable systems. They're undercutting our subscriber fee." Alexander Kidd rose from his desk and walked over to the sliding glass doors that led out to the wide garden on the fifteenth floor. The lawn was immaculately clipped, and shrubs and flowers bloomed along the geometric paths. Judith had been responsible for the initial layout when KWEN first moved into the building six years ago. "We have two options," he said, his back to Page Shepard. "Double our international news staff or lower our fee to the systems."

"Neither of which we can afford," Page commented sourly.

"Neither of which we can afford," Alex repeated softly. "But," he said as he turned, "there is a third alternative."

"I knew there would be. I take it that this is where the risk comes in."

Alexander Kidd nodded. "We take our existing sports channel, keep the news channel exactly as it is, and use the third transponder in the satellite to add a third channel, a really first-rate culture channel. We'll make a package deal with the systems they can't afford to turn down: Sports, news, culture. Page, it would be like selling them a complete tier at a bargain price. They should flip for it. Well, what do you think?" His enthusiasm pervaded the office.

Page Shepard sat thinking for several moments. "The systems are already carrying culture channels," he said, playing devil's advocate. "They have to carry PBS by law. There's no market for a new one. The CBS service and the Entertainment Channel went bankrupt trying."

"We'll out-PBS PBS, the rest are all shit. We'll sign up the top programming around the world."

Page fought against Kidd's excitement, trying to maintain an objective perspective. "Most of the kind of programming you're talking about has already been committed. The BBC has signed with—"

"So we'll unsign them," Alex rushed on. "And we'll sign up all the good Broadway stuff, give the producers a cut."

"Money, Alex, money. Where is all the money going to come from?" He pointed to the balance sheets spread across the desk. "We're borrowed up to the hilt right now. We'll have to give away the store to get more."

"I'm going to dilute my equity in KWEN," Kidd said softly.

"You're going to do what?" Page shouted.

"Only for a few years," Kidd insisted. "It'll be done quietly and I'll buy it all back as soon as we get things rolling."

"You can't, Alex. If you borrow against your stock, you'll lose control."

"Not if the members of our syndicate stick with me." He was referring to the other five partners who with him had put up the initial sixty million dollars to launch the KWEN satellite. Each of the five held eight percent ownership in Kidd's network, Alex and Judith held sixty percent between them.

"You have no guarantee they will stick with you."

"They should, those bastards. They've made back their initial investment three times over."

For more than an hour Page Shepard fought against his friend's plan to raise additional capital. "Damn it, man, you can sell a lease on the satellite's fourth transponder for at least fifteen million dollars today."

"No," Kidd said bluntly.

"Then at least borrow against it."

"No."

"What's so damn sacred about that transponder?" Page

demanded. "You won't use it, you won't lease it. It's been floating around up there for nine years without transmitting a single signal. Alex, that thing is a valuable asset."

"I know, I know," the other said, defensively. "So call me stupid, call me whatever you like, but let's leave the satellite out of this discussion, okay?"

Page looked up at the ceiling in exasperation and said nothing while his frustration eased. Ever since the satellite had been launched, Alex had remained strangely evasive about the mysterious fourth transponder. "Exactly how much of your stock are you planning to put up?" he asked finally.

"Nine percent of the network."

"That puts you in control of only forty-seven percent of the stock."

"Fifty-one percent, counting Judith's four."

"Does she know?"

Alex shook his head.

"You're out of your mind."

"I like risks." There was little humor in his voice.

"To whom are you entrusting our future?"

"A bank group in the Bahamas. I know the men running it; we can trust them." He looked down at Page. "And I can trust you. No one must know, just the Freeport bankers and you. I don't want raiders sniffing around."

"When?"

"If all goes well, by the end of the week."

Standing, Page Shepard sighed. "I guess that's that. I might as well go and start pulling together plans for KWEN's brand-new, phantasmagorical culture channel. Anything else I can do to help along this insanity?"

"Just remember that old nautical saying, 'A slip of the lip can sink a ship'—my ship."

Page smiled. "Right ho, mein cap-i-tain." They were off again on another showstopper so typical of Alexander Kidd, one that would keep the communications industry buzzing for years.

CHAPTER 5

Sweat poured down Miklos Androssy's face as he sat in the sauna in the basement of his New York mansion. His well-toned body glistened with the moisture of the steam. He ran his hand across his chest, taking pleasure in its firmness.

He looked over at the flabby, aging body of Anatoli Butov, who dozed on the cedar bench built into the opposite wall of the small room, and smiled at the comparison. Emerging from relative obscurity, Butov had been given a position in UNITAR, the United Nations Institute for Training and Research, which concentrated its efforts on the developing countries. It was a suitable cover for the KGB agent. As he studied Butov, Androssy mused upon the quirk of fate that seven years ago had delivered into this man's hands and, through Butov, into Androssy's own hands and those of the Soviet Union the power to change the course of the political history of the world.

After the Russian invasion of Hungary, Miklos Androssy seized the only avenue open to him in which to restore his shattered life. He offered his services to Moscow and vanished without a trace for two years. The baron's Russian benefactors had worked long and hard to help establish him as a leading and respected international figure, a man well placed within the world power groups, a man above suspicion. Androssy turned up in Beirut's chaotic banking circles, and his career exploded upward with unexplained good fortune. He transferred his expanding financial operations to Brussels, the headquarters of the European Economic Community and NATO, where he moved with grace and ease among the representatives, diplomats, and ambassadors of Europe. Then to New York where his reputation for financial genius had preceded him. From the beginning, New York, home of the United Nations and the financial heartbeat of America, had been his objective. It soon became his base of power.

Early on, his great potential value to the KGB had become well established and so his connection to the organization had been cloaked in secrecy. Today, few outside of the chairman of the KGB knew of his real connection to the Kremlin. While other KGB and GRU agents scurried about the world gathering information, plotting and counterplotting, Baron Androssy had been left alone to concentrate solely on building and consolidating an international empire. He had been held in readiness for an operation of only the greatest importance to the Soviet Union. Looking at Butov, he shook his head. After all the years of relative independence from Moscow, this minor agent from Albania had been the flint that ignited the flame under that operation and drawn him back to the KGB.

For two days he and Butov had pored over every detail of the latest information supplied by Vladimir Savich. They were searching for the identity of the last of the three Furies. Butov had looked for any possible match between the backgrounds and occupations of those attending the Warren funeral service and the drugged meanderings he had wrung from the late President while under his "care" in Albania. Baron Androssy had approached the same material from a more rational point of view, trying to determine how each man or woman could fit in with the many facts they already knew about the Acheron Plot. They had devoted their attention initially to the military and government officials as they seemed most likely to have some connection with America's spy satellites which Androssy was certain had to be at the core of the plot. And then only an hour ago they had reexamined the file on Alexander Kidd.

"Tell me, Butov," Androssy asked, seeing the other's

eyes flutter open, "why did you not kill Warren instead of returning him to the Americans?"

Butov stretched and reached for a towel to wipe his sweat-covered face and belly. "I did not have the time." He thought back to the night of the great storm.

When he had rolled the President over on the beach, his medical training told him at once that the man's back was broken. It would have been best for Warren if he had left the President immobile and summoned help from the village to take him to the nearest hospital. But this heaven-sent opportunity to hold in seclusion and question the President of the United States could not be lost by the KGB. Under his direction, the fishermen had lifted Warren and carried him back up the treacherous cliff path while Butov carefully supported his head and neck. He knew that a cash gift would insure the silence of Drin and Shkumbi.

For three and a half days he and Shura had alternately nursed and questioned the man, keeping him sedated and floating in an undefined world of shadows. As the monumental significance of the information they were learning became apparent, so too did the fact that John James Warren could never be returned to his countrymen to warn them of the security breaches he had made.

The bodyguard was useless to them and was disposed of at the end of the first day. Securely bound with soft linen to avoid marking his body, the drugged man had offered no resistance as Butov secured the plastic bag over his head and Shura filled it with seawater from an old bucket. He had drowned within minutes, struggling vainly in an instinctive effort to live. That night they carried his body to a deserted cove about a mile from the villa and wedged it facedown in the water between two rocks.

On the morning of the third day, the President's incredible scheme to prevent American weapons in the Middle East from ever being used against U.S. interests began to emerge. It had been prompted by Butov's interrogation concerning the name Acheron that Warren had first whispered on the beach. The name was obviously exceedingly important to the President, but it was something that Butov had overlooked in his initial greed for information on U.S. military deployment.

Warren's foreign policy in the Middle East had vacillated back and forth, depending upon events of the moment. Under great pressure to not only increase the supply of arms to maintain Egypt's strength in the area but also to assure Israel's security, Warren also sought to placate Jordan, Saudi Arabia, and other oil-rich states. But Warren had no way to maintain control over how these weapons would be used. All too easily he could imagine a time when the Mideast nations would turn their planes and missiles against the U.S. Probing deeper and deeper, Butov learned that the President had found a way to assure that none of the weapons he supplied would ever be used in contradiction of the terms under which they were sold. He had found a way to immobilize them.

Butov knew his mythology well and so had found it easy to understand the significance of the code names Warren mentioned in his drugged delirium and to relate them to the President's co-conspirators and the type of hardware they had developed to put their ingenious plan into effect. Later in New York, working with Androssy, Butov and the Hungarian baron had filled in the details.

Warren himself was Acheron, the name of the river across which the dead passed into Hades. And Acheron's daughters, the three Furies, were his co-conspirators, the only others with any knowledge of the plan and how to put it into operation. After much investigation, Butov and Androssy correctly linked General Carmody to the code name Megaera. Carmody's Pentagon position enabled him to isolate those planes and missile systems that were to be sent to the Middle Eastern countries. The appropriate modifications were included in the specifications for their directional and guidance systems.

From Carmody, the step to uncovering the second Fury was not difficult. Simon Felton, code-named Tisiphone, was an electronics expert. His small manufacturing company led the industry in computer-chip technology. Intrigued by the problem presented to him by the late President, he had modified a standard guidance circuit by placing within it a tiny, ingeniously complicated chip. When a special code was radioed to it on an ultra-high frequency, the chip was activated. Antagonistic current surges were generated to block normal operation of the circuit, thus rendering entire systems inoperable. So complex was this chip that seven years of study by a team of highly trained Russian technicians had not been able to unlock the secret of its activating code.

The entire circuit was code-named Cerberus by the Furies, but appeared simply as 120044C in the specifications of manufacture. Cerberus was the monstrous three-headed dog in mythology whose neck bristled with serpents. Never sleeping, he guarded the gates of hell to stop the spirits of the dead from escaping. Butov had found it a fitting name for an ever-alert electronic circuit waiting for a signal from its master to bring to earth a threatening warplane or misdirect an enemy missile.

The identity of the third Fury had eluded them. He was presumed to be in the Pentagon or with NASA, since this Fury must control one of the many American spy satellites. His job was to maneuver the satellite over an area of potential conflict in the Middle East and order it to radio down the preset code that would activate the Cerberus circuits to knock out all U.S.-supplied weaponry in that area. The target area could be as small as a few hundred square feet or as large as an entire country. But which satellite? Warren had not referred to it by name. Only he and the third Fury, Alecto, would know. Butov had been in the process of wresting the satellite's name from John Warren when the door to the villa had burst open. Looking back, he remembered the moment well.

Mrs. Warren's pleas had finally been heeded by the Albanian rulers and the villages along the coast had been ordered to search their shoreline for wreckage or bodies from the American President's yacht. The body of the

Secret Service man assigned to Warren had been found and brought to the village. Beqir Drin and Enver Shkumbi had recognized the dead man. They knew the rich Greek must have killed him, but why? For some reason their rulers wanted to find him and the other foreigner they had carried up the face of the cliff on that stormy night. There must be a way to profit from their knowledge. The two fishermen had debated. They needed help. And so they went to the head of the village, Mehmit Scutari, with their version of what had happened on that stormy night. Scutari was an old hand at blackmail; few of the villagers had managed to escape his demands for tribute in one form or another. Taking his gun and followed by the fishermen and several of the local militia, Scutari had walked boldly up to the villa of the man he knew as Demetrias Bralo and kicked in the door.

Alerted by his wife's scream and the scuffle in the hallway below, Butov had reached for the hypodermic needle on the table beside him and quickly filled it. All he could think of was that the man on the bed before him must never reveal what had happened to him, that he must die. Inserting the long needle in the delirious President's arm, Butov pressed down on the plunger just as a firm hand grasped his wrist. The spurting needle fell to the floor. The KGB agent looked up into the leering, heavily mustached face of Mehmit Scutari.

"Ah, Demetrias Bralo," the headman had said, "I think perhaps you have been very naughty. I think perhaps we should talk."

It had cost Butov and the KGB a great deal of money, but the village hailed the Greek as a hero for saving the life of "the man from the sea," and he and his wife were allowed to quickly leave the country. Butov was also hailed by his surperiors and finally assured a place of responsibility and authority within the party hierarchy. Steps had been taken at once to make use of the military information he had brought with him, but the more important implications of the "Acheron Plot" as Butov called it, were kept secret in the top echelon of KGB headquarters in 2 Dzerzhinsky Square.

As Butov recounted his last days in Albania, Miklos Androssy stared through the steaming mist at him, barely hearing his words. Butov was no longer necessary to the operation; he was expendable. The few other field operatives, including the resident, knew only small bits and pieces of the puzzle. But Butov knew the entire puzzle, knew far too much if Androssy were to turn the Acheron Plot to his own advantage. Right now the chairman of the KGB and the Secretary General were the only two in the Kremlin fully knowledgeable about this affair. They trusted only him, his empire, and his discretion to uncover the identity of the third Fury, the spy satellite capable of activating the Cerberus circuits, and the codes that manipulated the satellite. Secrecy was essential.

The baron had no basic loyalty to the Soviet Union. He regarded those in power there merely as business partners. And from his experience, the partner who was more clever, who kept the trump card up his sleeve, was the partner to survive.

Anatoli Butov and his wife's rapid rise within the Party had gone to their heads. They boasted, talked too much. And the baron did not trust the obvious comradery that had grown between the Butovs and the resident, Vladimir Savich, and his wife, Galina. Galina Fedorovna Savich was a skilled operative, one who could easily extract information from Shura Butov, who enjoyed too much the luxuries provided by her husband's position in the New York headquarters of UNITAR. No, Androssy thought, it is time for our fat friend and his wife to go home.

They had been in the sauna for nearly thirty minutes, and the baron noted with satisfaction Butov's heavy breathing. He had gradually been increasing the heat and steam in the small room.

"Have you plans for dinner this evening?" Androssy casually asked the KGB agent.

"Shura and I have been requested to dine with Vladimir and Galina Savich," Butov replied with a touch of pride.

"You dined with them last evening, if I am not mistaken."

"Yes. The women have become good friends, and Vladimir and I . . ."

"Are you feeling well?" Androssy asked, interrupting the boast he knew would follow. "You look ill."

"The heat," Butov replied, wiping his streaming face with a towel.

Androssy smiled. He too felt the pounding of his heart. They had been in the sauna much too long, but he knew the other's pride would not allow him to be the first to suggest leaving. Continuing their conversation, he paid close attention to the other's color and the sound of his labored breathing until he finally rose. "My friend, you are not well." Crossing the room, he solicitously helped the Russian rise dizzily to his feet and supported him as they left the sauna. Guiding him to a chair, the baron picked up the phone and handed it to the gasping man. "Here," he said, "I insist you call Shura and tell her you are not feeling well. Perhaps you should postpone your dinner this evening."

"I will be fine as soon as I catch my breath," Butov protested.

"At least call your wife and tell her you are returning home at once. Please." His request was an order which the other was not fool enough to ignore.

Taking the phone, the KGB agent reluctantly dialed and spoke in short gasps to his wife. "No," he replied to some inquiry the baron could not hear, "just a little out of breath." He paused. "We will discuss it when I get home." Another pause. "When I get home," he repeated, hanging up the receiver.

"You relax here, Anatoli," Androssy said. "I will have a taxi called for you. Unfortunately, Edith and the children have the cars this afternoon. I was not expecting to need the limousine."

"You are most kind." Butov leaned back, mopping his face.

Androssy smiled sympathetically. Thirty minutes later he accompanied Anatoli Butov to the door and saw him safely into the waiting taxi. Its driver wore a Hawaiian-patterned sport shirt and jeans.

Returning to his study, Baron Androssy contemplated his next moves.

On the face of it, Alexander Kidd's file had seemed innocent enough. But as soon as he had begun reading between the lines, Androssy knew that he had uncovered the third Fury. It suddenly had become so very obvious, even the similarity in the names—Alex and the code name Alecto. It was obvious, that is, if one knew exactly what he was looking for. Kidd's KWEN satellite had been launched during the Warren administration. Kidd would have needed powerful government backing to have pulled off a coup of such magnitude, getting his own satellite put up just after NASA's experimental communications satellite ATS-6, and before those of the major networks.

All the American satellites had been launched either under the auspices of, or in cooperation with, various government agencies and departments. Yet unlike the other satellites, the detailed blueprints and specifications of Kidd's satellite were held only by KWEN. The actual use of each of its four transponders was not a matter of public record, and control of the satellite was maintained only by KWEN in New York. Finally, Kidd's satellite was nick-named Charon II, a name that fit perfectly with the others in the late President's plot. Charon was the mythical boatman who ferried the dead across the river Acheron. Clever, Androssy mused, to use a commerical rather than a military satellite. Obviously John James Warren had wanted to make sure that the secrets of Charon II never fell into the hands of his own or later Presidents' military establishments.

Charon II obviously could receive and respond only to those messages that were beamed up in the proper frequen-cy and codes—just as it must beam down the preset code to activate the destructive Cerberus circuits. To control the satellite and its awesome potential meant to control those codes. And only Alexander Kidd would have them.

Leaning back in his chair, Baron Androssy looked at the photogrpah of Alexander Kidd in the file before him. He wondered exactly what type of man he would face in the battle ahead. The Androssy empire would have to move quietly and quickly to take over KWEN and its satellite. But he alone would take over the information Kidd must hold hidden in his brain. Only he, Miklos Androssy, must know the codes to command Charon II. Just imagine the bargaining power he would wield over the Kremlin—or for that matter, the U.S.—if he could pull it off. The baron smiled to himself as he contemplated the prospect.

Since uncovering the Acheron Plot seven years ago, with Androssy's behind-the-scenes help, the KGB had moved quickly to turn Warren's weapons against the United States. They had infiltrated Simon Felton's electronics company while simultaneously managing to have one of their top Pentagon illegals discreetly transferred into General Carmody's command. It had not been difficult, thanks to the Americans' dismantling and destruction of their own security services in the aftermath of Watergate, a childish act encouraged by the KGB's skillful use of disinformation techniques in the U.S. media.

Once inside Felton Electronics, they had discovered that no 120044C Cerberus circuits had been shipped for inclusion in any planes, missiles, or other weaponry after President Warren had been voted from office. In fact, the entire Acheron Plot seemed to have been dropped, but the potential to turn it from a plan for peace into a devastating blow against America and its allies still remained.

With characteristic effectiveness, one of the many companies in the Androssy empire launched a successful takeover bid for Felton Electronics. The price paid was excessive, but it stopped shareholder debate and sealed the fate of the company quickly. Given an unlimited research budget, Simon Felton relinquished all management responsibility and happily devoted himself to the development of new and more advanced space-age technology. The baron smiled to himself. It was technology that had been generously smuggled to the Soviet Union for years without its inventor being any the wiser.

Within weeks, under the new management at Felton Electronics, the complex chip contained in the 120044C circuit was incorporated silently into the standard 120044 circuit. That meant that for the next seven years every piece of sophisticated weaponry and its necessary replacement parts manufactured in this country for its defense and sold to other non-Warsaw Pact countries contained the potentially destructive Cerberus circuit. And that included most of the nuclear missiles—the long-range ballistic missiles in silos buried deep in the United States, those in submarines circling the globe, and those carried by planes and based on the European continent. During all that time Androssy had secretly led the search for the missing key, the satellite that would activate the Cerberus circuits and so make the Soviet Union impervious to attack while bringing America and its allies to their knees.

The sound of a door being opened distracted him. Edith Androssy bustled into the room from the garden carrying a large vase of freshly cut summer flowers. "Was that the man from the United Nations something-or-other research group I saw leaving?" she asked, setting the vase on the long library table and making a last few adjustments to the arrangement.

"Yes," he replied casually, watching her fuss with several obstinent blossoms. "How very thoughtful of you, my dear. You know how I enjoy flowers."

"The zinnias are perfect now." Edith stood back to examine her handiwork. "He looked quite pale. Was he sick?" she asked.

"Yes, he was. I doubt we shall be seeing him again. Our work is finished."

"Good."

"Why do you say that?" he asked, smiling at her.

"You know I never criticize your friends. . . ."

"Business associates," he corrected.

"Yes, business associates, but I really didn't care much for that man the few times we spoke. He is rather," she paused, searching for the right adjectives, "rather coarse and . . ."

"Common?"

"Yes, common, that's it. He's common. Is that cruel of me to say, Mickey?"

"No, not at all. That is exactly what he is. Now tell me, what are you going to wear tonight for the benefit?"

"Oh, darling, you must help me make up my mind," Edith Androssy said, crossing the room to him and kissing his cheek. "I love the red gown, the one you bought with me in Paris, but I've worn it once before this summer and . . . do you think . . . Of course there is the mauve. . . ."

The baron laughed tolerantly and put his arm around her ample waist. "My dear, whichever you choose will be absolutely perfect. Have you thought of the new blue gown? You look so cool and pretty in it."

"Yes, the blue one. Oh, Mickey, you are clever." Giving her husband a quick hug, Edith Androssy hurried across the room and left the baron to return to the file before him.

Having recovered, Anatoli Butov leaned back in the rear seat of the taxi. He looked out of the window, but his eyes focused on nothing, his thoughts on what he would have to tell his good friend Vladimir Savich at dinner that evening. When he had first arrived in New York more than six years ago, he had been instructed to report immediately to the resident all matters pertaining to the Acheron Plot. He had become aware that a far more senior person was pulling the strings concerning Acheron, but it was not until eight months ago that he had been shocked to learn that Baron Androssy, the international financial genius, was a Russian agent and the man in charge of uncovering the Acheron Plot in the United States. From that time on, he had been ordered to report only to Androssy.

The baron was obviously trusted and respected by the

chairman of the KGB and the top leaders in the Kremlin. He recently had heard rumors that the Premier had been a friend of Androssy, that the two had once worked closely together. Did the knowledge he had gained from the late head of the KGB and leader of their country contribute to the baron's power and seeming immunity from the rules of the Center?

Butov found himself in an unhappy position. His usefulness was beginning to wane, there was little more he could contribute to solving the Acheron puzzle. And he knew that Androssy hated him. On the other hand, his friend Savich was the resident, the top KGB man in New York. He ran many operatives and was involved in many areas besides this satellite thing. Butov and his wife liked New York. After the isolation and hardship of all those years in Albania, they deserved a post of merit. He had been wise to cultivate Savich, to drop him what bits of information he could. Tonight he would prove to Comrade Savich and his own wife, Shura, just what a clever and essential man he was. Because this afternoon he alone had found the key to the riddle of Acheron. He looked forward to presenting the name of Alexander Kidd to his host at dinner that evening.

Caught in the rush-hour traffic going uptown on Madison Avenue, the taxi veered left on Seventy-second Street and headed into Central Park. Aroused from his fantasies of grandeur, the KGB operative shouted out and banged heavily on the partition separating the two. Butov pointed in the opposite direction as the driver slid back the partition. He was still shouting when the seven-inch tube containing an ampule of prussic acid was shoved within an inch of his nose and the trigger pulled. The vapor from the exploded ampule briefly surrounded Butov's face as he gasped and slid forward, toppling off the seat to the floor of the cab. Prussic acid left no trace. Even the finest doctor at the Soviet Mission would say that Anatoli Butov had died of cardiac arrest. And his widow, Shura, would bear witness to the ill health in which her unfortunate husband had left the home of Miklos Androssy.

* * *

The following day, the baron sat relaxed and confident at the head of the long mahogany table in the elegant, Victorian-decorated dining room atop one of the many corporate buildings within his empire. To his left, the floor-to-ceiling windows, the only modern feature of the room, gave a dramatic view of Wall Street and the pyramidal domes and financial towers that surrounded it.

"Gentlemen," he said, addressing the seven dark-suited men lunching with him, "the cable television industry is one of the fastest growing segments of the market today. Nearly thirty percent of all homes in this country are now subscribing to cable systems. By 1990, fifty percent will subscribe. Systems are being built in Dallas and other cities offering up to one hundred channels. Gentlemen," he repeated for emphasis, "one hundred channels. Can you imagine?"

The men seated at the table were aware that if the baron had chosen this as a subject for conversation today, he was somehow interested in entering that market.

"And how will the cable systems fill all those one hundred channels? The answer is obvious. They cannot. Not today. Software, developing programming for cable television, will be the gold mine of tomorrow." He paused, lifting a crystal goblet of excellent claret to his lips as he looked from one man to the next. Taking a sip, he lowered the glass. "Gentlemen, it is time for our group to enter show business." He smiled.

"You obviously have something specific in mind," the distinguished banker to his right commented.

"I do."

"Our western conglomerate holds a major interest in Milo Productions in Los Angeles," another suggested. "The film facilities can be upgraded or we could merge it into a major studio. Two are ripe for takeover."

"Ah," the baron said, pleased with the other's statement, "you have put your finger on part of my idea. Milo Productions is the core, or shall we say the facade. It will be the screen behind which you will work to take over the Kidd Worldwide Entertainment Network."

The surprise and separate conversations that erupted between the men around the table gratified Androssy. Using a heavy sterling silver fork, he speared several pieces of endive from his salad plate.

"Why Kidd?" the banker asked. "Turner and the three major networks are squeezing it."

"Exactly," Miklos Androssy replied. "Right now it is a profitable enterprise with all the necessary hardware. But it must either expand quickly with new programming or be relegated to what you call the minor leagues. From what I have been able to learn, Alexander Kidd will expand. He does not like playing in the minor leagues." Several of the men nodded their agreement. "The entire network is owned by only seven principals and held together by a maze of bank loans. Kidd will need more capital for his expansion. Where will he get it? Gentlemen, that will be the key to your move."

"Once we've got it, what do you plan to do with KWEN?" his management consultant at the far end of the table asked.

"We will merge it and Milo with at least one major studio in this country and one abroad to become the fourth television network and to form the largest supplier of video software in the United States and, for that matter, in the world." He lied. Androssy knew full well that the Charon II satellite would never be used again for commercial purposes once he got his hands on it. "Gentlemen, as I said before, we have a gold mine waiting for us."

Once again separate conversations broke out around the table. The baron held up his hand to silence them.

"Tomorrow my office will distribute to each of you a portfolio containing all the information our researchers have been able to uncover to date on Kidd's network. In the meantime, put your ears to the ground. Find which banks hold the loans for every penny outstanding, which ones are friendly to our group or could be induced to lay off their loans. I want the exact financial position of each of Alexander Kidd's five partners, whether or not they might be coaxed into throwing in with us, how much it will take, and who should approach them. And above all, I want to know Kidd's plans for the future, what commitments he is making." The others at the table nodded their heads knowledgeably. They were old hands at the techniques for raping and pillaging unwary companies.

"Need I say, gentlemen," Baron Androssy continued, "your discretion and speed is of the utmost importance. We must remain anonymous. I believe Mr. Kidd is a street fighter. I do not like brawls. We will take him by surprise from all sides, render him helpless before he can so much as lift his hands to swing back." Placing his napkin on the table, Miklos Androssy pushed back his chair and stood, his eyes moving from one man to the other. "Our group has never lost a takeover, gentlemen, and I do not plan to bloody my nose on this one." Glancing briefly through the glass wall at the financial center of the city spread out below him, he left the room.

Later that night he met again with Vladimir Savich in the darkness between the abutments of the Triborough Bridge. "I wish to meet the German cameraman, your raven. Arrange a place where we can speak without being seen."

"Butov is dead," Savich said flatly.

The baron was silent for a minute and then asked without emotion, "The details?"

"Apparent heart failure," the resident replied, emphasizing his first word, "just after leaving you yesterday afternoon."

"He did not look well when he left," Androssy commented. "Where was he stricken?"

"In Central Park. Apparently"—once again he emphasized the word—"he left his cab on the way home for a walk. He was found beside a bench."

Androssy didn't miss the skepticism in Savich's voice nor his reference to a cab. How could Savich be sure that Butov had taken a taxi unless he maintained a constant surveillance of the house at Sutton Place? "This comes at an unfortunate time," the baron said. "We had not finished our work together. Have you reported it to the Center?" Androssy referred to Special Service II, one of the KGB departments responsible for penetrating foreign security and intelligence services.

The other nodded. "You found nothing in the reports I sent you?"

"Nothing."

"You still do not know the identity of the man called Alecto?" Again disbelief lay behind Savich's question. Butov had obviously been in close contact with him.

"No." Again Androssy lied to the resident to exclude him from the details of the Acheron Plot. Through his Zurich channel of communication with the KGB, Androssy had wired the chairman the vague message that he had identified the satellite and was taking steps to acquire the codes that controlled it.

"What about Alexander Kidd? I thought you were—"

"He remains one of my suspects," Androssy interrupted, "but there is no real connection other than his acquaintance with the general."

"But you want to question the German," Savich persisted, digging as he always did.

"He may be useful sometime in the future, Vladimir Savich," the baron replied smoothly, "nothing more."

CHAPTER 6

Sporadic bursts of gunfire and distant explosions were the only sounds that penetrated the heavy, tattered draperies pulled tightly across the windows of the large, once-beautiful salon overlooking a back street in the Moslem section of East Beirut. The uneasy cease-fire between the various Christian and Moslem groups was breaking down more and more frequently these days. There were rumors that the Syrians were massing troops and equipment both in Lebanon and along their fragile border with Israel. Jordan also seemed edgy and in a strangely aggressive mood since the latest failure to reach agreement with the Israelis. Israeli jets daily swooped low over their neighbors' territory in shows of force and to gather information. Alliances between the Arab states were made and broken every day. The entire area was in turmoil.

Although the moon shone bright over Beirut, none of its light reached the far corner of the shabby room where four men sat around a circular table littered with papers, coffee cups, and glasses. All four were in shirt-sleeves, collars open to give some relief from the heat of the July night. No military uniforms covered with rows of colorful medals were present to signal the prominence of those present. The rumpled suits of common businessmen were more suitable to mask the importance of the meeting. They spoke with urgency, their voices lowered.

"Proof," the Syrian demanded. "My president wants proof."

"He will get it," General Ivan Ivanovich Guryanov replied in an even, rational tone.

"When?" Ali Gemayel challenged. "We are tired of promises." The heavily mustached military adviser to the Syrian president brought his fist down on the table in frustration. "How can you expect us to base an entire military operation on this . . . this . . ." He paused, reaching for the right words. "This improbable—no, impossible feat. How can—"

"Ali," the large, broad-shouldered man sitting to his right interrupted softly, "be calm. Give our friend the chance to explain." General Saad Hassam, veteran leader of the Syrian armed forces, had been intrigued by the Russian plan when it had first been proposed to his president over two years ago. As his associate had just pointed out, it would be an impossible feat. But if the Russians were so sure that they could pull it off, he, for one, would go for it. The general relished the thought of being able to bring the Israeli army to its knees, rub their faces in the dust as they had done to his people. Not only would he take back the Golan Heights, but half their country as well. The rest could go to Jordan and the Palestinians. He smiled at Salim Chamoun, the fourth man seated at the table. Thin, intense, unshaven, Chamoun was the senior PLO representative in Beirut. He would lead his people in the uprising when and if it came.

Saad Hassam looked back at the middle-aged Russian. "This is the second time you have postponed the date in the last two years."

The Russian said nothing.

"General Guryanov, time is running out." His voice was precise and rational. "You propose that we and our brothers in Jordan, Libya, Gaza, and the West Bank launch an invasion of Israel, this time on September twenty-second." He waited for confirmation of his statement.

The heavyset, balding Russian nodded. "That is correct." His eyes moved from one man to the next.

"You have guaranteed that on this date not a single Israeli plane will fly, not a single missile will hit its target."

"Not a single *American*-supplied plane or missile," General Guryanov amended.

Saad Hassam looked at him with a mixture of fascination and doubt. "You say you will be able to sabotage them."

"Correct."

"All of them."

Again the Russian nodded.

"Why only the American weapons?" Ali Gemayel pressed.

Ivan Ivanovich Guryanov shrugged. "Does that matter? The Israeli armed forces depend almost entirely upon American-made weapons. You will find little if any opposition in the air."

"Can you tell us how you propose to sabotage such a large number of planes, missiles, and tanks? And almost simultaneously so that our attack will be a surprise?"

"Obviously I am not at liberty to disclose that," General Guryanov answered. In fact, the general himself did not know. He was only the Kremlin's military strategist and messenger boy in this operation. "For security reasons," he added.

"For security reasons," Ali Gemayel parroted in irritation. "This entire business is impossible. Twice before you promised, twice before you demurred."

"We need proof, Ivan Ivanovich," General Hassam said calmly. "We have already begun the necessary mobilization, but unless we have proof, some evidence, that you can do what you promise this time, we will call it off. Our Palestinian brothers agree."

Salim Chamoun nodded. "We will find other ways, other times to defeat our enemy."

"My friends," General Guryanov began, "do not be hasty. We—"

"Proof," Saad Hassam interrupted.

Ivan Ivanovich Guryanov reached for his empty glass and heaved his heavy, bullnecked body up from the chair.

Wiping his fat, sweaty face with a damp handkerchief, he walked slowly over to the large sideboard. Above it hung an elaborate, cracked mirror set into the wall. Unscrewing the top of the vodka bottle, the general filled his glass. In the dusty mirror he could see the eyes of the other three boring into his back as he poured the colorless liquid.

The Russians had expected this demand. "We will give you proof," he said without turning.

"When?" Ali Gemayel demanded.

The general's thoughts took him back to the complex of unmarked stone buildings at 2 Dzerzhinsky Square. That complex not only housed Lubyanka Prison where many a party official had been imprisoned, tortured, and executed, but the offices of the all-powerful KGB. Earlier that Sunday morning, he had stood in the chairman's third-floor office, receiving his final briefing. "Stall for time," the chairman had said. "The means of sabotage will soon be ours."

"You will have your proof," General Guryanov replied, his back still turned to the others, "two weeks before the invasion."

"That is not enough time, my friend," General Hassam countered.

"They are bluffing," Ali Gemayel scoffed in an aside to his fellow Syrian. He said it just loud enough for the Russian to hear. "It is a hoax to involve us all in a war that will only weaken us."

The KGB field operatives had been supplying almost daily reports on the preparedness of all the countries in the area. General Guryanov had reviewed them before leaving Moscow and, therefore, knew the extent of the Syrian and Jordanian buildups. As only the Syrian and Libyan air forces with their Russian-made planes would be involved, he saw no great timing problem there. Exactly how long would it take Israel's two immediate neighbors to complete the preparations they had already begun? Three weeks? Four? Certainly no more.

"Ali Gemayel," he said, turning, "you must trust me. We are your friends, your neighbors."

"Does the sheep trust the jackal?" the other retorted.

The attack had to be planned down to the last detail. Just at sunrise on September twenty-second, Libyan planes would swoop in from the west and Syrian planes from the east to hit major military and civilian targets. There would be no need to destroy Israeli air bases as their planes would be useless and the landing strips and facilities could be used later by the invaders. The Jordanians would put their few Russian jets bought since 1981 into action on the outskirts of Jerusalem while the PLO and their Arab sympathizers within the city would rise up and attack the foreign occupiers. In hours, the seat of Israeli government would be silenced. The PLO would also strike in Gaza and the West Bank. Egypt and Saudi Arabia had already agreed to look the other way in the conflict as their contribution to Arab unity and as the price of their acceptance back into the Arab League.

As Israel had controlled the air in 1967 to conquer its neighbors in five days, now those same neighbors would control the air and enjoy protection from Israeli land-based missiles. They would be able to move freely on the ground, knowing that their enemy's malfunctioning tanks would not be able to fire upon theirs. The elimination of Israel as a nation would be a magnificent military coup.

The general could not know that the inner circle in the Kremlin had decided to throw Israel to the wolves merely as an example to the United States and its NATO allies that all their heavy military equipment and nuclear missiles were impotent against their Soviet superiors. Capitulation was the only possible response in the face of complete annihilation. General Guryanov only knew that it was essential that he gain the cooperation of the three Arabs in the room.

"Very well, my friends," he said, returning to the table. "In late August we will prove to you our ability to destroy American weaponry."

"Give us a date," Ali Gemayel persisted.

"It will be sometime during the weeks of August twenty-one or twenty-eight." Those were the dates he had been given by the chairman of the KGB that morning.

"You are vague," General Hassam said.

"That is the best I can do. It will depend upon circumstances that we ourselves cannot control. But you will see, I guarantee."

"What form will your proof take?" Salim Chamoun asked.

"Again it will depend upon circumstances," the Russian replied. "You will be informed beforehand." He himself did not know how his country planned to supply proof.

A grudging silence fell over the room as the Syrian and Palestinian plotters eyed each other for some sign of accord.

"Until that time," General Guryanov said, "we expect you to continue your covert mobilization." He looked from one man to the other. "Those are the conditions of our offer. Take them or leave them," Guryanov said gruffly. "You will never get another chance like this to destroy your common enemy with so little risk to yourselves."

"He is right, Ali," General Hassam said finally. "What do we have to lose? If our friend does what he says he can do, we will divide Israel between us before the year is out. If not, we demobilize and wait until the time is right to strike. And you, Salim Chamoun?" he asked the PLO representative.

"I agree. We will wait for the proof."

His mission accomplished, General Ivan Ivanovich Guryanov nodded. "Good, then shall we get down to the details of your invasion plans?" He upended his glass and gulped the remaining vodka. As the Syrians spread out their war maps across the table, the Russian only vaguely wondered about the magnitude of the forthcoming massacre of the helpless Israeli army and civilian population. He heard the dull explosion of another grenade in a street nearby. The lights in the room flickered briefly.

"Fools," Baron Androssy cursed, rereading the telex before crushing it in his fist. The Monday-morning message had come from the small Stadthausquai 17 branch of one of his many banks in Zurich, the conduit through which he communicated directly with the chairman of the KGB. It stated simply, "TRANSFER OF FUNDS TO ISRAEL COMMITTED WEEK OF 21 AUGUST." "They are moving too fast," he exclaimed to the empty room. "Do the idiots not realize one needs time to maneuver in the capitalist world?"

Dropping the telex into the paper shredder beside the desk, he watched it disappear as he reviewed his next steps. Only a little over a month remained in which to accomplish a major takeover in the communications field, one which the government would surely want to review for antitrust violations.

"Fools," he grumbled again. But the chairman could not know the complications. Despite repeated requests for further information, Androssy had elected to send none.

Rising, he crossed his antique-filled office to the window and stared blankly down on the tiny figures bustling below on Wall Street. Did the chairman suspect the motives of his most trusted agent? Was his hand being forced? Was the twenty-first his deadline? After that, would the KGB move in to take over? What was Savich telling them?

Androssy liked to move cautiously, anonymously, covering all his tracks, finding and plugging all loopholes before striking, taking his victim by surprise. Until now he had enjoyed the game; to date no victim of his had ever survived. But now?

Not only was he being forced to move too quickly for a smooth, clean takeover of KWEN, but after that was accomplished, he still had to get his hands on the two codes needed to move Charon II and activate its transmissions to the Cerberus circuits. The first code used to move the satellite was obviously known to others, those who worked with Charon II on a daily basis and were responsible for keeping it in orbit. The second would be locked in Kidd's brain or elsewhere within his KWEN empire, probably both. But after its seven years of nonuse, Kidd would surely have forgotten the Cerberus code. It *had* to be written down or recorded somewhere. Androssy had to get that code, and until he did, none of the three Furies must ever suspect an

outsider knew of the original Acheron Plot or suspect that
the takeover bid for KWEN was aimed solely at gaining
control of Charon II and its destructive capabilities. At least
Kidd is in England playing with his yacht, Androssy
thought. That would make things easier.

With a fatalistic sigh, he returned to his desk and picked
up one of the many phones lining it to begin personally to
put together the financial consortium that would back Milo
Productions in its attack on Alexander Kidd and his network.

"Ready about," Kidd shouted, glancing once again at the
wind vane atop the masthead of the *Privateer*. The twelve-
man crew scurried over the deck, taking their positions for
the change of course that would take the boat across the
English Channel and back to its berth in Portsmouth. It was
August 15. They had spent the grueling day off the coast of
France carrying out a variety of maneuvers to perfect the
split-second timing so vital to the proper handling of sails
during a race. Two weeks ago a spinnaker wrap had cost the
Privateer the Fastnet race from the Isle of Wight to the Irish
coast. It was his first international race and he had lost.
Kidd was determined it would not happen again. Although
he had lambasted the crew for the carelessness that had
allowed the spinnaker to wrap around the headstay, in his
heart he knew he bore the responsibility for not having spent
enough time to weld them together into an efficient, well-
coordinated team. Most of his time and thoughts since
arriving in Europe had been concentrated not on drilling his
crew but on putting together KWEN's new international
culture-and-arts channel.

"Hard alee," he shouted into the wind, and spun one of
the twin wheels in the cockpit. The mainsail flapped only
briefly before refilling, and the graceful sixty-seven-foot
boat swung to port and came about to run before the
southwesterly wind. The captain of the *Privateer* watched
with an appraising eye as his crew repositioned the
spinnaker pole and set the sail. The great red-and-white-
striped chute billowed out to pull the boat ahead, its shiny

blue hull slicing neatly through the water. A capitalist through and through, Kidd loved the country that had given the boy from a poor Connecticut family the opportunity to become a millionaire. What other colors could he have possibly selected for his championship boat but red, white, and blue?

The maneuver completed to his satisfaction, Kidd turned the wheel over to his most trusted crew member, Hal Trevane, and leaned back against the cushions in the cockpit. He did not enjoy running before the wind because the boat always felt sluggish then. It bored him. Kidd preferred the challenge of sailing a close reach, heading into the wind until the sails were trimmed in almost as far as they could go, the boat heeled over at a steep angle, water racing past over the lower edge of the deck. And the wind. He loved its caress against his face. At times like those, he felt he, the wind, and the sea were joined together in a tenuous love affair. He respected their caprices and took satisfaction in holding firm his mastery over them.

Today, looking up at the dazzling white mainsheet and the blue sky beyond, Alexander Kidd allowed his tired mind to drift from the sea.

The negotiations with the European national television systems, orchestras, ballets, and even the art galleries had been far more difficult and complex than he had anticipated. It was mid-August and many people key to his plans were on holiday, the capitals virtually closed down. Alex had spent nearly a month working on the deals and still had a long way to go. The Europeans, aware of the tremendous demand in the U.S. for cultural softwear, were showing great reluctance to assign exclusive American rights to KWEN. Bastards, he thought. He had spent a little over ten million dollars to set up his entire sports channel, and these cultural hypocrites had already extracted nearly six million in advances and investments in new productions. He was being forced to go far over the budget he had set for himself. But no matter the cost, the Kidd network would produce and control the best damn cultural-and-arts channel in the world. Then he would come back and screw those intellectual twits to the financial wall.

Financial walls. That brought images of his tempestuous meetings with the Bahama bankers. Charming, soft-spoken, those perfect gentlemen in their white business suits had torn a strip of flesh off Alex. Had he been there, Page Shepard would have withdrawn from the negotiations after the first day, but Kidd desperately needed that eleven million. And so, swallowing hard, he had agreed to sign over eleven, not nine percent of the KWEN shares to the vultures as security for the loan. Together, he and Judith now held only a forty-nine-percent interest. They had him by the balls, but he would be free of their hold within three years when his cash flow increased from the many new cable systems that would carry KWEN.

Those two-faced Judases had pontificated morally on their plush terraces overlooking the golf courses, swimming pools, and casinos of Freeport while their banks busily laundered drug and organized-crime money from Miami. Kidd had had to restrain himself many times from throwing one of their pink gins into their faces.

Alexander Kidd felt the gentle sea breeze soothe his face. Why, he wondered, was he taking this risk? Up until last month he could have retired a very rich man. Now he had committed millions of dollars without even consulting his five backers.

"Head up slightly into the wind, Hal," he said, looking at the coastline of southern England in the distance. "And take in the mainsheet a bit. Let's get the wind to port quarter and go to a broad reach. Portsmouth will be coming up soon."

Nodding, Hal Trevane turned the wheel. "There's that speedboat again," he commented, pointing to the powerful black boat coming up to pass on their starboard side. "I've noticed it several times today."

Kidd looked over. "Probably timing us. Know who it belongs to?"

Trevane shook his head. "Only that it's moored across the harbor."

"Well, we should be flattered," Kidd replied, smiling. He felt the *Privateer* slowly responding. Once it was on its new tack, he sank back into his own private thoughts.

Judith was certainly being a stubborn bitch in New York. No, that wasn't fair. Judith might be infuriating, but she certainly was no bitch. Principled to a fault, talented—he had to admit that—and cultivated. Not flamboyant at all, serene and confident. With the exception of her confidence, she was everything he was not. Why had they grown apart? Certainly not because either of them had changed that much since first meeting at Yale. Maybe they just didn't need each other as much as they used to. She had been an art student, always deeply involved in some cause or other, waving the banner for right. No, again he was exaggerating. Judith was not an extremist, she did not wave banners. Instead she quietly and efficiently organized her causes and stayed in the background while others did the shouting. He smiled, remembering her admirable but unsuccessful crusade to rid the campus of its secret societies because she felt them too elitist. She did not know that on the day she stood in the Old Campus distributing pamphlets, Alex had stood within the gloomy temple not far away being initiated into the most elite of all the societies, Skull and Bones. Perhaps he had been wrong not to tell her, but there seemed no point at the time. They both had their own values, their own lives to lead.

Alex had not been caught up in causes, just in getting the best possible education he could at the best college that would give him a scholarship and, once there, making a name himself. He was tired of being on the outside; he wanted in. During his senior year, he had been elected to the prestigious position of head of the *Yale Daily News*. And he had made the varsity crew. Kidd had to admit that the only reason he had tried out for crew was that he thought it was a rich kid's sport and for once in his life he wanted to feel like a rich kid. He had not thought of it in years. That was how he had met Page Shepard. When he thought of Page and his original, selfish motivation for joining the crew, Alex felt a twinge of guilt. Page's family had welcomed him unselfishly, treated him like a son, lavished affection on him, taught him so much of the world.

That was a lot more than he could say for his own father, a proud, hard disciplinarian of the Old World style. He believed that once born into a class, you stayed there, satisfied with your lot, not looking above your position. That bastard, Kidd thought, that Bible-spouting bastard. In his mind he saw his father in that crummy little appliance repair shop, bent over the littered old workbench, waiting for his son to join him after school, waiting for his daughter to sweep up before helping her mother with the evening meal. Across the park on the other side of town, the kids went off to private schools, went to dances at the country club while Alex Kidd bent over that damn bench, learning how to repair cheap radios and, after supper, beat his brains out in the library teaching himself what he needed to escape the life his father felt good enough for them.

Again Alex relived that terrible afternoon when, with the long-awaited letter in hand, he faced his father in the gloomy shop.

"I'm going to college, Dad."

John Kidd spoke calmly, without looking up from his work. "No, you're not."

"I am."

"Who's going to pay?" The older man's eyes remained on the radio before him.

"I've got a scholarship. To Yale, Dad. A full scholarship to Yale."

His father's hands stopped their work. Alex saw the knuckles of his large right hand turn white as he clasped the screwdriver in it. Without looking at his son, John Kidd spoke in a slow, controlled voice.

"You are going to stay here. You are going to work here. You are part of this family; you belong here."

"No I don't. I don't belong here. I don't want to sit in this crummy shop the rest of my life."

His father looked up, looked him square in the eyes. "Is that the scholarship letter?" he asked, pointing to the paper in his son's hand.

"Yes." Alex held it up for him to see.

John Kidd reached out and took the envelope. Still holding his son's eyes with his, he slowly tore the letter into small pieces and let them flutter to the floor. "I promised the Corbins you'd have their radio repaired by six o'clock today."

Now in his midforties, Alex still did not know if his father had forgiven him for going to college. How the bastard had shouted when he told them he was going to marry Judith.

"No Jew will ever set foot in this house," John Kidd had cried, thumping his fist against the kitchen table.

"Only her father's Jewish," he had equivocated. Had his father's approval meant so much then?

"She's still a Jew. Never in this house," John Kidd raged.

"You're right," Alex had finally shouted as he stormed out, "no Jew ever *will* come into this house, because Judith and I will never come to this house, never again."

He never did go back and he never looked back. Years later, driven by guilt, he had bought his widowed father a home in Florida to retire to. Nothing fancy, but nice. John Kidd had refused. It stood empty today, a monument to their mutual stubbornness, a useless trophy in their contest of wills.

For Judith's sake, Jacob Singer had tried to hide his disappointment over the marriage of his only daughter to Alex, but he had gradually come to accept him and took pride in the successes of his daughter's husband. Jacob had risked his own future for his adored daughter in 1965 by lending Alex the money needed to take over his first radio station. "Like her mother, Rosalind," Jacob Singer often said, quoting Shakespeare's description of his heroine, "Judith is 'a gallant and witty girl.'" It was a good description of Judith, Alex had to admit.

"Do you want to take her in?" Hal Trevane asked, bringing his skipper back into the present.

Kidd nodded and took the wheel in preparation for a close reach into Portsmouth harbor. "Take in the mainsheet," he called, "and for Christ's sake, watch that spinnaker."

Sandra Bannister stood waiting on the pier at Portsmouth, shielding her eyes from the setting sun with her hand while the *Privateer* headed toward its berth. Aside from Page Shepard, Sandra alone knew of Alex's plans for the third channel. At his request, she had taken a leave of absence from the news staff of KWEN and had been acting as his right hand in the European negotiations since their arrival in England nearly a month ago.

Issuing his last commands, Alex jumped from the boat to the dock, leaving his eleven crewmen to secure the elegant yacht as he jogged toward her. "Any news from Paris today?" he asked, kissing her cheek.

"They'll make their decision next week. Legendre and Audibert want more money if they do decide to give you an American exclusive."

"Surprise," he said sarcastically. Alex took Sandra's hand and pulled her along behind him as he walked rapidly toward the parking lot.

"Where are you dragging me, O Fearless Leader?"

Yanking open the door to his small red Porsche, he plopped her inside. "To London. I'm in the mood for a good meal."

"But aren't you taking the *Privateer* out tomorrow?" she protested.

"Yep. I'll drive down in the morning."

"Darling, you're going to kill yourself. You can't keep going at this pace. Let's just grab something here at the Lone Yachtsman and call it a night."

"That hole? I said a *good* meal and while we're at it," he leered at her, "this fearless leader wants to fuck you in a *good* bed." He slammed his car door.

"You're crazy. You know that, don't you? Absolutely bananas," she laughed.

"Hell, girl, it's only seventy miles." The tires shrieked as the Porsche jumped forward. "We'll be at the Connaught in time for pink gins." Then he sobered. "I'm expecting a call from Page. Something funny's going on over there."

"What?"

"Not sure. But I smell a rat." He swung the car onto the A-3 and raced north toward London. Sandra studied his face. He was worried, very worried. She leaned lightly against him and put her hand on his thigh, hoping her presence and warmth would bring him some comfort.

Sandra Bannister adored Alexander Kidd and had from the minute she had joined the underranks of KWEN and first seen its dynamic owner across the studio shouting at several cameramen. A California beach beauty, athletic, well educated, and highly ambitious, it had not taken Kidd long to notice her. After all, she had taken every opportunity to be in his presence. To his credit, Alex had not taken her as his lover until she had proved she could make it on her own as a keen reporter and anchorwoman. She admired him for that. But she had hated watching him toying with the minor actresses and high-class hookers who threw themselves at him wherever he went. Sandra and Alex had been together on and off for almost four years. She wondered how much longer it could last. In his restless drive forward, Alex seemed in constant need of new stimulation, new people. He seemed afraid of ever dropping anchor, standing still in calm water. But they were together now, sharing his newest adventure, and if he dropped her for another sex partner, she knew she would still always be part of his life. Sandra Bannister could settle for that. Her mind pictured Judith Kidd—beautiful, elegant, gentle. Is that what she was doing? Settling for just being part of Alex's life? No, not Judith. She would want more than that.

An hour later the Porsche pulled up to the Connaught Hotel.

"You go on up to the suite and change while I pull a few strings to get us into the grill," Alex directed as they stood in the portico.

She nodded and passed through the revolving door into the lobby. Alex was about to enter when he froze. So too did the young man still in the lobby who had just motioned his date through the exit.

The beautiful black woman whom Alex had often seen in the pages of *Vogue* passed through the revolving doors and turned to speak to her escort who was not there. She looked over at Alex and smiled as she stood waiting in the portico. Alex stepped back and also waited as the young man slowly swung the door around and joined them outside.

"Mark."

"Alex."

"You know each other?" the young woman laughed. "I love it."

"Namba," Mark Kidd said, "this is my father."

"The *famous* Alexander Kidd?" She smiled. "Now, this *is* an unexpected pleasure."

"Very unexpected," Mark said wryly as the model extended her hand.

Alex took it and smiled. He looked over at his son. Mark had turned into a sturdy man since he had last seen him. His six-foot frame stood well-muscled and compact, and he was more handsome than his father, having inherited the dark hair and elegant features of his mother. "I didn't know you were in London. What are you doing here?"

"Working on a new commission, a sculpture." He glanced through the glass revolving doors at Sandra Bannister, who stood waiting in the hotel lobby.

Alex noticed the trace of animosity in his son's expression. "Are you staying here?"

"Too rich for my blood. I've rented a furnished flat on Neville Street in South Kensington."

The two stood facing each other nervously. Was this all they had to say to each other after four years, Alexander Kidd wondered—talk about changes of address.

"Sorry about the Fastnet," Mark said finally.

"Ran into trouble with the spinnaker."

"So I read. Surprised you didn't have a net up." The boy

had loved sailing as much as his father. They had been a real team years ago.

"Didn't think I needed one."

Again the awkward silence. Sensing the tension, the model stepped in. "How long will you be staying in London, Mr. Kidd?"

"Another few weeks. Getting ready for the Whitbread," Alex lied.

Her eyes grew round with respect. "You're going to race around the world?"

"I didn't think Alexander the Great had time for that," his son put in. "What happened to superstation KWEN and all the lovely ladies within it?"

"Watch it, Mark," Alex warned, trying to keep his voice light, "you're getting into deep water."

"That's right, I forgot. Only *you* walk on water." Before his father could reply, he took the model's arm and turned. "See you around, Dad," he said over his shoulder. After walking a few steps, he paused and turned back. "If you're interested, some of my work is being exhibited at the Gannet gallery on New Bond Street. It's only a few blocks from here." He bit his lip and looked long at his father. "If you're interested, that's all." He shrugged and walked away.

Standing in the portico, Alexander Kidd watched his son fade into the darkness. The two had lost the art of communicating with each other four years ago. Shaking his head, he turned and pushed his way through the door into the Connaught lobby. Damn good-looking kid, though, he said to himself with pride.

"Mark, wasn't it?" Sandra asked as he joined her at the porter's desk.

"The one and only," Alex replied cockily, covering up any feeling he might have shown. "He's doing some commission here in London. How did you like that girl he was with? A knockout, eh?"

"Like father, like son."

"Who are you complimenting," Alex asked, "my son or yourself?"

"I'll let you think about that one for a while," she laughed. "Get me a gin and tonic. I'll bring you down a tie when I come." Sandra stepped into the paneled elevator and nodded to the operator.

"Nice day, Miss Bannister?" he asked.

"Very."

Glancing at his watch, Alex asked the porter for his phone messages and skimmed through the batch. "Are you sure no call came in from a Mr. Shepard?"

"I'll check once again, Mr. Kidd." The elderly man thumbed back through the papers on his desk and picked up the phone to press Alex's inquiry. Putting it back in its cradle, he smiled apologetically at the American. "Sorry, Mr. Kidd, nothing."

"Probably too early anyhow," Alex mumbled, looking at his watch again. Thanks to the time difference, it would be only early afternoon in New York. "Will you see if you can squeeze us into the Grill Room for dinner tonight."

"Oh, Mr. Kidd," the other scolded, "you know how very difficult that can—"

"You've never let me down," Alex interrupted, "at least not yet."

The old porter sighed. "I'll do my best."

"We'll be in the bar." Turning, Kidd walked down the deeply carpeted hall and into the hush of the dim bar.

Slumping into a chair in a window alcove, he summoned a waiter. As he waited, Alex looked out across the shadows of Mount Street. Several couples strolled slowly past, looking at the displays in the expensive shops. A man stopped by Alexander Kidd's parked Porsche and admired it. He bent low and, with apparent interest, peered into its window before passing on.

CHAPTER 7

There had been little love, only need in their lovemaking that evening. Alexander Kidd looked down at Sandra's sleeping body curled against his, her face pillowed on his shoulder. He felt the gentle brush of her long blond hair on his skin and stroked it lightly with his free hand in an unspoken apology.

He had taken Sandra quickly, savagely. She had seemed to expect it, and accepted it willingly. Like so many of the others, she had given her body to him almost in sacrifice. What did his slaughter of it give to her in return? What need did it fulfill? He thought of his meeting with Mark that night and of Judith. With her there had been more sharing; each demanded and each gave, with more foreplay, more involvement, sometimes gentle, sometimes fierce. There had been emotion and there had been contentment when they lay exhausted, their bodies touching, independent but feeling as one.

How different they had become. His life was now one of strife, action, glamor, and hers involved art, tranquility, and humanity.

His mind snapped back to the present. Taking his hand from Sandra's hair, he squinted at the luminous dial of his watch. 1:32. It would be 8:32 in the evening in New York. Where in hell was Page?

As if by telepathy, the phone beside the bed broke the dark silence of the room. Kidd snatched it up. "Yes?" He listened. "Yes, yes, put it through. Page," Alex shouted into the phone, "what the hell took you so long, old buddy?" He fell silent, listening to the voice from across the Atlantic. "How bad?"

"Real bad," Page replied from the study of his Fifth Avenue apartment. "We've got a takeover bid on our hands."

"A what?" Alex shouted in disbelief. "Impossible!"

"Some small production company out in Hollywood. Ever hear of a Milo Productions?"

"No."

"Well, that's the one." Page took the double Scotch held out to him and glanced up, giving Helmut Bruck a brief smile of thanks. "They crank out a couple of TV movies every year and do a lot of television-commercial production." Helmut settled into a chair at the far side of the room and thumbed absently through a copy of *Cablevision*.

"Those silly-assed bastards," Alex sneered. "Who the hell do they think they are? What's their capitalization, one camera and seven cans of tape?"

"They're small. That's not what's worrying me."

"Then what? Page, sometimes you act like a frightened old lady."

Page covered the mouthpiece with his hand. "Helmut," he called softly across the room, "would you mind?" He motioned to the door with his head.

The blond German nodded and rose, casually dropping the magazine on the coffee table. "I'll be in your room."

Page returned to the phone. "Milo is small potatoes. It's what's behind it, Alex. From all I've been able to learn to date, Milo is the front for some large conglomerate. Alex," he said, shaking his head, "it's a giant octopus."

"How do you know? Which one is it? One of the networks?" The condescending humor was gone from Kidd's voice.

"I don't know exactly who's behind it yet. It's not the networks. I'm still trying to put things together. Alex, we had no warning. They hit us from all sides this morning. Practically all our outstanding loans have been layed off to four new banks, each with foreign headquarters. I can't get to them. Only Chase refused the offer. If those banks get together, and I have no doubt whatsoever that they intend to, they could squeeze the hell out of us; several of those loans are callable at will."

"Is a foreigner behind it?" Alex grabbed hopefully at the straw. "If so, then we've got no problem. Foreigners can't own a major communications company in America, you know that."

"The banks aren't the ones trying to take us over, although they've obviously got to be part of it. It's Milo, remember. And Milo is one hundred percent American."

"Who are the banks?" He didn't recognize a single name Page read off. "Has an approach been made yet to our partners?" He dreaded the answer to his question.

"Yesterday. All of them. Hamilton Jarvis was the first to call me for confirmation. That was the tip-off. I contacted the others."

"And?"

"They're all considering it." Page took a gulp of his Scotch.

"Bastards," Kidd swore. "How much are they being offered?"

"Nearly fifty percent above current market value. We can't match that. Even if we increase the quarterly dividend, we can't meet it."

Kidd slammed his fist against the wall. "Another loan? We could buy out one of the partners. That's all we need to hold control."

"No good. You're hocked up to your neck. That last transaction of yours in the Bahamas pulled the plug."

"You don't think they know about that, do you?"

"If they do, we've had it. We won't even be able to bluff."

"Who the fuck is it, Page?" Kidd's frustration doubled by not knowing upon whom he should vent his rage.

"I'm trying to find out, believe me. No one but Milo has come out into the open. Tomorrow an official offer for the stock will be made. We have only twenty days to reply. You've got to come back to New York."

"I can't, I'm almost finished wrapping up the third channel."

"Alex, forget it. You may not have a network left to put it on. Cancel everything and get back that eleven percent of your stock. Once you've got control again, it doesn't matter what the other partners do."

"Too late, Page. Over six million is committed with no way of getting it back. And I don't trust those bastards."

"Fucking hell."

"Look, Page, don't panic. All we need is just one of the others on our side. That shouldn't be difficult." Mentally Alex totaled the percent of shares held by each of the five partners in KWEN and those held by Judith and him:

Concord Investments:	8%
Hanley Trust:	8%
Hamilton Jarvis:	8%
Lavarre and Sidney Bolt:	8%
Myer Fisk:	8%
The Bahamas bankers:	11%
	51%
Alexander Kidd:	45%
Judith Kidd:	4%
	49%

"I'll call them from here. They'll hang in. Hell, we've made 'em rich."

"Don't bother with Hanley and Concord," Page said angrily. "They're both planning to dump their shares. The fifty percent is too good for them to turn down; they're afraid of a stockholder suit if they don't take it. And they're also afraid of the future of KWEN. Paul had the gall to complain that while the network was going down the drain you were off playing with your 'toy boats.' Several of the others said the same thing. Whoever's behind this thing is going after your jugular on mismanagement as well as financial incompetence."

Kidd whirled around, almost tearing the phone from the wall as anger raged through him. The glass and water pitcher on the bedside table crashed to the floor. "Those shitheads," he exploded. "*I* built that network from nothing. *I've* been the one filling their pockets with dividends for years. What the hell are they talking about?"

"The Bolt brothers are divided on the issue," Page continued, deciding not to react to Alex's outburst. "Those two Texans have been badly hurt by that commodity speculation of theirs, and the government is coming down hard on them. They may be forced to liquidate most of their holdings to pay it all off. Sidney's for taking the offer, but Lavarre is holding out in your favor."

"And Jarvis?"

"After his first inquiry, Mr. Hamilton Jarvis has been unable to answer my calls." There was no mistaking the sarcasm in Page's voice. "We're in trouble there. I happen to know that our former ambassador's investments were badly hit in 1981 and 1982. And a big chunk of his assets was confiscated by the Iranians. He hasn't been able to get compensation yet. You know, Alex, the publicity for KWEN hasn't been all that great recently, and he may want to get out while the getting's good. He never was much of a gambler. President Warren was the one who talked him into investing in the first place, if I recall correctly."

"Fuck," Alex muttered. "Myer Fisk? He's always been one of our biggest boosters. He knows the business. He'll stick."

"Call him, Alex. Call him now. It's still before six on the Coast. He'll still be at the studio. You've got his number?"

"Yeah, I've got it. Hell, with Myer's eight percent there's nothing those bastards can do to us." He took a deep breath, his confidence returning. "Look, let's not take any chances. As soon as they announce publicly, we'll attack. Get our boys to write screaming editorial advertisements about freedom of the airways, the evils of bigness, antitrust, a whole lot of crap like that and splatter them in the *Times* and the *Wall Street Journal*. And have a go at our pet senators. You know what I mean. If little McGraw-Hill could beat off American Express, we should be able to flatten Milo and its phantom backers. Call in that PR firm—what's its name? Yeh, Lazarus, Ryan, and Newbran. Get 'em, Page.'' Alexander Kidd was back in stride giving orders. "And while you're at it—"

"Alex," Page Shepard's reasonable voice broke in, "slow down and listen. I've called in Martin Granville of Winchall and Bleaker to help fight this thing. You know him?"

"Who doesn't? Tops in the takeover field, a real slick infighter, hardly ever loses."

"He says you are *not* to make any comment. If you're approached, say absolutely *nothing*. We've only got twenty days to pull together our fight plan. All our lawyers are trying to find out who's really behind this Milo bid."

"Get our reporters digging on it, too. And have Granville call me first thing in the morning."

"Right."

"And Page, here's the name of the Bahamas group." He read the name, address, and phone number carefully to his friend. "Feel them out and don't faint when they tell you the conditions of the deal I made with them. You hear me, Page?"

"I shudder to think," the other replied quietly.

"I'll call Jarvis, Lavarre Bolt, and Fisk. You keep on Hanley and Concord, okay?"

"I'll do my best."

"Goddamn it, I knew something was brewing. I felt it in my gut."

"I wish we'd had that gut of yours over here."

"As soon as I sign up Covent Garden and the Paris Opera, I'll fly right back. Hell, the news of a third superchannel may be all we need to bring those so-called partners of ours in line." He was about to hang up when another thought occurred to him. "Is Judith still in New York?"

"Saw her only two days ago."

"I'd better talk to her. Try to keep her there until I get over. How is Mary taking all the excitement?"

"She doesn't know anything about it; she's still closeted safely at Fishers Island with the boys."

"Well, at least you won't have any distractions. Keep up the good work. And Page, let me know if anything happens. We've got to move fast."

"Alex," the other countered, "remember, be careful what you say. Keep that mouth of yours shut."

Alex smiled as he hung up the phone. His mind was wide awake, ready to take on this new challenge. Across the Atlantic, Page stared at the papers scattered across his desk. In a sudden burst of anger, he brushed them to the floor with one hand and, picking up his drink, walked through the tastefully decorated apartment to the master bedroom.

"Hi," Helmut said, pushing back the phone on the bedside table to make room for the book he had been reading. "Problems, huh?"

"An understatement if ever I heard one," Page sighed as he sank down on the coverlet beside him.

"Well, now that you've put me on the news staff, maybe I can help."

Page leaned back wearily against the young German photographer. "I'm afraid we're going to need a lot more than just pretty pictures."

"You mean you're really going down to Portsmouth this morning?" Sandra asked in disbelief. "With KWEN blowing up all around you, you plan to jump on that boat of yours and sail off into the blue? Alex, for God's sake, be sensible."

"That, my love, is exactly what I am being." He nodded toward the morning papers scattered over the unmade bed. "As soon as the news of the takeover bid for KWEN gets out, this place will be swarming with reporters." He smiled at her. "And you, being a good reporter, would be one of the first. Right?"

Sandra smiled back. "Right. And Alexander Kidd is particularly good copy. You're not unknown for dramatic statements."

"Do I detect an understatement?"

"A gross one."

"Well, old Captain Kidd is going to continue to do just what he supposedly came over here to do. Sail." He pulled a striped T-shirt over his head and tucked it into his white denim trousers. "And that's that. I shall be the picture of perfect confidence." He struck a pose for an imaginary camera. "I might even manage a contemptuous smile for the pitiful efforts of poor little Milo Productions."

"Okay, Mr. Picture-of-perfect-confidence, what do you want me to do today while you're out being confident? Keep after the Paris Opera deal?"

Alex nodded. "And see what's holding up Covent Garden. I want the complete ballet schedule of both companies. I meant what I said to Page. This new channel could be our ace in the hole against Milo if things get rough." Tossing her a kiss, Alex headed for the door.

Much of Alex's confidence had faded by the time his Porsche arrived at Portsmouth. The early morning drive south from London through the rolling, green countryside had given him the chance to calmly consider all that Page had said and to assess his position in the upcoming battle. It could not have come at a worse time. Here he was, hocked up to his eyeballs and playing the role of a playboy while attempting to persuade his partners that he had the management of the network firmly in hand. Perhaps he should let them know why he was in Europe. But then he would have to tell them where the money was coming from and reveal his unauthorized deal with the Freeport group. Who could he trust with that information? Lavarre Bolt? He was a gambler and would probably go along. And Myer Fisk. He understood show business. And he understood Alex. All Alex needed was one of them on his side.

Swinging aboard the *Privateer*, Alexander Kidd greeted Hal Trevane and the rest of the crew. "Okay, men, let's take her out," he shouted merrily. "Hal." The other joined him in the cockpit. "I'm going below to make a few phone calls. You handle things topside."

"Not like you, Alex," Hal said. "Something wrong?"

"What could be wrong? I trust you, Hal, that's all," he replied with a shrug.

"I'm flattered."

"You should be, buddy." Kidd slapped him on the back and went below to the ship-to-shore telephone. But the only number he called was that of the flat at 19 Neville Street; his son had already left. Alex left a message for him to call his father at the Connaught that evening.

With only occasional trips topside to confer with Trevane and get a breath of fresh air, Kidd spent most of the morning below, his thoughts so completely occupied by the problems of KWEN that he had little enthusiasm for the rigors of putting the crew through a series of difficult maneuvers. He realized his temper would be short and only hard feelings would result from a day with him in command. Trevane, he knew, would do a more than adequate job in working with the crew. Instead he waited in frustration while the sun crossed the Atlantic, and America woke up.

Kidd was not surprised that his call to Hamilton Jarvis proved fruitless. He was informed politely by Mr. Jarvis' private secretary that her employer had left the day before for a tour of the family plants in the Midwest. No, she did not know where to reach Mr. Jarvis at this precise time, but she would be more than happy to have Mr. Jarvis return Mr. Kidd's call as soon as she contacted her. Alex resisted the urge to fling a few prize expletives at the well-educated voice and, instead, left the number of the Connaught.

An hour later he heard the familiar twang of the crusty old Texan, Lavarre Bolt. "You can count on me, Alex boy."

"Page tells me you've got a lot of pressure on you from the government, that they're coming after you and Sidney."

"Man, those folks down in Washington don't scare one

tiny little piece of hell out of me. Sidney and me have fought a shitload of worse villains than them."

"But you're pinched for cash," Alex pressed. "Be honest with me, Lavarre, no bulling around."

"Hell, man, we Bolts have been pinched for cash before, and we're sure as hell going to be pinched for cash in the future. It's the way we live."

"Sidney feels that way too?"

"Why, that little ol' brother of mine feels the way I feel. An' if he don't, well, there just ain't much he can do about it. I'll tell you this, Alex, and don't you go quotin' me, but that brother of mine is chicken, got no stomach for a gamble or a fight. Hell, man, you and me are more alike, and we ain't even kin."

"You're behind me then?"

"You ain't listenin' to me, boy. I'm behind you one thousand and fifty percent. Can't be much more behind a feller than that, can I?"

"I appreciate it, Lavarre."

"Don't go thankin' me. I kind of like looking up at that big ol' sky at night knowin' that I own a chunk of one of them itty-bitty lights up there." Lavarre paused and then his voice became serious. "When you gonna get off that boat of yours and come home to do some business?"

The question was blunt. It sounded more like a command. "Very soon, Lavarre. I've got a few more contracts to complete over here, and then I'll be back."

"Contracts? What contracts?" Bolt was cautious. "You up to one of your tricks, boy?"

"It's confidential, Lavarre. A new channel."

The Texan's *yahooo* almost deafened Alex. "I knew you weren't just lollygaggin' around over there, boy, not Alex Kidd. A new channel, eh? Don't that beat all. Now, don't you go worryin'. You got the Bolt guns right beside you. When you get back we'll kick the bloody shit out of them Milo folks."

Replacing the receiver, Alex leaned back with a smile. His votable forty-five percent of KWEN stock coupled with the Bolts' eight percent and Judith's four gave him a fat majority of fifty-seven percent. Milo Productions and whoever stood behind it did not stand a chance against him. One hour later that smile broadened. Myer Fisk assured Kidd that he stood firmly behind him. Although he chastised the headstrong president of KWEN for proceeding with a third channel without first consulting his partners, Myer agreed that Alex's decision to expand their network into the cultural area was the correct one in the face of the competitive threat from the three major networks. These words from the owner of one of Hollywood's largest studios were a salve to Alex's ego. Now he could count on sixty-five percent of the outstanding KWEN stock, maybe as much as seventy-six if the Freeport group backed him. Suddenly the thought of taking over command of the *Privateer* appealed to him. Even though he personally would not be able to go on the Whitbread race around the world later that month, Hal Trevane could do it without him. Do it, that was, if Kidd whipped the crew into perfect shape before leaving for New York.

"Fuck you, Hamilton Jarvis and all the little Jarvises," he mumbled happily as he climbed up on deck, "who needs you?" Inhaling deeply the fresh salt air, he turned laughing to Trevane. "Okay, Hal, what do you say we put these landlubbers through their paces?"

"I'm with you, Captain," the other replied, turning over the wheel to him while moving across to take charge of the second one. "By the way, that black speedboat has been hanging behind us all morning."

"Good, we'll show 'em just what a good crew and boat can do. You ready?"

Trevane nodded.

"Ready about," Alex shouted.

The *Privateer* tacked back and forth across the English Channel for most of the afternoon, its mainsail full, the colorful red and white spinnaker billowing out taut in the wind. It was just changing to a port tack that would bring it into Portsmouth when the call came from New York.

"When was the last time you talked with your Freeport pals in the Bahamas?" Page Shepard asked without preliminaries.

Alex was put on guard by the calm, level tone with which Page asked the question. "About a week ago," he replied. "Why?"

"Ever hear the name Credit Bank Schiller?" Page continued without bothering to answer Alex's question. "The address is Stadthausquai seventeen in Zurich."

"What's this all about, Page?"

"You don't know the bank then."

"Of course not. Page, so help me God, I'll—"

"Three days ago that friendly little group of Freeport bankers you once found so trustworthy ceased to exist." Alex stared at the receiver in his hand in disbelief. "They merged their interests with the Credit Bank Schiller. And so right now some eleven percent of KWEN voting stock rests with the gnomes of Zurich. How do you like them apples?"

Alexander Kidd said nothing.

"I assume from your silence that you do *not* like them apples."

"Let's cut the sarcasm, Page."

"Alex, believe me, I'm not being sarcastic. I'm being fatalistic. We're in trouble."

Regaining his composure, Kidd smiled. "Relax, buddy. You're only talking the bad news. I've got the good stuff here. Both Lavarre and Myer are with us. I've got their guarantees. We've got more than enough votes to carry the day. Stop worrying."

It was only noon in New York, but Page Shepard sounded exhausted. "I'll believe those guarantees the day after the vote."

"Call them yourself."

"I will."

"What does Granville think?"

"Too early to tell. He's finding it difficult to prepare a defense against the unknown."

"You still don't know who's behind Milo?" Annoyance showed in Kidd's voice.

"Alex, we keep uncovering one holding company after another. Milo's finances are so tangled, I wouldn't be surprised if they led us all the way back to Genghis Khan."

"Well, keep trying, Page. And don't worry so much, it's in the bag." Alex's words were encouraging, but his earlier optimism faded as he put down the phone. The Freeport double-cross had shaken him. The apparent power behind Milo's bid was frightening. He tried to rid his mind of Page's warning, "I'll believe those guarantees the day after the vote." He felt a new sense of urgency. That famous gut of his told him to get his ass back to New York as soon as possible.

In his current frame of mind, Alexander Kidd was in no fit state to meet the press, but meet the press he did as the sleek *Privateer* made fast to its mooring. Reporters swarmed around him as he jumped onto the dock and walked briskly to the end of the pier where he saw Sandra Bannister waiting.

"Would you care to comment on the rumors of the bid to take over your network?"

"I would not," Kidd stated firmly, pushing the microphone aside.

"They are more than rumors, aren't they?"

Alex turned away.

"Have you entered negotiations with Milo Productions?" another voice shouted.

"No comment."

"Then you intend to fight?" still another called out.

"No comment," he repeated, forcing his way ahead.

"Will this affect your plans to enter the Whitbread?"

"What the hell do you think?" Alex growled. Up ahead Sandra stood by the car, holding the door open. If he did not get to it soon, he knew he would slug one of these toads. He plowed on toward her as the voices attacked him from all sides.

"Is it true that most of your partners are in favor of the takeover?"

"No comment." Who in the hell was leaking information to these guys? They seemed to know as much if not more than he did.

"We understand the Bolt brothers are about to be indicted for fraud."

"No comment." That one hit below the belt. Was it true?

"Mr. Kidd, what will you do if you lose?" The voice was high-pitched.

"I never lose."

Another microphone jammed into his face. "Would you repeat that?"

Anger raged throughout his body. "I never lose." Alex pronounced each word clearly and with emphasis.

He was almost to the car. Watching his crimson face, Sandra Bannister crossed her fingers and prayed for the impossible.

"But if you did, what would you do?" the voice pressed.

Alexander Kidd stopped and glared at his questioner. "I built that fucking superstation," he snarled, "and I can blow it up."

Sandra uncrossed her fingers and closed her eyes.

CHAPTER 8

Helmut Bruck leaped from the Checker cab as it pulled to the curb at Fiftieth and Broadway. Leaning back in, he pulled his camera case from the back seat and winked at Page Shepard. "The ever proper Mr. Shepard," he laughed.

Page returned the smile.

"Dinner tonight?"

"I'll try," the KWEN executive promised.

"Call." Helmut slammed the cab door and began walking down the two blocks to Rockefeller Center, the same two blocks down which the taxi now moved with its sole occupant.

Looking back through the rear window at the young cameraman, Page wanted to laugh as several secretaries turned to ogle the handsome German. He felt flattered. He was still smiling as he entered the building that held KWEN's headquarters and took the elevator to the fifteenth floor. Crossing the richly appointed executive lobby, Page greeted the receptionist with the same perfunctory words with which he had greeted her for the last four years, and strode down the side corridor toward his office. His secretary handed him the morning newspaper as he passed.

"Mr. Granville is . . ."

His thoughts occupied elsewhere, Page failed to hear her as he passed by and entered his office. He was startled to see Martin Granville, the takeover expert, seated on the couch in the corner. A thin black briefcase rested beside him.

"Martin, good morning. I didn't remember we'd arranged a meeting this morning." Page walked toward the distinguished lawyer, his hand extended.

"We didn't," the other replied coolly. "I tried to reach you at your apartment this morning."

"I . . ." Page retreated a step and flushed. "I wasn't there."

Martin Granville's eyebrows lifted in amusement at Shepard's obvious discomfort. "So I gathered," he smiled, not too discreetly. And then his expression hardened. "Have you read the *Times* this morning?" he asked, pointing at the paper under Page's arm.

Page frowned. "Why, is something wrong."

"Obviously you haven't read the *Times* this morning. May I suggest that you sit down and do so?" There was no mistaking the annoyance in Granville's voice.

Slowly lowering himself into the chair across from his colleague, Page opened the paper. "Oh, my God," he moaned as he saw the headline halfway down the front page.

"I thought we had agreed," the lawyer said, "that you would muzzle our Mr. Kidd."

Page read aloud the offending headline in disbelief. "SUPERSTATION OWNER THREATENS TO BLOW UP NETWORK."

"The *Wall Street Journal* was a bit more restrained in its reportage," Granville commented icily, "but their article is no less damaging to our cause."

Across Manhattan, Edith Androssy looked up from her toast spread lavishly with guava preserve and stared at her husband seated opposite her at the breakfast table. "You certainly look like the cat who swallowed the canary this morning, Mickey."

The baron lowered his paper, a subtle grin playing about the corners of his mouth. "In a manner of speaking, I may just have done that," he replied, leaning forward to pluck a blue bachelor button from the floral arrangement in the center of the table.

"Something good in the news?" she inquired.

"Quite good." He carefully inserted the flower in the lapel of his immaculately tailored, pin-striped suit. "A competitor of mine has just walked into a little trap I had set for him."

"Oh, really, darling? Who? Do tell me." Edith Androssy pulled her patterned silk kimono tightly around her ample body and looked at him eagerly. "It sounds so exciting."

"Not very. Nothing for you to bother your pretty little head about."

Edith's face fell. "Mickey, you *never* tell me about the things you do." Her complaint was not a new one.

"It is just boring old business. Stocks, bonds, that sort of thing." He smiled at her and rose. "Now wipe that pout off your face. Do you not have a luncheon party today?"

Reluctant to leave the subject, Edith Androssy nodded. "At the Opera Club. But—"

"Had you better not start dressing? It is nearly ten, and I am sure cook will want your instructions for dinner this evening. How many will there be?"

"Fourteen," she replied, looking down at her plate.

He bent to kiss her forehead. "Now cheer up, my sweet darling. I promise to tell you about the first really interesting thing that comes along." Straightening, Androssy left the breakfast room for his study.

Somewhat mollified, Edith forced her mind to the upcoming activities of her day. She spread another piece of toast with butter and purple preserve and rang for more coffee.

As his employer entered the study, Robert Frankel, the baron's personal secretary of nearly nine years, looked up. Unshaven, his suit badly wrinkled, Frankel sat on the leather couch glancing through a sheaf of papers. He was average looking in all respects. Only the furtive look in his cold, snakelike eyes and the slight bulge of the holster under the arm of his jacket indicated that his services to the baron might involve more than just intellectual activity.

"Well done, Robert," Androssy said.

The other nodded his acceptance of the compliment. A

petty thug on the Marseilles waterfront in his teens, Frankel's natural cunning had soon brought him into the lucrative drug traffic moving through the port. His emotionless acceptance of murder earned him the position of enforcer, an undercover role he had carried out with dispassionate efficiency. Accused in the murder of his prostitute mistress, Frankel had stood trial and been acquitted for lack of evidence. In Marseilles on business at the time, Miklos Androssy's curiosity about the low life of the French port had lured him to the court during the last days of the trial. He had been fascinated by Robert Frankel and the ruthlessness that lay just beneath the tranquil facade of the killer's youthful face. At twenty-four, Frankel was obviously extremely clever and, more important, streetwise, both traits that could be very useful to Androssy if packaged correctly. The baron had found it relatively simple to have Frankel's official dossier amended and to obtain the necessary working papers and passports. The young killer had been like a chameleon, easily absorbing the education and culture of his new life while maintaining the cunning of his old. Frankel was now in his early thirties, and every inch of his wiry body beneath the tan fabric of his summer suit was tight muscle wound like a spring and ready to uncoil at a second's warning.

Like Robert Frankel, the baron's large, iron-faced chauffeur, Victor Kamera, also had been recruited from the depths of the European underworld. Fiercely protective and loyal to their employer, both men would have sacrificed their lives for him without thinking. Since learning of his connection with the KGB, Vladimir Savich had insisted that Androssy employ Russian agents within his household, but the baron would have none of it. Miklos Androssy knew the KGB too well and would have no one under his command with divided loyalties.

"When did you get in from London, Robert?" Androssy asked.

"Almost an hour ago. I came directly here." He brushed

a lock of unruly black hair back from his forehead. "As you predicted, Kidd exploded."

"So I see." The baron shook the morning paper at him as he crossed to his desk. "You have eaten?"

"On the jet." Androssy maintained several private jet planes to assure his presence and those of his underlings whenever needed anywhere in the world. "I've planted enough information with the press to keep them hounding Kidd for the next few days. The *Financial Times* was particularly cooperative."

"From what I know of Alexander Kidd, he will be returning soon. He will not be able to resist getting into the fight personally, and every outrageous word he utters will play right into our hands." Androssy smiled to himself. He too enjoyed a good fight and looked forward to besting the loud-mouthed American. "Did you bring the latest tapes with you?"

With his attack on KWEN, the baron had finally confided the name of the third Fury and the satellite to the chairman and requested the KGB bug Kidd's car and hotel rooms in Europe. Androssy had personally arranged the wiring of Kidd's and Page Shepard's home and office phones. Helmut Bruck, who had been easily suborned in this matter by the wealthy head of the Androssy empire, no longer reported to the resident.

"They are being sent to Savich by diplomatic pouch after—"

"After our Russian friends have had a chance to study them," the baron interrupted with a sigh. "I fear I am beginning to make them uneasy. Now I must again meet with Savich."

"Can't I do it?"

"No."

Robert Frankel let the matter drop. He never asked for reasons or questioned his employer's commands.

"Inform Victor that I will be needing him and the taxi this evening after dinner." Frankel nodded and sat waiting for further orders. "We have a very busy day before us, Robert.

Mr. Kidd has handed us a potent weapon to use against him. We must make sure we use it well." Androssy leaned back in his desk chair and stared at the ceiling as his mind reviewed various alternatives. A smile slowly spread across his face. "I think we should be able to convince those holding ownership in KWEN that it is in their best interest to petition the courts to remove Mr. Kidd from active participation in the management of the network until after the shareholder vote on August twenty-seventh. After all, he is an irrational man, is he not? And has he not made threats to blow up all their assets out of pure spite if he feels threatened? I would say that Mr. Kidd feels very threatened right now, would you not, Robert?"

"Very."

The baron leaned forward. "Contact Howard at once and have him pull together a representative of each bank holding paper on KWEN for a three o'clock meeting downtown."

At the nod of his employer, Frankel rose and crossed the room to swing open a portion of the bookcase running along that side of the study. He passed through the hidden door into his small office beyond, closing the panel behind him.

Baron Androssy picked up his phone and called various of his inner circle to explain his strategy and to arrange invitations to that afternoon's meeting for the representatives of Hamilton Jarvis, Hanley Trust, Concord Investments, and the Milo lawyers who were ostensibly handling the takeover bid for KWEN. He, of course, would not be present. By the end of that meeting, arrangements would already have been made to present the petition to a "friendly" court; all they had to do was sign it. Timing was essential. He wanted Kidd barred from the KWEN building in Rockefeller Center before his adversary had the chance to fight back and, more important, actually had the chance to harm the Charon II satellite or destroy the codes that held the key to his power.

Miklos Androssy sat thinking for several minutes before once again picking up his phone. His call to Washington assured him that the government's commodity-speculation case against the Bolt brothers would be pushed into the courts within the week. A second call to Los Angeles assured a more thorough investigation of Myer Fisk's and his studio's finances.

Later that evening Vladimir Savich stood on a street corner not far from his apartment, apparently attempting to hail a cab. Several slowed but were waved off impatiently by the resident. Finally one slowed to a stop and he got in, nodding to the heavyset driver. The taxi moved across town, weaving through what little traffic there was, turning and turning again until the driver was sure it was not being followed. Heading east, it swung up First Avenue and pulled to the curb at Fifty-eighth Street to admit another passenger. Miklos Androssy pulled open the door and slid in.

Both men settled back, not looking at each other until the cab had covered several blocks. Finally Androssy spoke. "Vladimir Savich, you have the London tapes?"

The other pulled six cassettes from his jacket pocket and handed them to Androssy without comment.

"Anything of interest?" the baron asked, smiling to himself at the resident's discomfort. He dropped them into a small, nearly imperceptible slit in the back of the front seat from which Victor Kamera would later retrieve and deliver them to him.

Rather than answer his question, Savich asked one of his own. "Why did you delay for two weeks before telling me of Alexander Kidd's involvement in the Acheron Plot?" His eyes stared straight ahead, the anger in his voice unmistakable.

"There was no need."

"I am responsible for all operations in this—"

"*I* am responsible for the Acheron business," Androssy interrupted. "I alone."

"We could have helped."

"I deal in subtleties. The KGB is not always known for its subtlety. I did not relish the idea of your agents running about sticking poison needles in people like that disgraceful affair in Germany, or of Russian generals racing cars through the streets of Washington like—"

"You prefer prussic acid," Vladimir Savich said.

"I beg your pardon?" Androssy asked. His voice was even.

"Prussic acid," Savich repeated, "a subtle method of murder. Untraceable."

"So I understand," the other stated flatly. "I too have received training at Dzerzhinsky Square. Why are you telling me this?"

"We continue to pursue the death of Anatoli Butov."

"And?"

The resident stared at his companion. "We continue to pursue it, that is all. I felt you should know."

"Your thoroughness is impressive." He turned to meet Savich's eyes. "Have our efforts to take over KWEN triggered any reaction from General Carmody?"

"None that we have been able to discern. Our mole reports no reaction to date. Perhaps the general has not made the connection between the KWEN fight and the potential loss to him of the satellite. He appears completely absorbed with the upcoming NATO meetings in September."

"Good. Your man is monitoring all phone calls?"

"All. As well as any meaningful correspondence."

Still smarting from the baron's earlier words, Savich added, "You see, we can be as subtle and efficient as even the great Baron Androssy." Before Androssy could comment, he went on. "Has our raven been of use to you?"

"Not really," he lied, wondering how much the resident knew of Bruck's work for him. The boy had pledged secrecy in return for the promise of an inside track within the Party and perhaps even within the baron's own organization.

Vladimir Savich remained silent.

"When can I expect to receive the next shipment of tapes from London?"

"On the nineteenth, in two days' time."

"Then let us meet at the south Brooklyn drop."

"As you wish."

Baron Androssy leaned forward and rapped on the glass partition separating them from the driver. Victor Kamera turned at the next corner and drew to a stop in midblock. Savich exited and walked slowly into the darkness.

CHAPTER 9

Alex watched his son as he entered the bar of Les Ambassadors, the exclusive club just off Hyde Park Corner. Mark Kidd seemed constrained by the traditional tie and jacket required by the club.

Father and son eyed each other nervously as Mark approached through the dim, richly paneled room. Alex stood to greet him. The young man smiled awkwardly. "Is it safe to sit down to lunch with the mad bomber of KWEN?"

"Not funny." Alexander Kidd sat back in his deep leather chair. Mark Kidd took the chair across from him.

"Sorry."

"Your fan, Page, was on the phone all day yesterday ranting and raging about that crack."

"How is Uncle Page?" Mark ordered a glass of white wine from the waiter who came to stand beside him. It was a far milder and more civilized drink, Alex noted with minor annoyance, than the double Scotch that sat before him on the small, highly polished table.

"Page is fine. Up to his neck in this Milo thing. Wants me to stay over here out of the way of his soft-spoken, goody-goody boys."

"You're not always known for your discretion, if I may say so."

"I'm a plain talker. I speak my mind."

Mark lowered his eyes, trying not to smile. The controversy over his father's pronouncements had surrounded him most of his life. "Are things really serious? Can they take the network?"

"No. I've got too many votes on my side."

"Counting Mother's four percent?"

"Your mother's and *yours*. That stock is in trust for you when and if you decide to get serious and come back to the States." He saw Mark's jaw clench and the too familiar thrust of his chin. Alex quickly changed the subject. While he recognized and basically approved of the other's inherited stubborn and independent streak, it also irritated him. And this was no time for another argument. "How are your grandparents? Judith said you visited them in Israel."

Mark relaxed. "Grandfather Singer is still teaching medicine at the university in Tel Aviv, and he's spending a lot of time at the clinic in Gaza."

Alex noted the pride in the young man's voice. "Jacob is a crusader," he commented, "always has been." Kidd liked his father-in-law. Nothing seemed to ruffle him. He was a giver, not a taker. He was not discouraged by disappointments; he just kept going forward.

"They're going to give him an award."

"He deserves it. And Rosalind?"

"Grandmother isn't very well. But she's still playing the cello and tours with her string quartet when she can."

Alex shook his head. "Well, it's obvious from which side of the family your artistic bent comes."

Picking up the mildly sarcastic tone in his father's voice, Mark rose to the defense. "Dad, the world needs more than just businessmen. I like art. I'm good at it, I really am. What's so wrong about wanting to paint, to sculpt?"

"Nothing, I guess, if you can afford the luxury of not having to earn a living." It was happening all over again. He was being drawn into the same old argument. Why couldn't he let it go?

The brief silence that fell between them was broken by Mark's bitter words. "You don't have to worry. None of your money has been wasted on me since I left."

"Mark, I didn't—"

"I borrowed the money for the Sorbonne from Grandfather Singer." That bolt out of the blue rocked and hurt
Alex. Judith had said nothing about the loan. "And before
you start preaching, I seem to recall that once *you* borrowed
from him, too." Mark scored twice. Before Alex could
counter, he went on, the hurt within him over his father's
disapproval and lack of support boiling up. "While we're at
it, shall we tell Mark again what a traitor to his country he
is? It's been nearly ten minutes, Dad, and you haven't
brought that one up yet."

"Christ, they weren't going to draft you. All they wanted
you to do was register. Don't you think you owe your
country something?"

Mark heard the American flags waving once again in his
father's voice. "Yes, I owe it a lot. I owe it enough to stand
up and speak out, not to help it get involved in another
politicians' war."

"You sound just like your grandfather Singer, damn it—
and your mother. They're turning you into a fucking saint."

"At least that's something you'll never have to worry
about," Mark shot back.

"And just what is that supposed to mean?" Alex
struggled to hold his temper.

"Nothing at all."

"Goddamn it," Alex growled under his breath, looking
around the hushed bar, "grow up."

"I'm not sure I want to. I don't like your definition of
growing up."

"Which is?"

Mark answered the question by avoiding it. "Where is
Miss Bannister today? Or have you found another one?"

The real trouble between them was out in the open at
last—Judith. "Okay," Alex said, "let's talk about it."

"Will it make any difference? Will it hurt Mom any
less?"

Alex stared furiously at his son. "Don't preach to me,
boy."

Mark rose. "Well, thanks for lunch. As usual, it was

charming. See you around." He turned and left. The untouched glass of white wine reflected in the polished surface of the table before his empty chair.

Kidd was still fuming thirty minutes later when he entered Sandra's newly rented flat on the top floor of an old red-stone building in Codogan Square.

"I see you and Mark have had another successful reconciliation lunch," she commented wryly. Alex glared at her and walked into the bedroom. "What's up?" She followed him in.

"I'm going to New York." Kidd began yanking clothes out of the closet. They had only been moved there from the Connaught the day before.

"I thought Page wanted you to stay here."

"Fuck Page."

"Oh, come on, Alex, he's only—"

"That's my network over there, not Page's. I'm tired of all this pussyfooting around. It's time someone kicked Milo Productions and their whole bunch of fucking lawyers in the balls."

"Lunch was *that* good, was it?" Sandra smiled. "Sounds like Mark took you by at least two rounds."

"Damn kid," he mumbled, jamming clothes into a small carry-on bag.

"He loves you."

"Ha," he snorted.

"And you adore him. I've seen the two of you together." He discarded a jacket. "That's the reason you two fight—neither will admit how much he cares. Hurt before being hurt. That seems to be a Kidd motto."

Alex looked up from his packing and held her eyes with his. What was it he saw in them? "Is that what I do to you?" he asked, understanding perhaps for the first time what she was saying. The anger seemed to drain from his body.

"I let you do it," she replied, lowering her eyes. "They're our rules."

"Oh, Sandy." Genuine softness entered his voice as he

moved to her and pressed her in his arms. "I love you. You know that."

"You *need* me, Alex," she whispered, caressing the back of his head as he held her. "You *love* Judith." She felt his body stiffen at the name. Sandra stopped him from pulling away, kept his cheek pressed to hers as she spoke. "It's all right. I'm happy with the part of you you can give. I don't expect more, I've never asked for more. Just having you to love has been enough." The compromise she had long refused to openly admit brought tears to her eyes; her breath was ragged.

Slowly Alex pulled back to look at her, their arms still around each other. He kissed the wetness on her cheek. "Do I deserve you?" he asked gently, touched by the truth he recognized.

Sandra hugged him tightly. "No, you bastard." She began to laugh and cry, grinding her hips forward into his, "but I deserve you." She pulled him back down onto the bed amid the tumble of his unpacked clothes. His lips moved slowly across her neck to the opening of the silk blouse. Sandra's fingers dug into his back as his encircled her breasts.

The wheels of the Concorde touched down on the tarmac of John F. Kennedy International Airport at 4:59 that afternoon. The mild jolt roused Kidd from his confused thoughts of Mark, Sandra, and her words about Judith. He was back in New York. It was time to fight.

Alex had not ordered the KWEN limousine to meet him, preferring instead to arrive at the office unannounced. That would shake them up. He was confident that his dynamic presence would galvanize the morale of the entire organization. Let the lawyers do their thing; he would do his. The Kidd Worldwide Entertainment Network would stand up tall and beat the shit out of its attackers. He felt like Sir Lancelot, armor flashing in the sun, riding forth to destroy Milo Productions and the anonymous multiheaded dragon that stood behind it. And he knew victory would be his.

Thirty-five minutes later, Alex jumped from his cab and walked straight into the bustling marble lobby of the towering Rockefeller Center building. Heading for the elevator, he nodded a familiar greeting to Frank and Ned, the two security guards standing nearby, and walked on. A confused expression spread across both guards' faces and, looking at each other, they both hurried forward.

"Mr. Kidd, I'm sorry," Frank blurted out, blocking the path of KWEN's president.

Ned came up on the other side. "We can't let you go up, sir." His face was a mirror of misery.

Alex pushed forward, not believing what he had just heard. Their arms held him back. Ned looked over his shoulder at two uniformed policemen who moved toward them.

"What in the hell are you talking about," Kidd snapped. He angrily wrenched Frank's hand from his arm.

"It's orders, Mr. Kidd. The court, they say you can't get in."

Alex stared the man down. "Get out of my way." Frank stood aside.

"Honest, Mr. Kidd," Ned pleaded. "You can't go up."

Alexander Kidd glared at the speaker. "I go where I please in this building." He moved forward only to feel both his arms seized from behind.

"This Kidd?" a deep voice asked.

A small crowd gathered to witness his brief, violent scuffle with the police. Kidd was pinned to the cold marble wall by them. "Sorry, sir, by order of the court you've been forbidden entry to this building and all property of Kidd Worldwide," the uniformed officer stated. "Sorry."

Kidd shook himself free. "For what goddamned reason?"

"Seems they're afraid you'll wreck the joint." Before the familiar face of the popular network executive, the officers too seemed embarrassed. "No offense, but you said you were going to blow the place up."

"I don't believe this," Alex shouted in dismay. "Call Page Shepard."

"Okay, sir, but you'll have to go over there with us."

Reluctantly, Alex let himself be led to the security desk. Ned had run ahead and held the phone in his hand. Within less than a minute Page Shepard hurried out of the elevator toward them.

"Alex, what in the hell are you doing here?"

"I didn't know I needed an engraved invitation."

"Why didn't you let us know? Come on." Page took his friend's arm and led him out onto the street. "Let's get a cup of coffee."

"Page, I don't want a cup of coffee. I just want to know what the fuck is going on around here." He followed Page a few steps and halted.

"It's those stupid threats you made in London," Page retorted, turning to face him. "I told you to keep your mouth shut. Milo took it to court six hours after the newspapers hit the street. Hamilton Jarvis, Hanley, Concord Investments, the banks, they all backed Milo."

"Those bastards."

"I tell you, Alex, this is serious. When I talk about being organized, this takeover is being orchestrated by a real pro. They seem to know our every move before we even decide to make it."

"You still don't know who's behind it?"

"All we have is Milo. We haven't come up with anything else but a bunch of mixed-bag holding companies and that Swiss bank." Page averted his eyes and lowered his voice. "Your office had been padlocked. Even *I* can't go in without a guard." He paused and then went on awkwardly, "And they've made me acting head of the network until the day of the vote." Page looked back to face his friend's angry glare. "Alex, believe me, I had nothing to do with this. I tried to reach you at the Connaught this morning, but you'd checked out. They didn't know where to reach you."

"You didn't think of getting hold of Sandy?"

"We . . . I . . . ." Page's face was contorted with the embarrassment he felt.

"I never thought it would be you, Page," Alexander

Kidd said in a low, even voice, his mind seething with ugly feelings of betrayal. "I never thought it would be you."

"Alex, I had—"

Raising a threatening fist, Kidd cut off Page Shepard's words. The struggle raging within him was obvious to the other. Suddenly turning on his heels, Alex walked angrily away down the sidewalk and turned into the first bar he came to.

The Bartok concerto floated softly through the air of the high-ceilinged music room and surrounded Judith Kidd as she sat trying to concentrate on the novel in her hands. Looking up, she reached for the long-stemmed crystal glass on the table beside her. The lights of the room shimmered like diamonds in the last of the pale dinner wine. After Page's concerned telephone call that afternoon, she had canceled her theater plans to wait for Alex. She had ended dining alone.

Judith's long raven-black hair fell free, framing her aristocratic features and delicate complexion. She wore a dark velvet, ankle-length skirt and white silk blouse open to a point midway between her smooth breasts. A long strand of simple black pearls hung from her neck. The wine felt cool to her lips, its bouquet light as she inhaled. She rested her head back against the sofa as her eyes moved slowly about the room, pausing on one beloved object after another: the concert grand, its ebony surface mirroring its surroundings; the Monet hanging over the fireplace, a gift from her parents after the birth of Mark. The music room had been her domain. Alex had his study and, attached to it, the television screening room where in the first days of the network he, she, and their associates had worked and argued, always struggling to improve the quality of KWEN's programming. In those days she had been an integral part of the small band who had supported him and helped lay the foundation of the superstation, as it was called today.

Putting aside the book, Judith rose and crossed the room, opening the double doors to the rest of the large, rambling apartment in the Dakota. She had always felt comfortable here, at home, a far cry from the castle in Tangier where she now spent much of her time. The castle had been bought as their summer refuge, one known to few people.

Strains of the Bartok followed behind as Judith wandered slowly from one room to the other. She had labored long and hard to convert the twelve-room apartment from the dark, paneled lair of an old railroad tycoon into a light, airy place with great open spaces where each room flowed into the next. Highly polished dark wood floors contrasted with pale walls and ceilings, the elaborate moldings high above blending in to give character but not weight. There was no clutter. Each room was decorated with carpeted islands of fine furniture, simple in construction, elegant in design. Paintings of the Impressionists and those of de Kooning, Picasso, Johns, Frankenthaler, and Lichtenstein hung across from each other, a skillful blend of schools. Works of pre-Columbian and Greek sculpture stood isolated; a Moore and three tall Giacomettis were grouped in one corner. The stark simplicity of the rooms was softened and warmed by the richness of the draperies at the windows and of the colors of the carpets and upholstery.

Judith stopped at the open door to Alex's study; he called it his sanctuary. In contrast to the rest of the apartment, this room seemed like a large, cluttered photograph album. A profusion of framed snapshots carrying Alexander Kidd from college to KWEN, from America to Europe and the Far East and from friend to celebrity covered the walls. Athletic trophies crowded the bookshelves. Papers and files were stacked in disarray about the room.

Smiling, Judith moved on into the master bedroom. She stared at the new Rauschenberg hanging above the bed. It was a good one, yet she frowned. Had it been Alex's choice or that of Sandra Bannister? She was standing before it when the hall door burst open. Alex's unsteady footsteps approached through the apartment. She turned to face him as he reached the bedroom door. Seeing her, he straightened and then leaned disheveled against the doorjamb.

Judith was the first to speak. "You had a rough day. Page told me."

"Fuck Page." He brushed his blond hair out of his eyes.

"You don't mean that, Alex, and you know it." She moved forward and, taking his arm, turned him back toward the living room. "What you mean is, Fuck Alex. It's your fault, not Page's."

Her use of the four-letter word amused him. "Fuck? Why, that's not at all like my Judith, the Judith I used to know. Since when have—"

"What have you been drinking, Scotch?" Judith left him and went to the bar, taking up a crystal decanter.

Alex slumped back onto the tan, suede-covered sofa and put his feet on the large glass and chrome Mies van der Rohe coffee table before it. "No." He waved his hand at the decanter. "Perrier, tonic, something—no booze."

"Are you sure?" she asked, turning. "Are you sure you don't want to drink yourself into oblivion?"

"Ease up, Judith." His voice held the warning tone she knew well.

Judith filled a glass with ice and poured soda over it, returning to place it on the table by his feet. Seating herself at the far end of the couch, she looked at him. "When did you get back?"

"This afternoon, on the Concorde." He took his feet off the table and leaned forward for the glass.

"And Sandra?"

"Still in London. Wrapping up my work there."

"The third channel?"

His eyebrows raised. "You know?"

"I know you well enough to know that you had more on your mind than just racing. I asked Page."

Nodding, he took a deep drink of the bubbling water. "Good old Page." There was sarcasm in his voice.

"You're lucky to have him as a friend," she said gently. "And so am I."

"I know." He raised the glass again.

"If they had to put the network in somebody's hands, at least they put it in someone's you could trust."

He nodded again. His anger earlier that afternoon and his feelings of betrayal by Page had long since worn off. After a quiet and logical analysis of events while sitting at one of the many bars he had visited that day, Alex realized that Page was doing his best. But hard as he tried, he still felt resentment and jealousy at the other's assumption of his position as number one at KWEN. He finished the soda.

"What are your plans?" Judith took the glass from him and rose to refill it.

"I'm flying to Houston tomorrow to talk to Lavarre Bolt, and then on to the Coast to see Myer."

Her back to him as she stood at the bar, Judith smiled. That was her Alex, back on his feet and fighting. "I like Lavarre." She crossed the room and held out the glass, feeling the touch of his hand on hers as he took it. "I really don't know why you and Page are so upset about this thing. Together your stock and mine add up to sixty percent."

"Forty-nine," he corrected. She stared at him in astonishment. "I see there are some things Page doesn't tell you." Alexander Kidd briefly explained his deal with the Freeport bankers and the defection of three of his partners.

"But surely you can count on Lavarre. He—"

"I'm taking Page's advice on this one. I'm not trusting anyone until the day after the vote."

"What can I do?"

"Nothing."

"But there must be something. Honestly." Judith looked down at him, waiting.

His eyes moved from her face down over her body, remembering past days and nights. He glanced back up and smiled. "You can vote your four percent with me."

The warmth drained from Judith's heart, she turned abruptly from him. "You felt you had to ask?"

"I . . ." He fell silent, feeling her disappointment in him, her anger. He had wanted to say other things, but instead he had hurt her. Why? "Hurt before being hurt," Sandra had said. He shook his head miserably.

Judith stood motionless, her hands rigidly pressed against her sides, her back to him. "Is it really over between us, Alex?" she asked softly. "You really feel nothing? Nothing's left?"

He had heard these questions before, but he knew this was the last time she would ever ask. Alex stared down at the ice cubes in his empty glass. He didn't answer; he didn't know how.

Judith suddenly whirled around. "You bastard," she cried, her eyes filled with angry tears. "Say something. Don't you know what you're doing to me? Please." Her voice broke. "Then at least let me go."

In the silence of the room, Judith heard the final strains of the Bartok concerto. The next morning she was gone.

Alex heard the heels of Lavarre Bolt's cowboy boots pounding against the tile floors of the ranch house long before he heard the familiar voice call out. "Swing your ass up on that horse over yonder and let's have us a little talk." The two men rode half the day, sometimes talking business, sometimes joking, sometimes in silence.

"Someone's out there squeezin' me, boy," Lavarre said, "but he don't know just how much squeezin' a Bolt can take. When I find out who it is, I'll put that bastard on a spit and roast his fat ass, treat us all to one hell of a barbecue."

"And Sidney?"

"He don't even know how to tie his shoes. Quit your worryin', Alex. I ain't gonna let you down, boy. You made me one hell of a lot of money in the past, and you're gonna make me one hell of a lot more. Besides, like I told you, I enjoy havin' my name on the lease of that little bitty star up there in the sky."

The next day Alex left his bungalow at the Beverly Hills Hotel and walked through the lush tropical foliage to his convertible. He reveled in the show business atmosphere of the hotel, its Polo Lounge crowded with producers, directors, and aspiring young actors and actresses hovering around small tables making their deals both business and romantic. Forty minutes later he drove into Myer Fisk's studio lot. Crossing the mammoth sound stage, he was surrounded by a maze of cables, arc lights, platforms, and the familiar swirl of milling carpenters, grips, propmen, stylists, makeup men, and extras dressed in elaborate period costumes.

Stepping around a vast, marble-looking staircase, Alexander Kidd continued across a replica of the ballroom in the palace of Fontainbleau toward the group of men huddled together arguing by the camera. Myer Fish looked grayer and more haggard than when they had last met.

The studio owner extricated himself from the group and took Alex by the arm. "You look well, Alex."

"Making a comedy or a drama?"

Fisk snorted. "The only comedy about this film is its budget."

"Trouble?"

"When am I ever not in trouble? A blank check, that's what directors want these days. Give me a good . . ."

"No, not that kind of trouble," Kidd interrupted.

Myer Fisk stopped and stared at him. "Why do you ask?"

"Quite honestly, you look like a man who, as our friend Lavarre Bolt would say, is gettin' squeezed."

"You've seen Lavarre?"

"Yesterday."

"How is he doing?"

"Fighting like a cornered bobcat. He doesn't know who, but says someone's stirring up problems for him in Washington. He's been indicted."

"I know." Myer Fisk paused. "You were right, Alex. I am being squeezed."

"How?"

"Your friends at Milo. They've left me with the strong impression that if they fail to win KWEN, they'll be in the market for a major studio. Mine."

Kidd whistled. "Could they pull it off?"

"Alex, why ask? You know the business. One day up, the next down. One day solvent, the next skating on thin ice."

"How's your ice?"

"Thin, very thin. Distribution of my last film is strangely delayed. 'No room in the theaters,' they say. I say shit to that. There was room before Milo got interested in KWEN. Alex, forty million dollars I have tied up in this new production. The king of France I should be to afford it. The king of France I am not."

"What are you telling me, Myer?"

"I'm telling you that like Lavarre, I too am caught between a rock and a hard place. I'm telling you that I'll stand behind you as long as I can. But I'm also telling you that if it comes to a choice between KWEN and a studio I have spent thirty-three years building . . ." He stopped. "Alex, don't look at me like that. I love you like a son. What am I to do? You tell me."

"We're going to lose Fisk," Alex told Page Shepard on the phone a few hours later, "and I don't need that famous gut of mine to tell me."

That night as Kidd sat at his table in the celebrity-filled Polo Lounge trying to appear interested in the conversation of the young actresses on either side of him, back in New York Baron Androssy tried to control his anger as he read another of the terse and persistent telexes from Zurich. "URGENT YOU CONFIRM DATE OF FUNDS TRANSFER TO ISRAEL. OUR CLIENTS ANXIOUS IN FACE OF POSSIBLE COMPETITIVE ACTION." Dropping the crumpled document into the shredder, he returned to the task before him.

Photographs littered his desk. They were copies of the documents in Alexander Kidd's office safe, the latest batch delivered to him by Helmut Bruck along with taped conversations from Page Shepard's office. In mounting frustration, Androssy had studied them for hours. He had met with no success. Nowhere could he find anything even resembling a radio code for the Charon II satellite. For days he had been poring over photos and the contents of Kidd's desk drawers and safe in hopes of finding the elusive codes. Bruck, a highly trained operative, had been methodically searching that office ever since joining the staff of KWEN. He had uncovered nothing. The baron's personal secretary, Robert Frankel, had done the same thing to Kidd's apartment at the Dakota with equally disappointing results. The codes had to be written down somewhere; Androssy found it inconceivable that Kidd would rely upon his memory as the sole custodian of such vital and complex information. Perhaps when he met Bruck at 9:30 that evening, the young KGB raven would have found something. This was to be his last delivery.

But the codes were only half of the baron's problem. First he had to take over control of KWEN and Charon II. He had only four days left before the stockholders' meeting on the morning of August 27, and Kidd still held the winning hand, but only by one card. Androssy had tried to remove that card through every economic and legal channel at his disposal. Now he would have to remove it in another way. Pushing a button on the small console on his desk, he waited as the panel in the bookcase silently opened and Frankel stepped into the room.

"Yes?"

"Tell me, Robert, can you ride a horse?"

The secretary frowned slightly. "No."

"Then perhaps you had better learn, Robert." Miklos Androssy smiled as he handed the younger man a folder which bore the name BOLT. "You are going on a business trip to Texas."

Frankel returned the baron's smile.

"It will be a very short trip, I am afraid. Only four days. Do you think you can handle it?"

"I'm sure I can, sir."

"Yes, I am sure you can."

Page sat waiting at the small out-of-the-way restaurant in the Village when Helmut Bruck entered. His frown faded as his handsome lover joined him at the corner table. "What kept you? It's after ten."

"Sorry, I wanted to check some footage I shot yesterday; the lab was late getting it to the screening room." He picked up the menu and scanned the entrées. "I'm famished."

"Wine?"

"Thanks."

Page reached across the table and filled Helmut's glass from the carafe. He was rewarded by the caress of the young man's leg against his.

As Bruck's eyes moved down over the Italian dishes listed on the card, his thoughts were far from food. They were in the back seat of the taxi he had just left, dwelling on the insistent words of Baron Androssy. He had not yet found the set of numbers for which the other searched, a code of some sort that had something to do with the KWEN satellite. It must be terribly important for the KGB to be so anxious to get it. The baron was upset with him. That was not fair; it wasn't his fault. His career within the Party organization would suffer if he failed, he was sure of it. He was in over his head and frightened. His only hope lay in keeping after Page Shepard.

"Can't you make up your mind?"

Helmut raised his eyes. "Everything sounds so good."

"I'm having the veal piccata, it was excellent last time."

"Good idea. What are you starting with?"

Page shook his head. "Not with this waistline."

"I have no complaints with it." Helmut winked. "Why should *you*?"

"Shut up," Page laughed, "and make up your mind before they close the kitchen."

"Fettuccine carbonara," he said decisively, lifting his glass in a toast to his host.

"God, you'll be a butterball."

"You forget I'm a growing boy." He suddenly realized he had entered the delicate area of the great difference in their ages which embarrassed Page, and hastened on, "Who's in love with another growing boy sitting across from him."

"Nice recovery," Page commented wryly.

Helmut smiled sheepishly. "I tried."

Page burst out laughing and waved for the waiter.

Halfway through his pasta, Helmut asked casually, "Do you ever move the KWEN satellite?"

"Sometimes, to make minor adjustments in its orbit."

"I thought it was a stationary orbit." Bruck sipped his wine, looking back to the fettuccine before him.

"It is, but . . ." Page continued to chat on about the techniques used to control the satellite. Nothing he said gave Helmut the slightest hint that he knew of the existence of any code.

"Why is it called number two? The Charon Two? Is there another one somewhere?" He picked up the carafe and filled Page's partially empty glass.

"Funny," Page Shepard said, nodding his thanks, "I haven't thought about that in years. Yes, there is another one." His mind reliving events in the past, he failed to notice the abrupt change in Helmut Bruck's expression. "Judith made it, a small bronze sculpture of Charon poling his boat across the river Styx. I remember the day we all christened it at Yale. She, Alex, and I got very drunk and poured beer over it to celebrate. It was her final class project."

"Where is it now?" The KGB raven tried to submerge the anxiousness in his voice.

"At the end of the garden outside Alex's office; its the top of the sundial. The pole in Charon's hand casts a shadow over the numerals around the disk in which Alex had it set." He smiled wistfully. "Those were happier days for Alex and Judith. We were all a team then."

Helmut Bruck's smile was far from wistful as he reached over to refill both his and Page's glasses. He had an intuitive feeling that Baron Androssy's long search was at an end.

CHAPTER 10

The morning of August 27 dawned hot and humid in New York. Shortly before eleven, Alexander Kidd and Page Shepard joined Martin Granville and two company lawyers in the cool lobby. They took the elevator to the fifteenth floor where a small group of men, most strangers to Alex, stood talking quietly in the foyer before the double doors leading into the KWEN boardroom. The receptionist looked up and smiled. "Nice to have you back, Mr. Kidd."

And indeed Alexander Kidd did feel back at the helm of the network he had struggled so hard to build. In his briefcase he held not only the voting power of his and Judith's stock—forty-nine percent of the company—but the proxy that Lavarre Bolt had sent him after his visit to Houston. Lavarre's eight percent gave him effective control of KWEN.

Precisely at eleven, the doors to the boardroom were opened and the men entered to seat themselves in red upholstered chairs around the long conference table. A pad of paper and a sharpened pencil rested neatly before each position at the table, and glasses and silver thermos pitchers of ice water were clustered in groups down the center.

Like contestants, the opposing forces in the battle for KWEN grouped themselves across from each other, Alex and his four followers on one side, the Milo representative, his lawyers, and those supporting him on the other. As the formal terms of Milo's offer were read in circuitous legal jargon, Alex looked from one man to the next, trying to guess what each was thinking.

The representatives of the Atlanta-based Hanley Trust and Concord Investments from Chicago were strangers to him. They sat cool and dispassionate, typical business school graduates, he thought. Hamilton Jarvis had shown up. That surprised Alex, but he guessed the New England-bred ethic of honor had forced the man to be present at the supposed execution. Jarvis tried to keep his eyes averted from Alexander Kidd, but his furtive, guilt-induced glances brought them in constant contact. Myer Fisk was not present. As Alex had suspected, the motion picture mogul had caved in to the pressure from Milo and thrown them his proxy. Myer had had the decency to phone him before he did it; no real explanation had been necessary. Looking at the faces across from him, Alex could not help wondering why this meeting was taking place. Was it just a formality? After all, he had won. Milo must know it did not have the necessary votes to take him over.

As the reading droned on and the lawyers raised and discussed various points in question, he caught the eye of the well-tanned representative of the Freeport group. The banker nodded pleasantly at him and shrugged his shoulders to indicate his helplessness. It was a futile gesture of friendship. How had that Zurich bank found out about the KWEN-Freeport deal, Alex wondered. How?

But Alex's interest lay more with the representative of Milo Productions. Perhaps forty-five, he sat silent, confident, controlled, his facade one of polished marble. Alex did not like that—the man was too sure of himself. Or was he? Why did his eyes keep glancing at the door as if expecting something? Alex himself looked at the two heavy wooden panels, half expecting to see their brass handles turn. He was slowly becoming aware that the Milo lawyers were stalling, taking longer than necessary to explain and expand upon the various points in their proposal. Leaning over to Page, he whispered, "What's going on? Why the delay?"

Page relayed the question to the KWEN lawyer on his right and, after a brief exchange, the man addressed the

group. "Gentlemen, we are all very aware of the terms in
the Milo proposal and understand them fully. Can we not
speed up this process and move for an acceptance or
rejection vote?"

The Milo lawyer turned to the KWEN secretary who sat
nearby recording the minutes of the meeting. "Let the
minutes show that we propose to conduct this meeting in the
manner prescribed under the law."

"Then get on with it." Alex sighed impatiently. He was
eager to get back to his office, get back to work. Kidd had
talked with Sandra in London earlier that morning. She had
managed to keep alive his plans for the cultural channel
despite the well-publicized fight going on over KWEN.

No sooner had the opposing lawyer resumed reading
when a commotion in the foyer outside interrupted him. All
eyes went to the doors. Angry voices were raised in debate.
Alex saw the brass handles turn down. The doors burst open
as a furious man tried to force his way into the boardroom
past the receptionist who attempted vainly to restrain him.
"Will someone tell this here person just who I am?" he
shouted. Alex turned to Page in stunned silence.

"Come in, Mr. Bolt," the Milo representative called,
rising. "We did not expect you."

The receptionist released her hold and stood back as
Sidney Bolt, brushing the wrinkles from the arm of his suit
jacket, straightened himself and entered. "Gentlemen," he
said, easing himself into the twelfth and last vacant chair at
the boardroom table, "I bring you very sad news, very sad
indeed."

Alex felt every muscle in his body tense.

"Lavarre, my dear brother Lavarre—we found him late
last night. He died sometime the day before yesterday out
there on the range he loved so much."

"Died?" Alex repeated, aghast.

"From a heart attack, they think. Fell from his horse.
When he didn't come back that night, the ranch sent out
searchin' parties. That poor horse was standin' beside him
grievin' when they found him." Sidney Bolt removed the

steel-rimmed glasses from his narrow face and polished them with his handkerchief. He waited for the murmured conversations around him to subside before continuing.

"Alex, I know how close you and Lavarre were. He used to say he loved you like a son. And I know that he was standin' behind you in this thing." With a nod of his head he indicated all those seated around the large table. "But Lavarre's gone now. I got to think about the family, about the future." Alex could feel it coming. For the first time in his business career, he actually felt sick to his stomach. "I got to run things professional. Can't let emotions get in the way like Lavarre did."

"He built a pretty big empire that way, Sidney," Alex said in defense of his friend and himself.

"We surely did, *me* and Lavarre." The reply was icy.

The king is dead, Kidd thought, long live the king.

"Alex, I'm afraid I'm going to have to revoke that proxy Lavarre gave you. As head of the Bolt family and its interests, I think Milo Productions' tender for our stock is a mighty good one. Even though the estate is going to be tied up for some time, I've been assured that I'm within my rights to accept it."

Martin Granville and Page looked at Alex. He sat motionless, his fists clenched, frozen, numbed by the inevitable. It was over. They knew it, he knew it. With great self-control, he slowly rose and stood erect, looking with contempt from one man to the next. "Handle the funeral, Page," he said softly. Turning, Alexander Kidd left his boardroom for the last time. Hamilton Jarvis looked away.

CHAPTER 11

In the brief two days following the takeover of KWEN, subtle changes were made within the staffing of the network, changes that went unnoticed by all but the technical staff. Page had refused at first to accept the three technicians who had arrived from Milo on the afternoon of the takeover. They were not needed, and he considered a Milo presence in the control rooms of KWEN premature at this time. The excuse that they were there only on temporary assignment to learn the operations side of the network seemed flimsy and dangerous to the morale of the other engineers. But that evening a phone call had changed Page's mind.

Working late in his office, the call came through on his private line, bypassing the switchboard. "Yes?"

"Mr. Shepard?" a cool voice with a slight European accent asked.

"Who is this?" Page replied. "How did you get this number?"

"Will you be good enough to look under the left-hand side of the blotter on your desk."

Page Shepard held the receiver away from him and looked at it in surprise.

As if his reaction had been anticipated, the voice repeated, "Under the blotter, Mr. Shepard. I assure you this is not a prank."

Looking down at the dark blue blotter edged in leather, Page frowned and lifted it hesitantly, almost as if a serpent might lie coiled beneath ready to strike. He saw no serpent, only a thin manila envelope. An unreasoning sensation of dread swept over him as he put down the receiver and slowly slid out the envelope, reluctantly opening the flap. A soft moan escaped him as he pulled out the large, glossy photograph and stared at it. The naked man in his arms had his back to the camera, but Page recognized Helmut's golden-blond hair and the pattern of the tousled sheets upon which their sweat-coated bodies sprawled. Still staring dumbly at the photograph, Page picked up the receiver.

"You have it, Mr. Shepard?" the mysterious voice asked.

Page nodded mutely.

"Mr. Shepard?"

"Yes, yes, I have it," he answered softly.

"We have many others, far less discreet. The voice paused, waiting for some reply, and then went on. "Your German lover is quite young, Mr. Shepard, not much older than your own sons. Their names are Quin and John, are they not?"

The mention of his sons pulled Page back from the numbing shock he felt. "Who are you?" he demanded weakly.

"Quin plans to be a lawyer, I believe," the voice went on, unperturbed. "A very respectable profession. And your wife, Mary, is spending the summer with friends at Fishers Island. She is a very lovely and social woman, Mr. Shepard."

The intent of the call was all too clear to Page. "I suppose you won't tell me who you are."

"That is correct."

"Then tell me how much you want."

"Not money, Mr. Shepard, just cooperation. This afternoon you rejected three technicians. Tomorrow morning when they return you will put them on your staff and rearrange the work shifts in the control rooms as they suggest. A simple request."

Page was frightened and furious at the same time. He fought to control his voice. "So Milo stoops to blackmail?

Is that how you guys operate, how you took us over? Is that—"

"Your pathetic outrage is understandable," the voice interrupted, "but of little value to you in your current predicament. The three men will be at your office precisely at nine tomorrow. I also require an unlimited security pass for a man named Pelton, John R. Pelton."

"Now wait just a minute, I can't—"

"You can do anything you please, Mr. Shepard, anything that pleases me. Look again at the photograph." The phone was silent for nearly a minute, then the voice said, "I will enjoy working with you, Mr. Shepard."

The following day a brief telex arrived at Credit Bank Schiller, and its message was relayed to KGB headquarters at 2 Dzerzhinsky Square. General Ivan Ivanovich Guryanov entered the chairman's office on the third floor and, accepting a small glass of vodka, sat in the chair opposite his superior. His eyes moved over the battery of phones lining the immense desk that provided immediate contact with the Kremlin and the high officials of the Politburo and Central Committee as well as KGB offices scattered about the Soviet Union and Eastern Europe.

"It has come, Ivan Ivanovich."

"Finally," the general replied. "When will it happen, and in what form?"

"Three days from today. The American carrier *Constellation* on the morning of August thirty-first."

Guryanov looked at him aghast. "The entire ship?" The general still remained in the dark concerning the details of how his country could actually cripple the Israeli forces, and knew nothing of its plans for the United States and the NATO forces after the destruction of the Jewish nation.

"Only a squadron of its fighters. The carrier will be at sea off the coast of Libya participating in the war games. Our friend Colonel Qaddafi will have a grandstand seat for the disaster." He raised his glass to the general and smiled.

"The Israeli funds will be transferred between seven and

eight A.M." the chairman continued, repeating the exact words of the telex.

Guryanov failed to understand the exact meaning of the phrase, but repeated the time. "Seven to eight on the morning of the thirty-first. It has come none too soon; the Syrians were about to pull out."

"You will be leaving shortly for Beirut?"

"This afternoon."

The chairman finished his vodka in a final gulp and nodded, dismissing General Guryanov. As the other rose and crossed the room to leave, he called out to him, "Ivan Ivanovich." The general turned. "Make sure our Arab friends understand that it was we, not Qaddafi's toy air force that downed the American planes. He will make the claim, of that you can be sure."

Guryanov smiled and nodded. Leaving the room, he walked quickly down the long, dull green corridor, the heels of his boots clacking loudly against the uncarpeted parquet floor. The general had much to do before his flight departed that afternoon for the Middle East.

They had not even permitted Alexander Kidd to enter his office after leaving the boardroom. It remained legally padlocked to him. Using that stupid threat he had made in Portsmouth as an excuse, they had escorted him politely but firmly from the building. Now Alex put down his glass and looked about at the paintings hanging against the walls of the living room at the Dakota. Well, what the hell did he care anymore? He was a rich man now, he'd buy more paintings. All he had to do was sell his stock to that Milo what's-its-name. It was time he relaxed, had some fun. The Whitbread—why not sail it himself? The twenty-seven thousand-mile race around the world would take about seven months. Why not? He had nothing else to do now. Poor old Lavarre, that poor old rebel. He'd miss him. These and many other thoughts ran through his dulled brain as he reached for the half-empty bottle on the coffee table before him and sloshed more Scotch into his glass. He looked up, and in his mind he saw Judith standing above him as she had done on the last night. He imagined he was taking his glass from her hand and gulped down its contents.

The room suddenly felt too cold and impersonal to bear. Lurching to his feet, Kidd moved unsteadily through the dark apartment to his study and sank back into the reassuring comfort of the old leather sofa. Across the room, the figures on the screen of the television set, dialed out of habit to KWEN, moved silently back and forth. He had turned down the sound three days after the announcement of his network's takeover and the appointment of Page Shepard as interim caretaker until a new management team could be installed. Kidd had not answered any phone calls, and his door had remained closed to all knocks. Page had been there twice; Alex recognized his muffled voice trying to reach him through the solid oak. He had gone out only once, slipping out late the previous night to a liquor store. On the way, a sleazy red-headed hooker wearing too much mascara had sidetracked him on Columbus Avenue. After fucking her brutally, Alex returned unshaven and in disarray to his self-imposed exile. He did not want to talk to or be with anyone from the real world.

At 11:53 that night, George Lunts and the other two Milo technicians moved into the KWEN control and transmitter rooms, relieving those at the consoles. The early morning shift was a routine and boring one, the work consisting mainly of transmitting prerecorded tapes up to the Charon II satellite. The older employees of the network had been only too glad to turn the shift over to the new men, all but Tom Petterson. He sat in the employees' canteen several floors below, sipping coffee.

There was something about the new men he did not like. Oh, yes, they were capable. They were actually overtrained for the job. He had been impressed by the speed with which Lunts had mastered every switch and dial as well as the circuitry behind them, and learned how to communicate with the satellite. Lunts had watched as Petterson made the monthly adjustment in Charon II's orbit. Of course, for reasons of KWEN security, Tom had not let him see the code he used to tap into that part of the satellite's computer brain. Lunts appeared an enthusiastic person, full of questions. There was no doubt in Tom's mind that he was a real electronic pro. But still he felt uneasy about him. Perhaps it was jealousy. Now that KWEN was no longer Alex Kidd's, Tom felt that he had lost his exclusive claim to his baby floating twenty-two thousand miles up in space.

While one technician remained at the consoles monitoring transmission of the network's news and sports programs to the satellite, Lunts bent over the dials on the panel that controlled the movement of Charon II. Pug Ballon, the third Milo technician, moved to lock the door to the outside hall and stood with his ear to it.

"We've got three hours to move that bastard ahead forty-five degrees latitude," Lunts said over his shoulder as he began beaming up the stolen first code to which Charon II's rockets would respond.

"You're going to lose all program transmission."

Lunts shook his head. "There's no other way. The earth dishes are all aimed at Charon II's current position. Unless they're moved, they'll lose us as soon as we move ahead a few degrees."

"There'll be all hell to pay," Ballon smiled.

"Let's hope most of the subscribers go to bed early," Lunts replied. "At fourteen thousand miles an hour, it will take about three hours to move it ahead and, thanks to the earth's rotation, only three-quarters of an hour to bring it back into position. We'll make the early morning news."

Both men watched the hands of the wall clock until they touched one A.M. Lunts took a deep breath and began the transmission to the satellite. Ballon stood behind him, his gaze alternating between Lunt's movements at the console and the screen of the monitor above as Charon II slowly moved ahead in its orbit.

Twenty-two blocks north in his Dakota apartment, Alex took another gulp of Scotch, his attention only briefly distracted by the snow and jagged diagonal lines that cut across his television screen to obscure the KWEN transmission of a basketball game. He smiled to himself. "Serves you bastards right," he mumbled, leaning forward to refill his glass.

Shortly after, Tom Petterson was roughly awakened from sleep in his chair in the canteen by one of the network's late night managers. "We've lost transmission."

"What do you mean 'lost,'" Tom asked groggily, rubbing his eyes. "We can't just—"

"Oh yeah?" the other retorted. "You tell that to the systems managers out there. Portland was the first to call."

Those words brought Petterson to his feet. "Jesus," he muttered, "she must be drifting." The old engineer headed for the door and the control room two stories above. "Tell them we're working on it," he called back over his shoulder. Taking the steps two at a time, Tom reached the operations floor of the KWEN building and, his heart beating wildly from the exertion, raced down the dimly lit corridor to the control room door. Grasping the knob, he turned and pulled. It did not open. Damn, he thought. But there was nothing strange about the door being locked; it was a security measure often taken on the morning shift. He banged on it with his fist and waited, gasping for breath. Banging again, he stood back impatiently. Again, the lack of response did not seem out of the ordinary; all the attention of those inside would be directed at getting the satellite back on course.

Inside, Ballon looked at his superior and then at the door.

"Find out who it is," Lunts ordered. "Tell 'em we're doing all we can, that everything's under control."

Moving across the room to the door, Ballon was about to speak when both men heard a key being inserted in the lock. "Damn," he muttered.

Tom Petterson was one of the few who had a key to the operations room of the network. Pulling open the door, he glanced quickly at the two new technicians and then up at the tracking screen. "What in the hell's happened?" he demanded, pointing at the blip on the screen overhead.

"She's ahead over ten degrees latitude. Use the rockets to slow her."

"Everything's under control, Tom," Lunts replied calmly, almost condescendingly. "We'll get it back."

"Here, let me at those controls." Tom moved forward, taking George Lunts's arm in preparation to pushing him aside. Lunts's eyes met Ballon's in a brief command and Ballon took Petterson's arms and gently pulled him back.

"Easy there, Tom, let's not get excited, okay?" His grasp tightened on the older man.

Tom stopped struggling. He was confused. He looked at Lunts maneuvering the dials and switches on the control panel. The man was an expert. Then why was Charon II moving forward in orbit? Studying the tracking screen, he saw the satellite gain another degree, and then he realized the truth. These men were not trying to correct Charon II's position, they were . . . "You're purposely changing the orbit," he exclaimed.

"That's right, Tom," Lunts stated flatly, his attention turned to the screen before him. "Just following orders. We're moving it ahead forty-five degrees for a few hours."

"Orders?" Petterson challenged. "Whose orders?"

"Our big boss, yours and mine, Shepard. They came down about an hour ago."

"Impossible. Page knows only I can . . ." And then the truth hit him. "The code! How did you get the code?"

Tom tore himself free from Ballon's grip in one sudden movement and lunged across the control room for Lunts. Just as his hands reached the other man's shoulders, Ballon's vicious blow to the right of his head sent him crashing to the floor, skidding across its polished surface to the far wall. Ballon reached behind him and relocked the door before coming to kneel beside the fallen man. Dazed, Tom Petterson stared up into the barrel of a small, deadly-looking gun.

"Sorry, Tom, didn't want to do that." His smile was cold. "We don't have time to fool around."

"Why?" the bewildered man asked. "Why are you doing this?"

Ballon glanced over his shoulder at Lunts and then turned back. "You know, Tom, would you believe me if I said I honestly don't know why?"

Petterson, rubbing the side of his face, looked up at the gun in the hand of the man kneeling above him. Over his head he could see the tracking screen. Charon II was now more than twenty degrees ahead in its orbit. It was past two in the morning.

Picking up the buzzing phone for perhaps the tenth time, Lunts answered. "Yes, I know, I know. We're doing our best. The transponders are on the blink." He listened. "Look, tell them we should have it fixed in the next few hours, certainly in time for the early morning news." Again he listened. Tom could not make out the words of the agitated voice of one of the members of the night skeleton force shouting on the other end of the phone. "No, there's no point in your coming up here. We've got everything under control. It takes time, damn it." Exasperation exploded in his voice. "Look, we weren't broadcasting anything interesting anyway, just a delayed-action basketball game and, for Christ's sake, there's nothing new on the news. Tell 'em all to go to bed and stop bugging us." Lunts hung up, mumbling an obscenity under his breath. "How's it going over there, Pug?" he asked without taking his eyes from the monitor.

"Just fine. Tom is behaving himself, aren't you, Tom?"

Petterson didn't answer. His initial confusion was giving way to fear.

At precisely 3:40 in the morning, John R. Pelton slipped out of one of the darkened offices on the editorial floor of the KWEN building and walked quickly to the staircase leading down one flight to the control room. Pausing briefly outside the door, he looked up and down the deserted corridor and knocked three times, paused, then knocked twice more.

Inside, Lunts nodded to Ballon, who slowly backed away from Petterson toward the door, his gun still pointed directly at the man's ashen face. Fumbling with the lock behind him,

Ballon opened the door to admit the stranger that neither he nor Lunts had ever seen before. Glancing at the weapon in Ballon's hand, Pelton frowned. He looked across the control room to Tom Petterson. "Who is he?"

"The chief engineer, Petterson."

"Why is he here?" Pelton's voice bore the trace of an aristocratic foreign accent.

"Barged in on us," Lunts replied. "This room is Tom's home. He looks on Charon II as his personal property."

Pelton stared at Petterson. "Did he give you any trouble?"

"He tried," Ballon answered.

"Pity," the other said, dismissing the prisoner. He crossed to stand behind Lunts. "Is the satellite at the forty-five latitude mark?"

Lunts nodded, looking up at the tracking screen "She's back at seven thousand miles an hour in a stationary orbit, just as you requested."

"Good." Pelton removed a piece of paper from his pocket and studied the coded numbers carefully copied upon it. From across the room, Ballon watched the stranger curiously out of the corner of his eye. John R. Pelton wore a nondescript, rumpled brown suit, his dark knit tie slightly off center. He stood a bit hunched over, but Ballon estimated his height at about six feet two. He found it hard to determine the man's age. His reddish hair was shaggy as was the mustache and beard that covered much of his face. Heavy, steel-rimmed glasses completed the picture. Mr. John Pelton was a distinct disappointment to Ballon, who had expected to meet a very sinister looking character. Aside from the slight accent, Pelton could have been one of a hundred people who were normally seen in the halls of KWEN.

"Are the spot-beam antennas set to cover the prescribed area?" Pelton asked.

"One hundred miles in diameter." Lunts repeated his instructions, pointing to an area in the Mediterranean seventy miles off the North African coast.

"Excellent. I wish to make the transmission at a very high frequency." He showed Lunts the setting on the paper in his hand and watched as the technician made the necessary adjustment.

"What the fuck are those clowns doing up there," the network's distraught night-shift manager grumbled to a nearby assistant. "It's been almost three hours since we lost transmission."

The other looked up from the papers spread on the desk before him and shrugged helplessly.

The manager fumed, staring at the large circular clock on the wall across the room. It read 3:50. "I'm going up there and—"

"Give 'em a chance. They're working on it."

"Shit, they're working on it." The night manager stood up and headed for the door.

"Petterson's up there now, Bob. What can you do that he can't? Shout and holler? Get everyone mad? Get in the way? Cool it."

The other hesitated, his hand on the knob. Sighing, he reluctantly turned back.

"I'll take over now," the mysterious Mr. Pelton said. "Exactly how long will it take to transmit my instructions to the satellite?"

"A quarter of a second up," Lunts replied, standing to turn over his chair to the stranger, "and the same down."

"Please leave me now."

Lunts nodded and moved across the control room to join Ballon. As a highly trained KGB operative, he knew how to follow orders without question.

The wall clock read 3:55, six hours behind the time of NATO's Mediterranean Fleet off the coast of Africa. The man who called himself Pelton sat down and began sending up to Charon II the code that he had taken so recently from the base of its brother boatman on the sundial in the garden outside Alexander Kidd's office on the fifteenth floor. As he sat there sending the complex, repetitive code to activate the satellite's transmitters to beam down to earth the preset radio message designed to knock out Cerberus circuits, Miklos Androssy could not help wondering if, after seven long years of disuse, the hardware and technology behind the Acheron Plot would really work, if he really held the balance of world power in his hands.

CHAPTER 12

Sweeping low over the Mediterranean, Commander Pete Ryan pulled his F-14A Tomcat out of its final dive in the mock dogfight between his and a second flight of three jet fighters comprising the squadron. Followed by the others, he soared up through the cloud cover toward the morning sun, rolling over in a victory salute. "Well done," he radioed the five silver jets behind him.

The sky was blue crystal, a sharp contrast to the murky fog and clouds masking the NATO task force floating on the sea far below. Ryan glanced at his watch. It read 9:46. They had only minutes before their scheduled landing back on deck.

"Silver Rooster to the chicks," he radioed. "Join landing formation. On your way in, swish your tails low at Chicken Hawk last seen at thirty-four north, seventeen east." (Chicken Hawk was the name given to the Russian spy trawler that had dogged the fleet for the last two weeks.) "You want to take her in?" Commander Ryan asked his co-pilot. These were the first war games in which the young man and most of the other rookie pilots had participated.

"Yes, sir," he answered eagerly.

Ryan smiled at the barely disguised zeal in the boy's voice. "She's all yours." He sat back, relaxed, looking out into the blue void, his thoughts back in Ohio with his wife and two sons, Charlie, six, and John only three and a half.

As the lead F-14A Tomcat slowly sank into the clouds, the other fighters followed, their pilots' eyes moving between the dials on the control panels before them and the mist below, searching for the dark shadow of the spy trawler. "There she is," the young lead pilot called.

"Captain," the Russian radar technician aboard the *Chernenkov* reported, "they are returning to the fleet right on schedule." The screen before him showed the bleeping lights of the approaching squadron.

"How many?" the bearded officer asked, putting down his coffee and picking up the log.

"Six."

"Six," the other repeated, noting them in his record. He vaguely wondered to what real use all the training schedules and other information he had been wiring back to Moscow over the last weeks was being put. The first jet roared close overhead. He cursed it, covering his ears against the next five.

"Squadron Seven is coming in," the radar officer on the carrier *Constellation* announced in a matter-of-fact tone into the microphone to his right. The deck crew scurried into position, every man looking westward in anticipation of the first of the fighters that would soon break through the low-hanging mist.

No matter how many times he had done it, Commander Ryan had never felt completely comfortable with instrument approaches at sea. "Take it easy, son," he said encouragingly to his co-pilot as his eyes moved between the altimeter and the other dials before him. "Just keep on the carrier's radio beam."

Suddenly the needles and gauges on the panel before him went crazy, whirling and moving back and forth erratically.

"We're out of control," his panic-stricken co-pilot cried. It was the same cry being echoed by the desperate young pilots in each of the other five jets following them in.

"Pull her up," Ryan shouted.

"I am," the other yelled.

"No!" Ryan fought for control. "Up, up, man." Speeding through the mist, it was impossible to tell which way was up, which down. The needles whirled. Ryan relied on instinct only. It was not enough. His cry joined the anguished shriek of the fresh young co-pilot as the F-14A broke through the mist, diving straight down at the carrier. The men on deck scattered in all directions as the fighter's right wing cut into the bridge of the control tower, exploding in a ball of flame and spinning into the sea.

The radar officer below deck stared in horror as one after another of the five remaining light blips silently disappeared from his screen.

Eighty miles to the east, a small child was the first to scream as a fully loaded charter DC-10 on a delayed tourist flight from Las Palmas to Nicosia slowly turned on its side and began its long plunge twelve thousand feet into a watery grave.

CHAPTER 13

Alex's head throbbed as he pushed himself up into a sitting position on the study couch. The midmorning sun cutting through a gap between the draperies hurt his eyes, his mouth tasted sour, and his tongue felt thick. Rubbing a hand across the stubble on his chin, the former president of KWEN rose unsteadily and supported himself on one arm of the sofa while squinting painfully across the room at the still-silent television set. The newsman was pointing at a blowup of an aircraft carrier. "So you bastards finally got the transponder working again," he mumbled as he turned and walked slowly to the kitchen. Orange juice, ice-cold orange juice was the most important thing on his mind at that moment.

Glass in hand, he took another deep swallow of the refreshing citrus juice and, out of habit, opened the back door of the apartment to retrieve the *New York Times*. Tossing it casually on the table, Alex slumped back in a kitchen chair to finish the rest of the glass, staring ahead vacantly. It must have been a minute or two before his eyes focused on the headline before him.

> MEDITERRANEAN AIR DISASTERS!
> 123 PERISH ON CHARTER FLIGHT
> 27 DIE IN MULTIPLE NAVY CRASH

"Jesus," he muttered, slowly leaning forward to read further. His instincts for a good story gained in the years of

133

editing TV news overcame his current antipathy toward the
outside world and its inhabitants. The lack of details, the
unstated mystery in all the reportage intrigued him. A
coincidence between the two disasters? Had there been a
midair collision of some sort? If a Navy jet had brought
down a civilian aircraft during war games, he could
understand the reason for the Navy's reluctance to speak
out. He reread the first paragraph of the lead article.

> "Three crewmen safely ejected before six Navy jet
> fighters crashed while preparing to land aboard the
> carrier Constellation in the Mediterranean Sea today.
> A United States military spokesman said that the
> cause of the simultaneous crashes was under investi-
> gation. Nine crewmen of the American F-14A Tomcat
> fighters and 18 aboard the carrier died in the worse
> peacetime NATO disaster since . . ."

The story continued, stating that the crash of the American
DC-10 was also "under investigation." The charter flight
had had only time to radio difficulty with its navigational
equipment before it went down. Wreckage found close to
the area of the NATO war games bore grim evidence to the
lack of survivors. Equipment malfunction, Alex thought. A
bad day for the American aircraft industry.

And then he turned the page, and his eye caught a small
headline in the lower corner of the third page.

KWEN SATELLITE LOST FOR 4 HOURS

The throbbing in Alex's head disappeared and his mind
slowly began to focus sharp and clear. "American planes,"
he said aloud, not really believing the connection he was
beginning to make, "Charon Two missing." He made the
mental time-and-distance calculations as he projected himself back over seven years to the office of President John

James Warren. "Acheron?" he asked aloud, shaking his head in disbelief. "It couldn't possibly be. . . ."

Grabbing up the newspaper, Alex rushed back to his study. Reaching the television set, he turned it up full volume to the KWEN news channel. Page—he had to talk to Page Shepard. And Paul Carmody and Simon Felton. It had to be a coincidence. It couldn't be the crazy thing he suspected. Alex reached for the phone and dialed Page Shepard's private number. It rang three times before being picked up.

"Page, it's Alex."

"Alex, where the hell have you been? I've been trying to reach you for days. The Dakota—"

"I know, I know," Alex interrupted. "Page, I've got to talk to you. Charon Two, what happened last night?"

Alex noted the discernible pause at the other end of the line. When he spoke again, Page's voice sounded guarded to him. "Alex, I can't now, I'm in a meeting. Perhaps—"

"Just tell me one thing. Did you move the satellite?"

Again, another pause. "I've got to go, Alex."

"Page, did you or didn't you?" Alexander Kidd demanded. "A simple yes or no, that's all I want to know."

"Of course not," Shepard snapped quickly, denying the question. "Look, I can't talk now. Later."

Before Kidd could say another word, the phone clicked, cutting off further discussion. He slowly replaced the receiver and then quickly snatched it up again to dial the KWEN switchboard. "Tom Petterson," he asked the familiar voice on the other end of the line.

"I'll ring Mr. Petterson."

Alex's fingers drummed impatiently on the side table as he waited.

"I'm sorry, sir, there's no answer. Mr. Petterson must be away from his office. May I take a message?" The operator's voice was flat and dispassionate.

"Maggie, this is Alex Kidd."

The voice brightened. "Oh, Mr. Kidd. Good morning to you."

"Will you please call operations and find out who was on duty last night."

"Oh, Mr. Kidd, I don't think I can—"

"Maggie McNally, you can do anything. You're the ears of KWEN and you know it. Please, Maggie, a favor."

After a brief pause, the operator relented. "Okay, Mr. Kidd. How are you anyway? We miss you around here."

"Fine, Maggie, fine." He held on for several minutes before her voice returned.

"Sam Wilton and Ben Tokor were in charge. Sam's in. Do you want to talk to him?"

"Yes, thanks, Maggie. I owe you one."

"Look, after all these years, I still owe you a hundred. Hold on, I'll put you through."

Several rings later, Alex heard, "Wilton here."

"Sam, it's Alex Kidd."

"Hi, Alex. Some brouhaha, huh?"

"You mean Charon Two?"

"Right. That's why you're calling isn't it?"

"What happened?"

"Something went wrong with the transponder; apparently it blacked out for nearly four hours."

"Were you in the control room? You're sure Charon Two didn't change orbit?"

"No, it was the transponder, Alex. That's what the boys up there said. Tom was with them until they got it fixed."

"Where *is* Tom? I tried to call him."

"Sick. I guess last night got to him. One of the control room fellows, Ballon it was, put him in a cab a little after five this morning. He looked terrible."

"You saw him?"

"Yeah. Ballon practically had to carry the poor guy. How old is Petterson anyway?"

"Don't know, Sam. Who's this Ballon? I don't remember anyone by that name."

"One of the new technicians on the early morning shift."

"One of the new . . . ? What happened to Johnson?" Alex was puzzled.

"Transferred. They're all new on that shift. Came in when KWEN changed hands. Didn't you know?"

Kidd didn't reply. "I'll give Tom a call at home," he said finally. "Thanks for easing my curiosity. Good talking to you."

"Same here, Alex. KWEN still in your blood, right?"

"Right, Sam." Alex depressed the contact bar on his phone and then dialed Tom Petterson's home. Tom wasn't there and hadn't returned at all the previous night. His wife was frantic. Giving what assurances he could, Alex hung up and sank back into the soft suede of the sofa, deep in thought.

"You wanted proof, you have it," General Ivan Ivanovich Guryanov stated bluntly. "Since the crashes this morning, not a single NATO plane in the exercises has taken off. They sit confused, helpless."

"And their missiles?" Ali Gemayel questioned.

"Had they chosen to fire them during our period of control not one would have reached its target." Satisfied with the impression he had made on his Moslem companions, the heavyset Russian stood up from the table and, mopping the sweat from his face, walked to the French windows for a breath of fresh air. The late afternoon sun cast a pink light over the torn buildings of Beirut. Few people walked in the heat of the street below.

"The Libyans claim they shot them down," the military adviser to the Syrian president persisted.

Without turning, the general answered, "Remember, my friend, it was we, not the Libyans, who predicted the exact time."

"He is right, Ali," General Saad Hasaam said. "Let us not belabor the point." He too rose and walked to the window. "And the American charter plane?"

Guryanov had expected the question and turned. "A further proof of our ability to render useless all American machines either of peace or of war. And a proof of our determination to aid your cause in this area."

"So be it," the Syrian general said aloud, and then lowering his voice to keep their conversation from the others, asked, "How was it done? You can trust me."

The Syrian's question pleased Guryanov. It was an indication of the general's complete faith in the Russians' ability to deliver what they had promised. "Another time, my friend," Ivan Ivanovich said softly, dangling the carrot before the other. "And you, Salim Chamoun, what do you have to say?" he called across the room.

The thin, intense PLO representative replied calmly and precisely, "Obviously we are impressed. I have been in contact with our leadership both on the West Bank and in Gaza. They are ready to move ahead with the uprising. This afternoon Jordan committed itself. They request more Russian jets—a loan if you will. Their air force consists mainly of American fighters. Can this be arranged?"

"I will advance the request to Moscow, although the Libyan and Syrian air forces should be sufficient to destroy all land targets. They will encounter no resistance in the air from either Israeli planes or missiles."

"Nevertheless, it is a simple request," the PLO representative pressed, "one that would make our friends feel a bit more secure in committing their land forces."

General Guryanov nodded and repeated, "I will advance the request." He detested the wrangling and haggling of the Arabs. To him, their statesmen sounded like the filthy rug peddlers in the bazaars. "Inform our Jordanian comrades that the arrival of Russian fighters in their country might well signal our plans to the Israelis."

"They could be disguised before arrival," Chamoun countered.

"I will advance the request," the general sighed. He detected a slight smile on his Syrian counterpart's face.

"Join me in a vodka," General Hassam said, pouring two glasses of the colorless liquid.

Guryanov accepted the proffered glass and took a gulp. The fire in his throat appeased his frustration. Changing the subject, he addressed Ali Gemayel. "What of the Libyans?"

"Completely committed to the war. They stand shoulder to shoulder with our president."

"Excellent. And the buildup?"

"It has been progressing on all fronts as we agreed. Slowly, but that is necessary to veil our plans from the Zionists. Many of our troops have infiltrated across their borders dressed as civilians and wait quietly under cover. Their presence should not have been detected. Mobilization of our land forces is nearing completion." Pride radiated from Gemayel's voice.

"Moscow has heard disturbing rumors that President Assad and Kind Hussein are again in dispute over your boundaries, that the two are at the brink of conflict." He waited for a reply to his statement.

Ali Gemayel and General Hassam looked at each other, a trace of amusement in their eyes. Sobering, Saad Hassam addressed the Russian sternly, "My dear friend, you must not expect to orchestrate this war completely from Moscow. In the end it is our battle, is it not?" The Russian flushed. "You will admit that we are, perhaps, more sensitive to the mentalities of this area than you and your strategists who sit in the Kremlin."

Guryanov held up his hand in protest. "I meant no—"

General Hassam raised his hand to silence the other's protestations. He clearly enjoyed the opportunity to put down the imperious Russian. "The dispute to which you refer is an old one which both our leaders have agreed to revive and escalate to divert attention from our true intent. Tell your strategists in Moscow not to be surprised to see Syrian and Jordanian troups in a series of skirmishes on September twenty-first, the day before we move together to slaughter every Jew that now breathes on our lands."

Swallowing his pride, Ivan Guryanov raised his glass in a salute to the Syrian general. "I congratulate you and your countrymen, General Hassam."

The other received the compliment graciously and nodded his approval of it.

"Alecto?" General Paul Carmody exclaimed in surprise at the use of the old code name. The call had come through to him at the Pentagon on the ultraprivate phone he kept locked in the bottom drawer of his desk. Kidd had never used the phone before and certainly never that name. Surely there could be no emergency of the sort that had first entered his mind upon hearing it, not now, not these days. "What is it?" As he spoke, he gestured to his aide, Major Peter Granger, indicating his wish for privacy.

"I've got to see you," Alex replied. There was no mistaking the determination in his voice. It had taken him nearly an hour after talking with Mrs. Petterson to decide on this call. "I'll come to Washington, or we can meet in New York. No one must know."

"What's this all about?" Carmody asked guardedly.

"The Navy lost six planes this morning," Kidd stated flatly.

"Yes, I know."

"KWEN lost a satellite."

"So I read."

"Lost it for four hours during the same period of time." And then Alex repeated the code word Paul Carmody never thought he would have to hear. "Acheron."

The general stared at the receiver in his hand, his mind flashing back in time. "Impossible," he protested, "a coincidence."

"Do I come to Washington?"

"But only you have control of . . ." Then he remembered the publicity surrounding the takeover of KWEN.

"Or do you come to New York?" Alex's tone left no room for argument.

General Carmody sat silent. He was at a loss for words.

"Megaera?"

Jarred from his thoughts by his own code name, he reluctantly replied, "I . . . I'll come to New York. When?"

"Tomorrow morning?"

"Where?"

"Strawberry Fields at noon."

"That's being a little dramatic, isn't it?"

"Being dramatic used to be my business, remember?" Alex paused. "An in civvies. Make sure no one, not even Joan, knows where you're going. I'm afraid we're in deep shit."

"Anything you can tell me now?"

"No, not until tomorrow."

Carmody looked at the phone long after he finished the short but alarming conversation. As he closed and locked the desk drawer, he pressed a button on his intercom. "Peter, what have I got on my plate for tomorrow?"

His ever-efficient aide read a list of the general's appointments.

"Reschedule them all."

"But general, even the meeting with the Joint Chiefs?" the major protested.

"Make some excuse. You're very good at that, Peter."

"Are you leaving Washington, General?" Granger asked.

Carmody paused before answering. "No, some extremely important personal things have just come up." He cut off the intercom and buzzed his secretary. "Cynthia, get me the Felton Electronics file."

"Felton Electronics?" she asked, repeating the unfamiliar name. "I don't believe I know that file."

"It will be in the procurement section, marked confidential. You have the combination. And Cynthia, I won't be in tomorrow." He released the button.

"Doesn't the general have a full schedule tomorrow?" she asked, glancing up at the good-looking thirty-four-year-old major who leaned cockily against the door frame between their two offices.

Major Peter Granger, or Peter Lobantz as he was known to his superiors in Moscow, was an illegal. Recruited in East Germany and trained for seven years by the skilled instructors of the First Chief Directorate of the KGB, he had crossed secretly into the United States from Canada in 1972 and joined the Air Force two years later after having firmly established his cover story, or his "legend" as Soviet intelligence called it. Peter had worked hard to move up through the chain of command, all the while awaiting the time when Moscow would call on him. That time had come soon after the Russian discovery of the Acheron Plot. The young officer had been ordered to work his way into the Pentagon and attach himself to the staff of General Paul Carmody.

Granger nodded and smiled. "The general has some personal things to take care of. By the way, Cinny, I may not be in either tomorrow. Cover for me?"

"What's it worth?"

"Dinner?" he suggested, approaching her with eyes narrowed in a lecherous grin.

"And?" she asked as he moved behind her.

"Who knows. Have you anything in mind?" Granger's hand moved from her shoulder down into the plunging opening of the attractive brunette's blouse. He rolled the nipple of her left breast between his fingers. "Now you'd better get that file, sexy," he said with a final, painful pinch.

Cynthia North gasped and her hand clutched his firmly and held it against her breast until he slowly released the pressure. "Bastard," she hissed as he pulled his hand free and moved away.

Granger smiled. "The file," he prompted, helping her up.

CHAPTER 14

"What in hell's all this Alecto, Megaera stuff, Alex?" Paul Carmody demanded. As arranged, they were meeting at a bench in the Strawberry Fields section of Central Park. Carmody's voice was filled with a blend of comradery, impatience, and more than a trace of annoyance. "By the way, you look terrible."

"Thanks, Paul," Kidd replied sarcastically. Leaning forward, he heaved himself up. "Let's take a walk."

"The KWEN takeover hurting?" Carmody asked.

"I'm not used to losing."

"We all do sooner or later," the general replied, recalling his many frustrations and disappointments in the Pentagon's halls of political power. "You'll get over it. Now, why am I here?"

Kidd took his arm and led him forward along the park path. The peaked rooftops of the Dakota across the street loomed high above them in the clear blue sky. "Someone's onto the boatman."

"Impossible."

"They used Charon Two."

"I don't believe it." He was adamant.

"Why did your planes crash?"

"We're still trying to determine that."

"Don't kid me, Paul," Alex chided. "You know. Three pilots ejected; what did they say?" The general hesitated. "Remember, you're not talking to Alexander Kidd, you're talking to Alecto."

"Instrument failure," Carmody stated flatly.

143

"And the charter plane?"

"Apparently the same thing. But hold it, Alex," he rushed on to say. "Don't get carried away. The fleet was in bad weather. We believe there was some sort of electrical storm in the area. This sort of thing has happened before and—"

"Seven planes? One forty or fifty miles away?" Kidd interrupted in disbelief. "Come on, Paul."

"It's happened before," the general persisted. "An entire flight went down in the Bermuda Triangle, remember. And in Germany in 1977, two—"

"Why won't you even listen to me?"

"Because I know what you're going to say and I refuse to believe it for a minute."

"Then why did you come?" Kidd challenged.

Paul Carmody did not reply. Reaching into the pocket of his tweed sports jacket, he pulled out a cigar and bit off the end. Alex stood by as the general lit it and took several puffs. Carmody always behaved the same way when he felt under pressure. "Because there might be some small chance—only a chance—that what you implied on the phone could possibly be true," he said finally. "That you might know something I didn't. After you called, I had a friend at the Federal Communications Commission contact KWEN. It's not for public record, but they admitted a temporary rocket malfunction that caused the satellite to briefly lose orbit, that's all. I also contacted our satellite tracking section."

"And?"

"They confirmed a forty-five degree eastern movement in Charon Two's position."

"Forty-five degrees back and forth in four hours?" Alex exclaimed. "That's no malfunction, that's a deliberate orbit change with all rockets working perfectly. And Paul, that would have put Charon Two in easy range of the *Constellation*."

"Even if it were in range," Paul Carmody protested, "Charon Two could not have caused those planes to crash.

One, they were NATO planes, not of the type shipped to the Middle East during Warren's administration. And two, they were manufactured long after the Cerberus chip was discontinued."

"You're sure?" Alex demanded.

"I checked the files yesterday. We haven't put one of those chips into any hardware for over nine years. They're not even *made* anymore." He looked deep into Alex's eyes. "And finally, you're the only one of the three of us who knows the code to the fourth transponder in Charon Two. Without you, the damn thing wouldn't have worked even if the Cerberus chips *were* in those F-14A Tomcats." He smiled. "The satellite may have been moved on purpose, but I have three good reasons to prove that had nothing to do with those Tomcat crashes." He walked on. Alexander Kidd didn't follow. Carmody stopped and turned to look back at him.

"If one of those 'three good reasons' weren't so good, Paul, would you question the others?"

The confident smile left his face. "What are you saying, Alex?" He walked back.

"I'm saying I'm no longer sure I *am* the only one who knows the code." The general stared at him. "I lost KWEN, remember?" The other nodded guardedly. "The code is hidden in that building, and I can't get in to get it out. Paul, what if someone had that code and knew how to use it, knew what it could do?"

"But how could anyone have found out about Warren's plan?" Carmody protested. "After all these years?"

"Hell, I don't know, but supposing he did?" He put up his hand to ward off the general's continued protests. "I've been thinking about nothing but this ever since those crashes, so give me a chance. That person would have to get hold of Charon Two, wouldn't he? And since it's controlled only by KWEN, he'd have to get hold of KWEN. Paul, someone *has* got hold of KWEN: Milo Productions, that funny little company fronting for some mysterious group we were never able to track down."

"But still, there are the Cerberus chips. He'd have—"

"Simon's company was taken over seven years ago. Think about it, Paul," Alex said evenly, watching the other's reaction. "Another coincidence? How can you be so sure that chip is no longer being manufactured? How can you be so sure that it is no longer being put into those planes of yours? Well, how can you, Paul?"

"The specifications, I—"

"Those are *your* specifications, the Pentagon's," Alex interrupted. "Maybe they're not someone else's. Do you personally check each plane? The Cerberus circuit is pretty small; the chip inside it is tiny."

"Do you know what you're saying? The implications?" the general asked.

Alex nodded slowly.

"No, it's impossible." Carmody whirled around, trying to avoid the very possibility he was denying.

"Paul, the night Charon Two changed orbit, it was being handled by a completely new control room staff, a staff put in only a few days earlier by Milo. My man, Tom Petterson, apparently went up to find out what was going on. He hasn't been seen since." The general stared at Alexander Kidd. "And when I call Page Shepard, the guy who should know what's going on, all I get from my old buddy is the runaround. He hasn't given me a straight answer since this thing happened." He paused. "Will you contact Simon, or shall I?" Kidd asked quietly. "We've got to know."

General Carmody sighed, resigned to the inquiry he had to put into motion. "I'll call. And that code of yours?"

"That's my job."

"Isn't there anyone at KWEN you can trust to get it out for you?"

"I used to think there was," Alex replied, shaking his head, "but now I'm not so sure. I'll think of something."

"Knowing you, I'm sure you will," Paul Carmody said. "You've got the reputation for it. But Alex," he warned, "don't do anything to blow this thing out into the open.

Everything we've been talking about is still supposition. We haven't a single shred of positive evidence."

"Aren't you at least going to alert any of your boys down there to the possibility?"

"No. Until we've got some facts, I'm going to let sleeping dogs lie." Alex was aghast. "There's no use in shaking things up now. Too many leaks, too many hot-head politicians who'd relish getting their hands on a juicy bit like this regardless of the consequences to the country. Right now the Israelis are bugging the President with reports of an imminent Arab invasion in an attempt to squeeze more hardware out of us. Can you imagine what they'd do if they found out we'd made it possible for someone to sabotage half their air force? Hell, it could be even worse. We're supplying them with guidance circuits for home manufacture. If that crazy chip is still being . . ." He paused. "Alex, they would be completely vulnerable. We'd have to replace every damn plane they've got, not to mention the tanks and missiles."

Alex stared at him in surprise. "I'd no idea you guys had been so thorough with the chip."

"You weren't supposed to. Remember Warren's plan. Alecto, Megaera, Tisiphone, three Furies with three separate spheres of responsibility. The less each knew of the other, the safer it would be. Poor old Acheron, he thought of everything."

"Everything but this," Alex retorted dryly.

"Everything but this," General Carmody repeated. "His boatman may be crossing the wrong river." He stubbed out his half-smoked cigar on the pavement. "I'd better get back to Washington. Can't say I've enjoyed seeing you, Alex."

Alex stood watching Paul Carmody walk up the path through Strawberry Fields to Central Park West. Even though the man was dressed in slacks and a casual sports jacket, there was no mistaking the military bearing beneath them. He would make a terrible spy, Alex thought.

Peter Granger thought the same thing as he slipped the miniature camera back into his briefcase. He was faced with a decision. Should he follow General Carmody or report at once to Vladimir Savich. The resident would be very interested in the conversation he had taped yesterday and these photographs. He elected to see Savich.

Alex also realized that he had many wheels to put into motion. Glancing at his watch, he knew he would be able to reach Sandy at her flat in Codogan Square before she got involved in evening activities. Fortunately, Page had continued her assignment in Europe to tie up the negotiations on the cultural channel that he had begun. Alex crossed Central Park West to the Dakota, unaware of the eyes watching him from the car parked across from its main entrance on Seventy-second Street.

"But darling, it's over," Sandra Bannister protested softly. "Why go on pursuing it? Who cares now who was behind the takeover?"

"That's not the newswoman Alexander Kidd trained," he chided, ignoring the sympathy in her voice. "Whatever happened to that inquisitive nose of yours?" His tone became serious. "Sandy, I can't tell you why, but this is very important, more important than you can ever realize. I'm calling in all the chips today. The lawyers couldn't unravel the corporate web behind Milo, so now it's time to set all the news hounds on it full time. I've got to know, and I've got to know fast. Fred and Bart from the New York staff have suddenly developed summer flu and are working flat out on it. So is Frank from the Los Angeles office. By the time I finish, the new management of KWEN is going to think a plague swept through the place."

"When do I come home and start sneezing?" she asked. Sandra tried to keep it light, but all her instincts told her something very important was up. "Has this anything to do with the failure of our satellite?" she asked. His hesitation answered her question. "What do you suspect?"

"I suspect nothing, because I know nothing," he said defensively. "Don't press me. Somehow I think it may be too dangerous to know too much."

"Dangerous?" The word surprised her. "By dangerous

do you mean politically or career-wise dangerous?" She paused, waiting for his confirmation of one of the first two choices. When he didn't speak, she continued, "Or bang-bang dangerous?"

"I'm afraid it might be closer to bang bang."

She swallowed, her throat tight. "I see. When do you want me in New York?"

"Not New York. I want you over there. I want to know all you can dig up on a little bank in Zurich called the Credit Bank Schiller."

"The one that holds KWEN stock?"

"The same. I want to know who their customers are, who sits on their board, what connections they have in the States. I want to know everything. Lean on our economic advisers in the City and around Europe. Enrico Montagna in Milan should be a help, and he owes me."

"What am I looking for? Can you give me any clues?"

"Shit, I don't know. Just dig. And Sandy, take off the gloves, but be careful at the same time. Okay?"

"Are you coming over here anytime soon?"

"Did you hear me? I said be careful." Alex waited for her answer.

"I heard you," she replied. "Did you hear *me*? I miss you, Alex. I miss you so very much."

His voice softened. "I'll try to get over as soon as I can. I miss you too."

"Sound like you mean it, you bastard."

"Bitch," he laughed.

"Bastard," Sandra retorted, "magnificent bastard. Okay, chief, I'll ruin my manicure for you digging in the Swiss Alps, but remember, when I get back you owe me one whole day at Elizabeth Arden."

"You've got it." He hesitated. "Look, Sandy, don't call at the apartment anymore. I'm using a neighbor's phone while they're off for the summer."

"Do I ask why?"

"I think you've probably guessed by now. I'm not taking

chances." They spent the next minutes arranging how and when they would next contact each other.

"Have you seen Page?" she asked when they had finished. "Is he coping?"

"Strange you should ask," Alex replied sarcastically, "I've been trying to reach him all day."

"Tell Mr. Kidd I'm out," Page Shepard said miserably.

"But he's been calling you all afternoon, Mr. Shepard. He said it's very—"

"I don't care what he said, Miss Pruit, I'm out of the office and that's that."

"He doesn't believe me," she protested. "I can tell by his voice. He insists on coming here to see you."

Page glanced at his watch and stood up. "Very well, if it makes you feel any better, I'm *really* out." Snatching up his briefcase, Page stormed across the office. His hand on the door knob, he turned back to glare at the confused woman. "I'm taking a very early and very long weekend, Miss Pruit." The door slammed behind him.

Guilt. He had never felt so guilty in all his life. Page could not face his best friend, the man with whom he'd worked since college days, the man he trusted more than his own brother. What could he say to Alexander Kidd? Only lies. He could not bear to do that again, not to Alex. In his mind he saw the compromising photograph that had lain beneath the desk blotter and heard the menacing voice on the phone that directed his activities more and more each day. Charon II had been deliberately moved, but why? Tom Petterson, the only one who knew what had really happened that night, where was he? Page was frightened. In his heart he was sure Tom was dead. Someone had actually come into the KWEN building and abducted and murdered one of its loyal employees. It could happen to him. Who was doing all this? And for what reason?

Waving aside the company limousine, he hailed a cab and jumped into the back seat. "La Guardia," he called to the driver through the plastic partition. He studied his watch.

With luck he could just make the afternoon flight to Groton, Connecticut. From there it would just be seven minutes by charter plane over to Fishers Island, a small, verdant strip of land off the eastern coast of Connecticut. Mary and the boys would be there. Page pictured them on Chocomount Beach, Mary and Quin lying on their towels, deep in their books, and the ever-active John would be swimming. Then he pictured the disillusionment and revulsion on their faces and those of their friends should they ever see that photo. They must never see it, never.

The departure of the small Pilgrim plane to Groton was delayed, giving Page more than enough time to phone ahead to tell Mary of his surprise arrival. "Darling, marvelous. We missed you." He listened as she excitedly relayed the calendar of social events that lay before him in the next few days: cocktail parties, dinners, and a formal dance at the club. That life was so alien to the fears and pressures of the last weeks that hearing about the once-detested activities now made him feel safe. He was fleeing back into the warm and secure cocoon of the island that would insulate him from the photograph and that foreign voice. Those things just did not happen in places like Fishers Island.

And then he thought of Helmut. His young lover had been as horrified as he by the photograph and its implications. He had blamed himself for placing Page in this position and, tears streaming from his eyes, had proposed to leave the country and never see Page again. The young German's selflessness endeared him all the more to the older man.

They had planned to meet briefly in the coming weeks, not having seen each other for five days. It would be necessary to tell Helmut of his change in plans. Page took another coin from his pocket and was about to insert it in the pay phone when he hesitated. That quarter represented a tie to Helmut and the world he sought to escape. Sanity and peace of mind lay less then two hours away. Page stared at the thin coin in his fingers for more than a minute before inserting it in the slot.

* * *

Thousand upon thousand fairy lights twinkled through the branches of the trees in the large garden of the Androssy home at Sutton Place. The lawn spreading down to the iron railing overlooking the East River had been carefully manicured to the consistency of soft green velvet. In its center, an elegant pink and white candy-striped canopy rose into the star-filled night. The polished dance floor beneath glistened in the light of crystal chandeliers suspended above as couples dressed in long gowns and white dinner jackets swirled to the music of a ten-piece orchestra. Around the edges of the garden, pink cloths on circular tables fluttered gently in the evening breeze, and candles enclosed in hurricane lamps softly illuminated the fresh faces of young men and women and reflected in the delicate champagne glasses they held.

"Oh, Papa," Katherina Androssy exclaimed, squeezing her father's arm before returning to the receiving line in the marble hall, "it's so beautiful, so wonderful I can't stand it."

"Nothing is too beautiful, Katty, when a beautiful princess comes of age. Am I not right, my dear?" he asked, winking at Edith Androssy.

Before she could answer, Edith was distracted by another surge of chattering birthday guests entering the hall along the red carpet that stretched from the curb outside to the receiving line. Behind them several older couples from the United Nations arrived. In all, nearly eight hundred were expected that evening. Beckoning to his oldest son, Stephen, the baron removed his white gloves and took a glass of imported champagne from the silver tray held by a nearby waiter.

"Stephen, do the honors for your old father for a few minutes, will you? It is nearly eleven-thirty and I want to circulate and check things in the garden." He paused and then spoke softly into his son's ear. "The couple—she is wearing green and white—are Lord and Lady Wittleton.

Very big in the City. Could be of help to our London office."

"Do you ever relax?" his son asked, smiling.

"Yes, when I sleep. Take good care of your mother and Katty now." The proud father patted his son's shoulder and left the hall.

Instead of going to the garden, Androssy quickly descended the stairs to the lower hall of the mansion and, substituting his black dinner jacket for the white coat of one of the caterers, entered the kitchen and moved unnoticed through the chaos of shouting waiters and chefs carrying platters of elaborately garnished food. He exited the house through the service door. A dark caterer's van stood waiting around the corner. He climbed in beside the driver. "Little Italy, Victor."

They had been parked on one of the bustling side streets in the district no more than a few minutes when Vladimir Savich approached the van. Victor Kamera opened the door to the resident and left to take a table in the window of a small coffee-and-sweet shop across the street.

"Moscow is well pleased."

"So my sources have indicated," Androssy replied.

"Ah, yes, *your* sources," the resident repeated with obvious distaste. "What your sources may not have told you is that Kidd and General Carmody suspect."

"Oh? And what exactly do they suspect?" the baron asked. He too took no pains to hide the contempt in his voice for the other.

Almost with pleasure, Savich opened the black leather briefcase on his lap and handed several photographs of General Carmody and Alexander Kidd to Androssy. "Here is a transcript of their phone conversation yesterday morning. I am sure you will find it interesting."

"Where and when did they meet?" Androssy asked, skimming the paper.

"Central Park. This morning," the resident replied.

"Do the KGB operatives normally carry sensitive material of this sort in their briefcases?" Androssy asked, stalling for time to digest the import of this new piece of information.

"Only when it can be destroyed quickly." Savich reopened the case to indicate an electric razor and cord lying among the other papers. "One touch here," he said, pointing to a spot close to the handle of the case, "will ignite the magnesium flare within the razor to incinerate instantaneously and completely the contents."

"An interesting toy," Androssy commented. He made a mental note to acquire one.

"Well?" the resident asked, nodding at the photograph in Androssy's hand.

"Interesting," the other replied calmly.

"Interesting? Is that all you can say? They are on the verge of discovering that we brought down their planes yesterday, that we can manipulate their weapons in the Middle East."

"No, they are not," Androssy lied. He was annoyed that Vladimir Savich knew so much about the Acheron Plot. Just as he had feared, Butov had talked far too much over his dinner wine. "They can have no facts, only suppositions. Those seven planes are at the bottom of the Mediterranean. The satellite is back in operation and there is no one who will contradict our story to the FCC. Officially, the KWEN control room lost control of the satellite, it left orbit, and it was returned to orbit. The company did not wish the real reason for the transmission interruption published for fear that it might damage confidence in the new management of the network. Mr. Shepard will make that announcement should I require it. Does that ease your fears, Vladimir Savich?"

The resident remained silent for a minute. "And Felton? General Carmody tried to phone him today from Washington."

"Tried," the baron asked lightly, "or succeeded?" Androssy attempted to hide his concern on this point. He knew that Simon Felton was the weak link in his plan. Although the odds were against it, given the incentive,

Felton was the only man who might discover that the discontinued 120044C Cerberus circuit was in fact the widely used 120044 circuit. General Carmody could give him that incentive. He would have to be eliminated. A pity, as his electronic ingenuity had inadvertently been of great help to the Soviets. Rather than further involve this ferret of the KGB, the baron's personal staff would have to attend to the matter themselves.

"The two did not talk. Felton is backpacking in the mountains."

"How did you learn that?"

"From the same man who took these photographs," Savich replied. "The illegal on the general's staff."

"Good. Although there is nothing Felton can do to expose us," Androssy lied again, "make sure your man stays close to the general. I want to know exactly what Felton tells him if they do make contact. And I want to know every move Carmody makes from now on. Is that clear?"

Again the imperious tone in which the orders were delivered made Savich cringe. He nodded.

"And alert your illegal that we might have to terminate General Carmody should he decide to act upon supposition rather than fact."

"What of Kidd? He too is dangerous."

"Of the three, he is the most helpless," Androssy stated. "A quick mind, resourceful, and highly charismatic, but right now, emasculated. No one would possibly believe him should he shout Acheron Plot from the rooftops. His reputation for braggadocio and sensationalism speaks against him. Who would believe his—as the Americans say—sour grapes story. You will recall, Vladimir Savich, that he threatened to blow up the network long before those Navy planes fell mysteriously into the sea."

"But he knows the code."

"I very much doubt that. It is too complicated to be remembered, and from the dramatic hiding place in which I found it, I am sure there are no other copies. Kidd's frantic attempts to get back into his office confirm my belief."

"I repeat, he is dangerous to us. And our friends in Moscow agree."

"Agree with whom, Vladimir Savich? May I remind you that I am in sole charge of this operation, not you."

"And may I remind you that as resident here, I will do what I think necessary to protect the interests of my country and its agents," Savich flashed back.

"I, not Kidd, have the code, you fool. His elimination at this time would certainly attract undesirable attention and lend credence to his suspicions in the eyes of General Carmody. It would send the general scurrying to others in the government. Is that what you believe to be in the best interests of your country, Vladimir Savich?" Androssy shook his head in disgust.

Then Savich pulled his trump card, the one he had been waiting to play all evening. He spoke quietly. "I have been requested by the chairman of the Komitet Gosudarstvennoy Bezopasnosti to get the code from you and send it to him at once by diplomatic pouch. He does not trust your usual channels of communication through Switzerland in this matter."

The request hit Miklos Androssy like a crowbar. He had expected it to be made sooner or later, but that it should be Savich who delivered it surprised him. The time for the confrontation had come sooner than expected. He must stall a little longer until his plans were completely finalized. It was time for the greatest gamble in Androssy's career.

"Comrade Androssy?" Savich pressed. "The code."

"No."

CHAPTER 15

Beneath the fairy lights, the elegant young couples circled each other, gliding around the dance floor in an old-fashioned waltz, the prelude to the birthday music that was soon to be played on the last stroke of midnight. As she turned round and round in the arms of her escort, Katherina Androssy looked anxiously about her at the faces of the guests standing in groups at the edges of the canopy, trying to see the face of her father. Where was he?

"I can't find Father anywhere," Stephen whispered to his distraught mother. "Tibor and Andras are still looking. He's probably locked up in some business talk with one of the guests and lost track of time."

"It's not like him, Stephen," Edith Androssy replied, shaking her head in dismay, "and certainly not on Katty's birthday."

"He'll be here, Mother, don't worry."

Looking at the tiny diamond watch on her left wrist, Edith shook it to assure herself of the correct time. "Tell the orchestra leader not to play happy birthday until we tell him, Stephen. Oh, and alert the kitchen not to bring up the cake." Edith Androssy gazed up at the many lighted windows in the mansion. "Where can your father be, Stephen? Where?"

"I repeat," Miklos Androssy said coolly, "your request is quite out of the question."

"And I repeat, comrade, the chairman wishes *me* to send it at once—for security purposes." Savich was aware

157

of and savored the discomfort of the other. "Perhaps the strength of your special relationship with the chairman and the immunity you seem to enjoy are not as strong as you had supposed."

"My relationship, as you put it, with the chairman is as strong as it ever was." Androssy looked out of the van window at the people passing on the narrow, crowded sidewalk and across the street to the window of the coffee shop where Victor Kamera sat watching. He turned back to the resident. "I trust no one but myself in this. The chairman will understand."

"I have been ordered to obtain it from you." Vladimir Savich's voice was firm and level.

"You have no authority in this matter," the baron countered. "I alone will make all decisions concerning the Acheron Plot."

"My orders are to—"

"I do not take orders from you, Vladimir Savich," Androssy interrupted. "Remember that." He sensed the other falter.

"You would disobey an order directly from the chairman?"

"The order did not come to me directly from the chairman. I will discuss it only with him."

"You equivocate," Savich snapped angrily.

"And you forget your place," the baron returned. "You know nothing of the true importance of that code or the purpose to which it will soon be put. I alone know the code, and for the sake of security, I plan to keep it that way. You may inform the chairman of my decision and that I stand ready to put the operation to which we both agreed into effect upon receiving his message through my regular Swiss channel, a channel which has never yet failed us."

The resident fought to control his rage. "You overestimate your importance to the organization, comrade." Savich purposely emphasized the last word. "And you overestimate your exemption from our control."

"You *under*estimate it, Vladimir Savich."

Savich stared at him in silence for several minutes and then spoke aloud what he had begun to suspect over the last few weeks. These suspicions had prompted him to persuade the chairman to request the Acheron code from Androssy. "Because you hold that code, do not make the mistake of considering yourself what one might term a 'free agent.' No man is a free agent, comrade. No man with a family."

Androssy stared hard and deep into the eyes of the resident. He saw not Savich, but his daughter in the twinkling lights of the garden. When he spoke, his voice was like ice-blue steel, his words pronounced precisely and slowly. "If you and your butchers so much as touch any member of the Androssy family, the Acheron Plot is dead. There will be no bargaining. It is automatic."

"Are you threatening the Komitet Gosudarstvennoy Bezopasnosti?"

"Regard it as a statement, Vladimir Savich, a simple statement of fact." Turning from him, he nodded to Victor Kamera across the street. The hulking chauffeur rose obediently and placed money on the table. Androssy returned his attention to the resident. "And now if you have no further news of General Carmody and Felton to give me, I have obligations at home."

Dismissed, Vladimir Savich angrily opened the van door and stepped out while saying, "I shall report our conversation."

"I would appreciate your doing so," Androssy replied imperiously.

Turning, the resident leaned down and spoke his warning softly through the open window. "Remember, comrade, in this little game you are playing, there is, to quote our American friends, many a slip between the cup and the lip."

"Keep me informed of the general's moves," Baron Androssy replied with finality, making no acknowledgment of the other's words. He nodded to Victor as the resident moved aside to allow the chauffeur to enter the driver's side. The motor growled into action and the van moved slowly into the flow of traffic crowding the street.

Turning on his heels, Vladimir Savich stormed down the sidewalk, colliding with a careless pedestrian. He directed his anger not only at Androssy but also at his own superiors in Moscow. Had they not made an exception in the Acheron matter by giving the Hungarian agent a free hand, this current problem would never have arisen. What relationship, what knowledge could Androssy possibly have of the Kremlin leaders to have justified the strong hand the KGB had dealt him, a hand now highlighted by his exclusive knowledge of the Acheron code. He must find a way to weaken that hand, remove that exclusive card. Unlocking the door of his car, Savich slipped behind the wheel and stared straight ahead in deep thought. He would mount an undercover operation parallel to that of Androssy's. While appearing to cooperate with the agent, he would move into a position of readiness. If worse came to worst, he and his own agents would jump in to capture all three of the Furies and physically wring from them the information he needed. Certainly there must be a way to break Androssy's exclusivity on that code. He would have his revenge, revenge for the humiliation to which he had been subjected by the autocratic baron, and revenge for the murder of his agent, Anatoli Butov, which he laid solely on Androssy's doorstep.

Their voices raised in another chorus of "Happy Birthday," the guests applauded as Katherina Androssy began the delayed ritual of cutting her cake. Stationed beside his daughter, Miklos Androssy beamed with pride as he watched the antique silver knife cut deep into the pink sugar roses clustered in creamy white frosting. He looked up at the radiant faces of his wife, Edith, Stephen, the eldest, Bela, Tibor, and Andras as they sang to their younger sister. Standing tall and proud, the guests saw Baron Androssy only as a handsome, polished aristocrat. None saw behind the human shell to the cunning and ruthless animal lurking within that was trained to kill without emotion, an animal inbred with the instinct to protect his cubs at all cost.

Well, my darlings, he thought to himself, it is out in the

open, your father's bid for great power, a greater power than one man has ever held in his hands before. The schism with Moscow had come. But as long as he alone held the key to the Acheron Plot and its ability to tilt the balance of world power to the East or the West, he stood invincible.

As the birthday orchestra played on for the pleasure of the early morning revelers, across the city Alexander Kidd paced restlessly back and forth in his study at the Dakota. Stopping, he picked up the phone for the hundredth time and punched the buttons. Again the metallic voice on Simon Felton's private line announced that he was not in and would the caller like to leave his name, number, and message upon the beep? "I must have monopolized his entire tape by now," Alex grumbled, slamming down the receiver only to snatch it up and punch a new number. "Where in the hell are they all?" he muttered impatiently. The phone in Page Shepard's New York apartment rang endlessly without answer. Alex took another gulp of Scotch.

He had to find out if the Charon II codes were still in their hiding place in the sundial at the KWEN offices. He needed that evidence to convince himself and Paul Carmody that someone really had breached the security of President Warren's plan. Alex wondered if Mary Shepard knew where to reach Page. It was nearly two in the morning, but what the hell, Mary was used to calls at all times of the day and night, and she was a fan of his.

Mary wiped the sleep from her eyes as she lifted the receiver. "It's Alex, dear," she said across the darkness separating their twin beds. "Says it's urgent. Is something wrong?"

Page pushed himself up into a sitting position. "No, not that I know of," he replied reassuringly, but he was filled with dread. Everything he had tried to escape in New York was now back in the bedroom at Fishers Island. "I'll take it in the living room. You go back to sleep." Rising, he slipped into his silk robe and left the room. Mary could hear the distant mumble of his voice on the phone before she drifted off.

Replacing the receiver, Page lit a cigarette and stood deep in thought at the French doors, looking down across the lawn to the moonlight playing on the water. What was Alex up to? First were all the questions about Charon II two days ago and now a simple request for authorization to visit his office to pick up a few personal things. No request made at two in the morning was simple. Questions tumbled about in his mind for nearly an hour when the phone rang once again. Quickly crossing the room, Page reached for it before it woke Mary. "Now what do you want, Alex?" he demanded. It was not Alexander Kidd.

"Mr. Shepard," the now familiar foreign voice said softly, "it would be very much against your interests to allow Mr. Kidd entrance to the KWEN building now or at any other time."

"Who is this?" Page demanded. "How did you know I was here?"

"We know a great many things, but that is beside the point. You are not to allow Mr. Kidd to enter the building."

"It's too late. I've already said yes."

"Then merely change your mind, Mr. Shepard. It is really quite simple. People do it all the time."

"Fuck you," Page shouted in frustrated rebellion against the anonymous voice. "Alexander Kidd is a friend of mine, and if he wants to get into his office, he gets into it."

"Your expletive is a very appropriate one, Mr. Shepard. It brings to mind several photographs in my possession. Perhaps you would enjoy showing them to your two sons. I am sure they would be understanding."

Page closed his eyes and slumped against the wall.

"Mr. Shepard?" the voice inquired softly. "Are you still there, Mr. Shepard? Ah, yes, I can hear you breathing. From your silence I assume that you are in complete agreement with my request?"

"Yes," Page answered dully.

"Good. I hope you enjoyed your evening at the club dance."

"How in the hell did you—"

"Please give my warmest regards to your charming wife," the voice interrupted. Page heard the click on the other end of the line cutting off further conversation. He stood hollow and alone in the darkened room, the only sound that of waves breaking on the sandy beach beyond the garden.

Six days later, on September 7, Dr. Simon Felton emerged from the Colorado forest, slipped off his knapsack, and dropped it on the porch of his primitive log cabin. Several weeks' growth of beard further darkened his tanned face. Stretching his hard, lean body, the electronics genius looked once more at the gold-and-red streaked sunset. Bed would feel good. Hauling his knapsack into the cabin, Simon lit an oil lamp, carefully trimming the wick for a constant flame.

A small mouse scurried across the floor and disappeared under the woodpile beside the large stone fireplace. "Hey there, little fellow," Felton called gently, "don't get upset. I won't get in your way. Come on out, it's dinner time." Smiling, he sank into the padded rocking chair by the hearth and surveyed his humble surroundings, built completely by his own muscle and the sweat of his brow. No one, just a few rangers, knew of his retreat, the place where he meditated, where his mind could concentrate on physics and electronics unencumbered by petty interruptions and the details of business. The only contemporary pieces in the room were his slanted drafting table by the south window and his specially designed portable radiophone in the canvas carrier in the corner. It connected to a radio tower at the northeast side of the cabin that extended just above the treetops. He stared at the canvas bag and, running a hand through his thinning dark hair, reluctantly reached for his steel-rimmed spectacles. "Well, little friend," he said sadly to the wee occupant of the woodpile, "I might as well find out what's been happening in the world since I've been gone." Simon started to rise but changed his mind, settling back. "No, I think we can stand one more evening free from the cares of the world. Tomorrow is soon enough." Turning his gaze from the radiophone, he reached for the half-read report on quark research.

One hundred and fifteen miles across the Colorado mountains, Robert Frankel sat slumped in a black Honda looking up at the darkened windows of Simon Felton's apartment outside Boulder.

CHAPTER 16

"Tisiphone, urgent you contact Megaera." Mixed in with the other messages, those words had been recorded by his answering machine every day for the last seven days. Like Paul Carmody, Simon Felton first heard the code names with a combination of surprise, remembrance—and then dread. Oh, shit, he thought as he looked through the cabin window at the sun rising over the mountains. Resigned to the obligation implicit in the coded message, Felton poured another cup of coffee and reluctantly put through the call on the scrambling device he and the general had developed years ago.

"What's this all about, Paul," he asked after the two men had confirmed each other's identity. "We haven't gone through this ritual in years."

"The Cerberus circuit. Any chance it could have got in some Navy F-14A Tomcats by mistake?" the general asked.

"Our planes?"

"Ours."

"The chip went into only those planes you specified," the scientist replied positively. "As to the location of the planes, only you knew that." He paused, his rational mind leaping ahead. "I take it that one of our F-14As has crashed, and you fear it might have been caused by the Cerberus?"

"Correct. Only six, not one, went down in the Mediterranean on August thirty-first."

"Six?" Simon repeated in surprise. "Bad news. Did they contain the circuit?"

"Not unless there was a screw-up."

"Well, I haven't shipped any since Warren lost the election. Besides, the Cerberus is harmless until activated by the code in the Charon Two transponder, and only Alex has the code to turn on that transponder. Have you talked to him?"

"It was he who first contacted me. The satellite was missing over the sea during the time of the crash; he no longer has control over it, you know."

Felton nodded. "Yeah, that's right, I read about it." And then he smiled. "Still, Alex is the only man with the code. I destroyed my copy as soon as the satellite was programmed and launched. Wiped my slate clean, so to speak."

"We're not so sure Alex is the only one," Carmody replied calmly. He briefly outlined his and Alex's suspicions, putting aside one after another of Simon Felton's overly rational objections. "Simon, all I'm asking is that you check. If you find nothing, then we can all relax. How many circuits are left?"

"Oh, about a hundred circuits and a couple thousand of the chips. They're locked in my vault."

"You sure none are missing?"

"Christ, Paul, I don't count them every day. Of course they're all there," the scientist replied testily. He felt most uncomfortable in the world of espionage into which he had been pressed. He wished it would all go away and leave him alone. "I'm the only one with the combination to that vault; I keep all my prototypes, notes, and experiments in there."

"Simon, we thought Alex was the only one with the code. Now we're not so sure," the general replied, his tone one of mild rebuke. "If by any chance someone got those circuits out and is using them, you, Alex, and I have a hell of a lot to answer for."

Felton scratched his head. "I wish I'd never gotten into this," he said.

Carmody spoke gravely. "At the time you did it to save lives, remember?"

"That's what Warren told us," Simon answered miserably. "It seemed right then. But this cloak-and-dagger stuff just isn't my line."

"Let me put it this way," the general countered, "you are still in it to save lives. Simon, along with those six jet fighters, a hundred and twenty-three innocent passengers on a charter plane went down." He paused. "Men, women, children, Simon. All dead."

"Oh, shit," Dr. Simon Felton swore, his stomach churning. He was being hooked once again.

Felton sat for a long time after the conversation staring at the woodpile and the little dark space into which the wee mouse had run the previous evening. "What a crock," he said aloud. Acheron, Megaera, Alecto, Tisiphone, they were all in the past. It was all over. This is now. Good old Alex, he was probably just being melodramatic. And Paul Carmody was in his element. Okay, so he'd check the circuits and chips to please the Pentagon, but that was it. He looked at his watch. It was time for him to end his backpacking holiday and return to the laboratory and the new computer circuitry he had been working on. It would take about forty-five minutes by jeep to the Gunnison County Airport where he kept his small private plane. After a beautiful flight through the mountains, he'd land in Denver around noon. Suddenly eager to roll up his sleeves and get back to work, Simon elected not to go first to his condominium in Boulder to change clothes, but to go directly to Felton Electronics, situated only a few miles north of the Denver airport. What did it matter how he dressed, he thought. They were used to the eccentric scientist by now. And besides, he owned the second largest chunk of stock in his company. He paused, wondering briefly who exactly owned the largest piece. He could not actually recall ever having met the heads of the conglomerate that had bought him out. The lawyers had handled the entire transaction. It had been most favorable to him, at least that's what everyone had told him.

Shortly after twelve, Dr. Simon Felton presented his identity card at the entrance to Felton Electronics and drove through the gate into the parking lot beside the building that bore his name. Having to identify himself every day to his own company had initially irritated Simon, but after all these years it now seemed just as normal as brushing his teeth.

The building itself was contemporary in design, a deceptively small looking two-story structure in the form of the letter E constructed of stone and glass. The stone surface of the long front facade was broken by vertical ribbons of narrow windows extending up the entire two stories. This section contained the executive offices and development laboratories, some of which extended beneath the earth's surface for several levels. Three wings extended back from the front of the building to complete the E design. Constructed almost entirely of thick, burglar- and shatter-proof glass, they contained the assembly lines producing the wide variety of Felton electronic circuits and systems found in much of the country's weaponry, computers, and communications systems. A high electrified chain-link fence circled the entire complex, which was only thinly disguised by ornamental shrubs and trees.

Striding across the lobby, Simon waved offhandedly to the attractive blond receptionist who returned the gesture with a smile of amusement. She found it hard to believe that this man, dressed in faded jeans, scuffed hiking boots, a yellow T-shirt emblazoned with Smokey The Bear, and the floppy remains of a once-proud ten-gallon hat, was Dr. Simon Felton, the guiding genius and founder of the large, respected, and important electronics company for which she worked. His tattered briefcase in hand, Simon sprinted up the stairs two at a time, snatched the handful of phone messages his secretary held out to him, and entered his corner office. "I'll deal with the mail tomorrow," he called over his shoulder as he closed the door.

Simon flung his briefcase across the room onto the sofa and quickly sorted through his messages. Nothing that could not be put off, he thought, eager to get to work. He headed for the spiral iron staircase that led from the office down into his private laboratory on the ground floor. The door to his lab from the lower hall was always kept locked as a security precaution. As he descended, Felton looked about him at the long workbenches below and the electronic equipment and computers that lined its walls. He felt welcome in this environment. But instead of stopping, he continued on down the staircase to a reinforced-cement basement room below the laboratory where his personal, walk-in vault had been constructed, invulnerable to all but the inventor.

Dialing the combination with his right hand while pressing his left to a plate of glass through which his palm print was being electronically verified, he waited for the hollow robot voice to say, "Good afternoon, Dr. Felton."

"Good afternoon," Simon replied. Verification of his voiceprint would be the final obstacle to pass before the vault door automatically swung out. The human touch had been added by the scientist as a whim, and he smiled as he waited, not knowing that for years a plastic print of his hand and a tape of his voice had been used in the same sequence to gain admittance by operatives of the KGB. The thick steel door slowly swung open to him. Reluctantly tearing his eyes from a current project on the shelf to his right, Simon walked on past to the filing cabinets lining the rear wall of the vault.

Pulling open the third drawer from the left in the bottom row, Simon knelt down to examine its contents packaged neatly in small hermatically sealed plastic envelopes. Laboriously, he counted out 126 complete 120044C circuits; that matched exactly the number shown on the inventory list that he personally initialed with each withdrawal of one or more of the circuits. Putting them aside, he began on the envelopes containing the tiny chip which responded only to the highly complicated code built into Charon II's fourth transponder. That transponder, in turn, was activated only by the code given to Alexander Kidd over seven years ago. The two codes were then combined and radioed down to the Cerberus circuits. Thus, in effect it took two codes—one from Earth and one from space—to set off the destructive force of the chip and the circuit in which it rested. Its complexity had brought its inventor great pride, but he had not stopped there. As an added precaution, he had given Alexander Kidd the power to destroy the Charon II satellite itself merely be reversing the numbers in his code. No one aside from the two of them, not even the late President, knew of this twist. It was born out of their mutual concern that other, less trusted men than Carmody in the Pentagon might fall heir to Warren's plan.

It took him more than an hour to count the chips. They totaled 3,249, only two less than listed on the initialed inventory. He put it down to error in his counting; the envelopes had probably stuck together. Besides, the difference was not statistically significant and did not warrant a time-consuming recount. Closing the drawer, Felton stood up and took off his glasses. So much for the wild fantasies of Paul Carmody and the theatrical Alexander Kidd. It was an immense relief. He was about to leave when curiosity made him reopen the drawer and remove one of the 120044C circuits. He made the proper notation on the inventory list. Would time, he wondered, have had any effect on the complex action of the chip? Slipping it into his pocket, Simon left the vault after collecting his notes and the prototype of a new invention. The heavy steel door slowly swung shut at his touch.

Placing the prototype and notes on one of the work-benches in the lab, Simon continued up the circular stairs to his office and put through a scrambled call to General Carmody.

"Megaera? Tisiphone here."

The other identified himself.

"Well, you've got nothing to worry about, Paul. The Cerberus circuits and chips are all accounted for," he said cheerfully.

"You're absolutely sure?"

"Absolutely. Counted them myself."

"And they're no longer being manufactured out there? You've checked?"

"Paul, I personally saw to the destruction of the molds, locked the only blueprint in my vault—it's still there—and removed the 120044C designation from the books. Trust me. As far as the world's concerned, that complex little devil does not exist and never existed." Felton leaned back in his desk chair. "Satisfied?"

"Thanks, Simon. Yes I am," he replied. Simon noted the relief in his voice.

"Good. Then tell Alex to calm down," Simon cautioned. "He's been watching too many of his own made-for-TV movies for his own good. Next time you're out this way, come up to the cabin with me and go hiking."

"That will be the day," Carmody laughed, looking down at his ample girth. "I'll settle for a couple of drinks."

"You're on. Until then." Dr. Felton replaced the phone and closed and locked the desk drawer containing it. He wondered why he had kept it all these years. Well, Charon II was bound to fall out of orbit within the next few years. He'd get rid of the phone then.

"I don't care what Felton says," Alexander Kidd raged that evening when he talked with General Carmody, "the chips brought down those Navy planes."

"Be reasonable, Alex. You have absolutely no proof, nor do I. And I, for one, am glad you're wrong."

The brief but infuriating conversation left Alexander Kidd all the more determined to get into his office to find the boatman and discover once and for all whether the Charon II code still lay in its place. For some reason, Page Shepard had reversed himself and refused to help him—or even to speak to him. Alex poured another Scotch and sat back on his study couch staring at a large framed photograph of the KWEN office building that hung on the opposite wall. There had to be a way. His eyes moved up the building, studying the windows of the KWEN floors and of the leased floor above. Kidd suddenly leaned forward. As a plan began to form in his mind, a smile spread across his face.

* * *

Back in his laboratory, Simon Felton straightened up on the workbench and stretched. Absorbed in his drawings, he had lost all track of time and was surprised to find it just after eleven. Coffee time, he thought, and then back to the drawing board. Mounting the stairs to his dark office above, Simon let himself out and locked the thick, opaque glass door behind him.

"Working late, Dr. Felton?" the old guard asked as Simon passed in the hall on the way to the canteen.

"Just catching up, Jerry."

"Tom," the guard corrected. "Tom Crandel."

"Oh, yes, sorry," Simon apologized. "The typical absentminded professor, eh?" He pushed through the doors into the dark canteen. Reaching into his pocket for change for the coffee machine, he felt the forgotten 120044C circuit and remembered the reason for its being there. Simon inserted his coins and collected a cup of steaming black coffee.

Instead of heading back down the hall to his office after leaving the canteen, the scientist turned left and made his way toward one of the darkened assembly wings and, walking past long rows of silent machines illuminated only by pale blue night lights, he withdrew his master key to unlock the door of a storage room. Scanning the shelves, his eyes fell on the object of his search, a bin of 120044 circuits. Signing the inventory list beside it, Simon pocketed one of the plastic envelopes and walked back toward his lab, again passing the guard station. The face of the guard was not familiar to him, distinctly hostile, he thought as he glanced at the man's bull-like shoulders sloping down from a thick neck. "Where's Jerry?" he asked pleasantly.

"Jerry's on his break," the other replied gruffly. He watched the scientist walk past and then picked up the phone to report the actions of the man he had been ordered to abduct when he left the building.

Simon was nearly back to his office when it struck him that the old guard's name was not Jerry. It was Tom something-or-other and the new security guard most certainly should have known it. Most strange. It gave Simon a funny feeling, but he brushed it off, attributing his unease to all General Carmody's talk about spies and threats to national security. However, he did make sure to double-lock his office door before descending to his laboratory, and made a mental note to report the strange behavior of the security guard to his superiors in the morning.

Outside, parked in his black Honda on the other side of the chain-link fence, Robert Frankel watched Simon Felton through the windows of the corner lab with a pair a powerful binoculars. Felton had caught him off guard by going directly to the plant instead of first stopping at his apartment. During the days he had waited for the scientist, Frankel had had plenty of time to thoroughly search the apartment for any clue to the other's whereabouts. So too had the other two men who most certainly were KGB operatives. Frankel could smell them a mile away. His orders were to kill Dr. Frankel before he got to the plant and anyone else had a chance to get hold of him. It was a harder assignment than he had anticipated. His two KGB rivals obviously had access to Felton Electronics, and Frankel could not get through security. He would have to make his move when Felton left. What in the hell was the man doing now? Frankel wondered as he watched the scientist pull two things from his pocket that looked rather like small brown candy bars.

Carefully extracting the two identical-looking circuits from their plastic envelopes, Simon labeled each of them with chalk to avoid possible confusion. He wired both to a monitoring screen that would record the degree of resistance and almost infinitesimal heat each would create when he passed an alternating electrical current of sufficient strength through them. The 120044C circuit with the chip implanted in it would generate over twice the heat than the regular 120044 before being destroyed. This was how Simon had personally tested each of the Cerberus circuits before shipment. The monitor would show the great difference in resistance and heat between the two circuits if the chip were still operable.

Taking a sip of his now cold coffee, Felton slowly turned on the electric current and watched the two lines, one from each of the circuits, form on the screen of the monitor before him. They registered identical resistance and heat-generation levels. He increased the current to both. As expected, the 120044C line registered double the heat generation. Dr. Simon Felton did not know how long he sat staring at the monitor without taking a breath. "Oh, shit," he finally mumbled. The 120044 circuit registered the same.

Tearing the 120044 circuit loose from the wires, Simon frantically began prying away its thin top layer. As it broke away, his eyes saw what he feared. The tiny Cerberus chip glistened under the magnifying glass. How many, he wondered in panic, how many of these circuits contained that bastard chip? Was the one he held only a fluke, did it lie undetected in dozens, hundreds, hundreds of thousands? Had it been in those Navy Tomcats? "Oh, shit," he repeated softly as he realized that Paul Carmody and Alex had been right in their fears. Felton stood up abruptly. He did not hear the stool upon which he had sat clatter to the tile floor behind him. He had to check the 120044 blueprints; they would be in the main drafting room files in the west wing of the building.

Taking the spiral stairs two at a time, Simon Felton mounted to his office and started across the darkened room to the door whose opaque glass glowed from the hall lights on the other side. He froze as the shadow of a man cast itself against the glass. Simon recognized the bull neck and sloping shoulders of the new security guard and watched with almost hypnotic fascination as the shadowed hands moved to the lock on the door. The gentle scratching noise made by a key being inserted into the lock seemed shatteringly loud in the silence of the dark room. It galvanized the scientist into action.

Simon moved quietly back down the staircase to his

laboratory. Turning off the sole light over his workbench, he tiptoed to the door, an exact replica of the one above in his office, and stood listening. Unlocking it, he slid quickly into the hall and moved stealthily toward the entrance to the west wing, keeping alert for approaching footsteps. If a guard came, even one he knew, could he trust him? Was there anyone in the building at this time of night whom he could trust, turn to for help? These questions raced through Dr. Felton's mind as, unobserved, he reached the double doors to the west wing.

Opening one of them a crack, Simon peered through at the silent rows of machines in the ghostly blue light. He closed the door behind him and moved quickly down one of the shadowy assembly lines to the staircase at the far end which led up to the employee lounge and the main drafting room beyond on the second floor. He was at the doors to the lounge just as the entrance doors to the west wing were thrown open. The bright shaft of light from the hall silhouetted the dark forms of two security guards, one with the distinguishing bull shoulders. Simon could not catch their mumbled words as they moved down the line, but he knew their intent. To them he was an animal, an animal being hunted in its own lair.

Simon had so little time. Within minutes he was leaning over the detailed blueprints of the 120044 circuitry spread out on a table in the corner of the drafting room. The pinpoint of light from his pocket flashlight moved over the complicated drawing, following one line and then another until it stopped at a point where several dozen converged, coming together at the chip that should not have been there. He flashed the tiny light to the date on the lower right-hand corner of the plan. It was dated nearly seven years ago, not long after he had sold the controlling interest in Felton Electronics. "For seven goddamn years," he mumbled. He moved the light back to the drawings of his brainchild chip that he realized now rested at the core of the electronic systems in almost every weapon produced by the United States in the last seven years. The red phone in the bottom drawer of his desk flashed before his eyes.

Resisting the urge to tear the blueprint before him into shreds, Felton carefully placed it back in the files and moved silently through the maze of small dark laboratories and halls on the second floor of the west wing back toward his office, pausing at every turn, listening for following footsteps. He wondered what The Bull, as he had come to think of the alien security guard, had been after in his office and if he would be back there waiting for his return.

The hall leading to his office appeared deserted as Simon peered up and down it. Removing the keys from his pocket, Felton selected the right one and, taking a deep breath, sprinted for his door. The key was not necessary—the door stood ajar. So they've come out in the open, he thought as he moved through into the darkened room, closed and locked the door after him. Sliding behind his desk, Simon turned his pocket flashlight to the lock on the bottom left-hand drawer. Once again a key was not necessary; the drawer had been forced and, when he opened it, Simon saw that the phone had been torn from its wires. Well, he thought, now's the time to find out whether or not I'm a coward. He reached for his regular phone and quickly dialed, knowing that his call would flash his whereabouts to anyone watching the switchboard.

Although poor with names, Simon Felton's memory for numbers was astonishing. From the depths of his mind, he managed to pull out Carmody's unlisted home phone number. His eyes glued to the opaque glass panel in the door across the room, the scientist waited impatiently for the phone to ring, praying that his friend had not moved homes or changed numbers during the years, praying that he would be there. What a fool, he cursed himself. Why in the hell hadn't he taken Paul more seriously that afternoon? Why hadn't he . . .

"Hello?"

Felton heard the sleep-filled voice with relief. He also heard running footsteps coming down the hall outside.

"Tisiphone," he croaked into the receiver as he slid down behind his desk. "Tisiphone," he repeated, thinking as fast as he could. "Disregard previous conversation. Cerberus is out!"

"Who? What?" Carmody's voice sounded confused. It was nearly 2:30 in the morning in Washington.

Simon's office seemed to explode with shots as the lock and the glass door shattered simultaneously.

"You were right, goddamn it," Simon shouted into the phone and then, throwing it aside as the Bull burst through into the dark room, leaped for and down the spiral staircase toward his lab and the door in the lab that opened into the ground-floor hallway.

"What was it, dear?" Joan Carmody asked sleepily as she rolled over in bed and looked up at the dark form of her husband, who sat staring at the receiver he held in his hand. "Darling?" she asked again.

Paul Carmody stood without answering and, pulling on his robe, left the bedroom. Grimly, he descended the stairs in his Georgetown home and strode across the foyer to his study and the red phone in the drawer of his desk. Why had Simon not used the scrambler phone? Why the regular phone? What had he meant in that garbled conversation? Something about Cerberus, something about being right. Right about what? And the noise? Sounded like shots.

As the general worried over these questions, Simon Felton raced down the hall to the main lobby of Felton Electronics. A security guard, one strange to him, ran forward to cut him off from the entrance doors. Simon could hear the Bull shouting after him. Snatching up a metal ashtray stand as he ran, Felton swung it with all his might at the guard blocking his way. The man tried to duck, but the heavy base caught the side of his head and blood burst from his torn face as he fell backward against the doors and crumpled to the floor. Kneeling, Simon quickly forced his key into the lock at the bottom of one door, twisted it and pushed out into the cool early morning darkness.

Glancing over his shoulder for the Bull, Simon ran

desperately toward the parking lot. Robert Frankel watched his flight through his glasses. Rounding the corner of the building, Simon raced for his car, wrenching open the door. Don't fail me now, he pleaded silently as he jabbed his key into the ignition. The engine roared into life. Throwing it into reverse, he backed out and then shifted into first, the tires screeching as the car shot forward down the short drive to the security gate. In his desperation, he failed to notice the car without lights that rounded the corner of the building behind him.

Alarmed by the commotion, the guard at the gate ran from his small house drawing a gun. Was he one of them? There was no time to find out. Simon floored the accelerator. The man lowered his arm to fire but, recognizing the scientist at the last moment, jumped aside as the car flashed past, smashing through the chain-link gates in a spray of sparks and flying metal. The dark car followed in pursuit.

Simon turned onto Interstate 270 and headed southeast toward the airport. He'd call Carmody from there and then fly to the safety of his cabin retreat until things had blown over. And then, for the first time, he noticed the car moving up behind him and realized who must be inside. He could never make the airport phones or his plane now; there would be too many delays. Swinging to the right at the interchange to Route 35, he sped southwest, glancing into the rear-view mirror at the dark car following. Another vehicle came into view, moving up beside his pursuer. Its bright lights reflecting in his mirror blinded Simon, and he looked away for the next interchange, the one with Interstate 70 that led west to the mountains. It was coming up on his right.

As his speeding black Honda pulled alongside, Robert Frankel looked over at the thick-necked KGB agent behind the wheel of the other car. He quietly thanked him for delivering the fleeing rabbit to the fox. Slowly Frankel raised the gun in his hand and aimed through the open car window. The agent's eyes opened in astonished realization of the other's intent as Frankel's weapon barked three times in rapid succession, shattering the window of the Russian's car and the head of the man behind it. The vehicle weaved drunkenly for a second or two and then swerved sharply to the right, overturning and somersaulting end over end as it exploded in a gush of flames.

Frankel looked back coolly at the empty highway. "Another one for me, Savich," he said softly, and then he looked ahead to the interchange. He frowned. Baron Androssy's killer could no longer see the taillights of the scientist's car. The rabbit had once more eluded him. Robert Frankel sped along Route 35 for several more miles in hopes of spotting the car before pulling over to the side to think. What had happened back at Felton Electronics to make Felton flee like that? Why had the KGB moved against orders? Had Felton discovered something, something Frankel's employer should know? Would his prey go to ground, he wondered, or go to the police now that he knew his life was in danger? If Felton did the latter, Frankel was helpless, but if he went to ground, Frankel would find him.

The killer knew that Simon Felton had a cabin hidden somewhere in the mountains and that he also had a plane; Frankel had seen photographs of the Cessna in the scientist's apartment in Boulder. While waiting for Felton's return, he had used his time well by making discreet inquiries at the Denver airport and at all the other airports within several hundred miles. The well-known eccentric's flight plans most often listed the Gunnison County Airport as a destination. If Felton's retreat were in that area, it would take the scientist between two and three hours to reach it by car at this time in the morning. Frankel could reach the Gunnison airport in far less time by charter plane and make further inquiries from there. Smiling, Baron Androssy's private secretary gunned the engine of his Honda and drove the few miles back to the entrance of Denver's Stapleton International Airport.

CHAPTER 17

Startled by his approach, a lark bunting took flight. Simon watched it flutter among the branches of a blue spruce and settle, its call alerting others to the invasion of the human. Totally exhausted from the stress of the last twenty-four hours and the long, arduous hike up the mountain, Felton lowered himself wearily onto a large boulder and looked around at the forest. Its absolute stillness and the scent of its trees acted as a soothing balm to his aching mind and body.

By this time in the morning, the sun's first rays should have turned the night sky into a delicate pink glow behind Castle Peak and the other mountains stretching far to the north and south of him. Instead, large thunderheads hovered above, the distant rumbling a prelude to the heavy rain that would soon sweep through the valleys and cascade down over the rock faces of cliffs to the rushing streams below.

Several larks shrieked angrily behind and to his left. Simon did not bother to turn to seek the source of their agitation.

He had left his town car at the Gunnison Airport, swapping it for the jeep he had left there only yesterday. Yesterday morning, he thought with a wan smile. It seemed as though a year had passed between then and now. From the airport, Simon had driven thirty miles north to Crested Butte, where the paved surface ended, and then continued several bumpy miles farther along a rutted dirt road before pulling the jeep into a small clearing. The hike up the steep trails from there had taken him less than an hour, hastened by his urgent need to reach the radiophone in his cabin.

From where he sat, Simon could just see the top of his radio tower through a break in the trees overhead. He had obtained permission to erect it on the condition that the National Park Service would have access to it as an emergency backup should the radio in their fire-watcher's tower atop the mountain go out. Up ahead, another lark called its annoyance, its final cries drowned out by a crack of thunder from the approaching storm. Lightning flashed up the valley, signaling Simon to move on.

The first drops of rain splashed on the trail ahead as he rounded the bend just below the cabin retreat. His watch read 6:20. Turning, Simon looked back at the curtain of water moving rapidly toward him and sprinted the last hundred yards to the shelter of the porch. Another crash of thunder and flash of lightning greeted his arrival. Branches thrashed overhead as the wind drove the rain horizontally at him. Gasping for breath, the scientist fumbled with the heavy padlock on the door, finally snapping it open. He pushed quickly through into the dark cabin and slammed the door behind him.

Rain beat down loudly on the roof and again thunder sounded above. Shaking the water from his wet hair and shirt, Simon crossed the room to light the oil lamp on the mantel. He turned toward the radio. Fortunately, the storm would not materially affect transmission of his call to Washington on the sophisticated equipment he had assembled here in the wilderness. He knew exactly what had to be done. He, Paul, and Alex had to destroy the Charon II satellite before it could be used against their country. Simon froze at the sound of another's voice.

"Dr. Felton, how very nice to finally meet you after all this time."

Simon whirled around and stared at the clean-cut, young-ish man dressed in a business suit who sat comfortably in the rocking chair by the fireplace. The electronics genius did not miss the cold, steel-blue eyes or the lethal-looking revolver that lay on the table within reach of the stranger's hand.

"Who the hell are you?" Simon's challenge was nearly lost in a clap of thunder that rocked the cabin.

"A friend, Dr. Felton. A very curious friend. Won't you sit down?" Robert Frankel indicated a straight-backed chair on the other side of the hearth.

Simon shook his head. "How did you get in here?" he demanded in a voice far more brave than he felt at the moment.

Frankel picked up his gun and rose. Reaching slowly forward, he relieved Simon of his oil lamp and put it back on the mantel. The baron's secretary was much too wise in matters of this sort to allow an intended victim any possible means of defense. "I followed you from the Gunnison airport," Frankel answered pleasantly, again indicating the chair with a nod of his head. "What a happy coincidence that I should have been there when you picked up your jeep. A nice vehicle, isn't it? For getting around in places like this, that is."

Felton stood his ground. "How did you get in here?" he again demanded, knowing the answer full well. The forced window in the kitchen area gave evidence of the other's means of entry. But he had to stall for time, time to think. His eyes glanced briefly at the radiophone on the other side of the room.

"Does it really matter, Dr. Felton? I'm here, that's all that counts." He smiled at the scientist. "Well, if you don't want to sit down, I do. You set quite a pace coming up the mountain." Frankel reached behind him for the arm of the rocker and slowly eased down into it, his eyes not once leaving those of the other. "Tell me, Tisiphone, did you talk with Megaera today?"

"I beg your pardon?" he managed lamely. "I . . . I don't know what you're talking about."

"Oh, I'm sure you do, Dr. Felton. May I refresh your mind?" He waited, and when the other said nothing, continued, "Megaera is General Paul Carmody, a very influential friend of yours at the Pentagon." Again Simon's eyes darted to the radiophone. "Ah, you'd like to make a call right now, wouldn't you?" Frankel asked, teasing his captive. "Didn't you get a chance to do it earlier today?" The sarcasm in his voice was barely concealed by his pleasant tone. It was a tone that Simon found more frightening than that of an outright threat. "Is there something very important that you want to tell your friends?"

The anguish on the scientist's face told Frankel all he needed to know. So, he thought, the fool waited until he got back here to alert the police and Carmody. He stared at Felton, the wind and driving rain the only sounds in the room.

"I'm very sorry, Doctor, but you won't be able to use that phone over there." He nodded to the corner. "You see I had a little accident, and the wires seemed to have got all torn out. Perhaps you'd like to tell me what you wanted to say to your friends." He smiled.

Lightning flashed viciously around the peak of the mountain and thunder again shook the cabin, rattling its windows. The heart of the storm was directly overhead. Simon's thoughts had been centered on how to trick and overpower the man so that he could get to the phone. With this new revelation, his thoughts were now directed solely on escape. He saw no way of leaping through a window; they were too small and solid for that. If he could get through the door on the other side of the room without being shot, he could certainly make it down to his jeep. Even though the stranger was younger and obviously more agile than he, Simon knew the shortcuts down the mountain through the forest and, in this rain and mist, he could lose the man.

Watching him carefully, Frankel saw the scientist's eyes reach out for the door, and read the message in them. "I am only going to ask you once more, Dr. Felton. Sit down." The pleasantness had vanished from his voice. It was now a command. He saw Frankel glance at the woodpile to his right, his attention attracted briefly by an ever so slight movement, that of a small mouse poking its head out from between two logs. Frankel looked back to Simon. "I mean what I say, Doctor." Casually raising his gun, he pulled the trigger. The deafening explosion splattered the small animal into nothing more than bits of blood and fur. Sickened, Simon slowly sank into the straight-backed chair opposite the intruder.

"That's much better, Dr. Felton," Frankel said, smiling. "Much better. Now, shall we talk?"

"About what?" the scientist asked, cowed by the brutality he had just witnessed.

"General Carmody asked you to check the 120044C circuit. What did you find?"

Aghast, Simon stared at the man. "How could you possibly know—"

"Please, Dr. Felton, I am very tired of playing games with you. What did you find?"

The desperateness of not only his own situation but that of his country swept over Simon Felton. He *had* to escape. He sat silently, the noise of the wind-whipped trees and rain on the cabin roof replacing his unspoken words.

"Your last chance, Doctor." Frankel slowly raised his gun and pointed it at the scientist. "I really don't have to know. It won't make any difference one way or the other. I'm just curious, that's all."

Staring into the muzzle pointed at his face, Simon slowly rose, steadying himself with the back of the chair. He would die standing. The muzzle followed him up.

"Just curious," Frankel repeated. His fingers tightened on the trigger.

The hair on the back of Simon's neck suddenly stood up. It was not fear induced, but something else, a growing surge of electricity in the air. He recognized it from his long experience in the mountains. "All right," he gasped, desperately buying the few seconds of time he needed. "All right, I'll tell. . . ."

Frankel's finger hesitated on the trigger and, in that brief instant, a great, blinding bolt of lightning pierced the sky, striking the radio tower, its violent energy twisting and following it down, blasting like a fiery bomb into the cabin. In wide-eyed terror, Frankel rose as its untamed force hurled both men across the room like dolls and shattered the place in a ball of exploding light and heat. Having anticipated the violence, Simon was first to his feet and bolted for the door, yanking it open as Frankel, stunned and blinking, fired wildly at the figure he could barely see. Two slugs bit into the door by Simon's head, and another tore painfully into his left thigh. He crashed down onto the porch outside, grinding his teeth against the pain that shot up through his body. Scrambling to his feet, the scientist half ran, half limped into the heavy fern growth behind the cabin and pressed up into the concealing forest. Wounded as he was, Simon instinctively knew he would stand no chance of beating the stranger's gun to his jeep in the valley below.

Frankel stumbled from the smoking cabin into the little clearing before it. He stood reloading his revolver while looking frantically about him, searching the downpour for his fleeing victim. The jeep, he thought. Felton will go for the jeep; it's his only way out. Even though he had put the vehicle out of commission before following the scientist up the mountain earlier that morning, the road leading back to Crested Butte still offered an avenue of escape he had to block.

About to run down in that direction, Frankel's eyes fell on the cabin porch and the red spot by the door slowly dissolving in the rain. Mounting the two steps, he knelt down to examine the pool of blood. How badly hurt was the man? he wondered. His eyes slowly moved over the rough wooden floor on either side of him. Another patch of rain-diluted blood lay at the far end of the porch. He moved to it and looked up at the dense fern growth shrouded in mist and rain behind the cabin. So, he thought, the elusive Dr. Felton is going up, not down. But why? In this rain there would be no easy trail of blood to follow. He would have to sniff him out. It was going to be a longer and more difficult hunt than Robert Frankel wanted.

Felton limped on painfully, using his arm muscles to pull

himself up over boulder flows and the rock ledges blocking his way. He had to put distance between himself and the killer before the storm passed and the sun came out. He hoped to be well hidden in one of the maze of caves farther up before that happened. Later he would use the cover of night to climb across the bare rock crown of the mountain to the Park Service fire-watcher's tower. There he would find safety, weapons, and the all-important radio. Shivering, Simon pulled off his shirt, tore away one of its arms and folded it into a pad. He used the other sleeve to hold it tightly to the gaping wound in his thigh. He felt dizzy and weak from shock and loss of blood. But he had to keep going. He had to reach those caves before the rain and mist cleared. The thunder and lightning now rumbled and flashed far to the east, and the sky had already started to lighten.

Forcing himself up, Simon continued his agonizing climb as Robert Frankel squatted on his haunches on the cabin porch, planning his next move. He tried to put himself into the head of the prey he sought. Why, he asked himself, would a wounded man go up the mountain instead of down to the safety of the people living below? What refuge could possibly lie on top of a mountain? The answer would be his key to finding and eliminating Simon Felton.

"Damn it, Alex, I don't know where he called from last night, and I don't know where he is today. I'm just as worried as you are," General Carmody exploded into the red phone in his hand. "I've done everything I can." He swiveled around in the large chair behind his desk in the Pentagon and stared blankly out the window across the Potomac at the Washington Memorial standing tall and white against the clear blue noon sky.

"George, don't wait. Go to the Joint Chiefs or the Secretary of Defense today. Tell them everything."

"Not without some tangible proof," the general answered stubbornly.

"But Simon found something. You said so."

"I said I *thought* so," the other corrected.

"He said you were right about those chips being in the planes and he—"

"He said I was right, but not what I was right about."

"And the shots?" Alex pressed. "Why in the hell would anyone shoot at Simon if he hadn't found something important?"

Were they shots? Carmody was reluctant to stir up a hornet's nest only to discover the eccentric Simon Felton in another laboratory working on an experiment that made a lot of noise that he could have mistaken for gunfire. "Alex, be patient," Carmody counseled. "As soon as I hear from him and determine exactly what he knows, I'll go to the Secretary—that is, if Simon's information warrants it."

"Today, George. Go today."

The general sighed. "When I hear from Simon, not before. Things are already frantic at the White House."

"Why?" Alex's newsman's ears perked up. "What's up?"

"The Middle East is heating up, and no one knows why or what's really going on." He paused. "Not for others' ears, Alex?"

"Right."

"Syria and Jordan are taking potshots at each other and massing troops along their borders. The other countries in the area are jittery, putting themselves on military alert."

"What about Libya and Egypt?"

"Qaddafi is strangely silent. I don't like it. We've monitored a lot of training flights in his country recently. Egypt is quiet. Something's brewing."

Alexander Kidd thought of Jacob and Rosalind Singer. "And Israel?"

"Sitting in the hot seat. They don't know what's going on any more than we do. Their intelligence is pretty damn good, and it reports buildups everywhere. Poor bastards don't know which way to turn first, if, indeed, there's any need to turn at all. They can't afford another first strike like the Lebanon thing in 'eighty-two; the world would crucify them. Besides, with all the states arming, which one would they attack? It's a puzzle."

"Sounds fishy to me."

"Very. Have our best people working on it twenty-four hours a day. The Secretary plans a visit to the area in the next few weeks to see if he can cool things down a bit."

"Ha," Alex snorted. His contempt for the Secretary of State's abilities was well-known. The Middle East news served to distract Kidd only briefly. He returned to the matter at hand. "But Simon, we . . ."

"No, Alex, not until I hear from him. Then I'll decide what to do, not before. I'm not about to recommend that the Army march into KWEN and send their multimillion-dollar satellite crashing into the Atlantic on pure speculation."

Alexander Kidd hesitated only seconds before making up his mind. "I'm coming to Washington."

"Your being here isn't going to find Simon any faster."

"Paul, I just can't sit here doing nothing," he blurted out in frustration.

"Come on ahead," Carmody sighed, "but for Christ sakes, keep that famous mouth of yours closed until we've got some hard proof."

"Proof," Alex said aloud as he replaced the red receiver and slumped back angrily in his study at the Dakota. "Well, Paul George *Megaera* Carmody," he mumbled, "I don't need you and your damn generals to bring down Charon II. Simon and I know something you don't. I'm giving you two days—no more. Then, blam!"

Baron Miklos Androssy crossed the narrow Zurich street and walked toward an old, nondescript stone building. Among the other names listed on small brass plaques discreetly affixed to the left of the door was that of the Credit Bank Schiller. He slowed his pace and moved closer to the wall to allow two others exiting from a side door of the building to pass. Their eyes made contact. He continued on, pausing briefly before entering the main door.

"You recognize him?" Enrico Montagna asked.

Sandra Bannister nodded. "The last time I saw him was with Alex at President Warren's memorial service in New York. Do you think he recognized us?"

"Me, no. But you're pretty visible on TV back in the States." The second in command of KWEN's Milan office hurried back to reenter the building's main entrance and stood in the small marble foyer watching the elevator indicator. He smiled as the arrow stopped on the third floor. So, he thought, the illustrious Baron Miklos Androssy has dealings with the Credit Bank Schiller. Returning to Sandra, he took her arm and steered her to a small shop across the street. "Come on, we're going to get a cup of coffee."

Inside the bank building, Androssy exited the iron cage of the elevator and, glancing at his watch, pushed the small brass button by a pair of heavy, highly polished wooden doors. It was precisely 6:30, the exact time set for his meeting with Andrei Ryabov, a shadowy figure who moved about the corridors of power at the KGB with no title or apparent responsibility but, rumor had it, was the unofficial right-hand man of the sinister organization's chairman.

As it was after normal banking hours, the doors were opened to him by the president of the bank himself. "Baron Androssy, a pleasure as usual," the short, plump man said, bowing to the majority stockholder of the private institution.

"You look well, Horst."

"Thank you."

"And Frau Diebitsch?"

"Very well, thank you. I hope we may have the honor of entertaining you during your visit to Zurich."

"A very short visit, I am afraid, my friend. Perhaps the next time." He paused. "I passed two people leaving by the side exit a minute ago, a man and a woman. She was blond, he dark. Were they by any chance here?"

"Why, yes," the president replied, preceding the baron across the elegant but conservatively decorated reception room of the bank. "He is a correspondent for an Italian publication doing a study of private banking in Switzerland."

"And the woman?"

"His assistant." The Swiss opened the door to a long, carpeted hall lined with thick, secure-looking doors of the same highly polished dark wood as the front entrance. "But I would assume she is more to him than that," he said with a lecherous, man-to-man wink at the baron.

"Did they see my visitor?" he asked, unsmiling.

"Certainly not. As you requested, I put him in the small conference room." Accustomed to the anonymity with which so many of those using the bank insisted, the president did not find it unusual that his superior, Androssy, had not told him the name of the man he was meeting or that the stranger had not introduced himself earlier. It was standard practice in the world of private banking. Why else would they have a separate entrance and exit, except in order that those entering would not see those leaving.

"You have been discreet with the reporter?"

"But of course," the president replied in a tone of injured dignity at the thought the baron could possibly think he might deal loosely with any of the secrets of the bank or its clients.

"Do not see them again," Androssy said shortly. He left the heavyset banker standing by the door and proceeded alone down the hall to the seventh door on the right. The baron paused briefly before reaching for the knob. This is it, he thought. The time has come.

"What's got you so excited?" Sandra asked as they sipped their coffee.

"Androssy deals with the Credit Bank Schiller."

"You think he may be connected with the Milo group?" Her eyes sparkled with hope.

"Sorry," Montagna apologized, deserting his train of thought. "I wasn't really thinking about that."

"Then what?"

He leaned forward. "From all the dirt our informants

have been able to dig up to date, we know that the Bank
Schiller has a reputation for dealing very kindly with the
Eastern bloc."

"So?" she pressed.

"A couple of years ago Androssy's name popped up in
connection with the Banco Ambrosiano default in Milan.
Although we were never able to pin anything on him, we
researched the man pretty thoroughly. Hungarian nobleman
whose family was wiped out by the Nazis, fought in the
underground, a hero, apparently quite ruthless. He disappeared during the Russian occupation. Years later he
surfaces in Beirut and from then on seems to have the Midas
touch, piling up more and more money, more and more
power." Enrico Montagna scratched his head. "The Russians, Androssy, the Credit Bank Schiller; there could be
some connection." He smiled at Sandra. "It would be
fascinating if our capitalistic friend were involved with the
Ruskies."

"That line of investigation certainly isn't going to help
Alex very much," she commented dryly.

"One never knows where a lead will take one."

"Well, *is* there a chance he could be involved with
Milo?"

"He's certainly got the money for it. But we'll never find
out. The man has holding companies that do nothing but
hold other companies. He always stays in the background."

"He's all I've got so far, Rico. All the other leads have
gone absolutely nowhere."

"So will this one."

"But we've got to do something."

"Who did you say was working on it back in the States?"

"Fred Sangster and Bart Wilton in New York, Frank
Lawrence in Los Angeles."

"Good men."

"And I'm sure they've pulled in others to help," she
added.

"If you're so hot to trot, have them run Androssy through
the master computer. And have Barlow in London do the

same thing. Maybe they can come up with some link between him and Milo, but it's a long shot." Sandra started to rise and then sat back down when she saw Montagna had no intention of leaving. "No, go ahead," he said. "I'm going to hang on here a little longer. Give me that mini-camera of yours." He smiled at her. "Just in case."

"You're up to something, Rico." Sandra looked at the reporter curiously as she took the camera from her pocket and handed it to him.

"Every once in a while you get a hunch. I'm going to play this one for a bit." He turned back to look through the coffee shop window as she rose.

"Call me later at the hotel?"

"I'll pick you up for dinner at nine-thirty." He waved absently to her as she left. From his vantage point, Montagna could see the side entrance of the Credit Bank Schiller. He watched it for several minutes, and then his eyes scanned the third floor of the building. The shade in one of its windows had just been drawn.

The room behind that window was far more spartan in decor than the rest of the bank. Its plain white walls held several undistinguished landscapes in heavy frames under one of which stood a simple wooden cabinet displaying a silver tray with glasses and an assortment of mineral waters and fruit drinks. A rectangular mahogany table dominated the place. It stood centered on a worn Oriental carpet whose colors had long since faded. Three uncomfortable-looking chairs with leather seats and backs lined each of the two long sides of the table, and a more formidable leather chair rested at each end. Andrei Ryabov sat in one of these chairs, looking the length of the room through narrowed eyes at Miklos Androssy as he entered. Ryabov lived up to the description that Androssy had often heard of him: "the vulture of the KGB." He sat there, tall, thin, and gaunt. His long, hooked nose overshadowed a sunken face. Heavy black eyebrows pushed forward over dark, beady eyes that reflected the light from the lamp in the center of the table.

The Russian's black hair had been cut to no more than a half inch from his tight scalp, giving him the skeletal look of death. His black suit and tie hung loosely from his frame as if no flesh lay beneath.

Placing his briefcase on the table before him, Androssy took the chair at the opposite end. The two men stared at each other for some seconds without speaking. Androssy finally broke the intimidating silence. "We meet at last, Andrei Ryabov."

"We meet at last," the other repeated in a tone meant to convey threat.

The baron noted it and smiled. The mere presence of this man at the Credit Bank Schiller indicated to him the strength of the hand he held. "How is my good friend?" he asked, referring pointedly to his long association with the President of the Presidium of the U.S.S.R. Supreme Soviet. "In better health I trust."

"Contrary to rumors, the President is in very good health," the other replied. "But he and your other supporters are disturbed by your unexpected betrayal in this Acheron matter. He had wished to speak with you personally, as did my chairman."

"Under the circumstances, a trip to Moscow and the Center seemed imprudent," Androssy countered. "You are their official representative?"

Ryabov nodded slowly. "I am." He pushed the thin document case that had been lying next to his right hand down the length of the table to Androssy.

Reaching forward, the baron picked it up and opened the leather flap. He scanned the two simple documents it contained. "And your word is binding in this meeting?"

"Negotiation is, perhaps, a more accurate term," the vulture corrected, his hatred for Androssy scarcely concealed. "I am empowered to commit my country in certain matters. In others I am not. It will depend upon your terms for returning to us the code you have, in effect, stolen from us."

The baron smiled. "Vladimir Savich, as usual, has

misinformed you. I have no intention of giving you the code."

Andrei Ryabov's face showed no sign of emotion at the surprise announcement. He had anticipated something like this. He leaned forward and spoke in a low, even voice. "Beware, comrade, you are walking into the very flames of hell, you and your entire family."

"To the contrary," Androssy countered, "we are walking toward power and paradise. And to assure it, I will not relinquish that code. Andrei Ryabov, I am not naive enough to imagine that after you have the key to the Acheron Plot the Center will not exact its punishment for, as you call it, 'my betrayal in this matter.' " He stared into the other's eyes for several moments. "Tell me, given the opportunity, would you not be tempted to strip me of all my power and put a bullet into my head?"

The vulture of the KGB returned Androssy's stare. "A temptation to which I would gladly yield."

"Thank you for your honesty. Now it is time to put our cards on the table. I am sure that, as in the past, the Kremlin will find my terms very acceptable—even advantageous."

"Proceed, Miklos Androssy," Ryabov said evenly. "We, not you, will determine what is acceptable."

"First, I will remain the sole possessor of the Acheron code. I will use it in concert with Moscow. The Charon II satellite will be moved to the Middle East as planned in thirteen days time, on September twenty-second, to immobilize the Israeli war machine during the Arab invasion as proof of the power we hold over the weapons of the Western alliance. After all, did not I myself recommend the strategy to your chairman nearly seven years ago?"

Ryabov nodded coldly.

"After that, and in consultation with the Kremlin, I will place the satellite in permanent orbit over Moscow to destroy the guidance systems of any incoming Western missiles while Moscow either forces the West to dismantle its entire missile network under threat of immediate attack, or actually eliminates several major U.S. cities and has done with it."

The penetrating eyes of Andrei Ryabov burned with contempt and anger. "'In concert with'? 'In consultation with'?" he asked. "What are you suggesting is tantamount to membership in the Politburo."

"*Anonymous* membership. My second condition. I do not wish to jeopardize my current international position."

"Ridiculous! Impossible!" Andrei Ryabov snapped, taken aback by the presumption of the man opposite him.

Taking advantage of the other's surprise, Androssy continued, "Should you reject my conditions and move against me or any member of my family in an attempt to wrest the code from me, the only duplicate of that code and a full explanation of our operations over the last seven years and Moscow's future plans for the satellite will automatically and instantly be sent to the appropriate person in the United States cabinet. Let me assure you that I no longer have control over the sending of those documents. It rests in independent hands. To move against the Androssy family is to give up the most effective weapon for world domination that the U.S.S.R. has ever had."

"You fly high, comrade," Ryabov stated flatly. He had had a chance to recover and digest the other's threat. "The Greek, Icarus, burned his wings and fell to his death when he flew too close to the sun."

"My wings are made of something more substantial than wax and feathers." Androssy smiled. "I do not come empty-handed. In addition to my cooperation in the Acheron matter, I will continue to use my very large and diversified financial organization to handle and manipulate the more discreet foreign investments of Moscow in the Third World and in the West. As in the past, I will continue to siphon revenues from the Androssy operation into the coffers of the Kremlin." He paused, watching Ryabov's reaction. "Or perhaps, Andrei Ryabov, you are not fully aware of the great sums that flow annually from me to feed the Russian economy and build its war machine?" He smiled at the KGB man's displeasure. As he had anticipated, the cards were truly stacked in his favor. He played another. "And I shall continue to finance the Center's very profitable and subverting drug operations in Europe and North America, laundering the funds generated through the proper channels to your agents. The KGB needs those funds to maintain the scope of its operations abroad, does it not, comrade?" Again he paused to read the Russian's reaction. "Certainly the very essential services I perform for Moscow warrant the high position in the Party hierarchy I request."

"You are not born Russian," Ryabov snapped angrily.

"I am sure my birth will not stand in the way."

Ryabov sat silently. He had expected a difficult meeting with Androssy, but not this. He sat looking at the baron, or rather, looking through him as his mind sifted and analyzed all that had been said. He could not dispute the fact that Androssy not only controlled the code that would deliver the Western alliance into the hands of the Kremlin, but also did perform other invaluable financial services for his country. Was his threat of exposing the Acheron Plot valid? Knowing the ruthless history of the man opposite him, even the vulture of the KGB had to admit he had met his match. Androssy was already suspected of murdering several of Ryabov's agents in the U.S., including Anatoli Butov.

The vulture stared at him, looking for some crack in his armor, some point from which to bargain. "Obviously I am not empowered to commit to what you request, Miklos Androssy." Ryabov was forced to respect the man even though he wanted to see him and his whole decadent clan dead. "I will report our conversation to the chairman."

"You may well do that," Androssy replied confidently, "but more important, transmit it word for word to my good friend, the President."

The vulture stared archly at him.

"And while you do, please transmit my third and final condition." He enjoyed the power he felt at this moment. "I wish control over the Eastern bloc's gold reserves and production."

Andrei Ryabov's fist slammed down hard against the

polished mahogany table. "You go too far, Androssy," he spit out. "You . . ."

Fending off the angry words with an uplifted hand, the baron explained, "I do not demand ownership, Andrei Ryabov, only *control*. With that control and my empire, I will be able to manipulate and dominate the international monetary markets and be able to create a financial dynasty richer and more powerful than the world has ever known. And . . ." he hesitated and smiled at the KGB vulture, "I will do it all for my country, Mother Russia. I will destabilize the economies of our enemies while pouring more wealth into your hands than you ever dreamed possible. Tell that, comrade, to the chairman and my good friends in the Politburo."

After nearly two more hours of debate and discussion, Miklos Androssy stood up and, nodding to the dark figure at the far end of the conference table, left the room a victor in an uneasy truce.

Minutes later the side door of the bank once again opened and two men emerged—the short bank president and a tall, gaunt man with a hat pulled down to obscure most of his face. Enrico Montagna smiled. This was even more than he had hoped. Raising Sandra's minicamera to his eye, he snapped several pictures and then watched the men shake hands briefly and walk off in opposite directions. Thanks to his days in the Moscow news bureau, the shadowy form of Andrei Ryabov was well etched in his mind. Quickly dropping some change on the table, Montagna left the shop to follow the Russian.

Another patron sitting in the rear, a heavyset man wearing a houndstooth jacket, also dropped some francs on the table and slowly rose. Leaving the shop, the baron's chauffeur, Victor Kamera, sauntered nonchalantly after KWEN's Milanese newsman in the gathering darkness, pretending interest in various store windows whenever the Italian looked back.

Enrico Montagna never showed up for his dinner engagement with Sandra Bannister.

Sandra was informed of Rico's death by the police the next morning. They had tracked her down at the hotel after finding her name on the most recent pages in Montagna's pocket diary. The cause of death was officially listed as accidental drowning in Lake Zurich. She knew that could not be true. He must have been onto something, something that somehow was connected with Baron Androssy.

Returning from the Zurich morgue after making the identification, the KWEN reporter slumped into a chair in the Baur Au Lac's bar and ordered a double Scotch. She desperately needed it to settle her stomach; the sight of her friend's empty, gray face had been unbearable. Before leaving, however, she had braced herself to examine his personal effects. Her pocket camera had not been among them.

A laugh from across the room interrupted her thoughts. Looking up, she recognized Baron Androssy and several business associates enjoying a preluncheon drink. Sandra studied his face as he talked, interested to see that his eyes darted furtively in her direction from time to time. Why? she wondered.

On a sudden impulse, she left the bar for the phones in the hotel lobby. Dialing the number of the Credit Bank Schiller, she asked to be put through to the president. His secretary intercepted the call and politely but firmly informed Sandra Bannister that Herr Diebitch would be unable to meet with her and Signor Montagna that afternoon as previously arranged or, for that matter, any other afternoon for several months. So, she thought, slowly replacing the receiver, Androssy had recognized her and got to him. What was he afraid she might find out at the bank? Then another thought came to her. Was that smiling, urbane nobleman behind Rico's death?

Returning to her table in the bar, Sandra once again seated herself facing the baron. Taking a sip of her Scotch, she looked across the room and smiled bitterly. I think you just made a goof, big man, she said to him silently. And if you did, I'm going to get you. Sandra studied him for nearly half an hour before leaving the bar. She tried to reach Kidd at the three numbers he had given her, but he had left for Washington. She'd call his favorite hotel there when she got to London. Sandra reached for her suitcase and pulled open the closet door.

"Are you sure?" Miklos Androssy asked Victor Kamera as the two drove to the Zurich airport later that afternoon.

"Yes, the Bannister woman had the concierge at the hotel change her flight plans just after you saw her in the bar."

"And she's going to London?"

"This evening," Kamera confirmed.

The baron thought in silence for several minutes and then made his decision. "Have our men there meet her plane at Heathrow and keep an eye on her. I want to know where I can lay my hands on that woman morning, noon, and night. Clear?"

"Very. I'll phone them from the airport."

"The jet is ready?" Androssy asked.

The other nodded.

"Good, I have a great deal to accomplish in New York tomorrow." He poured himself a small cognac from the bar in the back of the limousine. "Any word from Frankel?"

"No, sir, not so far."

"Damn the man. He has had more than a week to do the job."

"He'll do it. He has never lost one yet."

Miklos Androssy leaned back into the soft leather of the limousine seat and closed his eyes. It had been a dangerous and tiring trip, but he had won. Even he had underestimated the importance Moscow placed on the Charon II satellite and its potential. Before leaving the Baur Au Lac, Ryabov had phoned him with the simple phrase, "It is done."

CHAPTER 18

"There's no point in your hanging around, Peter," General Carmody said to his aide. "It's nearly midnight. Go home. That pretty young wife of yours should get a chance to see you once in a while."

Major Peter Granger smiled as he dropped several more ice cubes into a glass of bourbon. Turning from the general's private bar, he replied, "To hear *her* talk sometimes, you'd think she'd seen enough of me to last the rest of her life. Another cube?" He lifted the glass.

"No, that's plenty." The general looked over at the cot in the corner of his office. "I have a feeling it's going to be another long night."

"You haven't left this place in two days. All outside meetings canceled. Meals brought in." Granger handed the general the glass and returned to the bar. "The call you're waiting for, it must be pretty important." He watched Carmody in the mirror over the bar.

"Vital," the other replied.

"What's it all about? Can you tell me?"

The general shook his head, not bothering to look up from the blueprints and specification lists arranged in precise piles on the top of his desk. "Sorry, Peter." Carmody closed the folder before him. "Look, Major," he said, a note of impatience underlying the good humor he tried to affect, "go home. And that's an order. I don't want to be hauled up in a divorce court as the other person."

"Really, I'd rather—"

"Out," the general broke in, pointing to the door.

Smiling, Major Granger gulped the remains of his drink and headed out. "I surrender."

"And Peter, turn off the lights in the outer office when you leave and lock the blasted door. I don't want the cleaners wandering about out there."

"Right," the younger man replied cheerfully. "Actually, I *could* use a bit of shut-eye. See you in the morning." Granger closed the door behind him and, after several minutes of loud and purposeful puttering around, turned off the lights and slammed the hall door without leaving. He stood in the outer office listening and then moved silently across the darkened room to take a seat behind a group of filing cabinets to the left of the general's secretary's desk. From there he could monitor the miniswitchboard in comfort. It would be his second night of such activity.

General Carmody rose from his desk and stretched. The grandfather's clock across the room read 11:43. Where the hell was Simon? Why didn't he call? Reaching down, he picked up one of the phones on his desk; a red light blinked bright in the darkness of the outer office and Peter Granger leaned forward. The general dialed and waited. "Carmody here," he said to the answering voice. "Put me through to the President. He's expecting my call." Granger's body stiffened at the words, and he reached for the soft leather briefcase beside him. The gun inside felt hard beneath his touch. "Mr. President," the major heard his superior say, "as yet I do not have all the information on the subject Mr. Kidd and I want to bring to your attention."

"When will you have it, George?" the President asked.

"I . . . I'm not sure. Soon, I hope."

"You are being very mysterious."

"I'm sorry, Mr. President."

"Very well. I will be up for another hour or so. If you get it within that time, call and I'll meet with you. If not, it will have to wait until tomorrow afternoon. I'm making an appearance at the Senate in the morning."

"Yes, sir. Good-bye." General Carmody heard the click as the President hung up, and was about to replace his own

receiver when he heard a second click. Frowning, he looked
at the instrument in his hand and then at his office door. No
light showed beneath it from the outer office. He hung up
and walked out into the darkness. He saw no movement,
heard nothing. His secretary's desk sat deserted. Shaking
his head, General Carmody closed the door and, recrossing
the room, slumped down behind his desk to wait. As his
eyes moved slowly over the weapons-specification forms
piled nearby, his fingers drummed impatiently on the
polished wood before him. He was committing political
suicide by going around the Joint Chiefs to the President,
but after much debate, he and Alex had finally agreed they
would get a more sympathetic hearing and faster action by
going straight to the top.

Pain shot through his body with each movement. Weak
and shaking, Simon Felton pulled himself through the last
of the scrub vegetation bordering the edge of the rock cap of
the mountaintop and fell panting while surveying the terrain
ahead of him in the moonlight. The base of the metal ladder
leading up the ranger's lookout tower lay less than two
hundred yards ahead and above him. But aside from a few
rock ridges, no cover existed to shield the last minutes of his
agonizing journey to safety and the radio.

He had lain unconscious in the caves below for more than
a day. Loss of blood, pain, and general exhaustion had
conspired to steal precious time from him. Awakening that
afternoon, Simon had waited for dark before attempting to
climb to the summit, a climb made more torturous and slow
by his swollen, useless right leg. He looked up at the moon
floating silently in the clear night sky. Where was a cloud to
cover his advance? He saw none. But maybe he needed no
cover. His pursuer might be miles away from here.
Certainly yesterday's downpour had obliterated any trace of
his trail. Could a complete stranger have followed him here,
have read his mind?

A dim light shone in the windows atop the tower, a small
cabinlike structure with a porch running around all four

sides sitting on sixty-foot steel columns. From there rangers kept a twenty-four-hour vigil over the surrounding peaks and valleys, their eyes ever alert for any wisp of smoke, any glow from an unauthorized campfire. Should he call out for help? No, he thought. Don't take chances now. Simon pulled himself to his feet and, stifling a cry of pain, began a limping run toward the ladder.

Another pair of eyes—those of Robert Frankel—looked up at the lighted windows. He squatted in the scrub on the other side of the rock clearing. A smile slowly spread across his face as he watched the painful progress of the man limping toward the tower. The long day's wait had paid off at last. Frankel could have brought Simon down on the spot but decided not to alert the ranger in the tower above with a shot. He would have no cover in the moonlight should the man decide to fire upon him from his superior position. Frankel would bide his time.

Reaching the ladder, Simon looked about and then began to pull himself up rung by rung. He had been right, he thought. The stranger was nowhere near. Cold sweat bathed his body as he struggled upward. His brain was nearly numb with the pain by the time he finally pulled himself up through the opening in the porch floor and crawled to the cabin door. Unnoticed, Frankel ran from the scrub across the rock cap to stand under the tower itself. The ranger whirled around in surprise as Simon fell through the door.

"Simon," he gasped, jumping up and running forward. "Jesus Christ, what in the hell happened to you?"

"Shot, Ben," he panted. "Some madman, yesterday."

"Your leg." Kneeling, the ranger began to tear away Simon's trouser leg; it was completely soaked through with new blood. "Don't move, I'll get—"

"No, no," the scientist protested. "Later. The radio-phone, I've got to use it."

"But Simon," the other argued, "you—"

"No—now," he gasped. "It's important, Ben."

"Okay. Okay." The ranger helped him up and supported

him across the small room to the chair before the radio. "You want me to put it through for you?"

Simon nodded weakly, giving him the Acheron number.

Outside, Robert Frankel slowly began his silent climb up the metal ladder.

General Carmody jerked upright in his desk chair as the phone locked in the lower left-hand drawer of his desk buzzed into life. "Thank God," he mumbled, pulling the key from his pocket and unlocking the drawer. He snatched up the receiver and practically shouted into it, "Megaera here."

"Tisiphone," Simon replied softly. The ranger looked at him with a puzzled expression. "Listen carefully, no time to talk." He paused, taking several deep breaths. "They tried to kill me."

"Who, Simon, who?" The general was on his feet now.

"Don't know. Listen. Important." The room was swimming before him. Through the window they failed to see the dark form straighten up on the porch outside. "The Cerberus chip is still being made. It's in all the 120044 circuits. For seven years—"

The door burst open. Frankel's gun barked, exploding the receiver in Simon's hand and sending the startled scientist toppling over backward, bringing the chair with him as he fell at the feet of the wide-eyed ranger. Before either could speak, Frankel reached over with his free hand and snatched up one of the four emergency oil lamps sitting on the ledge to his left. The ranger lunged forward as Frankel smashed its top off and, in one fast, continuous motion, flung the oil from its base into the other's face. Crying out, the ranger staggered backward, frantically rubbing his blinded eyes as the contents of the second splashed over him and the man lying on the floor. Androssy's private secretary pulled a Zippo lighter from his pocket and flicked the flint.

"You guys like to look for fires," he laughed derisively as the little flame danced in his hand. "Well, here's one of your very own."

"No," Simon shouted.

Frankel threw the lighter at him.

The scientist's clothes burst into flames as he tried to roll away. The floor exploded around him. Simon's cries blended with the shrieks of the ranger, who stood back against the large window, his hands pressed to his face as his entire body ignited in a vertical sheet of fire. Turning round and round trying to escape his incredible agony, the ranger plunged flaming through the glass onto the porch and, staggering up, crashed through the railing, his long, piercing scream carrying across the mountains as he plummeted down onto the rocks far below.

"Simon," General Carmody shouted into the dead phone in his hand again and again. "Simon, what's happening? Simon."

Frankel backed slowly toward the door, away from the burning form writhing on the floor that uttered little screeching sounds through missing lips while flailing at the flaming clothes encasing it. The fire spread across the entire far side of the cabin. "You should have let me shoot you when you had the chance," he said unsmiling to what was left of Simon Felton. Turning, Frankel left the blazing cabin and climbed quickly earthward. Below him he could make out the smoldering body of the shattered ranger. Looking up, he saw the flames now reaching high into the sky. It struck him as a rather beautiful sight, far prettier than that of the buildings he had torched from time to time along the Marseilles waterfront. And there would be no hint of murder. The Park Service would think the two men had been trapped in an accidental fire. An autopsy would show no bullet wounds in either of the charred bodies.

Carmody slowly put down the phone in frustrated misery. In his heart he knew the first of the three Furies must be dead. And now he had his proof; all that Alex had feared was true. "For seven fucking years," he mumbled under his breath as he stared at the piles of military specifications before him. "Practically every goddamned missile and plane we've got." Taking up one of the phones on his desk, he dialed and turned his attention to the civil voice on the other end. "The President. This is General Carmody again."

He listened for a few seconds and then broke in, "No, he's expecting my call."

Again he listened to the cool, impersonal voice.

"Well, I don't give a damn," Carmody roared impatiently into the receiver. "You wake him up and you tell him I'm on my way over." Glaring at the instrument in his hand, he bellowed, "And that's an order." The general slammed it down only to snatch it up again to dial the Watergate, where Alexander Kidd would be waiting.

"Put me through to Mr. Kidd," he demanded of the hotel operator. Tucking the receiver under his chin, the general began to jam into his briefcase those papers he would need to verify his story with the President and his estimate of the country's dire military situation. They contained a summary of the planes, missiles, and other sophisticated weapons depending on electronic guidance systems manufactured in the United States over the previous seven years in addition to those produced during the Warren years. They also showed the probable deployment of those weapons in the United States and abroad.

"Megaera here," he said upon hearing the phone lift at the other end.

"Alecto," came the expected answer.

"Get your ass over here fast," Paul Carmody said. "We're going to the President."

"You've heard from Simon?"

"Yes. They've killed him."

"Killed?" Alex gasped. "Who?"

"He confirmed the Cerberus circuit is still in production. It's been substituted for the 120044 for over seven years."

"Oh, my God," the other exclaimed. "Where is—"

"Not now, Alex. Get over here. With Simon's confirmation, I've got a briefcase full of evidence that can't be refuted. See you in what . . . ?" He glanced at his watch. "Fifteen minutes." Replacing the receiver in its cradle,

General Carmody continued the job of sorting out and filling his case with top-secret procurement documents while Alex rushed from his room in the Watergate to the basement garage. Finished, Carmody was about to snap the case shut when he heard a slight noise in the outer office. He froze, listening.

Certainly not the cleaners, he thought. Peter Granger had locked the hall door when he left several hours ago. Had he imagined it? That and the click on the phone earlier? His skin tingled, and cold sweat broke out all over his body. Switching off the desk lamp, he threw the office into darkness and slowly eased his ample frame back down into the large swivel chair. They, whoever they were, had got to Simon. They had to be onto him as well—and Alex.

Carmody looked across the dark room. It seemed incredible, but there on the other side of the door in the heart of the Pentagon, the country's secure and impregnable military center, might stand an agent capable and ready to kill him. Slowly, quietly, he opened the drawer to his right and reached in. The feel of the cold metal barrel of his service revolver felt reassuring. Withdrawing it, General Carmody aimed the weapon precisely sixteen inches above the doorknob, exactly where a man's heart would be. Then, picking up one of the desk phones, he called the Pentagon's security section.

"Joe?" he said to the familiar voice. "Send someone up on the double to check my office. I think I . . ."

He paused as the lights in the outer office were switched on. The general could see the thin, bright line under the door. A knock sounded, followed by Major Granger's voice. "General? You awake?"

"Yes, Peter," Carmody called out, heaving a sigh of relief as he lowered the gun. "Joe," he said into the phone, "forget it. My mistake."

"You sure, sir?" the voice queried.

The door opened, silhouetting Peter Granger in a shaft of light that fell across the general's desk. "Very sure," Carmody replied.

"Hope I didn't disturb you," Granger apologized. "Left some things I wanted to work on." He looked at the bulging briefcase and then the gun lying beside it on the desk. "Going somewhere, sir?"

"Yes," Paul Carmody answered, standing up and snapping the case shut.

The major walked forward. "Why the gun? Haven't seen that out in years."

The general smiled. "Guess I'm just getting a little nervous these days." He watched as Granger reached over and picked up the pistol to examine it. "For a moment, Peter, I thought you were a spy." Carmody did not detect the subtle change in expression that crossed the other's face at his words.

Still holding the gun, the major moved around the side of the desk. "Can I drive you?"

"No." The general glanced at his watch. "I'm being picked up. No need to bother yourself."

"No bother at all," Granger pressed. "The White House is on my way home."

Carmody didn't miss the slip. He slowly turned to the young man. "How in the hell did you know I was going to the—"

Before he could finish or move, Peter Lobantz, alias Peter Granger, flashed the pistol up to the general's right ear and pulled the trigger. The back of the startled man's skull blew off in an explosion of blood and gore. His eyes frozen open, Paul Carmody crumpled sideways across his desk, the glistening red pulp atop his neck spilling out over the polished mahogany surface.

"I know a great many things, General," Lobantz said softly as he quickly and methodically wiped the gun clean of his fingerprints and reached down to press it into the dead man's dangling right hand. "I would have preferred an accident on the bridge, but a suicide will have to do." It took the East German illegal only seconds to transfer the incriminating papers in the general's briefcase to his own. Making a few final adjustments to the body, Major Granger of the U.S. Air Force closed the office door behind him and was about to leave when the general's phone rang. He hesitated and then quickly snatched up the phone on Carmody's secretary's desk, flicking the connect switch. "Yes?" he asked in a gruff voice similar to that of the late general.

"Security, sir. We've got a Mr. Alexander Kidd down here who insists on seeing you."

"Right," Lobantz replied. This was an amazing stroke of lucky timing for him.

"He seems pretty steamed up, sir. Shall we come with him?"

"No, send him on alone. He knows the way."

"Yes, sir."

Replacing the receiver, Lobantz smiled. Holding tightly to the briefcase, he opened the door to the hall and slipped through, leaving it ajar, and headed down the long Pentagon corridor in the opposite direction from which Alexander Kidd would come. Surprise, surprise, Mr. Kidd, he said to himself as he turned a corner, intending to lose the contents of the case in his hand in the nearest paper shredder he could find in the great five-sided building.

Striding down the hall toward Carmody's office, Alex reran the brief conversation he had had with the general again and again in his head. Simon dead. The Cerberus circuits implanted in U.S. weaponry for the last seven plus years. He had so many questions. At least the threat to the country and its allies—far greater than even he had first imagined—would soon be over. With Presidential backing, and that of the Joint Chiefs of Staff, the government would certainly move quickly to take control of KWEN and let him destroy the Charon II satellite before it could do further harm. All he needed was the code hidden at the network to do the trick. The other set of codes and the second transmitter, known only to Alex and Simon, lay far across the Atlantic out of range.

Although nearly two in the morning, the light shone brightly in the hallway, reflecting off one after another of the seemingly endless number of antiseptic doors he passed on either side. Up ahead Alex saw the partially open door that led to the several rooms occupied by his old friend and his staff. Pushing through into the outer office, he called out, "Paul, it's me, Alex." The door to the general's inner office stood closed. Alex rapped sharply and opened it. "You ready to . . ."

The room lay dark, silent.

"Paul?" His eyes tried to pierce the darkness.

With his left hand, Alex groped for the light switch. The floor and table lamps about the traditionally decorated room blinked on. Alex's attention was immediately drawn to the colorful American and Air Force Academy flags flanking the general's desk across the room. And then his eyes lowered to . . . What was it? Alexander Kidd's normally strong stomach suddenly wrenched tight as he realized exactly what that disgusting, slimy pile of gore on the desk before him was. "Oh, God," he gasped, trying to swallow the wave of nausea surging up from within him. Turning away, he fell to his knees, forcing his handkerchief over his mouth.

Gagging, Alex reached out to one of the heavy colonial wing-back chairs in the room and pulled himself slowly to his feet, keeping his back to the grisly scene at the desk until he could bring his stomach spasms under control. He had steeled himself to all types of carnage around the world during his news-gathering days, but the sudden and unexpected confrontation with this shocking sight caught him off guard. He forced his mind not to personalize what he saw, forced it to erect an impersonal screen to protect him from it. That pile of gore was not his old friend, it was some third person with the name of General Paul George Carmody. He tried to regard it with detachment, as just another story for KWEN's morning news. He could not.

Kidd was too personally enmeshed in the events of this

room, events that like a surging tide had caught him up and were sweeping him inexorably toward some terrible conclusion in the mist of the future that he sensed but could not see. *Paul Carmody had been murdered just before going to the White House.* Alex sprang into action. Moving to the desk, he tried to avert his eyes from the blood while searching for the briefcase with its incriminating evidence that Paul had assembled for the President. With that in his hands he might be able to explain Warren's original plan for Mideast peace and how it had been subverted. The leather case he found in the closet was empty. It did not really surprise him.

Alex knew he now could never convince the President and the Joint Chiefs of Charon II's wild, science fiction threat. To try would just waste time, and he sensed he did not have much time. First Simon. Now Paul. He was the last of the three Furies. He would have to destroy the satellite single-handed.

Looking down at the gun in Carmody's lifeless hand, he wondered if others would think the general had taken his own life. It certainly looked that way, and it would certainly be a more convenient theory than to admit the possibility that one of the country's top generals had been murdered by an unknown assassin in the heart of the country's high-security Defense Department building. He was about to take the gun out of Carmody's hand to make certain that all would know he had not committed suicide but had died for his country when Alex realized that he would be caught up in a murder investigation and pinned down. No. For the present, Paul's "suicide" suited him as well as it did the murderer. "Sorry," he said sadly to the dead man.

Crossing the room, he switched off the lights and closed the door, abandoning the general's untouched body to the darkness. Alex left the lights on in the outer office just as he had found them, but locked the hall door behind him. He wanted as much time as possible before the discovery of the body.

"General Carmody's still up there working," he told the Pentagon guard casually.

"So Major Granger said. That man never seems to sleep." The guard looked strangely at Alex. "You all right, sir?"

"Yes. Yes, fine." Alex smiled as he handed over his security pass and left the building.

CHAPTER 19

"Shit," Alex muttered as he looked up at the flash of lightning through a window in the darkened law offices of Craft, Hassler, Hennes, and White situated in the tower ten floors above those occupied by KWEN in Rockefeller Plaza. "That's all I need tonight, a fuckin' light show." The low-pressure system that had brought the violent storms to Simon Felton's beloved Colorado mountains three days before had moved east and now held the entire coast in its grip. Rain had pelted New York City since early morning, delaying the arrival of his shuttle flight from Washington and slowing traffic on the expressway into the city from La Guardia to a near standstill. After leaving the Pentagon, Alex had driven directly to the airport and taken the first available flight out. The personal effects left back in his room at the Watergate would keep any federal agents who might wish to talk with him guessing about his whereabouts in Washington for a while, hopefully long enough for him to get to the code that lay hidden high above the streets of Rockefeller Plaza and use it to destroy Charon II. Failing that, he would go to Tangier for it and return.

Years ago, he and Judith had bought a romantic old castle on top of a hill in the center of the Casbah, the old native quarter in Tangier. They had remodeled it into a luxurious summer home overlooking the city and the entrance to the Mediterranean Sea. During the renovation, he and Simon Felton had built into it the second transmitter designed to pick up Charon II as it was sent across the Atlantic by KWEN New York and stabilize its new orbit due south of the Middle East. From Tangier, Alex would have been able to trigger the transmission that would activate the Cerberus circuits to knock out American-made weaponry in any country in the area President Warren felt was in violation of its arms agreements with the United States. Unfortunately, his transmitter in Tangier was out of range of Charon II's current stationary orbit over the Americas, and so Kidd could not use it now to trigger the satellite's self-destruct mechanism.

His first stop upon arriving in New York had been a visit to a mountain-climbing supply store on lower Broadway where he purchased the ice ladder now neatly folded beside him on the floor. Then after a shave, he had met Tom Hennes for lunch and talked him into smuggling him through the KWEN lobby to the rear bank of elevators feeding those floors above the network. It had not been too difficult a task thanks to the lunch-hour crush of secretaries and executives who had surrounded him and the fact that Alexander Kidd's face was no longer uppermost in the minds of the lobby security force. Alex had done a little amateur mountain climbing years ago; his macho image had taunted him into trying every type of sport at one time or another, the more danger, the better. At the age of forty-five, Kidd was still in excellent physical condition but not as fit as he had been while clinging to the face of the Matterhorn in Zermatt. He stared down from the window at the rain-swept terrace garden and its sundial ten floors below and wished himself a younger man. It would take all his strength to hang on to the flimsy ladder against the gusting winds that whipped through the caverns between the glass and stone towers of the Plaza. Another flash of lightning and a crash of thunder echoed over the city. He swore and looked at his watch. Alex did not plan to make his descent until after two in the morning. With luck, the worst of the storm should have passed by then.

Turning up the radio, Kidd sat back to listen to the latest on the evening news. The details of General Carmody's death still were not forthcoming; the afternoon news had announced only that the general had been found dead in his office by an aide and that the cause of death was not known at the time. Bullshit, he thought, the man's head was blown half off. They're trying to keep a lid on things until they can get a pat story for release that everyone agrees on.

As he waited in the darkened room, Alex reviewed and made minor modifications in his plans. If he were really clever about it, he could bring down Charon II without anyone knowing he was behind it. Anyone, that was, but the people on the other side. Why, he wondered, had they not come after him? He was the only Fury left who knew about the Cerberus circuits. Alexander Kidd had no idea that earlier that day Baron Androssy had been wondering exactly the same thing as he sat behind his desk, contemplating Alex's future.

The baron believed himself in sole control of Charon II and so felt no threat from Kidd on that score. But Kidd might conceivably find some way of obstructing his plans before it was time to move the satellite. He might somehow use the deaths of his fellow conspirators to get others to listen, even though he had absolutely no proof that the Cerberus circuits actually existed—the Baron knew this from Alex's intercepted conversations with Paul Carmody—or that Charon II was anything more than a normal communications satellite. Still, one could never be sure how politicians might bend in a wind. He could not risk his ticket to political power within the Soviet Union or chance his family's fortune being destroyed by a nervous government.

Equally important to him was the fact that his anonymity in the affair might have been compromised by the accidental meeting in Zurich with the Bannister woman. Her appearance at the Credit Bank Schiller had certainly been no coincidence. Kidd had sent her. But why? Murdering her companion had been a regrettable but necessary action to erase any possible connection between him and the KGB;

Ryabov had obviously been recognized. He did not like the way she had studied him at the bar in the Baur Au Lac. What had been going on in her mind? Kidd and his friends were no fools. Were they about to breach the veil of secrecy that he had so carefully wrapped around himself all these years? He had an uncomfortable feeling that they were closing in on him.

And so it was with cold, emotionless logic that Baron Miklos Androssy had condemned Alexander Kidd to death. The sentence would be carried out by his own men. He did not want the KGB to suspect any weakness in his absolute control in the Acheron matter. Frankel would be returning from Colorado later in the day.

At four in the morning, Alexander Kidd stopped pacing and stood staring out the window overlooking his old terrace garden. The rain had failed to slacken, but he could wait no longer. Far below in the street he could see only one person, a man who was clutching his raincoat about him as he leaned into the wind. Alex slowly rolled up his shirt-sleeves. Here we go, he thought, the beginning or the end of a great adventure. "Sorry, Tom old boy," he said aloud to the room as he picked up a heavy floor lamp and swung the bronze base at the sealed window. The heavy single pane exploded outward, a flutter of loose papers from a nearby table sucked out by the wind after it. The sound of glass shattering in the garden ten floors below was barely audible from where he stood. He leaned out and peered down, feeling the suction of the wind pulling at him. No lights showed in the KWEN windows or through the glass doors on the terrace level.

Using a stone sculpture, Alex quickly chipped away the sharp edges of glass that remained in the window frame and then secured the sculpture firmly to the bottom of the ice ladder to keep the light contraption from blowing too wildly in the wind. He slowly lowered it out and watched as it snaked down the wet side of the building, scraping against the stone and bumping against successive window ledges as it moved lower and lower from one floor to the next until finally reaching the rhododendrons bordering the edge of the garden. Tying the ladder to a radiator in the office, Alex straightened up and flexed his arm and hand muscles in preparation for the descent ahead.

Slipping over the window ledge, he searched for his first footholds on the ladder as he hung hundreds of feet above the streets of the plaza. The rain beat fiercely against his body, gluing the drenched fabric of his shirt and trousers to the muscles beneath. Alex began his slow climb downward. The light nylon ladder hung so close to the side of the building that he had trouble getting and keeping a toehold on the narrow rungs. His shoes slipped again and again, dropping his body down, jerking his hands and arms painfully as they strained to hold him. The rough stone surface down which he scaled scraped his knuckles raw as he continued on, precarious step after step, slipping, saving himself, gaining another toehold and lowering himself down rung after rung.

A maddened gust of wind caught his bulk and swung him and the ladder far out and away from the building, twisting him around. His feet slipped completely free, and he held on desperately only with his hands as the wind flung him back viciously against the wall. Alex's head cracked hard into the stone. Stunned, he fought numbly to hold on and regain his foothold. That done, he rested, leaning his aching head against one arm. "Come on, big guy," he mumbled to his Creator, "give me a break. I'm doing this for mankind, remember?" In answer, the wind seemed to abate a little. "Thanks," he said, a wild thought flashing through his mind. Could someone up there really have heard and moved to aid him? Smiling to himself, he again began the treacherous descent, passing one dark office window after another, pausing to stand and rest on each sill before lowering himself down to the next slippery rung.

At last Alex felt the branches of the rhododendrons brush against his legs, and, sighing with relief, he dropped free of the ladder into the mud of the terrace garden. Glass from the broken window crunched under his feet. Flattening himself against the wall, he looked about him, studying the darkness in his old office. Could someone be sitting in there watching him? Had the shattering glass alerted a guard? There was only one way to find out. Crouching, Alexander Kidd ran forward to the sundial that stood exposed at the opposite end of the terrace.

The bronze sculpture that Judith had created years before rested on a stone pedestal nearly three feet tall. An outline of a simple rowboat rose up from the center of the circular face of the dial with Roman numerals etched around its rim. Standing eight inches high in the center of the boat, the legendary boatman, Charon, strained against the pole in his hands, pushing it down into the bed of the river Acheron to ferry his human cargo into Hades. The sinewy arms and legs of the grim figure extended from the shroud it wore. The pole reached from the watery surface of the dial at a forty-five-degree angle to a point above the head of the boatman, the shadow it cast across the numerals on the dial pointing to the time as the sun moved across the sky. In the drenching rain, Alex had no trouble visualizing the mythical hell in which the little figure dwelled.

Crouching at the base of the sundial, he pulled a small wrench from his pocket and quickly loosened one of the two bolts that held the bronze dial to its base from beneath. The bolt he twisted was designed to come free. The other, directly across from it, was fixed into position and acted as a pivot around which the dial swiveled to expose the plaque beneath that Kidd had personally built into the base. The bolt came free and Alex swung the top open and peered in.

"Shit," he mumbled. The beam of his small penlight confirmed what he had feared from the beginning. The metal plaque upon which he had engraved two codes—one to move Charon II, the other to trigger the Cerberus circuits—lay mutilated. All the numbers had been gouged and scraped away. It was his final proof that the plane crashes in the Mediterranean were not accidental, that the continued manufacture of the Cerberus circuit was not a mistake, that Paul Carmody and Simon Felton had been murdered by someone, some group dedicated to the destruction of the U.S. To Alex everything was indisputable. To the world, he had not one shred of proof, not a leg to stand on.

But his course of action was clear. He must now go to Tangier to retrieve the set of code numbers hidden there. That done, he would return to the States and blow that damn satellite out of the sky. Swiveling the dial back into position, Alex replaced the bolt, hopeful that no one would be the wiser about his failed assault on the garden terrace. The broken glass could be explained by a fault in the office window that, after many years, had finally capitulated to the suction caused by the turbulent winds of the storm. Crossing the lawn, Alexander Kidd found the narrow ladder. His eyes followed its length up the ten stories. With a resigned sigh, he grabbed hold of it and took the first step upward. Through the dark, rain-filled night, the window above looked a hundred miles away.

By the time Kidd pulled himself over the windowsill into the offices of Craft, Hassler, Hennes, and White, he had little energy left. Stripping off his wet clothes, he fell exhausted on the couch in the reception room of the law firm. The radio alarm in Hennes' office woke him with a start several hours later. Glancing at his watch, he tuned the radio to the eight o'clock news, and as he shaved and slipped into his still damp clothes, he listened to the commentator drone on about the worsening crisis in the Middle East. They're always having crises there, he thought abstractedly, his mind centered only on the greater crisis his own country faced if he did not get to the Tangier codes fast.

The imperative nature of his mission was further emphasized when the network anchorman announced the suicide of Paul Carmody, "one of the Air Force's most respected generals." Seemingly endless speculation about the reasons for Carmody's action followed. They ranged from disappointment over his career path within the military establishment to domestic problems. Shaking his head in disgust, Alex repacked the nylon ladder. He would have blasted any one of his newsmen or editors for engaging in this type of sensationalism. "Report the news, goddamn it," he mumbled under his breath, "don't make it."

Straightening up, Kidd looked out the broken window at the beautiful, cloudless sky. The streets of the plaza below were filled with men and women scurrying to their offices. The lobby of the building would now be open to him, his passage masked by the arrival of the day's work force. Scribbling a brief note of apology to Hennes, he let himself out of the law offices and walked quickly to the elevators. His first stop would be his apartment at the Dakota to pick up his passport, and then to Kennedy International Airport to grab the first flight to Europe.

"Good morning, Mr. Kidd," the porter behind the reception desk of the Dakota said. "You're a bit out of shape, sir, aren't you?" The eyes of the elderly, white-haired Irishman roved over Kidd's disheveled clothing.

"Got caught in the rain last night, Tim, that's all." He started to hurry past when the porter's words brought him up short.

"A lot of people here looking for you yesterday."

"Oh?" Kidd turned back. "Who?"

"Wouldn't say, sir."

"What did they look like?"

"Well, let's see." The old man rubbed his chin. "One group—two men they were—came in the morning. Average-looking types, you know. Nothing out of the ordinary. They kept coming back on and off all day. Came in only a few minutes ago. I let them wait upstairs on the landing outside your door."

Government men, Kidd thought, wanting to talk to him about Carmody's death. "Nothing out of the ordinary" was a perfect description for government agents. "And the others?" he pressed.

"Only just one, sir. Wouldn't leave no name. Tried to sneak by me, he did, but I called him right back." The Irishman shook his head. "Not very nice that one, not like the other two gentlemen. Had mean eyes. Cold and mean they were."

"When did he show up, Tim?"

"Late afternoon, I think it was. Never came back after I caught him trying to sneak in."

Alex thought for a moment and then turned on his heels.

"Hey, sir, aren't you going—"

"Thought I'd cut through the courtyard, Tim," Alex replied as he walked from the small reception room down several steps to the large iron gate under the main entrance arch that led into the spacious interior courtyard of the old building. "Buzz me through, will you?"

The old man pushed the button beside his desk to release the lock. "Cut through the courtyard," the porter mumbled to himself. "As it seems to me, that's taking the long way around." Ah well, there's no accounting for the whims of these rich folks, he mused. Always doing crazy things, they are.

Kidd pushed open the entrance door to the stairwell and elevator diagonally across the courtyard from the one leading to his and Judith's apartment. The elevator rose with agonizing slowness to the top floor where a narrow corridor ran along all four sides of the great building to connect the small rooms once assigned to the servants of those occupying the lavish suites below. Moving silently along the passage, he came to the top landing of his stairwell. Peering down cautiously, he saw the backs of the two government agents leaning against the railing on the fourth floor. He had no time to get mixed up with the FBI. Kidd continued on, following the passage to the next stairwell that would take him down to the rear door of his apartment. Descending quickly, he pressed his ear to the kitchen door and then inserted his key into the lock. Turning it slowly, he gently lifted the dead bolt and edged the door open. The sooner he got in and out, the better. Having government agents looking for you was one thing, but strangers with "cold, mean eyes" were another. He thought of Simon Felton and Paul Carmody. Had men with eyes like that tracked them down?

Slipping into the kitchen, Alex stood listening for the slightest sound. Only the hum of the refrigerator to his left intruded on the silence. Walking as quickly and quietly as possible, he entered his study, cursing himself for insisting on having so few carpets in the place. Going directly to his desk, Alex pulled out a bundle of various sized and shaped documents from the upper right-hand drawer. He extracted his passport and a letter of credit and crammed them into his inside jacket pocket. Retracing his steps through the silent apartment, Alex was halfway across the kitchen when a quiet voice stopped him dead in his tracks.

"Good morning, Mr. Kidd."

Whirling around, Alex stared into the eyes of the man leaning almost casually against the sink. Then he looked down at the gun in his hand. It had a very large silencer attached to it.

"I was afraid we might miss you," Robert Frankel said, an innocent smile playing across his face. "Won't you sit down? I have a brief phone call to make."

Alex slowly lowered himself into one of the chairs at the kitchen table as the other moved across the room to the wall phone. Without taking his eyes from Alexander Kidd, he removed the receiver and punched the buttons with one hand. Alex could only hear the sound of the voice who answered.

"I've got him," Frankel said flatly. "Plan one or two?" He waited for the answer and replaced the receiver. "Plan two," he said to Alex. "You've bought yourself some time. Would you like a cup of coffee while we wait?" Baron Androssy's henchman nodded pleasantly to the Mr. Coffee machine on the nearby counter. Hesitantly, Alex stood and reached for the coffee can next to it as various alternatives for escape whirled through his mind.

"Oh, and Mr. Kidd, one sound from you and you're dead and I'm out the door. Is that clear?"

"Very," the ex-president of KWEN replied.

CHAPTER 20

"May I ask where we're going?"

Frankel opened the taxi door for Alex. The gun he held in his jacket pocket assured Kidd's cooperation.

Alexander Kidd slid across the seat to make room for his traveling companion. "I repeat, where—"

"To see someone who very much wants to meet you," the other replied archly, cutting off his question as he slammed the cab door with a finality Alex did not like. He also did not like the fact that the driver pulled away from the Dakota without waiting for directions, seeming to know their destination without orders. Obviously he would be no ally in any escape attempt he might contemplate. And indeed he would not. Victor Kamera made a U-turn on Seventy-second Street and headed down Central Park West toward the entrance to the park.

"And who," Alex pressed, "is the someone who wants to meet me?"

"You'll know soon enough." Robert Frankel did not feel comfortable with this man. Like his employer, Alexander Kidd had an imposing presence that put him on the defensive even though it was *he* who held the gun. He did not trust him.

"Lovely day for a drive through the park," Alex commented sarcastically. From the corner of his eye, he saw Frankel slowly pull the gun from his pocket and hold it ready. Kidd leaned back into the seat and folded both his hands in his lap in plain view of his captor. No use taking chances with some trigger-happy, hopped-up freak, he thought.

Exiting the park at Sixty-fifth Street, Victor Kamera continued east to York Avenue. "Well, your mysterious friend certainly lives in the high-rent district," Kidd quipped as the cab turned south toward Sutton Place. The newsman in him was consumed by curiosity, pushing aside temporarily his concerns for his life. This was no ordinary thug they were taking him to. He was, as the media would say, Mr. Big. A wave of excitement mixed with apprehension swept through Alex as the taxi pulled up before one of the most elegant town houses on the block.

"Okay, *Mr.* Kidd," Frankel said coldly, emphasizing the mister, "out." He made a pretense of paying the driver and, opening the door, slid out. The gun was back in his pocket but still pointed at his captive's head as he stood holding the door for Alex with a broad smile for the benefit of any onlookers. Nodding his head, Frankel indicated the door of the town house. Alexander Kidd walked to it and waited as the other inserted his key, unlocked it, and pushed it open. Feeling the barrel of the gun prodding him forward, Alex enter the house.

Frankel's smile dissolved. "Over there," he said softly, indicating an impressive set of double doors across the marble foyer of the mansion. Crossing together, Frankel knocked. "Remember, *Mr.* Kidd"—again he emphasized the mister—"I am a very good shot and I have very quick reflexes."

"I'll keep that in mind," Alex commented with a casual tone that rankled the younger man.

At Frankel's knock, Baron Miklos Androssy looked up from the papers spread across his desk and stared at the doors of the study. With the exception of his two henchmen, the house was completely empty. The servants had been quickly given the morning off, Edith and his favorite daughter Katherina had been sent on a shopping spree to be followed by luncheon at La Cote Basque. He knew he was taking a chance on bringing Kidd here before having him killed, but he wanted to find out exactly how much his opponent and his friends had learned about him and his connections with the Acheron affair and Russia.

"Come," he called. The doors opened and his reluctant guest walked in followed closely by Robert Frankel. Rising, the baron moved around his desk and toward them with an open smile. "Mr. Kidd," he said graciously, extending his hand, "it is indeed a pleasure to meet you. I am—"

"Baron Androssy," Alex interrupted, instantly matching the face to the many newspaper photos he had seen. "A pleasure to meet you"—he took the other's hand—"out in the open for a change."

The baron's smile did not falter, but Kidd felt the brief hesitation of his enemy's hand in his. So, Androssy thought, you are taking the offensive. We shall see just how long you can hold up your bluff. The game of life and death had begun.

"Please," the baron smiled, indicating a comfortable chair before his desk. He walked behind the desk and seated himself, leaning back confidently. "Robert," he said to Frankel as he opened the middle drawer and placed a gun on the blotter before him, "you can leave us. I am sure our guest will not cause me the embarrassment of having to use this macabre little thing." He patted the shiny black weapon disdainfully and looked back at Alex. "A necessary precaution, Mr. Kidd, for one in my position."

"And a very interesting position in which to be," Alex answered, noting Frankel's exit through the sliding panel that must have some sort of a peephole in it. "A Russian agent who is also owner of an American television network." The charge was unsubstantiated and based solely on supposition, but the other's reaction could prove him right or wrong. He had used this technique on interview shows in the past.

"You do not mince words, do you?" Androssy answered pleasantly, masking his concern over the Russian connection. How much *do* they know, he wondered, and how many of them are privy to that information?

"In *my* current position," Alex countered, "there is little reason not to mince words."

"I assume your information comes from Miss Bannister?" he asked, trying to trace the source. "We met briefly in Zurich."

It was Alex's turn to be surprised. He had not spoken with Sandra for several days. Her involvement concerned him. Kidd smiled. "No, from Rico Montagna." He cast another fly.

"Impossi—" Baron Androssy caught himself and then smiled. "You are *very* good, Mr. Kidd, very good indeed. But why do we bother to spar. As you obviously know, Mr. Montagna was killed before he could talk to anyone." Again Alex had to hide his surprise at this new blow. "Why do we not speak openly? We need have no secrets from each other."

"*You* need not," Alex retorted wryly. "Any secret you share with me will soon be a secret again. I assume you plan to kill me in the very near future." He looked at the gun. "I have an idea. Why not give me that little toy of yours and then I'll start sharing secrets."

Androssy laughed. "I enjoy you, Mr. Kidd. I knew I would."

"I'm glad I've been able to brighten your morning." He continued without pause. "Did you take over KWEN just to get your hands on Charon Two?"

The baron nodded silently.

"You killed Tom Petterson, my engineer?"

Again he nodded, the smile still there. "Not personally."

"Good," Kidd snapped sarcastically, "then we can be friends."

"Any other questions?" Androssy asked. "We might as well clear the air."

"Why did you bring down those planes in the Mediterranean?"

"A little test," the other replied.

"*Test?* A little *test*?" Alexander Kidd exploded. "You killed twenty-seven American Navy men and one hundred and twenty-three innocent men, women, and children, and you call it a little *test*?" He gripped the arms of his chair, the knuckles of his hands white with his rage.

Androssy took back control of the conversation. "Your satellite is most effective," he said without emotion. "My compliments to you and Dr. Felton. But tell me, why did you do it? What did Warren really hope to accomplish?"

"Peace. Stability in an unstable area," Kidd spat out, thinking of his dead friend. "Words quite alien to you and your bosses in the Kremlin."

"How disappointing," Androssy commented. "I had hoped for something more interesting than that."

"Such as?"

"Control of the oil fields," the baron answered as he mused over the various possible motivations of the late President, "Control over Israel. Blackmail."

"Is that what you and *your* friends have in mind?" Kidd asked.

Miklos Androssy looked at him for some time before nodding his head. "But on a much more grand scale."

"Oh, I'm sure of that." His sarcasm was not lost on the baron.

"First of all, Mr. Kidd, as one businessman to another, let me make it perfectly clear that *I*, not the Soviet Union, control Charon Two."

"What's the difference?" Alex protested rationally. "You're one of them."

"Wrong," Androssy retorted sharply and proudly. "I am *me*! And as long as they want control of that satellite, *I* control them."

Alexander Kidd had fought with many ruthless men on his rise to the top of his profession, met and dealt with corrupt, power-crazed politicians, but this man was in another league. He was taking on the whole fucking Soviet Union single-handed. He stared at Androssy, drank in the absolute, chilling power that seemed to permeate the air about him. "So you are you," he said to goad the other, "a great and powerful man. And what grand-scale plan do you have for Charon Two?''

Androssy smiled, his vision of the future in his mind. ''In permanent orbit over the Soviet Union, your satellite will assure Russia immunity from American-made missiles with their nuclear warheads. None will ever find its target, no aircraft carrying nuclear bombs, no submarine, nothing will be able to inflict strategic damage.'' He chuckled. ''Nor will the weapons of your allies. Due to the manufacturing efficiencies my people introduced into Felton Electronics, that company has been exporting Dr. Felton's ingenious little chip within the competitively priced 120044 guidance circuit to most of your country's friends. It now lies in their home-brewed weapons.''

''So what? No one plans to attack Russia.'' It was a stupid statement and Alex knew it. But he wanted to buy time, time to find a way out of the deadly mess he was in, and the best way to get it was through the other man's vanity.

''Come, come, Mr. Kidd,'' Androssy chided. ''I credited you with more imagination. Of course you don't plan to attack the Soviet Union. But we plan to dominate you. And if the United States and NATO were forced to dismantle their nuclear arsenal, they would be helpless to resist domination.''

''That's where your blackmail comes in?''

''Exactly. Get rid of your arms or Russia systematically destroys one of your great cities after another. And you and your allies, Mr. Kidd, could not retaliate, not with Charon Two sitting high above Moscow.''

''No one would ever believe you,'' Alex challenged.

''My friends in the Kremlin do,'' Androssy smiled. ''I gave them proof.''

''Your little Mediterranean test?''

The baron nodded.

''Well, the Americans won't believe it. Nor will our allies. What do you plan to do, invite us to send over a missile and then zap it with Charon?''

"The idea had occurred to us, but then we thought it not dramatic enough. No, Mr. Kidd, we want to provide the world with a much more graphic demonstration of what resistance to our simple request will mean to their populations. A demonstration under conditions of war."

"And may I ask where you plan to drop the first bomb?" Alex was finding it increasingly difficult to control himself. He itched to smash the smug grin off the face of the man sitting across the desk from him.

"Oh, much too crass. No nuclear bombs, Mr. Kidd, and not a single Russian soldier will be involved." He enjoyed the puzzled expression on Kidd's face. "Our Arab friends will supply the proof of the Soviet Union's power." Alex could not hide his surprise. His expression encouraged Miklos Androssy to boast of the plan in which he had so much pride. "On September twenty-second, just before sunrise, a joint Arab attack will be launched against Israel from all sides. With Charon Two overhead beaming down its destructive little messages, not one Zionist plane will get far off the ground, and few, if any, of their missiles will reach their destination." The date burned into Alexander Kidd's brain. It was only eight days away. "It is too bad that your President Warren did not live to see his plan actually put into effect in the Middle East."

Remembering Paul Carmody's statements on the confusion in the area, Kidd shook his head. "It will never work, Androssy. Your Arab pals are busy cutting each other's throats right now. How do you expect them to get together and organize in a few days?"

The baron's smile widened. "Yes, clever, are they not? It was their own idea to simulate border skirmishes to throw off Israeli intelligence. You may rest assured, Mr. Kidd, that their cooperation will be absolute." He shrugged. "At least until they have completely annihilated the Jews. Then I am sure the seven tribes will be back at each other's throats as before. But then who will care? They will have served their purpose."

"Supplied your proof," Alex volunteered.

"Precisely," the other replied. "And knowing the passions of the area, the massacre will be most impressive. They will seek vengeance for the Sabra and Shatila camps in Beirut. Men, women, even little children." He sighed, but the smile remained. "It will not be a pretty sight, but it most certainly will be an effective one."

Alex's stomach felt cold and empty. Judith's parents, Jacob and Rosalind Singer were living just outside of Tel Aviv. When they were last together, he remembered Judith speaking of plans to visit them—Mark too. "And you?" he asked. "What do you get out of all this?"

"Does that really interest you, Mr. Kidd?"

"Curiosity, that's all," Alex replied with apparent casualness, but as he continued, his voice became noticeably harder. "A man has to have some pretty big incentives for murdering hundreds, thousands of people. What are yours, Androssy?"

Again the baron shrugged as if to demean any potential rewards. "Considerable financial gain—and power. Tell me," he asked, switching the topic of conversation, "where is the second transmitter?"

"I beg your pardon?" Alex replied naively.

Androssy replied patiently. "The transmitter you planned to use to control Charon Two after moving it to the Middle East."

"I don't know what you're talking about." Alex stared the baron directly in the eyes.

"Really, Mr. Kidd, you must not take me for a fool." Picking up his gun, Androssy rose and walked to a large antique globe of the world. He spun it to the Middle East. The center of that region fell along the latitude of forty degrees east. "I am very aware of exactly how far that satellite can travel before losing contact with a ground station. You and your friends could not possibly control it from New York if it were in orbit over this area." The two men looked at each other in silence for a moment. "On your yacht?" Androssy prodded.

"I thought you had everything worked out," Alex

replied, admitting to the obvious existence of a second transmitter. "Why are you so interested in my little radio?"

"Like you," Androssy said lightly, "just curious. I have already duplicated the KWEN transmitter on one of the islands off the Spanish coast. I do not need yours." He smiled. "The yacht?" His finger touched the globe at the English Channel.

"Why not?" Alex answered with a shrug. "It's as good a place as any." Androssy had obviously decided that the boat was the hiding place of the transmitter, so why disabuse him of the idea? "A moving target is harder to find."

"And destroy," the baron agreed smugly.

It was only then that Alexander Kidd realized the danger into which he had just plunged the crew of the *Privateer*. Again his eyes swept the baron's library and the grounds outside for a means of escape. The overweight blond woman he had seen earlier in the garden had vanished. "You know you don't stand a chance in hell of getting away with it," he said.

"Oh? And why is that?" Miklos Androssy asked.

"Because in order for it to work, you and only you must have the codes to control Charon Two."

"Granted," the baron confirmed.

"And," Alex continued, "the U.S. government can't know about the satellite and destroy it before it leaves."

"Are you suggesting that your government does know about Charon Two and has the codes?" Androssy asked in a bemused tone.

"Yes."

"Mr. Kidd," the baron said, shaking his head, "lies. All lies. You and your late friends Megaera and Tisiphone never got the chance to tell anyone else about Acheron, Charon, and Cerberus. We have listened in on every conversation you have had since we first learned of your connection to the Acheron Plot. Your apartment in New York, hotel rooms, the Porsche in London?" Smiling, he went on. Androssy enjoyed the discomfort of his antagonist. "The red phones in your, Felton's and Carmody's homes and offices? We even know the quiet whisperings of your lovemaking, Mr. Kidd. Of everything, those, perhaps, brought us the most amusement."

Angered almost beyond endurance, Alex struggled to control his temper. "Microphones can record voices, Androssy, but not from public phones, neighbors' phones. And can they record the words from the banging of a typewriter? Can they record the sound of a stamp being pressed onto an envelope?" He stopped and watched for the other's reaction.

The smile left the baron's face. "And when did you put this stamp on an envelope?"

"This morning."

Androssy stood looking at him for a moment and then burst out laughing. "Oh, Mr. Kidd, you disappoint me. It is all so childish. You and I know there is no letter containing the codes. If there were, then why did you expend so much energy earlier this morning scaling ten floors down to look for them? Yes," he said, nodding, "your athletic endeavors were captured on videotape. You, Mr. Kidd, do not know the codes anymore than your government does. And," he continued, "we both know you have no physical proof that they or Warren's scheme ever existed. Carmody's records are gone as well as Felton's. Your playmates are dead. In this, you stand alone."

Miklos Androssy moved back to his desk. "Thank you, Mr. Kidd, I have enjoyed our conversation. You have told me all I needed to learn." He pressed a button. Almost immediately the panel in the bookcase swung open and his personal secretary stepped into the room. "Robert, Mr. Kidd will be leaving us now."

"Just like that, Androssy," Alex asked, realizing the finality of the other's words. "You push a little button and poof, Alexander Kidd ceases to exist? Is that how it was with Simon and Paul?"

"Precisely," the baron answered, all humor gone from his voice. He raised the gun and pointed it directly at Alex's face less than three feet away. His finger tightened on the trigger, and then relaxed. "Robert," Androssy said, stepping back, "Mr. Kidd is looking very flushed. Do you think it could be his heart?"

Frankel moved forward. Alex looked between the two men, not knowing from which side the attack would come. The younger man withdrew a thin tube from his pocket and was about to thrust it in Alex's face when the doors to the library burst open.

Startled, Androssy quickly hid the gun behind his back, and Frankel slipped the metal tube into his pocket. Their actions did not go unnoticed by Alexander Kidd. "Oh, dear," Edith Androssy exclaimed in embarrassment, "I didn't know you had company, Mickey." She began to back from the room.

Quickly sizing up the situation, Alex moved toward the woman as Frankel tried to insert himself between them. Kidd brushed his restraining hand gently but firmly aside. "Baroness Androssy," he said charmingly as he took her hand and brought it to his lips, "what a pleasant and welcome surprise." As he spoke, he maneuvered Edith around so that she stood between him and the others.

Looking over her shoulder at the frown on her husband's face, she apologized for her presence. "Katty met some of her friends and they went off together, so I came home. I really didn't need anything anyway." She turned back to Alex, who still held her hand.

"I am Alexander Kidd. What lovely flowers," he purred, looking at the blooms she held in her left hand.

"Why, thank you, Mr. Kidd, I—"

"Mr. Kidd and Robert are leaving, my dear," Androssy said coldly. "We must not detain—"

"And what a beautiful garden you have, Baroness," Kidd broke in desperately. "I could not help admiring it earlier through the window. You must be a veritable magician."

"Why—why, thank you," Edith Androssy stammered, her face flushed from his compliment.

"Would you do me the honor of a brief tour before I go?"

He felt the glare of the baron's eyes burning into him. "I believe I saw some cosmos?"

"Oh, dear me, no," she replied, flattered by his interest. "They're much too fragile for the river winds." Kidd's mind fastened on the word "river." "Perhaps you saw—"

"Dear," Androssy interrupted, "I must insist. Mr. Kidd and Robert have a very important meeting to attend. They have no time. Robert, please—"

"Now, *I* must insist," Alex countered. "I may make quite a scene if you don't let me inspect those gardens with your lovely wife." The pleasant tone in his voice overlaid the threat both Androssy and Frankel heard beneath it. "My arm, Baroness?"

Alex extended his arm to the somewhat confused woman who could not refuse. She looked questioningly at her husband's dark face as she moved into the hall toward the garden door. It was his only chance—Kidd knew it. But just how far could he push Androssy and his henchman in the game called "Don't let your wife know what a bastard you really are" before a trigger was squeezed, a needle jabbed? Like Simon several days before, the hair on the back of Alexander Kidd's neck tingled, waiting for the explosion. The baron followed along behind as Frankel dashed to the front door and motioned frantically to Victor Kamera, who sat waiting in the cab at the curb.

Emerging into the heat of the day, Alex and Edith Androssy began a leisurely stroll along the luxurious flower borders with the baron only two steps in the rear, his eyes and ears alert to any sudden move or compromising statement Kidd might make. As Edith gushed effusively over one exotic plant, one double bloom, one feathery leaf after another, Alex's thoughts were far from flora. From the corners of his eyes, he could see Frankel and the burly Kamera moving slowly behind the shrubs and trees on either side, keeping pace with them. They effectively cut off any escape he might try to make through the grounds and homes neighboring the Androssy mansion and garden.

". . . and there is no other plant quite like it anywhere in the world," Edith said, pausing before a black lily.

"How can you be sure?" Alex asked.

"I bred it right here in New York," she answered. "The gardener and I."

"I once developed a one-of-a-kind plant," Kidd said. "Called it Charon." He glanced at the baron with a faint smile.

"What a strange name," Edith commented.

"It was a very delicate plant. Only I knew how to feed it to keep it alive."

"Really? Does it need some sort of special fertilizer?"

"Very special. I had the formula written down, and then I lost it." He felt Androssy's eyes boring into him as he spoke. "Actually, someone stole it from me."

"Oh, what a terrible thing to do," she said, shaking her head in dismay. "Why on earth would anyone do something like that?"

"Beats me," Alex replied, taking her arm and moving farther along the border toward the foot of the garden. "But it's not really serious; I have the formula written down somewhere else."

"That's very interesting, Mr. Kidd," the baron commented with apparent casualness. "Then all you have to do is go and get it." He glanced reassuringly at the half-hidden figure of Victor Kamera nearby. Frankel stood alone off to one side, his hand in his jacket pocket.

"Oh, I will, believe me." They had come to the end of the garden, and Alex leaned against the iron fence. The murky water of the East River flowed swiftly by nearly fifty feet below them. "It's a tricky formula, Baroness," he continued, "and so is my plant. Both very complex and very tricky indeed." He looked Androssy square in the eye. "If I alter its diet just a fraction, it will die"—he snapped his fingers—"poof, just like that."

"How extraordinary," Edith Androssy said. "I should like to see it one day."

Still looking at Androssy, Kidd replied, "I'm afraid you

won't be able to. You see, I intend to alter its diet." He saw the question in Androssy's eyes, saw them narrow in speculation over his threat. Alex turned to his wife again. "And when it's dead, the man who stole the formula will have done it all in vain. I'll bet he'll even be in for a lot of trouble." Edith Androssy was puzzled by his conversation. It made no sense to her, this talk about killing plants and strange formulas. Alex extended his arm once more. "Shall we go?"

She reached out for it, and her husband started to turn. In that brief instant Edith's calm and sheltered life erupted into confused pandemonium. Alex suddenly grasped the top of the iron fence and vaulted himself up and over. She screamed. Her husband called out as he lunged for Kidd knocking Edith to the ground. Victor, her chauffeur, plunged from the nearby growth and raced past her, and Frankel ran forward waving something—God, it was a gun.

"Go to the house," Androssy shouted at her.

"But he—"

"To the house, damn it."

Cowering before Androssy's outburst, Edith pulled herself up and fled the length of the garden in terror. Kamera mounted the fence. All three men stared down into the polluted gray water, their eyes searching for the head they knew must soon bob up. "Go after him," the baron ordered. The burly chauffeur launched himself into a clumsy dive, splashing into the water below. "Can you get him from here, Robert?"

"I think so," the other replied, checking the tightness of the silencer on his gun. "Where the hell is that bastard?"

"Damn, damn, damn," Androssy muttered as he beat his fist impatiently against the iron. "Damn that man." Below him Victor Kamera surfaced and, turning his head around and around, treaded water as the current carried him downriver. Kidd's last words ran through Miklos Androssy's brain: "I intend to alter its diet." Of course, he must have the codes hidden with the other transmitter outside the United States; he would not have bothered to climb ten

stories down the side of the KWEN building if it were in
this country. And what of his boast that he could use the
codes to destroy Charon II? Androssy had never considered
the possibility that the satellite could self-destruct. It was
not logical. Why would Warren have wanted the option of
destroying it? It made no sense to him. Was it another Kidd
bluff? He could not take the chance.

Androssy's entire master plan and that of the Soviet
Union now depended on finding and killing Alexander Kidd
before he got to those second codes. The two men were in a
race. Leaning far out, he searched the water one last time
and then turned. "Come, Robert, leave him to Victor. We
have work to do. You are going to Portsmouth. I want you
to go over every inch of Kidd's yacht. I must meet with
Savich. Unfortunately, I need all of his men now."

With lungs ready to burst, Alex finally surfaced among
the pilings supporting the FDR Drive; they ran above and
along the side of the river at that point. Holding on to the
rough, oily wood against the swift current, he lay low and
watched as Victor Kamera swam toward the pilings and
began to move between them. Alex took another deep
breath and pulled himself down nearly ten feet beneath the
surface. He looked up at the rays of sunlight glittering down
through the dirty water. It seemed hours before he saw the
dark shape of the chauffeur pass above him. Gritting his
teeth, Alex waited as long as he could before coming up for
air. He kept the piling between him and the killer. When he
peered around it, he saw Kamera a good forty yards
downriver. Wouldn't do to mix with that one, he thought.
He has the weight on me, not to mention muscles that could
crush an ox.

Once Androssy's man was lost from sight, Alexander
Kidd let go of the piling and began to look for some way up
and out of the foul water. He was a strong swimmer, but
handicapped by clothing it took him nearly twenty minutes
of struggling along the water's edge before he came upon a
primitive ladder made of horizontal boards nailed to a

piling, obviously the work of slum children who had swum in the polluted river many hot summers ago. He gingerly pulled himself up the unsteady and rotting contraption, thanking God that his son, Mark, had never had to face poverty while growing up. "Shit!" A board tore loose in his hand; Alex caught himself before falling back into the river. A few more feet up and he pulled himself over the edge of a derelict pier and sat in a pool of water, looking at himself.

"You're a wreck, Kidd," he mumbled as he tugged off his sodden suit jacket and went through its pockets. He sighed with relief. His limp passport, letter of credit, and wallet containing credit cards and considerable cash had all made it through the dive from Androssy's garden. So too had his watch. It was nearly eleven in the morning.

Several taxis passed before one deigned to stop for the dripping passenger. "Hey, man," the youthful driver said dreamily, "only Jesus kin walk on water. You jus' ain't got 'nough religion." The cab smelled of marijuana.

"Cool it, mac," Alex retorted. "You just worry about getting me to Brooks Brothers, three forty-six Madison. I'll worry about my ties with the Almighty."

"Jive, jive, jive," the cabbie said, rolling his eyes, and swung into a sharp turn with a screech of tires.

Alexander Kidd made quite a sensation as he pushed through the doors into the hallowed, dark-paneled halls of the respected gentlemen's clothing store. Over the years it had probably outfitted more potential Presidents and industrial giants during their climb to fame than any other establishment of its type. Shoppers turned from the glass-topped counters supporting neat rows of ties, shirts, and sweaters to stare at the man striding confidently down the center aisle, his hair plastered wet across his forehead, his suit a sodden mass of clinging cotton. Alex's shoes left small, moist spots on the marble floor as he walked. Unfazed by the attention, Kidd snapped his fingers at one of the clerks. "Franklin, I need you," he said, and turned right toward the elevator.

Reacting to his customer with a courteous but aloof bow,

the tall young man picked up his order book and hurried after Alexander Kidd.

Less then an hour later, Alex stood immaculately attired in the manager's office, busily stuffing additional clothing into a small carry-on flight bag. Although his new, off-the-rack suit did not have quite the cut and sartorial elegance of his costly custom-tailored clothes that now lay in a damp pile in the corner, only the most discerning would have known Alexander Kidd had gone slumming.

Returning to his apartment at the Dakota was out of the question. And so, taking full command of the manager's office, Kidd dismissed its owner and the clerk while picking up the phone. He had two vital calls to put through before jumping into a cab for the airport. First, he called Sandra Bannister at the Codogan Square Flat. He had to warn her that the gloves were off and that she stood smack in the middle of a slugfest. No answer. Damn, he thought, it was too early, not yet five in the afternoon in London. His call to the *Privateer* went through with little problem.

"Hal, Alex here."

"Where in the hell have you been, Captain?" Kidd's second in command shouted over the ship-to-shore line.

"New York."

"You're going to be with us for the Whitbread?"

"Hal, listen carefully," Alex ordered. No one could mistake the seriousness in his voice. "I want you and all the crew to sleep ashore when the *Privateer* is in port. Not even a guard left aboard. Is that clear?"

"Clear, Alex, but it's madness. Portsmouth is swarming with rip-off artists. We could lose every piece of electronic equipment we've got."

"Hal, that's an order. No one stays aboard the *Privateer* while she's in port."

"May I ask why?" Hal Trevane's voice betrayed his anger.

Alexander Kidd thought for a moment. "Someone wants to find out exactly what we're carrying on the yacht. I want him to know we've got nothing out of the ordinary. If one of the crew gets in his way, he could get hurt. It's that simple. Understand?"

"Understand," Trevane replied. "I just hope your mysterious friend doesn't walk off with something we need for the race."

"Don't worry, he won't."

"When will we see you?"

Alex paused. He hadn't had time to complete all his plans. "Don't know. I'll call you tomorrow, Hal. Have you seen Sandy?"

"She was down yesterday."

"How was she?"

This time it was Trevane's turn to pause. "Not sure, Alex. She seemed nervous, not the same old Sandy."

Alex frowned. "Did she say anything?"

"She's working on a story of some sort. I think she's scared. Do you know what it is?"

"No." Alex's denial sounded almost like a protest, a protest against the concern he felt for her. He took a chance that the *Privateer*'s communications systems had not been compromised by the KGB. "Look, Hal, I've been trying to reach her. Will you keep calling the Codogan Square Flat until you get through and tell Sandy to check into the Connaught or Claridge's and stay there until I contact her? If she puts up an argument, just say it's orders."

"Sure, Alex." Hal Trevane thought a moment and then asked, "A storm brewing?"

"You might say."

"Serious?"

"I've got to go now," Alex said, evading the question.

"Alex, we've got a right to know," Trevane persisted. Kidd sighed. "It's a typhoon, a real lollipaloozer."

"Anything we should do over here?"

"No, just act normal," Alex replied. "And," he emphasized, "stay off the *Privateer* when you're in Portsmouth. You'll be in the Whitbread in two days, safely out of the way. Don't worry."

"Then you won't be joining us?"

"No, Hal, I'm afraid not. I've got something important I have to do. You're the skipper. I'll call tomorrow."

Slowly lowering the receiver, Alexander Kidd looked absently down at the congested traffic in the street below. His mind raised and rejected the alternatives open to him. Whatever he did, he would have to do it quickly before Androssy and his Russian-backed network moved to stop him. Picking up his flight bag, Alex headed for the door. The first thing he had to do was get out of the country, and that might not be so easy.

"We must stop him before he leaves the country," Miklos Androssy said softly out of the corner of his mouth to Vladimir Savich as the two stood near each other ostensibly looking at the same painting of Monet's water lilies hanging in the Museum of Modern Art.

"So it is 'we' now," Savich replied sarcastically, looking about to assure himself no one was nearby. "Has something gone wrong?"

"Absolutely not," the baron scoffed.

"When I insisted upon removing him earlier, you refused. Why is Kidd's immediate liquidation suddenly so vital to the welfare of my country?"

"I had to know everything surrounding the satellite and its operation, had to be sure no one else knew of its interesting capabilities."

"And?" the other asked.

"Now I am sure." Androssy glanced about him at the few visitors in the gallery. "He has linked me to the Center. Unfortunately, his people saw me with Ryabov in Zurich."

"The Italian was killed."

"There was another."

"You plan to kill him?"

"Her," Androssy corrected. "She and Kidd could cause me and the Center considerable embarrassment. I am sure the sensationalistic American media would enjoy a scandal of this magnitude. You have killed people for far less reason, Vladimir Savich," he ended coolly.

"I will send agents to the airport. London, you said?"

Again Androssy nodded. In his mind Kidd would go for the *Privateer* where the baron was sure the other had hidden his second transmitter and, if he were not bluffing, the second set of codes. "The first flight anywhere to Europe this afternoon is TWA at seven."

"The necessary gates will be covered. And you? What are your plans?"

"I have been invited to attend an international banking conference in London."

"One of your own making?" Savich asked.

"If Kidd should slip through, I will handle things on that side," Androssy said without bothering to answer the resident's question.

"When will you leave?"

A large group of tourists entered the gallery and engulfed them. The two men drifted apart only to meet again in another less-filled gallery to continue making their plans for the elimination of Alexander Kidd and all those connected with him.

CHAPTER 21

Over the years, Alexander Kidd had stored up a good many "you owe mes". Now was the time to start calling them in. As his taxi pulled into the maze of internal roads that snaked through the various terminals and parking lots in the John F. Kennedy International Airport complex, he directed his driver not to the glamorous, glass-faced terminals, but toward the hangar area. An international traveler, Kidd knew that, thanks to the six-hour time difference, nothing flew across the Atlantic except in the mornings and evenings.

Kidd looked about the area as the cab stopped before a hangar on the southern edge of the airport complex. The last place Baron Androssy and his thugs would think to look for him would be on one of his old KWEN jets. By the time the first commercial flight left Kennedy later that day, he was sure the baron's KGB friends would have the terminals under surveillance. He did not relish the thought of a needle or some other Russian death trick being jabbed into him by an innocent-looking tourist while he waited in line. He wondered briefly what had been in the metal tube Frankel was about to use on him back in Androssy's library.

Tipping the driver, Alex entered the side door of the structure. Chuck Saunders stood there waiting for him with a crooked smile spread across his craggy face. "What the hell you up to this time?" the veteran pilot asked, slapping him on the back. "Smuggling more show girls in from the Folies-Bergère?"

"Sorry to disappoint you." Alex returned his smile. "You've filed the flight plans?"

"Yep, as soon as I got your call. We can take off in a couple of minutes. Boy, if the company ever finds out about this, they'll have my ass in a sling."

"It's been there lots of times before, if I recall."

"But that was when *you* were head of the place. Page has been a real bastard ever since he took over."

The reference to his old friend and his current position at KWEN hurt. Alex still could not understand the other's complete refusal to talk to or see him. No matter what the business circumstances, at least he could have tried to keep their long-standing relationship going. Alex shrugged. "He's been under a lot of pressure lately." No sooner had he made the statement than a thought suddenly flashed through his mind. Pressure, Androssy, the Russians. My God, Page was caught smack in the middle of this whole thing? Did he know what was going on?

"Come on, Alex, let's shove it before some hotshot from the network bumps you." Chuck Saunders' words cut short Kidd's thoughts on Page Shepard, but they would return later during the flight across the Atlantic.

"Who's your co-pilot?" he asked.

"Some new guy they assigned a couple of weeks ago. Got rid of my regular."

"How come?" Suspicion suddenly rose within him. Since Androssy's group had taken over, a lot of new men had been brought in.

Saunders shrugged. "Mine not to reason why."

Alex finished the quote in his own mind. *"Mine just to do and die."* "He doesn't know it's me, that I'm the one you're flying over, does he?"

"Do you think I want to buy an early retirement? Told him you were a visiting VIP on the way to the London office for a look-see."

"Good, let's keep it that way—for *both* our sakes." He thought a moment. "Look, Chuck, I'll just hole up in the back sleeping compartment for the flight. No need for him to see me at all."

The pilot's face sobered. "What's going on, Alex? You in some sort of real trouble?"

"No," the other assured him, "just don't want to get *you* in trouble."

Saunders stared at Kidd for a few seconds, not believing him. He had known the man for too many years; he could read him well. Hell, they had shared the controls of the plane for hours, their talk rambling about their lives, ambitions, problems. But if he wanted to play it this way, it was up to him. Chuck Saunders' grin reappeared. "Well then, okay, let's get going." He grabbed Alex's flight bag and turned toward the hangar door behind which sat the KWEN jet, checked, fueled, and ready. "England, here we come."

At 2:30 on the morning of September 15, just one week before the planned invasion and slaughter of Israel, the KWEN jet touched ground at Gatwick Airport south of London. Alex and Chuck Saunders left the plane and walked together through the darkness across the tarmac toward an official who waited for them in a small car. As they crossed the beams of the vehicle's lights, the co-pilot who peered curiously from the cockpit window frowned. That was no ordinary VIP. He recognized Alexander Kidd.

During the trip, Alex had finalized his plans for the destruction of Charon II. First he would send Sandra Bannister out of London to safety. Then he would visit his old friend, the current American Ambassador to the Court of Saint James's. Even though there was little chance that his story about the satellite, Androssy, and the Russian blackmail attempt on the U.S. would be believed, at least he wanted someone with a sympathetic ear to hear it. Should he be killed, his death might act as proof of the truth of his story and spur the government into action before it was too late.

Then he'd catch the first plane to Tangier and the transmitter and codes hidden there. He had enough of a start on Androssy to make it. His foe obviously did not know the location of the second transmitter and so would not know where Alex was heading. He'd lie low for seven days. When Androssy moved Charon II, he'd be waiting in Tangier. As soon as it was over the Atlantic and within range, he'd radio the self-destruct code and blow the damn thing to smithereens. He saw only three potential flaws in his plan: keeping out of Androssy's net while getting Sandra out of London, keeping alive until Charon II was destroyed, and keeping alive after that. He held no illusions about Androssy and his pals seeking vengeance, as there would still be no evidence of the Acheron Plot after the destruction of the satellite, who would listen to and protect him from his "imaginary" villains?

But first things first. While waiting for his rental car, he phoned both the Connaught Hotel and Claridge's. Sandra Bannister was not registered in either. Alex swore under his breath, his curses more out of worry for her safety than anger. He started to dial the flat at Codogan Square but paused, remembering Androssy's admission that his people had tapped the phone. Alex replaced the receiver in frustration. He could not call Sandra without letting the Russians know he was in England. "Damn that woman," he muttered, "can't she ever obey a simple order."

And then a thought came to him. Maybe Androssy's men had already taken her. He had to know. Picking up the receiver again, Alex dialed the flat and waited as the phone rang. A sleepy voice finally answered. He sighed with relief.

"Hello?"

He said nothing.

"Hello?" Sandra Bannister asked. "Is anyone there?" The sleep had gone from her voice and Alex noted her agitation. "Hello? Hello?" she demanded. "Who is this?"

Quickly pulling a handkerchief from his pocket, Kidd wrapped it over the mouthpiece and tried to disguise his voice as he spoke slowly and purposefully. "Don't say a word. Follow Trevane's orders." He paused and then added, "Now." Alex slammed the receiver down loudly, indicating that there would be no further conversation, discouraging her from speaking his name should she have recognized him.

The two KGB agents monitoring the brief conversation looked questioningly at each other. Was it a significant call or not? Should they report it now or wait until the Soviet trade mission opened later that morning? Electing to wait, they took no chances. One pulled on his jacket and left the flat across the square to take up a position in the car across the street from Sandra's lighted window.

Wide awake, the reporter sat on the edge of her bed. The voice had been Alex's, of that she was sure. And he was in England. The connection had been too good to have been an overseas call. But what did he mean, "Follow Trevane's orders"? She had not talked to Hal Trevane since yesterday, and he certainly had not given her any orders. Oh, my God, she thought, the answering machine. Sandra had not returned to the flat until after midnight and in her exhaustion had fallen into bed without first checking her messages. She turned on the machine and listened. Sure enough, Trevane had been calling all night, but had left no messages. Picking up the small leather address book beside the phone, she thumbed its pages for the number of the Lone Yachtsman Inn in Portsmouth. Sorry about the hour, she thought, but this has to be important.

After nearly three minutes, the phone was answered by the night porter of the inn who, with great irritation, plugged her call into Mr. Trevane's room phone.

The last days had been bad for her. She was sure she was being watched, followed wherever she went. The two men at the KWEN office who had been helping her had both suddenly been given assignments outside the country. The coincidence frightened her. She felt her allies in England were being systematically removed one at a time. The sound of Trevane's voice was reassuring.

From the car below, a pair of eyes looked up through the early morning fog that slowly undulated about the towers and chimneys of London, looked at the waiting figure silhouetted against the light in the Bannister woman's window. A cab pulled up before the building and the light above blinked off.

Alex did not wait for the American Embassy to open that morning before contacting the ambassador. He called the official residence in Regent's Park in hopes of meeting his old schoolmate privately. The name of Alexander Kidd cut through all the red tape at the residence, and soon he heard the familiar voice of John Sherman. "Alex, what the fuck are you doing here?" There was no comradery in it.

Kidd was taken aback. "Hey, John, it's me. Alex. Take the wind out of your sails, I want to talk to you. Meet me at the Dorchester for breakfast."

"Breakfast at the Dorchester?" Sherman asked in disbelief. "Are you out of your mind? The whole Secret Service is looking for you and you want to have breakfast at the Dorchester?"

"What in hell is this all about?" Alex demanded.

"Murder," the other replied.

"What?" Kidd shouted. Now it was his turn for surprise.

"Or suspected murder," the ambassador said, amending the charge. "They want to talk to you about Paul Carmody's death."

"I thought they put that down to suicide."

"They had until an aide of Carmody's came forward and implicated you."

"Oh, oh," Alex said, somewhat subdued. He thought they would certainly want to question him sooner or later, but never as a suspect. He had planned to contact them after this whole thing was over, but now the call was out.

"Alex, you've got to—"

"I've got to talk to you, John," Alex cut in. "I can't tell you how important it is. Please."

Sherman said nothing. Kidd could almost hear the wheels of his mind turning.

"John?"

"Will you talk to the FBI afterward?" the ambassador asked, keenly aware of his position as representative of his country.

"No, John, I can't," Alex replied. "I don't have the time. I only have time to talk to you."

Again there was a long pause on the other end of the line. "What do you know about Carmody's death?" Sherman asked.

"I know who killed him, John."

"Oh, my God," the other exclaimed.

"Will you let me tell you?" Alex asked. "John, as a friend, see me. Christ, man, you've got to see me. What I've got will blow your socks off."

It was a phrase John Sherman had heard Kidd use many times in the past. Seldom had the newsman exaggerated. "Where are you now?" he asked reluctantly.

"In a phone booth. Meet me in fifteen minutes at the Lyons on Notting Hill Gate. Do you know it? It's not far from you."

A long silence followed. "I'll find it," the ambassador replied. Alex did not like the tone of his voice. "Fifteen minutes sharp."

Kidd hung up, glancing down the street at the old brick hotel. Sandy had checked into Claridge's earlier that morning; he would make plans to get her safely out of London to friends near Hull after his meeting with John Sherman.

Fifteen minutes later, Alex stood back in the doorway of a shop on Notting Hill Gate not far from the tube station. Through the glass of its show window he could see clearly down the street to the Lyons. It buzzed with men and women picking up coffee and sweet rolls on their way to work. The tables inside were nearly all taken. Perhaps it had been the ambassador's tone of voice, but Alex's famous gut told him to be careful.

The official embassy car did not show up. Instead an ordinary-looking black sedan pulled into a parking spot a hundred feet from the Lyons. "You bastard," Alex mumbled as John Sherman emerged from the back seat with two men. They were halfway to the Lyons Corner House when a second sedan, identical to the first, pulled up to the curb on the other side of the small restaurant. Kidd pressed himself farther back against the shop door and watched as the ambassador entered the Lyons. His two companions took positions outside the door, one pretending to read a newspaper, the other waiting for a bus. That did it. Moving into the traffic of office-bound clerks and secretaries on the pavement before him, Alex allowed himself to be carried along to the entrance of the tube station. Taking a quick look over his shoulder at the FBI agents, he entered and bought a ticket to the Bond Street station only three stops away. As he stood on the escalator carrying him deep belowground, he pondered his current dilemna. Not only were the KGB agents bound to be after him with their needles and guns, but now his own people were out to pull him in for murder. His private flight on the KWEN plane out of the States would not look good for him, nor would the false trail he had left in Washington. "Fool," he muttered under his breath, causing the young woman standing in front of him on the escalator to turn and stare indignantly at him for several seconds. Not only was Androssy stacking the cards against him, but Kidd was doing it to himself as well. There was not much time left, and he could find no sympathetic ear. He was completely on his own.

He boarded his train. It roared through the labyrinth of underground tunnels and into the Bond Street station. The doors rumbled open and Alex pushed out, still lost in thought. He arrived at Claridges slightly after nine and headed straight for the house phones, making sure to keep his back to the lobby.

"Well, it's about time," Sandra exploded. "I've been pacing this damn room ever since I got that crazy call of yours. What the hell—"

"Hold on," he said firmly. "What's your room number?"

"You all right?" she asked, her voice suddenly solicitous after her initial outburst.

"Fine. Order me breakfast. I'll be right up." Sandra gave him the number. Rather than take the elevator, Alex crossed the lobby and walked up the wide carpeted staircase to the third floor. A swarthy, heavyset man sitting in the main reception room off the lobby watched over the top of his morning paper.

Folding the paper carefully, the man rose, adjusted his dark suit coat, and picked up the attaché case beside his chair. Walking to the phones, he dialed and waited only a few seconds before speaking. "He is here. You were right. The girl drew him out into the open." He listened to the muffled voice on the other end of the line and then asked, "Both of them?" Nodding gravely to the answer, he replied, "It will be done."

Throwing the door open on the first knock, Sandra Bannister pulled Alex into the room and hugged him to her. "Oh, darling, I'm so glad to see you," she murmured. "I've never felt so alone before. I've . . . I've been frightened." She raised her face and kissed his neck, cheek, face, and then, finally, his lips, feeling the strength of his body next to hers. "But now you're here."

He responded to the fragrance of her hair, the warmth of her body through the thin silk dressing gown and pressed her even more tightly to him, returning her kiss. "Too long," he murmured, "too long." The seriousness of the situation was momentarily lost in his arousal as his hands caressed the curves of her body under the smooth silk. Sandra's tongue flicked his ear, and she mouthed it as her hips undulated against his groin.

The gentle rap on the door startled them. Alex pulled back, looking over his shoulder. "Who the hell is that?"

Sandra disengaged herself and smiled, trying bravely to affect her old casualness. "I'm afraid my big seduction scene has just been cut from the script by the arrival of your breakfast. Come in," she called.

A passkey rattled in the lock, and the door was pushed open by the uniformed waiter who wheeled in an elegant cart. Averting his eyes from the two who stood watching him, he bent low to swing up the half-moon leaves to form a circular table. As he smoothed the spotless white tablecloth, arranged the silver and napkins, twisted the rose in the bud vase slightly, and laid out their breakfast, Sandra told Alex of her problems.

"All my leads about Androssy have dried up. Everyone who was helping seems suddenly to be invaluable on other assignments."

"No surprise. You don't have to dig any farther. The baron has come out in the open." Alex handed the waiter a pound note to hurry him out of the room.

"Thank you, Mr. Kidd," the man said with a bow.

"You know me?" Alex was surprised.

"Oh, yes. You're going to sail in the Whitbread. We all know you."

Alex handed him a ten pound note. "Well, forget you saw me today."

The other bowed again and left, closing the door softly behind him.

Alex turned back to Sandra. "Androssy tried to kill me yesterday."

"He what?" Her eyes were wide in surprise.

"Sit down. I've got a lot to tell you, and it's going to take a lot of believing on your part." She sank into the chair he indicated at the table. For the next half hour, Alexander Kidd unfolded the plan of the late President Warren in great detail, explained Androssy's and Moscow's involvement and intentions, the violent methods used to take over KWEN, and the murder of the other Furies. She sat staring at him, not touching the food before her.

"Why haven't you told anyone?"

"No proof," he replied sourly, "not a single shred of evidence."

"But *I* believe you. Why won't they?"

"You're you, darling."

"But Paul Carmody's murder surely proves what you're saying is true," she protested.

He gave a short, sardonic laugh. "I'm afraid all it proves

is that I may be some kind of madman. They think I killed him, Sandy."

"But they can't. Why?"

"I think our chess master Androssy may be able to explain that one better than I. All I know is that the FBI has its net out for me. Almost got me this morning; John Sherman tried to turn me over to them."

"You can't be serious. He's your friend. He—"

"He's a politician," Alexander Kidd interrupted. "And I'm afraid I'm a bit too hot to handle right now."

"What are you going to do?"

He poured himself another cup of coffee and, while finishing his bacon and eggs, explained about the second transmitter, careful not to give its location. "I'm going to blow the damn thing up before they get a chance to use it."

"Then why are you here? Why not go and get it over with?" she asked logically.

"Because I've got to wait nearly a week before they move the satellite." He paused and smiled. "And because of you. You're leaving for Hull this morning. I want you out of Androssy's reach, fast."

"Oh, no, I'm going with you," she protested.

"Aren't you frightened enough as it is?" he asked seriously. "You feel you've been watched. Obviously you have. Those goons can start shooting at any moment." He shook his head. "No, my little news hound, this is one story you're going to write from the sidelines. Now go pack." He sat back and watched her reaction. Sandra rose reluctantly and moved to the small suitcase on the stand across the room.

She said nothing. To go with him was impossible, he was right in that. But how would she know if anything had happened to him, if Androssy and his men had captured—or killed—him? The only thing she knew for sure was that she was desperately afraid for him and for herself. "Will you drive me up to Hull?" she asked softly.

"No, you're taking the train. John and Gay will meet you, it's all arranged."

"Then this is it for a while," she said flatly.

"Until it's over. Even then I may have to stay low for quite awhile."

"You won't come to Hull?"

"If it looks safe. I'm not sure."

She did not know what to say. As she slowly began to fill her case, Sandra tried to pretend this wasn't really happening. She grasped for normalcy. "I ran into Mark yesterday," she said, her back to him. Alex's eyes rose expectantly. "His show at the Gannet has been a great success, he's sold nearly everything."

"Of course, he's a Kidd." There was no hiding the pride behind the flippant statement.

"He's staying in a basement flat on Neville Street just off the Fulham Road."

"You've seen it?"

"No, but there's an open invitation."

"Still with that model friend of his?"

Sandra absently folded a blouse and put it in her case. There must be more important things for us to be talking about, she told herself, like, don't die. "I guess so, I didn't ask. He's just back from Jerusalem."

Alex frowned. "What was he doing there?"

"Visiting his grandparents and"—she tried to keep her voice as casual as possible as she turned toward him and watched his face—"Judith."

Just as she feared, his reaction was still strong. "She's there?" he cried, jumping up. "Now?" And then Sandra made the connection between Jerusalem, Judith, and Androssy's planned Middle East massacre. She put her hand to her mouth.

Alex crossed the room and snatched up the phone in what seemed to her to be near panic.

"What are you doing?"

"I'm going to get them out. Operator," he shouted into the mouthpiece while jiggling the phone bar impatiently.

"Alex, you said you had a week. There's time."

"No! They might move it up. Who knows?"

Sandra started to cross to him when she heard a discreet rap on the door. Pulling her robe about her, she turned back and called, "Come in," to the waiter she presumed had returned to gather up the breakfast things.

The door did not open. There was no familiar rattling of the key in the lock. Shaking her head, Sandra Bannister moved forward and pulled it open. Her eyes grew wide with terror. She barely saw the figure behind it, only the tube coming forward toward her nose. In one desperate attempt, she tried to slam the door, shut out the ampule as its lethal vapor exploded around her face. Her cry for help was no more than a gasp. The KGB agent pushed in as Sandra's already dead body collapsed at his feet.

It had happened so fast, just a blur of movement. Alex stood transfixed, the phone in one hand, receiver in the other, staring in disbelief, yet knowing beyond all doubt that Sandra was gone. And then he moved. Flinging the phone at the attacker who rushed toward him, he dropped to the floor on his side of the bed and lunged for the partially open bathroom door. The other dodged to one side while raising the pistol in his hand. Alex hit the cold tile floor in one rolling movement, pulling the door closed with him and reaching up to lock it as the silenced bullets punctured the wood, showering his face with splintered fragments. More slugs tore through the panel inches from his hand. Scrambling to his feet, he looked wildly about the small room for escape. Pushing up the small frosted-glass window, Alex looked down into the mews below. Heavy black plumbing pipes ran up the old brick walls at the rear of the hotel. Another bullet slammed into the door lock, then another as Alexander Kidd pulled himself through and, balancing himself on the narrow ledge outside, jumped for a pipe several feet to his left. His fingers scraped painfully against the rough brick as he grasped it. The door of the bathroom was kicked open. Pressing both knees to either side of the pipe, Kidd used it like a fireman's pole to slide quickly down into the mews below. As his feet hit the cobblestones, he looked up at the swarthy face of his assailant at the window and then at the arm with the gun. Kidd jumped to one side as a stone by his foot disintegrated into fragments. Turning, he ran, dodging from side to side down the narrow mews. One or two deliverymen stopped to look at him with mild curiosity. Alex dared not look back until he reached the corner of Avery Row. When he did, he checked over his shoulder and saw that the window was empty.

Cursing under his breath, the KGB agent moved quickly across the bedroom to Sandra Bannister's still-warm body. Hoisting it, he carried her into the bathroom and dropped the dead woman onto the floor. Picking up his gun, he looked down dispassionately. With the toe of his shoe, he flipped back the silk robe to expose her body. His dark eyes moved over the soft white skin and then stopped at her left breast. Stepping back to avoid being splattered with blood, he aimed and fired into her heart.

Removing the silencer, the Russian agent carefully placed both it and the gun into a special compartment in his attaché case. Straightening his jacket before the mirror, the killer quietly let himself out of the room. His exit from the hotel went unnoticed.

Alex had never been so shaken. He leaned against an iron railing, panting and sweaty, seeing again Sandra's horrified face and falling body. Her face remained before him as he stumbled forward. What was the name of the gallery? The one holding Mark's exhibition? Yes, the Gannet. He knew the place. It lay just a few blocks ahead down New Bond Street.

His slide down the outside plumbing of Claridge's had done nothing to improve Alex's appearance. One of the directors of the Gannet, a tall, prissy gentleman, gave him a brief, haughty, you-don't-belong-here look as he entered and then, studying the familiar face a second time, broke into a smile and approached. "Alexander Kidd, isn't it?" he inquired. Before Alex could answer, he continued, "How can I help you?" Alex started to say something but the man interjected, "Your son, Mark, isn't here. Were you expecting to meet him?"

"Where is he?"

"I beg your pardon?"

"Where is he?" Alex repeated, trying to control his voice.

"Why, I couldn't possibly know," the gallery director replied.

"I mean, where is his flat? Where does he live?"

"You don't know your own son's—"

"His address, damn it," Alex demanded sharply. "And phone number."

Cowed, the director hurried off. Alex looked about him. The walls of the gallery were hung with a variety of artists. He recognized several Hockneys. A room to his right was devoted completely to one painter. Several landscapes looked familiar to him. Alexander Kidd glanced to the rear of the gallery where the director had vanished, and then walked into the room. Of course, they were his son's paintings. Two views from the castle in Tangier were particularly striking. All the work was strong and vital, and almost all bore the little red dot in the lower right-hand corner indicating a sale.

The voice behind startled him. He whirled around sharply, bumping into the elegant director, who held out a slip of paper to him. It floated to the floor. "Oh, dear, I *am* sorry," the man said, kneeling to retrieve the paper. "I hope I didn't—"

"Yes, you did." Kidd took the proffered paper and glanced at the address and number. "Thank you." He stuffed it into his trouser pocket and moved toward the entrance of the gallery.

"You must be very proud," the director called after him. "Your son's works are going for three to four thousand pounds."

"Yes," he called back vaguely, distracted by a Slavic-looking man staring through the window. Alex backed away and turned. "May I use your phone?"

"Please," the other replied, bowing slightly and pointing

to the small office at the rear of the gallery. Kidd followed him, glancing back quickly at the man outside.

Taking the receiver from the Englishman, who discreetly left, Alex closed the door and dialed. He waited. Finally he heard the click at the other end. "Mark?" he said, and then paused to listen. "Well then, call him to the phone." Again he listened to the woman. "I don't care what the hell he's doing, tell him it's his father," Kidd barked.

Nearly a minute passed before he heard his son's sarcastic voice. "Same old dictatorial style as ever, I see."

"Mark, I've got to see you. I'm coming over."

"You can't, not now. I'm right in the middle of—"

"Mark, it's your father." Kidd paused and swallowed. "I'm in deep shit." He did not bother to cover his desperation.

Only silence met his statement.

"Sandra's dead. They've murdered her, Mark. I need you."

There was no hesitancy. "I'll be waiting. You know how to get here?"

Alex nodded. "Nineteen Neville Street. And Mark, alone. Please."

"Of course."

Alexander Kidd paused, looking at the receiver in his hand. He wanted to say more to his son but instead slowly lowered the phone.

The foreigner had gone by the time Alex walked back through the gallery. Nodding at the director, he left and hailed a passing cab. Within ten minutes the taxi pulled up before one in a long row of identical white town houses with black wrought-iron fences before them. "Here we are Guv'nor, nineteen Neville," the Cockney driver called back.

Glancing at the meter, Alex pulled two pound notes from his wallet and handed them through the sliding glass partition. "Keep the change," he said, jumping out and slamming the door behind him. He looked up and down the street and then quickly crossed and descended the stone steps to the basement flat. The door opened before he had the chance to ring. Alex slipped in past his son.

"Dad, what's going on?" Mark demanded, closing the door. "You said Sandra's been killed?"

"Murdered."

"When did—"

Kidd held up his hand. "We're alone?"

Mark nodded. "I sent Namba out to visit friends."

Too tense to sit, Alex leaned against the wall. "First we have to call Jerusalem. We've got to get your mother and grandparents out." He saw the puzzled expression on his son's face. "The whole place may go up in flames at any moment."

Had it not been for the desperation in his father's voice, Mark Kidd might have scoffed at what seemed to be an overreaction to the Middle East war rumors the press was reporting. He answered seriously, "Grandfather Singer's in the hospital, that's why I went. Grandmother will never leave him."

"How bad is it?"

He shook his head. "Only a matter of time."

Kidd reached for the phone and handed it to his son. "Judith can talk them into coming out with her."

"Too late, she left when I did."

"Thank God," Alex murmured, "at least *she's* safe. Where is she now?"

"Mom has some meetings in Switzerland and Paris and then is going on to the house in Tangier." The young man saw his father close his eyes. "Why, what's the matter?"

"When is she due in Tangier?" Alex demanded, disregarding his son's question.

"In a couple of days, maybe a week."

Kidd's gut clenched into a knot. "Where can we reach her?"

Mark shook his head helplessly. "Her plans were up in the air when I left. I don't know."

Alex banged his fist against the wall in frustration. From the frying pan right into the fire, he thought miserably, and I put her there—right along with Sandy. How long, he wondered, would it take Androssy and the KGB to track down the castle. Once found, they would not be gentle with its inhabitants. They could leave no one alive who might know Alexander Kidd and his intentions.

"Dad, what's going on?" Mark begged. He sensed fear in his father for the first time. "For Christ's sake, tell me."

Alex stared at his son. "The last time we met you said you owed your country a lot, that you wanted to help save it from war."

"That's right." Mark returned his father's gaze, his hackles bristling briefly at the remembered challenge. He had a sinking feeling he was not going to like what he was about to hear.

"What if a war had already started, if American cities were about to be bombed, if your mother and grandparents were about to be killed?"

"That's not going to happen," he countered defensively.

"But what if it were?"

The young man looked at Alex curiously for a moment, trying to probe behind his father's words. "I'd have no choice. I'd have to fight."

"Well, you have your chance to prove it," Alex said evenly. "Mark, I need your help. You're the only one I have left."

Mark Kidd thought he would never hear his father say those words.

CHAPTER 22

Baron Miklos Androssy's private jet touched down at Heathrow International Airport outside of London just as Alexander Kidd began, for the second time that day, to explain the details of the Warren plan and how it had backfired on America and its NATO allies. As Alex spoke, Mark Kidd sat full of awe, yet with growing pride in his father and the behind-the-scenes role he had played for so many years in his country's foreign policy. Mark had always thought of him more as the traditional, conservative flag-waver than an active participant in government. But his father had literally put his life on the line for his country. It explained the strength of Alexander Kidd's reaction when he had refused to register for the draft.

"I was planning to fly out on the four o'clock plane this afternoon," Kidd continued, "but now that the FBI knows I'm in England, I'll never get through passport control." He put his hand on his son's shoulder. "Can you still use a radio transmitter? Tom Petterson said you were quite a pro."

Mark shook his head. "Tom exaggerated for your sake, Dad, and that was a long time ago. I haven't touched one since I left New York. They must be a lot more sophisticated now."

"Not the one at the castle."

"Sorry. I honestly wouldn't know where to begin. Until today I'd actually forgotten about that hidden room and your equipment."

"Damn." Alex rubbed his fist across his lower lip as he pondered the alternatives.

Mark's eyes lit up. "I could get someone else to do it for me."

"No," Alex said vehemently. "I wouldn't trust those codes with anyone but you."

"So it's you or no one," Mark stated bluntly.

"That's right."

"And passport control?"

"Portsmouth," Alex said. "It's my only way out."

"We'll go on the *Privateer*?"

"*I'll* go on the *Privateer*. You'll fly to Tangier and intercept your mother before she gets to the castle. I want her completely out of this."

Mark stood and went to the makeshift bar in a nearby bookcase. "I could use a drink. How about you?"

"Scotch," Alex replied, "a double."

The younger Kidd poured a healthy slug into a glass and turned. He froze in his tracks. Through the curtained window behind his father, Mark saw two pairs of legs standing on the sidewalk above. They were clothed in dark flannel, the shoes not in fashion. "Your FBI friends?" he asked softly, nodding to the window.

Alex whirled around and cocked his head to look up. Thanks to the net curtains and the light reflecting upon them from the outside, he could see out but those standing above could not see in. "They're certainly not English," he said. "Either FBI or . . ." He suddenly recognized the man who had burst into Sandra's room at Claridge's in whispered conversation with the other. "We're in trouble. Is there a rear way out?"

"Through the garden, over the back wall. Who are they?"

Alex moved quickly to the door and silently eased its interior bolt into place. "Some of Androssy's KGB buddies, if I'm not mistaken. Grab your passport and money." Moving shadows fell across the curtains. "Quick," he called softly, "they're coming down."

Mark was already in his room digging into the top drawer

of a bureau. Alex closed the door to the living room and locked it. He walked on to the glass-paned door leading into the small walled garden and opened it. "Speed it up, will you?" he urged, looking back at his son.

As he fumbled under gloves, handkerchiefs, and other assorted clothing for the small blue passport, Mark heard the bolt of the front door tear loose from the jamb under pressure of a jimmy. The brutal intrusion brought with it the stark realization that this was no cerebral cops-and-robbers game he and his father were involved in; it was real and it was a matter of life and death—his death. Frantically snatching the little blue book, he ran to join Alex in the garden, knocking over a small table in his haste. The men in the living room looked to the bedroom door.

"Which way?" Alex whispered urgently.

"Over there," Mark said, pushing his father forward toward the back, northwest corner. "We can get over into the Taylors' garden and through their house to Onslow Terrace."

Both men dashed to the six-foot-high brick wall and pulled themselves up and over, dropping down into a cluster of ornamental bushes on the other side. Behind them they heard splintering wood as the door to Mark's bedroom was kicked in. Father and son reached the rear door of the Taylor house in a squatting run. It was open. A startled woman turned from the sink in the kitchen.

"Only me, Sarah," Mark called as he and Alex walked quickly past. "Sorry, but we're in rather a rush."

"Mark," she called down the hall after them. "Mark, what the . . . ?"

He turned on the front stoop. "If anyone asks, you didn't see us," he called back to his neighbor and slammed the door.

"You've got a car?" Alex asked Mark.

"Come on," Mark said, pulling him up the pavement. "It's parked on Neville Street."

"Dangerous," his father cautioned, running after him.

"It's far enough away," he said as they rounded the corner, "and those guys should be busy inside for a bit."

"There could be others."

"There it is," his son called back.

By the time Alex reached the small black MG, Mark was behind the wheel and had reached over to unlock the door for him. He jumped in as the car pulled away from the curb and turned into Onslow Street. "Portsmouth?" Mark asked.

Alex nodded.

Turning into the Fulham Road, Mark wound through traffic toward the bridge south over the Thames. Across, they sped on past Wimbledon Park and continued south on the M-3 toward Portsmouth. Neither man said much to the other. Although he tried to plan his next steps, Alex's thoughts kept drifting back to the morning, Sandy's face, and the killer rushing at him. For his part, Mark was still trying to come to grips with his role in the destruction of the Charon II satellite.

Alex returned his thoughts to the *Privateer* and the Whitbread race that would start that afternoon. Hal Trevane was scheduled to up anchor at two and head around the world. Being an avid sailor, Kidd genuinely regretted that the crew of his boat would lose their chance to win. But it gave him the cover he needed to get out of Britain. No one would realize that the *Privateer* had dropped out until he had been safely landed in France near Cherbourg. Thanks to John Sherman's betrayal, the FBI would be looking for him now only in England. The Paris airports would be open to him. He should be in Tangier no later than a day after Mark.

The little MG was on the outskirts of Portsmouth when Alex's plans went up in flames. The one o'clock news on the car radio made sure of that. He sat stunned as the somber and proper voice of the newscaster reported the brutal shooting of Miss Sandra Bannister, the well-known American newswoman, at Claridge's that morning, presumed murdered by her lover who had bribed the hotel staff to remain discreet about their assignation. The police were looking for Mr. Alexander Kidd, the highly controversial yachtsman who had recently lost control of his American broadcasting empire, to "aid them in their inquiries." Both Alex and Mark Kidd and all of the British Isles knew the last phrase meant the police wanted Kidd for murder.

"Shit!" Alex shouted, remembering the ten pound note he had given to the waiter that morning. "That Russian bastard must have shot her and sneaked out. God, how obvious it must look to the police."

"They'll be swarming all over the *Privateer*," Mark Kidd said. "And the press too. What are we—"

"Pull over when you can. I've got to think this thing out," Alex said. "Thanks to Interpol, every fucking airport in Europe will be on the lookout for me now. There goes France."

They sat at the side of the M-3 for nearly fifteen minutes thrashing out the various alternatives for getting Alex to Tangier and the changing roles his son must play to pull it off. Finally Mark put the sports car back into gear and started off toward the docks of Portsmouth. Stopping nearly a half mile from the *Privateer*'s anchorage, he turned the wheel of the MG over to his father and got out to walk the rest of the way on foot.

"Don't let Trevane give you any back talk," Alex warned. "Make sure he understands the importance of that note."

"Don't worry," Mark answered. "Your timing is going to be tight. Are you sure you can make it?" he asked through the car window.

"If the winds hold. Remember, you're the key to this thing. Shoo your mother off and get that old smuggling bastard Pinto to bring me over from Tarifa."

Mark nodded. "And if you don't make it? What then? You let them kill off Israel and the rest of the world?" The challenge was clear in his question.

Alex searched his face. "To know the location of those codes is to sign your own death warrant."

"Would the Russians believe me even if I didn't know where they were hidden?" the younger Kidd countered. "If you don't show up, I'll try to find someone to radio them up."

Alex smiled. "So it's *us* now, is it?"

His son returned his smile.

Five minutes later he left Mark and drove at high speed toward Lizard Point on the western tip of England.

It took Mark nearly an hour to push his way through the crowd and reach the gangplank to the *Privateer*. A uniformed policeman and what he decided must be either FBI agents or plain clothesmen blocked his way. Identifying himself and repeatedly lying about his knowledge of his father's whereabouts or even existence in Britain, he finally managed to get aboard with the help of Hal Trevane after promising to report to Scotland Yard for further questioning. It was a promise that only a day ago, as a law-abiding citizen, he would have kept. Not now. Swept up in his mission, other people's laws no longer seemed important if they stood in his way. The maverick nature of Alexander Kidd began to bloom within his son.

"Where's Alex?" Trevane asked as soon as they were alone belowdeck.

"Before I answer, let me ask you two questions," Mark replied, doing exactly what he and his father had rehearsed.

"Ask."

"Did anyone come aboard last night. Anyone search the boat?"

Trevane looked at the young man with a surprised expression on his face. "How did you know?"

"How do *you* know?" Mark countered, returning the question.

"Someone went over the boat from stem to stern. Nothing missing, but we could tell. One thing or another slightly out of place. You can sense it."

"Good."

"What were they looking for?"

"I wish I could tell you, Mr. Trevane, but I can't, believe me. Dad will explain everything to you."

"Alex? When? Where the hell is he?" Trevane burst in. "Is it true? Sandy being murdered?"

Mark shook his head. "She's dead." He lowered his voice. "Dad needs your help. He asked me to ask you this. Will you and the others give up the Whitbread to help him?"

"What has the Whitbr—"

"A simple yes or no." Mark Kidd stared deeply into the older man's eyes. "An awful lot depends on you, Mr. Trevane."

When he had last met Alex's son, the young man had not impressed him. Now he did. "Well . . . well, of course," Trevane stammered.

"And you speak for the crew?" Mark pressed.

"Doug, Shep, the others, they're all friends of your father."

"Friendship has many shades," Mark Kidd replied. "A lot more than my father's life is at stake here."

Hal Trevane stared at him. "Look, Mark, what *is* this all about?" he demanded.

"Nothing Dad wants you to do is really illegal, I swear. There is risk, however."

"What kind of risk?" the other asked. "God, I knew something was brewing when Alex called from New York. And last night . . ." He left his thought hanging.

"A group wants to kill him. They've framed him for Sandy's murder. He's got to get out of England. They may come after him if they think he's on the *Privateer*. They're professionals."

"What is this group?"

"Only Dad can tell you." Mark put his hand on the other's knee as they sat beside each other on the bunk, and implored him with his eyes. "You've got to save him. Can he count on you and the others?"

"I said he could, and I mean it," Trevane said, standing.

He was uncomfortable. Vagueness always made him uncomfortable.

"Then show me your chart," Mark said, moving to a small table fastened beside the galley.

"Since when have you become a navigator?" the acting captain asked with a wary smile.

"Since an hour ago," Mark Kidd replied.

CHAPTER 23

Androssy stood on the balcony of his duplex penthouse overlooking Berkeley Square. There was no mistaking the anger in his voice as he spoke with his private secretary. "The fool," he ranted. "Is there no one from the Center I can trust in this affair?" His hands clenched the railing. "It was our best chance of catching Kidd. Now we have no lure left. How long has it been since he escaped?"

Robert Frankel consulted his watch. It was just past seven in the evening. "A little over nine hours. Kidd got away from Claridge's just before ten. They think he went from the hotel to his son's flat in southwest London."

"Think?" Androssy questioned impatiently. "What do you mean, 'think'?"

"When the Center's men broke in, whoever was there got out through the garden. They didn't see either, but presumably it was Kidd and his son. There were two half-filled glasses on the bar."

"I assume they bothered to check to make sure one didn't have lipstick on it," the baron sneered. Incompetence irked him.

Frankel said nothing.

"His son," Miklos Androssy mused. "My reports said the two were estranged, had not spoken in years."

His secretary shrugged.

"A painter, is he not? The son, Mark Kidd?"

"Studied in France."

"Find out all you can about the boy, Robert, and have him picked up and taken to the back house in Essex. We may be able to make use of him. And the *Privateer*? Our man found absolutely nothing on board?"

"Clean. Only the normal type of radio equipment one would expect on an ocean-going yacht. Certainly nothing sophisticated or strong enough to reach and control the satellite. No codes."

"Chalk one up to you, Mr. Kidd," the baron admitted grudgingly. "You are sure he is not aboard, hidden in the bilge or some other place?"

Frankel nodded. "The police took it apart before it left harbor this afternoon. I'm told they had men swarming all over the area looking for him."

"Well, at least that damn boat will be out of our way for nearly a year." He looked up as a gust of cool air ruffled his immaculate silver-gray hair. The sunny sky of morning had turned leaden. Androssy turned and walked back into the living-room of the penthouse with Frankel close behind. "We have a serious problem, Robert. I did not want the British police mixed up in this until Kidd was dead. Now we have to get to Kidd before the police do."

"At least they've bottled him up in this country for us. The only way he can get out is to swim," Frankel replied.

"Mr. Kidd does quite well with water, if you recall, Robert." His tone was biting. The secretary lowered his eyes over Alexander Kidd's embarrassing escape from the Sutton Place town house. "Let us see what the news has to say about our friend." Androssy crossed the room and switched on the television set.

"We will have missed the major news stories by now," Frankel commented.

Nodding his agreement, Baron Androssy reached back for the control knob of the set when the cameras switched to Portsmouth and the entrants in the Whitbread race. Curiosity stayed his hand.

The two men watched as the camera panned over the harbor, the long shots interspersed with interviews with onlookers and the captains and crews of the competing yachts, all conducted in crisp Etonian accents. ". . . and the splendid *Privateer*, owned by the controversial Alexander Kidd for whom the police are now searching," the commentator said as a hand-held television camera moved toward the yacht. "Captain," he called, attracting Trevane's attention. Turning from the young man with whom he had been talking, Hal Trevane faced the camera with a smile as the interviewers continued to move in on him.

"That was young Kidd," Frankel said, touching the baron's arm.

"You are sure?" Androssy insisted.

"Yeah, yeah, that was him."

Both watched the television screen, eager to catch another glimpse of Mark Kidd.

"So they are not on speaking terms, are they?" the baron said with a smile. "Then why would that young man have been talking with the captain of his father's boat? I will tell you why, Robert. Because Kidd is on the *Privateer*."

"Impossible," Frankel protested. "I told you the police went through it with a fine-tooth comb."

"He may not have been on it when the boat left the harbor, but I can feel it in every bone of my body, Alexander Kidd is going to be on that yacht." He slapped the top of the television set in a rare show of emotion and said triumphantly, "I have him again, Robert. I have him again. Signed, sealed, and ready for delivery."

The seas were still high, but the winds had lessened. With great difficulty Alexander Kidd tried to hold his small sailboat in position half a mile south of Lizard Point. It was after midnight, and the *Privateer* was behind schedule. Or had they missed each other in the darkness? Kidd did not dare light a flare for fear of attracting the attention of the British coast guard. The running lights of the *Privateer* would have to serve as his only beacon.

Before leaving England, Mark had confirmed by phone that all the arrangements for his father's pickup at sea had been made. Then Mark boarded a plane at the small airport at Lydd on the eastern coast of Britain to fly to Ostend. From Belgium, Alex's son planned to drive to Amsterdam and catch the first flight connecting with Tangier to "shoo" off Judith and await his father's arrival. Hopefully, this circuitous route to the castle would throw off Androssy and the KGB goons who Kidd was sure must be out in force.

"Damn." Alex watched the first wisps of sea fog drifting toward him. The lighthouse on Lizard Point that he had used to hold course blinked through the mist, was lost, then blinked through again. He would not have the beacon for long. If it went before the *Privateer* arrived, he would be forced to lower the sail and switch to the motor, using the compass as the sole guide. It would be more reliable than tacking back and forth in the fog. The man who had sold him the small boat obviously relied more on the motor than the sail. Six one-gallon tins of gasoline were lashed under the gunwales on either side of him.

The fog grew heavier and the Lizard Point light vanished, the mournful call of its horn the only proof of its existence and that of the jagged rocks upon which it stood. Alex was about to start up the outboard motor of his boat when another sound came to his ears—the foghorn of the *Privateer*. It was somewhere ahead in the swirling gray air. Leaning forward, his eyes tried to penetrate the mist and search out the red and green running lights. Suddenly the yacht loomed above him, nearly running the smaller boat down as it broke from the fog and swept past. Alex's cry was answered by those of the crew as they moved quickly to bring in the sails and slow the *Privateer*. Bobbing up and down in its wake, Alex started his motor and gunned it, coming about and chasing after the larger boat that had already been swallowed up by the fog. Five minutes later he came alongside and reached up for Hal Trevane's hand. "Trying to kill me?"

"Who cares about you," the other countered, hauling him aboard. "I was afraid I'd scratch this beauty here."

"Can't fault you for that," Kidd replied, smiling confidently. He was on his way to Tangier.

"What about your boat? Set her adrift?"

Alex thought a minute. "No, take her in tow. You never know when she may come in handy."

"It'll cut down our speed," Trevane warned.

"We're in a different kind of race now, Hal."

The other became serious. "Mark told us next to nothing, Alex. What are we getting into?"

"I'll tell you what I can," Kidd replied. "But first, let's get that boat in tow and then set course due south for Ile d'Ouessant off the coast of Brest."

"Brest?" Trevane asked in surprise.

"And beyond. You're taking me down to Spain, my friend, and as fast as our baby here can make it." Alex patted the smooth varnished wood of the hatch.

The *Privateer* swung to port on its new southern course, and the crew began working to bring down the flamboyant red and white sails which were the yacht's trademark and replace them with the dark gray sails they often used in rough-weather practice. Alex occupied himself painting over the *Privateer*'s name on the blue hull, stenciling on it the name of a friend's boat with similar dimensions and rigging that he knew to be cruising off the coast of West Africa.

Looking up from his perch at the bow, he realized that they would soon break out of the fog bank blanketing the English shoreline. Already he could see a few stars overhead, the mist hanging low to the water had lessened, and the breeze seemed to be picking up. Alex did not know if the change in the weather was good or bad for them. The improved wind would certainly get them across the English Channel more quickly, but he rather liked the anonymity of the fog. The distant sound of a helicopter motor made him start. Pulling himself on deck, he moved back to confer with Trevane.

"I don't like it, Hal," he said in a lowered voice. "What in the hell is a helicopter doing out here?"

Trevane shrugged. "Maybe it's the coast guard out of Whitesand looking for a ship in distress."

"No go. We've been monitoring the radio all night, and no distress calls have gone out."

"Well," he replied as the sound grew louder and louder, "maybe . . ." Trevane said no more. The aircraft came into view above them and dropped down to look them over. The crew stood dumbly looking up, not knowing whether to wave or duck for cover. After a few seconds, the helicopter swung away and up into the night sky. "Wonder what that was all about?" Trevane asked. "It wasn't the coast guard."

"I don't think I like it, whatever it was," Kidd replied. Suddenly the sky lit up like day. "Now I know I don't like it," he said as the flare from the departing helicopter arched high above them. "How long do you think it will take to get us back into that fog bank?"

Trevane didn't answer. He was already in the process of calling commands to the crew and swinging the boat around.

With only half its sails operable, the *Privateer* acted sluggishly. "Caught with our pants down," Alex commented wryly. He moved quickly forward to help raise more canvas.

They had been at work for nearly twenty minutes when the sound of another motor penetrated the night. It was not that of the helicopter but of a powerful speedboat. Alexander Kidd looked eagerly ahead. They were almost to the fog bank along the southern coast of Britain. And then he looked to his right. He could see nothing to starboard, but the sound of the racing motor grew louder. It seemed almost on top of them. The stars above grew dim in the fingers of mist into which they sailed. "Where the hell is it?" Alex mumbled, looking again to starboard. He called out, "Everyone get ready to duck."

Almost like a bullet, the black powerboat exploded out of the darkness at them. Hal recognized it instantly as the boat that had followed them so closely during the trials. "Alex, it's . . ." he called.

"Down," Alex shouted as the boat swerved, throwing a wall of water high in its wake. A submachine gun sprayed the *Privateer* as it shot past. Wood splintered about them, and two of the crew cried out as the attacking boat continued its turn, readying to make another sweep at the helpless yacht. "Bastards," Alex yelled after it. "Below, everyone below," he cried, helping a wounded crewman across the deck. Trevane crouched low in the cockpit, holding the *Privateer* on course as they scrambled past.

"Here it comes," he shouted.

The roar of the black boat's motor and the machine gun deafened them as it made its second charge at the yacht and zoomed past. Shaking with rage, Alex climbed back up into the cockpit with Trevane. "We're sitting ducks," he cursed.

"Almost there," Trevane said, not looking at his friend, his eyes riveted on the fog bank that seemed to roll forward to embrace them.

Alex looked ahead and then back at the powerboat that was now completing its second full circle and readying to come at them again from behind. "Faster, faster," he urged under his breath, and then started forward over the scarred deck. "As soon as we're in, Hal, hard to port," he called back, taking hold of one of the forward winches. He looked back at the boat as it roared toward them, and then it disappeared behind a thick wall of wet gray air. The *Privateer* veered to port. Trevane saw the grim, triumphant smile on Kidd's face as they heard the twin motors of their attackers rush past somewhere off to starboard and then they were cut, the only sound that of water moving past the *Privateer*'s sleek hull as it put distance between the two.

Alex crawled back to the cockpit. "Thank God sails don't make noise," he said softly to Trevane.

"If it comes after us, at least we'll know where they are."

"It's going to be cat and mouse," Alex warned. "Oh, oh, here they come." Both men listened as the launch's motors rumbled into life.

Victor Kamera, the still-hot submachine gun in his hands, stood beside the captain of the powerboat. The light from the launch's radar screen illuminated both their faces as they watched for the telltale bleeps that indicated the position of the *Privateer*. "She's moving at a good clip," the captain said, looking at his companion.

"Go after her," Kamera stated flatly.

"Not all that easy in this weather," the other countered. "We'll take it slow."

With the exception of the two wounded men, the crew of the *Privateer* scrambled back up and over the deck, desperately untangling and getting the jib up. Others worked belowdeck to caulk bullet holes that had punctured the smooth skin of the hull.

"We're lucky they aimed above the waterline," Alex commented. "We're only taking a little water."

"They're on our tail, Alex," Trevane said evenly. His face was hard and tense. "The sound of their motor has been getting closer for the last five minutes."

"Change tack again. At least we'll give 'em a little run for their money."

"They're using radar."

"I know," Kidd said, nodding to the inevitable. "We can't outrun them. They're going to get us sooner or later. I'd give my eyeteeth for a gun."

"We've got a flare gun," Trevane suggested. "Maybe we could give them a blast when they get close. Who knows, we might set something on fire."

"The odds are against it, Hal. That only happens in the movies." Kidd turned in his seat in the cockpit and looked behind into the fog from where the sound of their pursuers' motors was coming. His eyes fell on the small sailboat the *Privateer* towed and the six one-gallon tins of gasoline lashed beneath its gunwales. "Hal, how much fuel are we carrying?" he asked excitedly.

The other looked at him in surprise. "Fuel?"

"I think we may be able to arrange a little surprise for our friends back there," he said, pointing to the sailboat. "A floating bomb." Trevane turned to look. "Got my drift?"

"Damn right I do."

"Carrington," Alex called, "get your ass up here and get ready to pump oil." He moved across the deck and grasped the tow rope of the small boat. "Griffin, give me a hand with this."

"They've slowed," the captain of the powerboat told Kamera. "I wonder what they're up to."

"You'd think they'd be running for shore," Androssy's henchman said to the KGB agent. "I would."

"Too smart for that. The draft of their boat is greater than ours," the captain explained. "They'd run aground and founder before us; we could run circles around them as they sank. With that gun of yours, not one would make it to shore."

Kamera shrugged. "I'm tired of this. Go after them."

The Russian agent slowly increased their speed. The sound came to the crew of the *Privateer*. "Just in time," Alex said.

"You sure you know what you're doing?" Trevane asked. "The odds are against you."

"I like high odds."

"We may never find you again in this fog. You'll—"

"Swimming has always been my strong point," Alex interrupted. He shoved off from the *Privateer* in the small sailboat that had been nearly filled to the gunwales with highly flammable fuel oil and, hoisting its sail, headed into the wind in a broad reach that would take him back toward the position he estimated the powerboat would be in when the *Privateer* changed to a port tack. The fuel oil filling the hull sloshed around his calves as he held the tiller. A watertight bag slung around his neck carried the flare gun which would set off the floating bomb in which he sailed. When the time came, he prayed that all those years shooting skeet at the country club would pay off. Leaning forward, he strained to see through the gray walls of fog around him. Where was that fucking powerboat? He hated uncertainty—he had to find the boat before he lost his nerve. Dark oil splashed over his thighs.

"They've moved to a port tack," the KGB captain said, slowly turning the wheel to follow. And then he frowned.

"What's the matter?" Kamera asked.

"The radar has picked up something between us and the yacht." He pointed at the electronic screen.

"What is it?"

Alex trimmed his sail as the small boat raced silently before the wind toward the sound of the powerboat's motors.

"Not sure. Driftwood. Or maybe they jettisoned something to lighten her." He slowed.

"What are you doing? Keep after Kidd," Kamera ordered.

"There may be a lot of flotsam around here we're not picking up. It could tear a hole in us."

"I said go after Kidd."

Alex saw the dim lights of the powerboat through the fog before they saw him. It was moving north. "Damn," he swore, quickly changing his course to intercept.

The captain scowled at the screen. "Whatever it is, it's moving this way." He gripped the throttle as his and Kamera's eyes tried to probe the fog to their left.

Kidd tied off the tiller and, waiting until the last possible moment, started to lower himself over the side of his boat while pulling the flare gun from its plastic bag.

"There," Kamera shouted in surprise as the small sailboat swept out from the wall of mist directly toward them. He jumped into action, inadvertently knocking the captain aside as he brought up his submachine gun to fire at the man just slipping into the water from the approaching boat. Regaining his footing, the captain grasped the wheel, spun it violently, and pushed the throttle forward. Too late. The oil- and gas-filled sailboat raced headlong into the starboard side of the powerboat just as Alex fired his flare at it from the water.

Stunned, Victor Kamera fired wildly at the blazing rocket shooting straight at him. He and the others ducked as it exploded against the speedboat and the oil-filled bomb alongside it. A searing ball of fire erupted around them, engulfing all in a shrieking agony. The second explosion of the black racer's own fuel tanks completed the annihilation.

The force of the final concussion knocked the wind from Alex's lungs as he swam desperately away. He struggled to keep afloat, moving one arm after another in an instinctive fight for survival until he lost consciousness.

Guided by the still-flaming wreckage, the crew of the *Privateer* pulled his limp body from the water minutes later.

"I'm not feeling too good," Alex gasped to Hal Trevane as he lay in his bunk.

"Not surprised," Trevane replied. "That was some bomb you rode in on."

"The others?" he rasped.

"The boat's gone. Nothing left but splinters."

"Where is this all going to end?" Carrington asked Hal Trevane as the other moved into the cockpit and once again set the *Privateer*'s course south across the Channel toward Brest.

"Your guess is as good as mine."

CHAPTER 24

The newspapers that morning announced the breakdown in the newly convened arms-limitation talks in Geneva. The Soviets inexplicably walked out, setting no date for their resumption. The American team was left in a state of confusion, their chief negotiator called home by the President for urgent consultation. The date was September 19, three days before the impending attack on Israel.

The winds had been strong and kind to the *Privateer* as she skimmed south across the Bay of Biscay. Under her new guise, her journey had not been challenged by the French coast guard. The rugged shoreline of northern Spain now rose before them as the sun reached its peak.

"You'll take the inflatable in tonight?" Trevane asked.

Alexander Kidd nodded.

"And after that, what then?"

"If all goes according to plan, a long, fast drive across Spain," Kidd replied. "Some not-so-savory friends of mine will take it from there."

"Where will they take it, if I may ask?"

Alex shook his head. "You may not." He put his arm around Trevane's shoulders. "How about a drink, my old friend."

"Welcome to London, Mr. Shepard," Baron Androssy said, rising from his desk in his Victorian office on Threadneedle Street in the heart of The City, London's financial center. It was 11:30, September 20. Banking circles were in a state of near panic over the fluctuations in the gold market and the American dollar caused by the collapse of the Geneva talks and the Middle East turmoil. Syrian troups had crossed the border into Jordan. Israel had announced a state of alert. The smile on Androssy's face belied the desperation he felt. Kidd had disappeared, literally vanished. That yacht of his could have dropped him anywhere along the eastern coast of Europe. He had to find him, take any risk to find him. And although Page Shepard did not know it, he was one of the baron's risks. "Would you care for tea?"

Page shook his head. "I've had enough tea in the last two days to float a battleship." With the news of Sandra's death and Kidd's involvement in it, he had dropped everything and flown to London to handle Sandra's funeral arrangements. It had been a trying and confused time for him. He could not understand Alex's disappearance. His apparent behavior was bewildering. Now, at the urging of several KWEN directors, he stood across the desk from Miklos Androssy, a banker about whom he knew next to nothing.

"I can sympathize, Mr. Shepard. The English seem to think that the remedy for everything is a cup of tea." He turned to his secretary. "You may leave us now, Robert," he said, then turned back to Page. "Please be seated." He indicated a comfortable chair with a nod. "And what can the Bank Androssy do for the new president of KWEN?"

"I believe you know," Page answered bluntly.

"Oh?" Androssy's left eyebrow arched. A trace of a smile briefly flickered across his lips.

"A member of our board, one of the Milo directors, led me to believe that you were very aware of the financial difficulties in which KWEN finds itself and our need to cover certain theatrical commitments made by Mr. Kidd in Europe before he lost control of the network."

"Ah, Mr. Alexander Kidd," Androssy said. "A most unusual man. A close friend of yours? Do you really believe he killed his mistress?"

Page pressed on, not answering the offensive question. "I was led to believe that you were very interested in these theatrical ventures and that if quick action were taken, you might wish to relieve the network of its commitments."

"I see," the baron said, playing his role to perfection. "Cultural programming seems less interesting to the American public than first thought. CBS Cable and the Entertainment Channel have both failed."

Page nodded agreement with his statement.

"And yet . . ." Androssy said tentatively, pausing as if reviewing plans of his own. "May I ask the amount involved?"

He was in a cat-and-mouse game. Page recognized it. But he, not Androssy, was the mouse. "Nearly nine million."

The baron did not flinch at the figure. "You have the papers with you?"

Nodding, Page lifted his black leather briefcase from the floor. "They arrived this morning."

Androssy waved his hand. "Later." He thought for a moment and then went on. "Your Mr. Kidd had many friends in the arts, it seems. He enjoys their society, visiting their ateliers, their lairs?"

Page could not help smiling. "Afraid not. Alex and the arts are like oil and water. They never mixed."

"But this culture channel of his?" Androssy protested.

"Purely business, nothing more."

"Nevertheless, he managed to assemble a remarkable list of names and projects. You can't tell me that—"

"Once Alex sets his mind to something, he does it, and does it well," Page interrupted. His words were not reassuring to the baron.

Androssy glanced at his watch. "Mr. Shepard, it is nearly time for lunch. Will you do me the honor of joining me at my club? We can discuss the KWEN matter further."

Page felt uncomfortable. "I would prefer to—"

"Please, Mr. Shepard," Androssy said, "I do not work well on an empty stomach."

Page caved in. "Thank you. I would enjoy dining with you, but I—"

"Excellent." The baron flipped a switch on the intercom

beside him. "Robert, have the car brought around. Mr. Shepard and I are going to the club." Both men rose. "I cannot remember, Mr. Shepard, someone somewhere mentioned that you were very close to Alexander Kidd's son, that he was your namesake. Am I correct?" He took Page's arm and walked him to the door.

"Your sources are, as one would expect, very accurate. My middle name is Marcus."

Androssy smiled. "Then perhaps you would enjoy dropping into the Gannet gallery on our way to luncheon. Mark Kidd is showing there. It is very close to my club. You would like that, no?"

"Thank you," Page replied as the baron reached forward to open the door for him. "Yes, I would like that."

"Excellent, Mr. Shepard, excellent."

"No, Mark, no. I absolutely refuse," Judith Kidd stated flatly. "And if you won't drive me, I'll take a taxi to the Castle."

The noontime heat outside the Tangier airport was unbearable. Judith raised her hand to summon a taxi and indicated to the porter who stood nearby to take her luggage to it. As the small Moroccan reached for the largest suitcase, Mark Kidd put his foot on it.

"Mother, please be reasonable," he pleaded.

"I *am* being reasonable. I want to go home and have a bath, a cool drink, and lunch," she countered. "Now, if there is some specific reason for my not going, then you'd better tell me what it is." She looked challengingly at her son. His face was torn between emotions. There was something, she knew, something very serious. And she would get it out of him. "Very well," she said, turning from him and lifting her hand for the taxi.

"Damn it," he cried, reaching down to take possession of her suitcase.

"It has something to do with Alex, and with Sandra's murder, doesn't it?" Judith stated the question as if it were established fact.

"You know about it?"

"Don't be naive, dear. The whole world knows about it." She smiled tolerantly at her son. "He's at the Castle?"

Although he shook his head in violent protest, the subtle change in Mark's expression confirmed her suspicion.

"Then he will be. Is that it?"

He said nothing.

Judith softened her tone. "Darling, I know your father is no murderer, so don't worry on that score." That said, her tone hardened once more. "Now, what is he up to? Mark, answer me."

"I promised, Mother," her son said miserably. "All I can say is that Dad's up to his eyes in something that might be— well, dangerous."

"Might be?" she countered boldly. "Sandra shot to death, your father dropped from sight, and you say '*might be*'?"

"In case anything does happen here in the next few days, he doesn't want you involved," Mark persisted. "Please."

"You're involved, aren't you?" she snapped bravely.

"Well yes, but—"

"If my husband and my son are involved, then, damn it, I'm involved too." Judith snatched up her jewelry case and walked to the waiting taxi. "When you two come to your senses," she called back, "I'll be at home soaking in a nice tub." She slammed the car door, and the taxi sped off, swirling dry, ocher dust behind as Mark Kidd watched in frustration. Judith looked back at her son. Her body was ice cold and her hands trembled. What, she wondered, has that bastard done to us this time?

The chauffeur held the door as Miklos Androssy and Page Shepard left the limousine and crossed the pavement to the Gannet galley. One of the directors broke away from two women clients to greet the men as they entered. "You've come back to look at the Kidds," he said to Androssy as he ushered them into the exhibition room.

Page looked at the banker with surprise. "Then you've

seen them before?" The baron nodded. Page's uneasiness grew.

"Striking, are they not?" Androssy asked. "You must be very proud of your namesake, Mr. Shepard."

"I am," Page replied as he walked slowly from one painting to the next. He paused before a seascape and smiled.

Staying slightly to one side, Androssy stood carefully watching the other's reactions. "It amuses you?" he asked.

"Not really, just brings back happy memories. If I'm not mistaken, it's a view of the beach before the house at Fishers Island. He must have done it from a sketch years ago." He pointed to several slashes of color. "Those would be my two boys."

"Interesting how he is able to obtain so much form and definition with so few strokes," Androssy commented. "A very talented young man." He walked past Page to a painting of a jumble of sun-drenched buildings that seemed to grow up the side of a hill to a fortress, and waited until Shepard joined him. "And this one?"

"Tangier," Page said almost to himself. "Gosh, I haven't thought of the Castle for years." Androssy's body stiffened.

"Tangier?" he asked casually.

"Well, it was really an abandoned prison. Judith and Alex bought it years ago"—he pointed at the tower of the walled building that capped the hill—"and fixed it up for a summer place. It's right at the top of the Casbah. Leave it to Alex to do the exotic," he said, smiling. Page walked on to the next painting. Androssy followed.

"Does he still own it?" This was the revelation he had hoped for. None of his research into Alexander Kidd had come up with a castle in Tangier.

"Yes," Page replied absently, and then corrected himself. "Actually it belongs to Judith. He put it in her name."

"Exactly when did they buy it?" Androssy tried to make his questions seem unimportant. "It is indeed a splendid place for a summer home."

"Oh, about nine or ten years ago." Page moved on and

stood before another painting. "Here's another one of Fishers."

Androssy barely heard him. His mind raced with the information he had obtained from Alexander Kidd's friend. Everything fit. An old fortress halfway between Charon II's permanent orbit over the United States and the Middle East. From there Kidd could help guide the movement of the satellite across the Atlantic and over the Mediterranean to Israel, Iran, Syria, the entire area. And from there he could direct its beam to the Cerberus circuits in the weapons on the ground and in the air with complete accuracy. One way or the other, it would be to that castlelike fortress that Alexander Kidd must be heading now. Androssy would beat him there. He would *have* to beat him there.

Excusing himself, Androssy left Page Shepard standing before one of Mark's paintings and went to the gallery phone. His words were brief and to the point. "Robert, Kidd has gone to Tangier. Get the plane ready at once." He paused. "Yes, Mr. Shepard will be joining us."

Page found out about the impending trip during his luncheon with Miklos Androssy. "I had hoped we could wrap up this thing today," the baron said, "but KWEN's commitments here in Europe are far more complicated than I had anticipated." He laid down the summary sheets that Page had given him to review. "However, from what I see here, I am still very much interested."

"Good, perhaps tomorrow I can—"

"Unfortunately," Androssy interrupted, "I must fly to Hamburg this afternoon."

Page frowned. "Well then, when you return."

"That will be too late, Mr. Shepard. I need agreement no later than the day after tomorrow." His expression brightened. "Perhaps you will join me on the flight. It will give us time to review everything and put together a proposal to telex to your board in New York for approval."

Page shook his head. "I'm unable to leave London now. Too many—"

"Mr. Shepard, we are talking of some nine million

dollars. Surely you could defer whatever other business you have here for a few days."

"Unfortunately, I cannot."

"I must insist," Baron Androssy said, leaning across the table to look him squarely in the face.

"I beg your pardon," Page countered. "Obviously you did not hear me. I cannot leave London at this time. That's all there is to it. I am sure if you really are interested in the KWEN deal, we can discuss it upon your return."

"No, Mr. Shepard," Androssy said firmly. "You obviously did not hear *me*. I said that I insist."

"There's nothing more to be said." Page crumpled his napkin in preparation to rising.

"Sit down, faggot," Androssy hissed.

Page slowly lowered himself back into his chair, feeling as if he had just had the wind knocked from him by a heavy blow to the stomach. He could hardly believe his ears. It was the blackmailing voice he had heard over the phone in New York. He stared at his luncheon host. "You," he gasped.

Androssy did not reply to the accusation. "In two hours you and I will be on my plane for Morocco. You are going to take me to your friend Mr. Kidd's castle there. Is that clear?"

"What do you want? Why do—"

"Is that clear, Mr. Shepard?"

CHAPTER 25

For as long as anyone could remember, the high, white-washed walls of The Castle, as it was known to the local residents, had been Tangier's crown. It rose above the jumble of sun-baked, tiled roofs of poor shops and crumbling hovels that crowded one against the other up the narrow maze of alleyways honeycombing the steep central hill that dominated the city. Alluring to tourists by day, sinister at night, this shadowy native quarter was the Casbah, a place where brother sold sister, father sold son. A former Moorish prison, the Castle stood on the northwest corner of the broad cobblestone square that topped the hill. Once-elaborate houses of the long-deceased ruling class and decaying government buildings, some now converted to museums, surrounded the other sides of the breeze-cooled square.

The only entrance to the Castle was guarded by a heavy, iron-ribbed wooden door set into an arch in the south wall opening onto the square. The west wall rose into space above a sheer cliff that fell hundreds of feet to the crashing breakers of the Atlantic Ocean. A tower stood two stories above the structure's northwest corner. From it, one could see nearly the entire waterfront of Tangier below and far across the strait to the Rock of Gibraltar rising through the salt mist along the Spanish coast. Crowding against and below that northern wall, smaller dwellings, some combined and converted into the luxurious summer homes of the jet set, shared the spectacular view. The east wall had nothing to recommend it. Twenty-five feet high, it overlooked the square and the entrances to the steep alleys leading down into the crowded Casbah.

Flushed with his success in launching his satellite network, and backed with unlimited funds from President Warren's secret war chest, Alexander Kidd had managed to buy the deserted and crumbling landmark for a fraction of its present value. Over a two-year period, he and his artistic wife had converted the building into a showplace, mixing the traditional fabrics and style of Morocco with the glass and stainless steel elegance of modern designers. A shallow reflecting pool deep enough for swimming now occupied the center of the small courtyard. Spray from its two fountains glistened under cloudless skies and cooled the midday air. Tall Moorish arches and palm trees ran around all four sides of the pool to shade the story-and-a-half-high, glass-walled living and dining rooms at the north and south ends of the pool. The shade offered relief from the glaring sun to clusters of gaily striped canvas furniture carefully arranged for the comfort of visiting friends.

Small guest bedrooms honeycombed the east and west walls at various levels, depending on the caprices of the stone staircases that wound up through these two sides of the old prison. Their small, vertically barred windows looked out on to the pool or, to the west, across the Atlantic. Hidden behind the outer symmetry of the whitewashed walls, the flat interior roofs of the Castle ran along all four sides, rising and falling depending upon the heights of the various rooms below. They offered a series of attractive surfaces upon which to sun on wide lounges, gather for luncheon under the shelter of bamboo shades, or to sip cocktails while gazing at the setting sun.

The tower had been Alex and Judith's retreat from the world. Only twelve feet square, the great Moorish arches in all four walls had been filled with glass, and a large square bed heaped with silk cushions had been placed in the center of the room. At night they had lain in each other's arms, looking down over the lights of the Strait of Gibraltar and the towns along the Mediterranean. Above, rested a large radio dish carefully hidden under the observation platform of the tower. Judith had considered it a whim of Alex's. She had no idea that it was the sole reason for his buying and converting the old landmark.

As their son had grown, he and his father had built a second, much smaller radio tower upon the roof of the Castle and a transmitter in a storage room off the courtyard next to Mark's bedroom. The Moroccan government had been informed of and given its permission for Mark's radio transmitter. They remained ignorant of the much larger one smuggled in piece by piece by his father.

Judith sat on the roof of the Castle, looking at Mark's radio tower. The last violet glow of the sun had long since faded over the Atlantic. Her son sat beside her, a small table with cups between them.

"Will madam require anything else?" the butler and manager of the house asked as he put down a fresh pot of thick, dark coffee.

"Thank you, no, Ahmed," she replied after looking at her son.

"The boys are on watch?" Mark Kidd asked. "Everything is secured?"

"Everything, sir. Mohammed, Houri, and I will take turns all night. No one will get by us," he assured the younger Kidd. "And there are the police."

"Thank you, Ahmed."

The old retainer bowed and left them, descending the narrow stairs from the roof to the courtyard and kitchens beside the main gate of the old fortress.

"When did you say Alex was due in?" Judith asked nervously.

"Hopefully midnight, assuming he made good time on the *Privateer* and getting across Spain."

Mark had relented, telling his mother the complete story except for the existence of the codes his father had hidden in the Castle. She thought Alex needed only the powerful transmitter concealed in a small, derelict-appearing shed wedged between the north wall of the Castle and the dwelling below. To an outsider, it looked no more than a decaying addition. It had surprisingly thick walls of cement and steel and was accessible only through a narrow door hidden behind the wine racks now lining one of the old cells of the Castle. Mark rose and walked to the wall. He looked over into the square. A policeman leaned against an arch of a nearby house. Looking up, he waved. Mark raised his hand in return.

"What did you tell the police?" his mother asked, reaching over to pour him another cup of coffee.

"That someone had tried to break in last night and could we have a little more protection for a few days."

"That's all?" Judith asked, surprised.

"That and a little financial contribution."

"I thought so," she smiled, filling his cup. Her eyes fell on the pistol he had tucked into the waist of his jeans. She was about to ask if it was really necessary when she remembered Sandra's murder. Mark had given both house-boys and Ahmed rifles. Like the radio, they had been smuggled into the Castle in case of emergency. The old cook and maid were unarmed, the men feeling it safer not to have nervous amateurs wandering around with weapons in the dark. Judith looked at the small pistol Mark had given her lying on the glass-topped table. She wondered if she could ever bring herself to actually kill someone.

Mark turned from the wall and came to sit with his mother. Neither he nor the two policemen had noticed the shadowy figures that had slowly materialized from out of the alleys of the Casbah and now loitered in the darkness around the square. The distant noises of radios and barking dogs drifted up from the jumble of houses below, and a cool breeze blew in from the Atlantic.

"Chilly?" he asked.

"No, I'm fine." Judith pulled the sweater over her shoulders more closely around her. "Pinto is bringing him across?"

"Yes."

"He's a terrible scoundrel, but he adores your father."

She smiled to herself and added, "I guess it takes one to know one."

"You've met him?"

She nodded. "His men brought in all that radio equipment in the shed and the disk in the tower. How they ever got it all up the old smuggler's trail, I'll never know." Judith referred to a narrow and treacherous footpath that had been hacked into the side of the cliff under the west wall of the Castle. It doubled back and forth from the beach below to the top of the Casbah. From the top or bottom it was completely invisible to all but the most knowledgeable villain. "Pinto hauled the pieces up by rope from the widest part just under the cells at night." She shook her head. "And all those years I thought the radio was just another of your father's whims, not a strategic outpost for the States."

"Well, it won't be for much longer. As soon as Dad blows up Charon Two, there won't be any more need for it." Mark stood again and walked back to the wall, peering nervously over into the darkness.

Judith looked up at the stars twinkling in the clear night sky and imagined one was the KWEN satellite. It held many memories, both sweet and sour, for her. She sighed. "I'm going to miss the old boatman," she said to her son.

"I used to use that trail too, you know," Mark said, absently looking down at the light of the policeman's glowing cigarette.

"You didn't," Judith said, turning to him in surprise. "What on earth for? It's much too dangerous."

"Did you think I only swam in that dinky little pool down there?" he asked, referring to the reflecting pool in the courtyard below them. "I like the ocean."

"When did you do that?" she demanded in a tone of outraged motherhood.

"Oh, when I was about fifteen," he replied with a mischievous twinkle in his eyes.

"Fifteen! You could have been killed."

"Up until last summer." He broke into a wide grin at her horrified expression barely visible in the flickering light of the hurricane lamp on the table. "If no one's moved it, I'll bet the rope ladder I made to get down to that wide part of the trail you were talking about is still in that storage bin under the banquette over there." He pointed to the yellow-and-white-striped canvas cushions running along the west wall. "A pretty nifty job, if I do say so myself."

"Did your father know about it?" she demanded.

He nodded. "I'm sure, but he never let on."

"Men," Judith mumbled, secretly proud of both of hers. But was Alex still hers? During their last time together, she had finally made the decision to give him the divorce he seemed to want so much. And she had meant to put it in the works. But somehow she just had not gotten around to it. If it would really make him happy, then perhaps she would release him no matter the hurt to her. How long, she wondered, can you go around loving someone who did not seem to need or want you anymore? Mark's voice interrupted her thoughts.

"It's awfully quiet down there." He leaned out through the notch in the thick wall and craned his neck in both directions. "Can't see that policeman." He looked across the square, trying to make out the other one.

"Probably attending to the urgencies of nature," his mother answered casually without thinking. "What time is it?"

"Nearly eleven-thirty."

"Shouldn't you be heading on down to the Tripoli?" she asked, referring to the seedy waterfront bar inhabited by the Tangier underworld and its hangers-on. "If your father is on schedule, Pinto will surely have made it across from Tarifa by now."

Mark Kidd hesitated. "I'll stay for a few more minutes."

Judith smiled, recognizing his concern for her. "Mark, stop worrying. Aside from the fact that it would take an army to break in here, you've got policemen stationed outside and three—no, four"—she picked up the small pistol from the table beside her—"armed troops inside. Go on." Despite her brave words and smile, Judith was more

afraid than she had ever been in her life. Had it not been for
her terrible concern for Mark and Alex and her fear for her
parents should Israel actually be attacked in the manner
Mark had described, she would have moved out and tried to
take him with her. But he was his own man now, and for the
first time in years, father and son were standing together.
She would stand with them.

"You're sure? You won't change your mind?"

"Off," she ordered. "And if that bastard old man of
yours is there, don't hang around having beers for the road.
Hurry on back—fast."

Mark came to stand by her and looked into her raised
eyes. "Love you," he said, leaning down to kiss her
forehead.

How Judith wanted to reach up and hold him tight.
Instead she said, "Beat it, brat."

She watched his back as he walked across the flat roof
and disappeared down the narrow steps leading through the
west wall into the courtyard. "God go with you," Judith
whispered to the darkness at the top of the steps. Suddenly
aware of the pain in her right hand, she looked down. Her
knuckles were white from the force with which she was
gripping the gun. Judith dropped it on the table in disgust.

A taxi rattled across the dark cobblestone square,
approaching the gate in the south wall. Its horn tooted in a
happy staccato, shattering the quiet of the night. Alex? she
wondered. Could that crazy man be actually . . . Jumping
up, Judith started toward the wall to look over but was
distracted by the angry voices—some Arab, some English—coming up from the courtyard. "Don't open that
gate," she heard Mark call out as he ran around the
reflecting pool. Again voices were raised in protest.

Mark Kidd, his gun drawn, brushed Ahmed and Houri
aside from the small, barred peephole in the main gate and
looked out cautiously. His face suddenly lit up. "Uncle
Page," he cried in surprised relief, using the title he had
always applied to this old family friend. Jamming his pistol
into the waist of his jeans, he motioned to Ahmed, and the

two began to pull back the thick iron bolts, heedless of
Page's anguished expression and unaware of the men who
stood hidden on either side of him. Averting his eyes, the
policeman across the square bent to tighten his shoelace.

Judith hurried to the edge of the roof to look down into
the courtyard. What was happening? Page? Page Shepard
here? She did not know why, but instinct made her cry out,
"Mark, no. Don't!"

Too late, the small door set into the larger gate burst
open. Page Shepard fell forward, shoved to the stone floor
as Robert Frankel and another rushed in behind, the bleats
of the taxi's horn momentarily covering their onslaught.

Running forward in a vain protest, Houri's scream was
cut short. His face exploded from the impact of Frankel's
bullet. Splattered with gore, Ahmed fell to his knees in
horror, a heavy blade slicing down through his neck before
he could even beg for mercy. Fumbling for his gun, Mark
Kidd only had time to take three steps backward before
Frankel's silenced bullet punctured his chest. Turning, he
staggered into the courtyard to cry out, "Mother, run,"
before collapsing. Page Shepard lay in shock, staring at the
carnage about him as Miklos Androssy moved quickly from
the taxi and entered. One by one, dark, shadowy figures
converged from their posts around the square and followed
him in, pushing the gate closed behind them. The taxi
moved off.

It had happened so fast. Judith, her hands pressed over
her mouth to keep from screaming, stared down at her fallen
son and the strangers cautiously moving forward around
him. She backed away from the edge of the roof, her lungs
heaving with fright and stifled sobs, losing herself in the
darkness.

Androssy's angry voice came up to her. "I told you not to
harm the boy." Another voice ordered, "Search the place.
Bring everyone here to me." Androssy knelt to examine
Mark Kidd. "He still has a pulse. Shepard," he called, "get
over here and help him. I need him alive."

"Alive." Judith repeated the word softly. She started

forward to go to him. Her mind reeling in confusion, she stood torn. Go to Mark. No, escape. Get Alex. He would know what to do. She looked about her. The flickering hurricane lamp. Running softly back to it, she blew out the candle. The bright yellow-and-white-striped banquettes across the roof met her eyes in the darkness. Judith remembered Mark's rope ladder. It was her only way out to Alex. She ran to them.

The wails of the two servant women came to her from below as she desperately raised the top of one banquette after another. Angry voices drummed questions at the frightened and bewildered wretches. Judith heard their sobs and the slap of hard hands across their faces as her own hands fumbled for and found the jumble of rope and pulled it out. Searching feet ran softly about the courtyard and from room to room as she frantically unwound and tried to untangle its snags. Done. She looked over her shoulder at the doorway leading up to the roof from the building below as she threw the ladder over the west wall near the tower and hooked its top rung over a stone merion of the parapet. Her mind was now clear and determined, all confusion gone. She knew exactly what had to be done. Turning, Judith ran back to the coffee table and snatched up the pistol, thrusting it into her sweater pocket. Back at the wall, she removed her sandles and forced them into the other pocket. The voices calling from one room to another below her were coming closer. Pulling herself up onto the parapet, she slid her feet over and, taking one look down at the foam thrown up in the dim starlight by the waves breaking on the rocky beach hundreds of feet below, began her dangerous climb down the uncertan ladder. Mark did it, she repeated over and over in her mind, so can I.

But Mark Kidd was far younger and more athletic than his mother. Judith struggled with the sagging rope rungs that tangled her feet and swung her painfully against the rough stone wall. More than once she lost her footing and hung dangling hundreds of feet above the waves below. Her beautifully manicured nails and hands were torn and

scraped raw by the time she reached the foot of the wall.
She had only twenty feet more down over the rocks to the
old smugglers' trail hacked into the cliff face. Judith paused
to catch her breath and regain her strength before making
the final descent.

A noise above and to the right turned her heart to ice, and
she pressed back against the wall. The dark head of one of
the Castle's invaders peered out through a crenel in the
parapet and looked to the right and left. The ladder was
looped around a merion no more than ten feet from him. A
gust of wind from the sea fluttered the full skirt of her dress.
The man looked down. His face, backlit from the lights
within, was black and featureless to her. Judith held her
breath. If he saw her, would he shoot? Or worse, would he
cut the rope and watch as she plunged down onto the rocks
below?

The west wall lay in complete darkness, the half-moon
not yet high enough to cast its pale light over it. The head
withdrew. Gathering her courage, Judith struggled down the
last feet to the smuggler's trail. The agony of her flight was
just beginning.

Difficult for the most surefooted man in daylight, in the
blackness the trail proved a nightmare. Narrow, uneven,
unpredictable, the rough surface was covered with dirt and
small pebbles fallen from the cliff face that made it slippery.
Judith kept the sandles in her pocket, her bare feet the surest
guide in the dark. With her back pressed to the cliff and her
hands groping for holds, she inched her way slowly along
the treacherous path. The sound of the surf pounding the
rocks below filled her ears—she dared not look down.

"Fools," Androssy hissed at two of his PLO henchmen
standing beside him atop the parapet. "What have you got
for eyes?" His right hand gripped the rope loop around the
merion; he pulled at it impatiently. "She cannot have gotten
far in the dark, not in this short time. You," he pointed to
the two men, "go after her."

The first, dressed in shabby street clothes, hoisted
himself up and through the crenel, swinging himself out

onto the ladder. His pointed leather shoes slipped on the rungs until he learned to angle them down so the rope would catch in their heels. Then he began a quick descent. The other waited, crouching in the crenel until his companion reached the trail below.

"Try to bring her back alive," Androssy ordered, "but if you cannot, then make it final. Hurry."

The Arab nodded and lowered himself down. His comrade steadied him as his feet reached the rocky trail and then, one holding a flashlight and the other a gun, they started after their fleeing quarry.

Looking over her shoulder, Judith saw the bobbing circle of light above and behind her moving down the face of the cliff. She knew exactly what it meant, and in her panic unwisely quickened her pace. Rounding an outcropping of rock, the wide, flat stone upon which she stepped tilted down slightly in the dry rock rubble holding it. Thrown off balance, Judith lost her footing, and her hands tore loose from their holds in the cliff surface. Stifling the scream in her throat, she grasped the stone with the toes of her bare feet and let her legs buckle beneath her to fall straight down and back on the stone rather than out into space. Struggling to find new holds, Judith felt the stone beneath slipping under her weight. In desperation she grabbed for an exposed root of a dead bush and dragged herself forward and off the deadly seasaw as a shower of loose pebbles from the rock face above fell over her bare legs. The stone slowly tipped back up into place.

Pulling herself up into a standing position, the trembling and terrified woman took several deep breaths and, gritting her teeth, edged on, not daring to look down to the broiling surf that had nearly claimed her. Judith tried to concentrate on the Tripoli and Alex, not the beam of the flashlight drawing closer and closer behind her.

"There, shine the light over there," the second of her two pursuers urged the other. "I think that is she."

The Arab aimed the flashlight in the direction his companion pointed, a hundred yards or so ahead and down to their left. He moved it slowly over the cliff face, searching. The faint beam caught Judith's figure, her dress flapping in the wind, and stopped.

Her heart leaped, she could almost feel the heat of the light that cast her shadow dimly against the rock to which she pressed herself. A voice called out to her.

"Come back, lady. We won't hurt you."

The cries of her son and those slaughtered up at the Castle echoed in her mind. Judith looked to the source of the light and then back. She continued to edge her way forward.

"Lady, come back," the first man called. He whispered to his companion, "Shoot the pig." The other raised his arm and took aim.

The steep trail led Judith into a shallow cleft in the cliff, hiding her temporarily from her pursuers' view. Cursing, the lead Arab brought the beam of the flashlight back to the narrow path upon which they stood and moved onward. "We will get closer. Come." An outcropping of rock seemed to bar their way. He shone the light down upon the wide, flat stone just beyond and, finding a handhold, swung himself around the obstruction onto it.

Loosened earlier, the stone tilted abruptly away. His leather-soled shoes skidded on the scattered pebbles and slipped from under him. As he cried out, the flashlight looped down through space. He grasped frantically at the face of the cliff and then back to his companion's leg. The other kicked back, trying to free himself from the hold that pulled him slowly toward the trail's edge. The struggle for life and death was brutal and brief. Judith closed her eyes tightly, trying to shut out the fading screams that followed each other down and ended abruptly on the rocks below. Her mind pictured what the darkness concealed. "Let me get through," she prayed softly. "Oh, God, let me get through." She drove herself onward along the treacherous path, feeling her way slowly down the rough face of the cliff.

It took Judith nearly an hour before she finally reached the cold, wet sand of the rock-strewn beach. The saltwater that surged up through them stung her torn and bleeding feet. Kneeling, she scooped up handfuls of water and splashed her face, rubbing the coldness across the back of her neck to refresh her exhausted body. Then standing, she looked far up ahead toward the waterfront of Tangier and the dark alleys twisting through its harbor district. The small pistol she clutched in her sweater pocket was little comfort.

CHAPTER 26

"He should have been here over an hour ago," Alex grumbled nervously for the dozenth time. He stared at the cracked glass in the wall clock at the end of the dingy bar.

His bearded friend reached over and patted his arm. "Drink your beer, Alex. He will be here." The smuggler, Pinto, raised his own glass and downed its remains.

"Something must have happened up there."

"I have sent my man to the Castle to look around. You worry too much, my friend." Pinto signaled across the room for another beer.

Alex rubbed the stubble on his unshaven face and looked about the dim, nearly empty bar. The uneven plastered walls had long since lost their paint, the wooden tables their polish. Several swarthy figures hunched over the bar conversing in low voices, and two overly painted women sat by a gaudy jukebox. The multicolored lights shining through its dirty glass panels illuminated the sweat stains under the arms of their dresses. Nearby, a beaded curtain hid the steps that led upstairs to small, cramped rooms where sex in any form could be purchased to meet the varying perversions of the Tripoli's patrons.

"It's after two," Alex growled, the concern for his son evident in his voice. He stared straight ahead over the flame of the candle on their table at an ugly, heavyset man with a shaved head and dark mustache who sat in the corner. The man returned his stare. "Who is he?"

"A regular, nothing to worry about," the smuggler replied. "His wife and daughter work upstairs."

"Jesus," Alex mumbled in disgust.

"It pays the rent," Pinto said flatly. He nodded his thanks as the barman set two bottles of beer on the table before them. Drops of condensation ran down the cold amber glass.

The flame of the candle flickered as the door across the room slowly opened. Both men looked up at the pale, bedraggled woman who entered hesitantly. She stood back against the wall in the gloom, looking about the place. When she saw them, she started forward. In a flash of recognition, Alex was on his feet and across the bar, sweeping her into his arms as she collapsed against him. "Thank God I've found you," Judith wept.

Supporting her, Alex turned back toward the table. "What are *you* doing here?" he demanded in a low voice. "Where's Mark?"

Pinto rose to help Judith sink into the chair between them and called for cognac from the barman. All eyes in the place were focused with sullen curiosity on the two Americans and their Moroccan companion.

"What's happened?" The agony in Alexander Kidd's voice evidenced the dread he felt.

"Give her a chance, Alex," Pinto protested.

"No, no, I'm all right." Judith wiped her eyes with the back of her hand and turned to her husband. "Alex, they've shot Mark."

"Who?"

"Page and—"

"Page?" Kidd cried in disbelief. "What in the hell is he doing—"

"No, he didn't do it. The others, a European and a lot of Arabs. They broke through—"

"Androssy," he spit out. Alex's fist clenched on the table.

"Is he dead?" Pinto pressed.

Alex had anticipated the worst. A wave of relief flooded over him as she answered.

"No, not yet. Alex, it's serious, we've got to get him to a

hospital, got to get him out." She looked at her husband, her eyes imploring him to do the impossible. "The servants . . ." Her voice broke. "They've killed the men. I heard their screams." Tears ran down her face. Alex once more wrapped her trembling body in his arms. Reaching for the cognac the barman had brought, he forced it to her lips.

"Just a sip, darling. Take a sip."

Pinto looked across the room as the door of the Tripoli once again opened and one of his men entered. He rose and crossed to join him at the bar where the two spoke softly for several minutes. When he returned, Judith had regained much of her composure and was explaining in detail everything that had happened that night.

"Your home is swarming with PLO scum," Pinto said quietly, looking down at them. "At least a dozen." He lowered himself into a chair beside Alex.

"Mark?" Judith asked. "And the maids?"

"I don't know. My man couldn't get much out of the police up there. They turned their backs when it happened. Bastards," he swore. "They're scared. You don't make enemies of those slimy PLO killers and their friends in Tangier if you want to live long."

"Go to the chief of police, Alex," Judith begged, "or the army. You know them all."

Grimly he shook his head. "You forget there's an international warrant out for my arrest. To them I'm a playboy killer on the run."

"Then I'll go." Judith Kidd sat up straight and determined.

Pinto was the one to reply. "They will kill everybody in the Castle and fade away at the first sign of that kind of trouble. I know them."

She sank back down in her chair.

Alex spoke his thoughts aloud. "We've got to get in to get Mark out. And I've got to get in to that transmitter." He looked at the wall clock across the room. He had only twenty-four hours left before the Charon II struck. "How? How?" he repeated, shaking his head.

"The smuggler's trail," Judith urged desperately. "We—"

"They know about that now," Kidd interrupted. "They'll be watching."

Judith turned to Pinto. "Your men. Couldn't they slip in over the walls? They're good at . . ."

Once again she was interrupted. Pinto reached across Alex and put his hand on hers. "My men will never go against the PLO openly," he whispered, looking cautiously about the room and then back to Judith. "We would isolate ourselves from our Arab friends in Tangier. We may not like the terrorists, but in our business we need them and their supporters." He lowered his eyes. "I am sorry."

She covered his hand with hers. "I understand." Her heart was breaking for her son.

Pinto smiled weakly, and then his expression suddenly changed. He turned to Alex. "But the transmitter, it is the one we brought up for you?"

"Yes."

"That is in the little house *outside* the Castle?"

Again Alex nodded. "But the entrance is from inside the Castle, from the old cells."

"Cannot a house have *two* entrances?" Pinto smiled. "The floor is thin metal, I remember. We will dig under and use a torch to cut up through it."

Alex stared at him, his mind turning over the possibility. "You mean break in from the main house below?"

Pinto was in his element. "No, my friend, do you know who lives there now? And the noise?" He made a face and shook his head. "We tunnel in from the alley."

"But that's directly beneath the north wall." In his mind Alex pictured the narrow cobblestone alley. "Androssy will see us."

"Of course he will. But he will see only the dirty, underpaid employees of the Ministry of Public Works, the one who makes sure all the drains in Tangier do not work, that the sewage clogs the pipes, that the water is not fit to drink." Pinto smiled. "My friends, in my business I have found that the best way *not* to be seen *is* to be seen."

"We don't have much time left," Alex cautioned.

"So? *We* have strong backs." Pinto looked hopefully at Alexander Kidd.

Kidd nodded with a half smile and completed the smuggler's thought. "And *I* will supply the financial incentive."

"It is not for me," Pinto assured him honestly.

"Of course not," Alex replied in mock sympathy. "It is for your 'employees.'"

"Exactly," the other confirmed. "It pays the rent."

Kidd thought for a moment and then shook his head. "It won't work. I still need to get inside the Castle."

"But you can, through the cells," Pinto replied, not understanding the other's problem. "Then you smuggle your son out through the little house when they sleep." It seemed so simple to him.

"I have to get up to the radio dish in the tower. The doors over it are locked. The transmitter's no good unless . . ."

"Unless I'm there to open them," Judith Kidd suggested. It was her chance, her rational excuse to be with her son.

Both men looked at her in surprise. "No way," Alex said. "Never."

"It's the only way," Judith protested.

"You're not going back into that place." He paused. "Page, we'll get Page to do it."

"And exactly how do you propose to do that?" she challenged. "Telephone him?" Judith remembered her son's cries from the courtyard. "And you're assuming Page is on our side. Right now I'm not so sure."

"Oh, come on," Alex said, deriding her skepticism, "you know Page would never run out on us, certainly not once he knew what we are trying to do. He's the most loyal, the most American American you can find."

"Then explain why he's sitting up there in the Castle with that baron friend of his," Judith whipped back.

"I can't. I don't know. Somehow Androssy's using him,

but believe me, Page doesn't know what's going on." Alex stood firm.

"Okay, I'll go along with that, but we still have to contact him and I'm the best way. Page can help me once I'm inside. After we've unlocked the tower doors, we'll try to get Mark down to you."

Alex was torn. Judith's solution seemed their only chance to save their son and stop Charon II, but it could mean her death. Androssy would certainly kill everyone in the Castle to cover up his identity and the role he had played in the kidnapping of the satellite and the destruction of Israel. With no one left to point the finger at him, he could resume his luxurious international banker role in New York and continue his operations there undetected.

On the other hand, if Alex were successful in destroying Charon II, the Russians would come down on Androssy like a ton of bricks. He alone would be blamed for the disastrous Middle East war and the loss of the U.S.S.R's world-controlling weapon. His elimination, apparently by his PLO compatriots in the Castle, could be instantaneous, and the Americans might escape. The two men were in a gamble against each other—and Judith was part of the stakes.

"I won't let you do it," he said firmly. His once supreme confidence in his ability to always win had been badly shaken in the last weeks. The terrible choice he was being forced to make brought to the surface his feeling for Judith, forced him to admit his continuing need and love for her.

She recognized it and put her hand over his. "You have nothing to say about it," she said softly. "I'm going back to the Castle and I will unlock those doors, whether you intend to do anything with the dish or not. I will be with our son no matter what else happens." She was now sitting straight and in control. "So, my darling, you had better make good use of my being there."

Alexander Kidd saw the Judith of their earlier years together, her determination that he had loved and admired, and then had come to resent. He had been a fool. Not knowing what to say, he turned to Pinto. "What do you think?"

The smuggler smiled and shrugged his shoulders. "It is your only way, my friend. The road of life has many turns that turn into turns that again turn into turns. Only Allah can lead you through without risk. Put your trust in him."

Reluctantly, Alex nodded. The three began to plot their next moves. Pinto was the first to leave. Alex and Judith remained, unwilling to break the first real contact they had shared for years. He raised his hand to signal the barman. Judith pulled it back down. "No, I should go now. You stay." She did not move.

"You'll be careful?" he asked stupidly.

She smiled warmly. "As careful as you."

"If this doesn't work out for some reason, I . . ."

Judith put a finger to his lips. "It will work out. Since when has Alexander Kidd ever not had things work out?"

She had always been a source of strength to him. Now he realized how much. She had encouraged him, worked side by side with him in the building of KWEN, been part of him. Looking at her tear-smudged face, dirty, torn hands, and straggling hair, he knew that behind the veneer of international sophistication, she remained the same Judith he had fallen in love with. She and her values had remained unchanged. He and his values were the ones that had lost their way.

"This could be the last time we . . ." His voice broke. "We may never . . ."

Judith leaned forward and kissed his lips, tenderly brushing a strand of hair from his forehead. "We're together, we always will be." Smiling softly, she stood and walked from the room without looking back. She was afraid to look back. Her shoulders were squared, her spine straight.

Farther to the east across the Mediterranean, gunfire erupted over the Syrian-Jordanian border at several points. Syrian tanks rumbled south through the night in what appeared to be a threat to Amman. Troops and armor, in an apparent counterbalancing operation, massed between the capital and Damascus only miles from the Israeli border. Jets from both sides engaged in showy strafing missions. Infiltrators on the West Bank and in the Gaza Strip gathered their forces together for final briefings before setting out for their positions along the roads leading to and from Jewish settlements. Libyan mechanics worked under cover of darkness to assure that the country's jet fighters were in top condition for the conflict that would explode in just twenty-four hours. And in Washington, lights burned as analysts gathered more and more information from U.S. and Israeli intelligence. Confusion greeted each new report, and anger. The Israelis were once again mobilizing.

CHAPTER 27

"Well, this *is* a surprise, Mrs. Kidd," Baron Androssy said, rising gallantly from one of the great white, overstuffed couches in the Castle's main living room. "I had not expected your return."

"Nor I your arrival," Judith countered. She stood cool and confident and immaculately groomed and attired in a stylish cotton dress borrowed from an English friend whose home she had visited earlier that morning. Behind her through the glass doors to the courtyard, the fountains in the pool were just beginning to catch the yellow glow of the sunrise in their spray.

"Touché." With a nod of his head, Miklos Androssy dismissed the Arab terrorist who had opened the gate to her. "Then you *were* here last night. The servants were confusing on that point."

"Yes."

"And escaped by that ladder?"

"Yes." It had been decided that the truth—or nearly the truth—was her safest course of action. Androssy was no fool.

"We wondered. Congratulations on your safe descent. Two of my group were not so fortunate."

"So I heard."

Androssy could not resist smiling at her rather cold-blooded reference to his men's death. In similar circumstances, his own wife would have retired to bed with a box of tissues and a headache. "And tell me, Mrs. Kidd, after

310

such strenuous efforts to leave this place, why have you returned?"

"I should have thought the answer would be obvious to you," Judith replied coolly. "I have returned to be with my son."

"Without bringing the entire Moroccan constabulary with you?"

"I wanted to see my son *alive*," she stated flatly.

"You have an excellent grasp of the situation, Mrs. Kidd," Androssy said with a smile. "You need not worry. Your son is alive but, I regret, still unconscious. A doctor is with him now."

"Doctor?" Judith was relieved and genuinely surprised.

"Oh, yes, you see I want your son alive right now as much as you do." He shrugged. "Or at least I did. Now that you are here, my need is greatly lessened. I am sure you will be able to give me the assistance your son would have rendered."

A chill went through Judith, but she stood firm. "And why *are* you here," she asked.

"To repeat your own words, 'I should have thought the answer would be obvious to you.' I am here to keep your husband from his transmitter and some codes that he has hidden here. I am sure he has told you the reason?" Androssy left the question hanging. Robert Frankel, who sat across the room in the shadows, watched her reaction carefully.

"My husband and I have not been together for some years," she replied. "I am certainly not the one he would turn to. I am not his confidante." Judith tried to inject bitterness into her voice.

"I thought that perhaps last night you and he . . . ?" Again the question was left open.

"Alex is in hiding somewhere in England. There is a warrant out for his arrest for the supposed murder of his . . ." She paused, and then added the contemptible word, "Mistress." Would he believe her? She went on to supply the credibility it needed. "My son, Mark, was with him in London when it happened."

Miklos Androssy stared at her. "But you know of my intentions," he stated flatly.

Judith nodded. "Mark told me."

He smiled. "But I forget my manners, Mrs. Kidd." He gestured to a nearby chair. "Please, please be seated. You must be very tired."

"I would like to see my son," Judith countered, still standing.

"In a minute. Please." Again he indicated the chair. As she crossed to it, her walk showed defiance. Judith sat. The baron sank back into the white sofa and crossed his legs, an infuriating picture of relaxed charm.

"And what do you think of my plan?" he asked.

"Ridiculous," Judith stated flatly.

He stiffened, the charming smile fading from his face. "Oh, really? And why do you say that?" The undercurrent of challenge in his voice was clear to Judith. She wondered if he had actually swallowed her bait.

"Alex may have convinced Mark of that cock-and-bull story, but I don't believe a word of it. He is just being his old dramatic self. But if you two want to play games with each other, go right ahead."

Androssy's voice was cold. "I assure you, Mrs. Kidd, that I do not play games."

Noise of picks and shovels came up through the open window over the alley below the north wall of the Castle. Briefly distracted, the baron glanced in that direction.

"Then why don't you just blow up Mark's radio tower and transmitter and leave?" Judith quipped, recapturing his attention. "That silly little thing isn't strong enough to reach a satellite anyway."

Androssy's eyes narrowed. When he had first seen the radio setup in the Castle, he had thought the same as Judith and had continued a fruitless search for a larger, more sophisticated transmitter which he now felt confident did not exist. "Oh, I assure you that it is powerful enough to reach a satellite if that satellite were to move along a line directly south of it over the equator—the same path Charon Two will soon follow."

He shrugged. "But that is beside the point. I am here solely to keep your husband from—shall we say—doing mischief to the satellite. And thank you. Your return has just doubled my bait."

Judith lowered her eyes. Increasing noise came from the alley below. "What is going on out there?" Androssy demanded sharply.

Walking to the window, Frankel looked down at the shoddy collection of men digging a trench in the alley below. The passage had been blocked off with official-looking signs and barricades. A stack of long pipes lay piled beside them. "They're putting in a new sewer or something," he said.

"Well, close the damn window," Androssy ordered. "I cannot think with all that racket."

Rising, Judith spoke. "May I go to my son now? I presume he is in his room."

"Yes, go. And Mrs. Kidd, remember that you are, shall we say, a prisoner while I am here."

He watched her leave the room and walk along the colonnade to the right of the courtyard to her son's room. "Robert," he called without turning, "come with me. I want to talk to the base in Minorca." Frankel left the window and followed his employer out across the courtyard to the room holding Mark Kidd's radio equipment. It adjoined the wounded boy's bedroom.

By the time she reached the door to her son's room, Judith's legs were trembling. The PLO guard stationed there stood back and permitted her to enter. Page Shepard and an elderly English expatriate, Dr. Evans, looked up from Mark's bedside.

"Judith, what are you doing here? I thought . . ." Page began, but she brushed aside his question.

"How is he?" Judith moved to her son's side, placing a hand on his feverish forehead.

"His right lung has collapsed, and there is internal bleeding," Dr. Evans stated bluntly.

"His chances?" she asked.

"Not very good unless we get him to the hospital. I've done all I can. He's barely holding his own."

She closed her eyes, absorbing what he had said with all the control she could muster. "Can he last for another twenty-four hours?"

"Perhaps. He's a strong young man." He took a gold watch from his white vest and looked at it. The time was just after seven. "Do you think they will release us then?"

"Yes, I think so." She replied positively for his sake. In her heart Judith knew the odds of getting out at all were slim. "What can I do to help?"

"Just be here if he regains consciousness."

Page came forward. "Judith, forgive me," he asked miserably. "I had no idea this was going to happen. I have no idea why it *is* happening."

"I know, dear friend," she replied, reaching up for his hand. "I hardly understand it myself."

Sweat rolled down Alex's back and chest under the striped work shirt as he labored alongside Pinto's men in the lengthening trench. The earth was hard and rocky and their progress slow, agonizingly slow. It was nearly noon, and they had covered only a third of the distance to the shack where his transmitter and the entrance to the Castle were hidden. Could they risk working through the traditional luncheon siesta period? They would have to.

He yearned to look up at the windows and parapet of the north wall in hopes of seeing Judith, but he dared not expose his face even though dirt had been smeared over it and a beret concealed his blond hair.

More than two stories above, Robert Frankel leaned over the parapet, studying with curiosity the activity below. Earlier he had sent one of the Arab terrorists out to investigate the purpose of the work. He had returned satisfied with the answer that a leaking sewage pipe was

being replaced. Frankel was not so satisfied. He had yet to
see a trace of that so-called leaking pipe in the trench
beneath him. His eyes moved over the straining backs of
each man, one after the other. What was it that did not seem
right to him? They were applying themselves, working
much harder than the normal street worker. Or was it his
imagination?

Several times that afternoon Judith Kidd accompanied by
Page Shepard mounted the steps to the Castle roofs and
wandered about the parapets, ostensibly for a breath of fresh
air. Frankel and the PLO guards lounging about in the shade
of the inner walls watched them with different emotions.
Had she, Frankel wondered, come back only to be with her
son as she claimed, or, as the baron suspected, was she
there for a very different purpose? By being given full run of
the Castle, would she in turn give away her real intent? The
terrorists regarded her with smoldering anger and resentment. They did not like her superior attitude so typical of
rich Americans and were sure that she was responsible for
the death of their two companions last night. Given a free
hand, they would gladly have flung the "American pig"
over the wall to the rocks below.

She and Shepard now stood at the north wall. Frankel's
eyes narrowed as they carefully followed her gaze. Not
once did she lean over the parapet and look down at the
laborers making so much noise. Not once. Shepard did, but
not Alexander Kidd's wife. Why? Instead her eyes scanned
the mosaic of roofs in the Casbah, the far-off shore of Spain,
and the sun that was beginning to set in the west. Frankel
leaned over the parapet once again and more carefully than
before studied the trench and each man working in it.

They were only two feet from the foundation of the
transmitter shack when the handle of the lead man's pickax
splintered as its iron head bounced off a large boulder.
"Merde," he swore, stepping back in the trench to let the
others at it. Using crowbars and shovels, the men pried
away the earth and rock debris covering the face of the

boulder and then attacked the sides of the trench in an effort
to find a way around or under it.

Pinto shook his head and spoke softly. "It is impossible,
Alex. That rock must go from under the Castle right across
the alley to the house on our right. It is too big."

"Under, can't we go under?" Kidd demanded, looking
up at the sky. The sun was sinking fast.

Pinto gave the order although he knew it to be useless.
Alex stood back and watched with growing frustration as
the others dug down along the face of the giant rock. So
close, he repeated over and over in his mind. So close.
Nearly an hour passed. He allowed himself a quick look up
at the parapet atop the north wall above, hoping but
knowing that Judith would not be there. How he yearned to
make eye contact with her. Had she risked her life in vain?
Anger suddenly exploded within him. Grabbing up a
pickax, he moved forward and swung it clanging again and
again at the base of the boulder before throwing it aside in
disgust.

Attracted by the noise, Robert Frankel again looked over
the parapet and smiled at the frustration of the large laborer
below. They'll need heavy equipment to get through, he
thought. As the angry worker turned away from the stone,
he removed his beret briefly to smooth back his sweat-
drenched hair. In that instant Frankel could have sworn he
saw blond hair. Was that possible?

"We have lost," Pinto said. "It was a good try."

"There has to be a way," Kidd insisted. He thought of
Judith and Mark and of the war that would start in less than
twelve hours, a war Israel had no chance of winning.

"Not this way," the other replied. "We must go. It is
long after normal working hours. They will become
suspicious." He called to the men, who began to gather
their tools with sighs of relief. The Tripoli would be a happy
place that evening with all the money the American was
going to pay them. "Come, Alex," Pinto said, putting a
sympathetic hand on his shoulder. "We will go back to the
shop and think things out."

"I'll have to go over the wall, that's all there is to it," Alex said, his voice a combination of determination and fatalism.

"It is a good way to get killed, Alex." The smuggler pushed him forward. Robert Frankel's eyes followed them.

"I'll need a diversion," Kidd said almost to himself, paying no heed to the other's warning. They turned the corner and walked down a narrow passage leading to the top of the Casbah. Frankel turned away from the parapet.

Shortly after, Judith Kidd walked along the same parapet toward the tower. With the exception of two PLO guards, none of the other inhabitants of the Castle were there. She was relieved that the baron's henchman, Frankel, had finally gone. With apparent casualness, Judith mounted the stone steps to the top of the tower as she sipped wine from the goblet in her hand. Comfortable banquettes had been built within all four sides to make the perfect place in which to relax with a predinner drink and watch the sun set over the Atlantic Ocean. Looking about her, Judith knelt and reached under one of the banquettes to slide back a bolt hidden beneath. Rising, she turned to cross the tower to release the second bolt on the doors over the dish antenna. As she leaned down, a voice froze her heart.

"Have you lost something, Mrs. Kidd?" Miklos Androssy asked. The urbane baron stepped forward from the tower steps and smiled as Judith straightened. He too held a goblet in one hand and a bottle of rich red wine in the other.

"No," she replied more calmly than she felt, "no." Judith touched the lobes of each ear, making a pretense of assuring herself that both dangling gold ornaments were in place.

"Good. May I join you?" Androssy asked.

"Of course," she answered cordially and then, as she carefully seated herself, added, "Under the present circumstances it is kind of you to bother to ask."

Androssy sat opposite her on the banquette she had indicated with a nod. It rested against the eastern parapet of the tower facing directly into the sunset. He was forced to narrow his eyes somewhat against the intensity of the sun. "Such a lovely view from here."

"My husband and I enjoyed it," she conceded.

"You use the past tense."

"The Castle no longer holds Alex's interest."

"Nor does he care about those in it?"

Judith shrugged. "As I said earlier today, my husband's emotions lie elsewhere." She changed the subject. "When do you plan to move Charon Two?"

Squinting down, Androssy studied his watch, his eyes taking some time to adjust from the brightness of the sunset. Judith noted it with satisfaction. Looking back up at her, he smiled confidently. "We began her change in orbit just fifteen minutes ago at precisely three in the afternoon New York time. The satellite should pass almost directly south of us at one this morning."

"Its final destination, Israel," Judith stated flatly.

"Over the Mediterranean, thirty degrees east at five o'clock tomorrow morning on the same latitude as three great cities: Alexandria, Istanbul, and"—he paused before finishing with a flourish—"Leningrad."

"Its signal can reach Israel from there?"

"With surprising precision. The country is only thirty degrees north and five degrees farther east."

Judith remained silent.

"You have many friends there?" he asked with callous disregard.

She nodded. "And my parents."

"Pity." There was not a trace of remorse in his voice. Judith thought of the small pistol she had treated with such disdain last night. How she wished it were in her hand right now. Instead she watched as he lifted the goblet to his lips and sipped the red wine. The light would soon fade, and Androssy showed no signs of leaving the tower. She would have to move quickly.

"Damn," she exclaimed, bringing her left hand up to her ear and spilling her wine. Before Androssy could react, Judith put down her goblet and knelt, her hands searching the tower floor under the banquette. Feeling the hidden bolt, she quickly slid it open and sat back on her haunches, lifting the errant earring she had palmed up to the light. "Ah, here it is." She started to screw it back on and then, changing her mind, thrust it into the pocket of her caftan. "Must get that clasp fixed," she mumbled to herself as she sat back on the banquette facing the baron. She wiped the spilled wine from the canvas cushion with her handkerchief.

"Any damage done?" Androssy asked, indicating her caftan.

"None," she replied.

"May I?" He lifted the bottle and leaned forward.

"No, no thank you."

"Ah," he smiled, "you do not drink with the enemy."

"I still have some," Judith countered, lifting her goblet to her lips. Her heart pounded in her breast. Her part of the plan was nearly done. Just the signal to Alex was left.

"It's been a remarkably clear day," she commented casually. "Not a bit of haze in the strait, rare for this time of year."

Miklos Androssy turned to look north toward Spain.

"Look there," Judith urged. She stood and moved to the north parapet of the tower, pointing with her right hand to Gibraltar. "The light on the Rock is perfect."

As she distracted the baron's eye, her left hand deftly wedged the tip of her wine-stained handkerchief in a cleft between the old stones where it would be visible to those looking up from below, but not from atop the Castle. She turned and pointed south. "With a telescope you should be able to see your killer satellite from here tomorrow morning," she added with unconcealed bitterness. Leaving the parapet, Judith walked to the whitewashed steps leading down from the tower. "The telescope's in Mark's room."

Androssy nodded. "Perhaps you would like to join me."

"No," Judith answered, "I think not. I'll let the conqueror savor his victory alone." And then, almost as an afterthought, she asked, "Do you plan to set the activating beam—or whatever you call it—from here?"

"Although it would give me great personal pleasure," Androssy replied, "that will have to be done by a most trusted representative in Minorca. The transmitter there is far more sophisticated than that of your son. I am not one to take chances."

"I'm sure you aren't," she said tartly and started to descend.

"Dinner is at eleven," the baron stated flatly.

"I would prefer to eat with my son."

"And I would prefer that you and Mr. Shepard dine with me."

"For the pleasure of our company or to keep an eye on us?"

"Whichever answer you prefer." Baron Androssy raised his goblet to her in a mock salute. "Eleven, Mrs. Kidd." As he watched her descend, back straight and proud, he again raised his goblet in a gesture of appreciation for her beauty and guts. Such a waste, he thought as he turned back to look at the last rays of the sun as it slipped below the horizon.

"Why commit suicide?" Pinto asked, not for the first time as he and Alexander Kidd debated in the small, cluttered ironmonger's shop buried deep within the Casbah. The calls of mothers to their children, arguments, and the general noise of the crowded area came to them through the steel-shuttered doors. "What you plan is impossible. You know that. You yourself rejected it only this morning."

"Just give me a diversion of some sort. You guys are expert at that sort of thing."

"You'll never make it over the wall unseen," Pinto argued. "Those men are experts, guerrilla fighters. They have eyes in the backs of the heads. They are the friends of the shadows."

"There is a way up and over," Alex fought back. "Just one. My only problem is getting across the roof and down to the radio without being seen."

"'Only,'" the smuggler jeered. "What do you expect,

Alex? That I fill up the square in front of the Castle with a
hundred naked prostitutes to keep them all busy? Put on a
bullfight? And all in an hour's time?" He shook his head.
"You don't think that would be a little bit suspicious, eh?"

"Damn it," Alexander Kidd shouted, banging his fist on
the rough workbench behind which he sat, "I've got to try.
It's all my fault. I'm the only one who can stop him. And
Judith and Mark are . . ." He stopped himself.

Pinto lowered his head. Of course the other had to try or
live with dishonor, with the death of his family on his
conscience for the rest of his life. "Let me think," he said
softly.

"I wouldn't bother," a strange voice said. Both men
looked up in surprise. Robert Frankel stood in the doorway
leading from the small, scrap-filled hall. He held the lifeless
form of one of Pinto's men before him with one hand and a
gun in the other. The dead man's eyes bulged and his tongue
hung from a gaping mouth; he had obviously been strangled
from behind. Frankel kicked the door shut and released the
body. It crumpled at his feet.

"Who?" Pinto asked without taking his eyes from the
stranger.

"Androssy's secretary. A killer," Alex replied.

The only way out of the shop was through Frankel or the
open door leading into a windowless storage room behind
them. Frankel held a gun and the storeroom door was a
good ten feet away, but it was the better of the two choices
open to them, and all three men realized it.

"Neither of you move so much as an inch." Frankel
waggled his gun. Having lost Alexander Kidd once before,
he could not resist the opportunity to gloat over his intended
victim. "Before you and your friend here die, Mr. Kidd, tell
me why you were digging that ridiculous trench?"

"Ah," Alex said, stalling for time as his mind raced
ahead, "a very good question."

"Then answer it." There was no mistaking the menace in
Frankel's voice.

"Well"—he glanced at Pinto, their eyes meeting briefly

in unspoken agreement—"I was hoping to see my son and wife."

"Try again, Kidd," Frankel sneered, slowly raising the gun. "I believe I heared you mention a radio. There wouldn't by any chance be a radio transmitter in that shack, would there? And some codes?"

Alex's body went cold, but he smiled, leaning back in his chair so that his hands moved to the edge of the workbench. Pinto braced himself.

"A radio transmitter?" he repeated. "Why, yes, a transmitter. And a movie house, a discotheque, a—" Both men leaped into action as they saw the anger explode in Frankel's face. Alex threw over the cluttered workbench at him and dived for the floor and the open door behind him as the smuggler's hand flashed out with a knife.

Pinto's throwing arm caught the first bullet, and the second bit into the wood of the door frame as Alexander Kidd rolled through. Frankel staggered back, the smuggler's knife deep in his shoulder, and fired again, this time hitting Pinto in the face. The Moroccan fell backward against a row of welder's hydrogen and acetylene tanks, knocking them down into each other like a jumbled pile of pick-up-sticks, his lifeless form sprawled on top of them.

"Pinto," Alex called and when no answer came, slammed the door between the two rooms.

"Well, Mr. Kidd," Frankel called, grimacing from the pain as he wrenched the knife from his shoulder, "it looks like a draw right now."

"I have a gun," Alex called back through the flimsy wooden door.

"I don't doubt that for a minute," Frankel replied. He had noted earlier the bulge under Kidd's left arm. "I can't get in," he said as he pressed his gun hand to his shoulder to stanch the flow of blood, "but, on the other hand, you can't get out."

As the two men faced each other through the closed door, the hiss of escaping gas from a crack in the neck of one of the tanks went unnoticed. The lighter-than-air hydrogen, odorless and colorless and highly flammable, rose to the ceiling of the shop. The flame of the oil lamp across the room did not flicker.

"A toast," Baron Androssy said, lifting his cognac glass. He looked at the three others at the formal table. Only Zaki Osman, leader of the PLO contingent at the Castle, raised his glass. Page Shepard did not look up; he sat to the baron's left, staring glumly at the undrunk coffee before him. Judith Kidd, cool and aloof, looked her host directly in the eye. "To Charon Two," he proposed, "and its new home, the Union of Soviet Socialist Republics."

"And to the massacre of thousands of innocents," Judith stated bluntly.

Androssy paid no attention to her souring addition. With the smile frozen in place, he nodded to Osman and drank. The cognac tasted bitter in his mouth. The destruction of Israel was not a personal thing with him, it was an expedient, a business maneuver to bring him the power he wanted. Besides, he rationalized, it was the Russians who had dreamed up the Middle East war, not Miklos Androssy.

"Where is it now?" Zaki Osman asked, his eagerness all too apparent to those at the table.

Androssy consulted his watch. "Eleven forty-three. It will be well out over the Atlantic, headed this way."

"You sound very sure," Judith said. "Perhaps something has gone wrong." Page Shepard looked up hopefully.

"My people in Minorca have been in contact with your people at KWEN, Mr. Shepard. At precisely eleven this evening, just before we sat down to dine, New York confirmed Charon Two had moved east sixty degrees and was well on its eight-hour journey over us to the Middle East. Nothing can go wrong now. My station in Minorca can take over its control any time it wishes now.

"You forget about us," Judith said evenly.

"I find that highly unlikely," Miklos Androssy replied, "under the present circumstances." He motioned to one of the servant women for more coffee.

Judith could not resist egging him on. The quick look she had taken over the tower parapet earlier that evening while the baron had been distracted showed her the trench below leading to the transmitter shack just as she, Alex, and Pinto had planned. The long shadow cast by the shack had obscured the rock blocking the excavation two feet from its destination. As far as Judith was concerned, Alexander Kidd now sat before the radio console waiting to beam the self-destruct signal up to Charon II as soon as it got within his range. Her plight and that of her son were momentarily forgotten. Her eyes sparkled with the excitement she felt.

Androssy sensed Judith's supressed excitement; it made him uneasy. "Zaki," he said, "personally make sure that your men are at their posts and alert."

"You need not worry, Baron," the PLO leader replied, smiling, taking another gulp of cognac.

"But I *do* worry, Zaki. Please." He waited for the other to move and then added sharply, "Now."

The smile faded from Osman's face, replaced by a resentful glare. Throwing his napkin onto the table, he stood, roughly shoving his chair aside as he strode angrily from the room.

Turning to Judith, Androssy spoke with a trace of apology in his voice. "I regret that when your Israel falls, it must be at the hands of these peasant barbarians."

She bit her lip to keep from answering and reached for her as yet untouched cognac. Having drawn blood there, the baron turned his attention to Page Shepard.

"Tell me, Mr. Shepard, how was your friend when you saw him last?" he asked ingenuously.

Page stared at Androssy dumbly.

"Helmut? Your friend?" Miklos Androssy prompted, "Helmut Bruck? Certainly you have not forgotten your handsome young lover."

Judith looked in surprise from the baron to Page.

Shepard gasped. "I . . . I . . ." he stammered.

Androssy smiled. "Come now, Mr. Shepard, we are worldly men and women at this table."

Androssy enjoyed toying with this defenseless man. He leaned back in his chair. "Mr. Shepard, Helmut Bruck is one of our most effective ravens." He read the confusion in Page's face. "Raven," he repeated. "Operative, spy, they are all the same, Mr. Shepard."

The impact of Baron Androssy's words crashed over him. Page felt sick to his stomach not only from the emotional loss and betrayal that tore at him, but also from the realization of the role he must have played in delivering Charon II into Androssy's hands. As they had sat by Mark Kidd's bedside, Judith had told him about the destructive power of the satellite and what Androssy planned to do with it. Paling he slumped into his chair.

"Come, come, Mr. Shepard," Miklos Androssy said, smiling, "I am sure you will find another nice young man just like—"

In a sudden rush of anger, Page snatched up his brandy snifter and flung its contents into the baron's face.

Still smiling, Androssy picked up a white dinner napkin and carefully wiped his face. "Well done, Mr. Shepard. It is nice to know you have a little masculinity left."

Judith closed her eyes.

The gas drifted up through the cracks in the ceiling, its hissing escape from the cylinder still undetected. "Mr. Kidd," Frankel said through the door, "I'm a far better, far more experienced shot than you. Although you might get in a hit, I would most certainly kill you if we were to shoot it out. Why not just give up now, throw your gun out, and let me take you up to the Castle? Baron Androssy is most eager to meet you again." He waited for a reply. "You could see your wife and son."

Alex had been feeling his way around the small, dark room, using one match at a time. As Frankel stated his last proposition, Kidd's eyes fell on the trapdoor. The cellar, he thought, of course. The subterranean system within the Casbah was honeycombed with passages and tunnels connecting houses and shops. And Pinto's smugglers would most certainly make good use of them. He lifted the trapdoor as quietly as he could while calling out, "What guarantees do I get, Frankel?"

"Quit stalling, Kidd," the other replied, his voice closer.

"Okay, okay," Kidd countered, "Just give me time to think. Stand back." Hearing Frankel's footsteps, Kidd moved. Holstering his gun, he swung his legs down into the black hole, grasped the ladder, and climbed down, lowering the trapdoor over his head. He did not have much time. Striking a match, he looked about the cellar. Through the stacked litter he saw an arch to the left and moved quickly to and through it. Another match and he found himself in the cellar of the house next door. Two low arches in the opposite wall called for a decision. Lowering his head, he took the one to the left.

"Your minute's almost up, Kidd," Frankel called. Reaching behind him, he picked up the oil lamp with one hand and with his gun in the other, moved to the door. Smiling in anticipation, the killer prepared to kick open the door and hurl in the lamp to take his victim by surprise. It would be simple. Frankel slowly raised the lamp over his head. The flame brightened and—

The force of the horrendous explosion and accompanying fireball took out both the front and back walls of the building, tearing through the two floors to shred and shatter the unfortunates living above. Razor-sharp shards from windows flew in all directions up and down the alley; those nearby were blown in splattered, bloody pieces against the opposite walls. The entire Casbah trembled under the force and deafening boom of the first blast. Terrified, all eyes looked skyward at the great column of flame as the other cylinders exploded in rapid succession, drowning out the screams of the wounded.

Judith clutched the arms of her chair. Miklos Androssy tried to stand, but the vibrations of the floor beneath toppled him back. The chandelier swayed wildly above them, and the entire room was lit by the flaming tower that illuminated the night sky and reflected in the courtyard pool beyond the glass doors. The servant women pressed themselves against the wall, and glass could be heard shattering from falling shelves in the pantry beyond. United in their surprise, the three looked dumbly at each other. Footsteps ran about in the courtyard outside.

The first to her feet, Judith ran from the room to her son. Androssy, followed by Page Shepard, mounted the steps to the roof of the Castle and the north wall overlooking the Casbah. They and the Arab terrorists stared wide-eyed at the twisting, undulating flames that soared above their heads in a slow-motion dance of violence. Bits of burning wood fell from the sky; they brushed them away. The air was rent with shouts, the cries of those trapped and dying, sirens, and the frightening roar of a fire out of control.

Surrounded by the fleeing, Alexander Kidd limped from the Casbah into the square. The left leg of his trousers was soaked with blood; he had been briefly pinned by a fallen beam. He looked up at the Castle. The parapet of the north wall was lined with the faces of its invaders; they glowed red in the reflected light of the holocaust. A small white handkerchief fluttered from the tower. "That's my girl," he muttered. He ran as best he could with the crowd to the southwest corner of the old prison where an ancient tree grew up from the cliff face, its gnarled and leafy branches overshadowing that part of the Castle where the family liked to lunch on hot days. His clothes and face were black with soot.

The trunk of the tree extended a good three feet out from the cliff face. Taking a deep breath, Alex leaped at it, one hand around the trunk, the other grasping for a branch to keep himself from sliding down. Down meant a long drop onto the rocks and waves below. How, he wondered, had Judith had the courage to follow the smuggler's trail down? His left leg was of painful little help to him as he struggled up the tree, inching his head slowly up to look over the parapet of the Castle's southeast corner. No one stood guard there; all, it seemed, were crowded at the north wall. Among them he saw the back of Miklos Androssy. And there was Page. Well, he mumbled to himself, I wanted a diversion, but I never bargained for anything like this.

Quickly hauling himself farther up the tree, he grabbed hold of the major branch that extended over the Castle wall and, hand over hand, moved out across it, his eyes all the while riveted on the backs of the PLO guards and Androssy. If they turned he would be a very visible target. Two more feet. He now hung ten feet above the Castle's roof. Just as he let go, one of the men turned, but he didn't seem to see him. Alex landed in a catlike crouch behind the luncheon table and a cluster of chaise longues. Slowly pulling his gun from its holster under his left arm, he rose to look over the chair back at the door in the west wall that led from the roof down to the cells beneath the Castle. It was a good thirty feet away, most of it fully exposed. He had no time to hesitate. Ready to spring forward, Alex suddenly froze. Someone approached quietly in the shadows not more than a dozen feet away to his right. He looked up, ready to fire.

"Page!"

"What in the hell are you doing here?" Shepard whispered.

"Don't look at me," Kidd snapped. Page looked quickly away at the fire, its intense glow illuminating his pale face. "You know about Charon Two?"

Page nodded slightly. "Judith told me."

"I'm going to kill it. Are you with me?"

The other's pause was brief. "Yes."

"Is everyone up on the roof?"

"I think so." Page kept his eyes straight ahead. "Don't move now, some of them have turned. You know about Mark?"

"Yes. How is he?"

"Barely keeping his own. Judith's with him now."

"Tell her I'm here, but keep her away. Have you the run of the Castle?"

"Pretty much."

"Can you meet me in the cells?"

"I think so. Why?"

"Later, Page. This is important. Go to the edge of the roof and look down at the mosaic tiles bordering the pool. From up here you'll see a series of Roman numerals blended into the pattern. Write them down, starting at the center of the north side. Go counterclockwise, Page, and bring it down to me. Got that?"

Page Shepard nodded.

"Tell me when I can go."

Another explosion rocked the Casbah, followed by a fierce gush of flames.

"Now," Page urged. "Now, they're all looking at it."

"Counterclockwise, Page," Alex whispered. "Remember, counterclockwise." Then, not bothering to even glance to either side, he made a limping run to one side of the open door and pressed himself against the wall. Alex peered cautiously around the edge. The way was clear. He vanished down the narrow flight of steps.

Page followed his progress from the corner of his eye and then moved to the edge of the roof and stared down. In the fire's glow it took him a moment to find the first Roman numeral cleverly woven into the multicolored pattern, then the next one and the one following. Page took a pen from his jacket pocket.

CHAPTER 28

"He's here," Shepard whispered minutes later as he sat down beside Judith. He was flushed with excitement.

She turned from the deathly white face of her son, her hand still pressing the cold compress to his forehead. She thought for a moment, wondering how much he should know. "Yes." Her tone was tentative, cautious. "How did you find out?"

"I talked with him on the roof. He climbed the tree and—"

"What?" Judith interrupted in surprise. "The tree? He . . ." She lowered her voice so as not to wake the elderly doctor who dozed across the room. "What are you talking about? Alex is . . ." She stopped herself. Their plan had failed. For some reason he had not been able to dig himself into the transmitter shack. He had had to come over the wall to get to the transmitter. Oh, God, she wailed in silence, that means we can't get Mark out through the trench.

"I'm going down to meet him in the cells," Page continued softly. "Alex wanted you to know." He rose. "Stay here"—he kissed her cheek—"and cover for me if Androssy noses around." Judith started to protest, but the door closed behind him. Crossing the courtyard, sparks swirled around him. The reflecting pool glowed red in the night. Sirens and the shouts of those fleeing the conflagration filled the air. Was it his imagination or could he actually feel the heat of the flames sweeping up through the Casbah on the other side of the Castle's high walls? Looking about

him with apparent casualness, Page nodded shortly to one
of the PLO terrorists who had come down from the roof to
take up his post by the Castle gate. Others now moved about
the place, some packing up their things along with the silver
and other portable objets d'art from the Kidds' summer
retreat. It was obvious that Androssy and his killers were
planning to pull out shortly. It was equally obvious to Page
that he, Judith, Mark, and the old doctor would not be going
with them. They had little time left, but hopefully enough to
blow Androssy's plans apart. He entered the west wall and,
making sure he was not observed, started for the stairs
leading down to the old subterranean cellblocks.

Already there, Alex knelt before one of the wine racks
attached to the stone wall. Several cases had been moved
aside to make room for the rack to swing open. Where in the
hell was the catch? He muttered under his breath as his
fingers searched under the shelves. It had been so long
since . . .

He stopped at the sound of footsteps coming toward him
across the rock floor. Page, he thought. But taking no
chances, he quickly blew out his candle and moved behind
one of the foundation arches supporting the Castle above.
Growing louder, the steps stopped as the beam of a
flashlight swung around the corner and played over the
racks of dusty bottles. Alex heard the murmur of satisfaction as the intruder moved forward. Then came the clinking
noise of one bottle against another as they were pulled from
the rack. Alex leaned slowly forward and looked at the Arab
who examined the wine. Selecting a bottle, the terrorist
smashed off the top and, taking a sip, settled down upon one
of the crates Alex had pulled out earlier. Shit, Kidd thought,
this looks like a long drinking bout. The man sat facing the
arch behind which he hid, there was no chance of his being
able to take him by surprise, and he did not have the time
just to stand there and wait. His hand played with the gun in
his holster under his left arm. A shot would echo throughout
the stone cellblock and bring Androssy and his killers down
in droves.

Page's entrance solved the problem. The startled American saw not Alexander Kidd, but an equally surprised terrorist who, dropping the bottle with a crash, jumped to his feet and drew his gun.

Page took a step backward. "Hold it," he called out defensively.

The Arab moved toward him, turning away from Alex who, in that instant, yanked a bottle from the rack and, stepping forward, brought it down with all his might on the back of the man's head with a sickening thud. As Page stared wide-eyed, the PLO gunman slumped to the floor, blood running from his broken skull.

"Get his gun," Alex called softly. He pulled off the Arab's jacket and wrapped it around his bleeding head and then dragged the dead man behind the arch, pushing several cases of wine forward to hide the body.

"Is he dead?" Page asked, picking up the gun and flashlight.

"As a doornail," Alex replied. "Look, buddy, better him than us. You've got the numbers?" He knelt back down before the rack, at last locating the catch.

"Yes." Page pulled the paper from his pocket.

"What's going on topside?"

"The fire's getting worse. This place is right in its path."

"Don't worry," Alex said, standing, "the walls are thick. Androssy, what's he up to?"

"Charon Two passes south of us at one. It's being controlled by a transmitter somewhere in Minorca. They're going to put it in a geosynchronous orbit at thirty degrees east latitude."

"It's going to strike from there, is it?"

Shepard nodded. "At three o'clock our time, five Israeli. It looks as if they've started packing up to leave."

"Bastards," Alex mumbled. "Come on, Page, give me a hand with this thing." He strained to pull out the wine rack. Page put down the flashlight and joined him.

"What's behind it?" he asked as the rack slowly swung

out, its hinges squeaking much too loudly for Kidd's comfort.

"A door," Alex answered, "and a pair of steps that go into a little radio command room I set up over seven years ago. Keep your fingers crossed that everything still works." Page saw a heavy steel door set into the thick stone wall. Instead of a lock, it contained a combination dial. Alex began to twist the dial to the right and then the left.

"Looks like a safe," Page said as he peered over the other's shoulder.

"For all practical purposes, it is." Alex completed the combination and pushed. The thick metal door swung soundlessly inward. Reaching to his left, he switched on the lights. Both men entered and then turned to pull the wine rack closed behind to cover the entrance. Alex shut and locked the metal door as Page walked down the seven steps into the small control room. He whistled his appreciation.

In comparison to the Castle that sat above, this room looked as if it had come from the twenty-first century. Its walls, floor, and ceiling lined with thin sheets of shining metal against the humidity of the area gave it the aura of a spaceship. Banks of electronic and radio equipment rose against two of the walls. A large screen with which to monitor the movements of Charon II sat above the main control board.

"It looks more advanced than the KWEN control room," Page said. "How did you ever assemble it?"

"I had a lot of help," Alex replied, sitting down at the console and hitting switches. He remembered the help late President Warren had made available to him, and the money. Lights began to blink on in the various pieces of equipment about the room. "Has a separate electrical source from the Castle's." He flicked another switch and a gentle hum filled the room.

"What's that?"

"Air filtration. The place is airtight; we couldn't last long without it. Those vents keep oxygen circulating. Give me that paper."

"What do these numbers mean?"

"They're the code to control Charon Two. A real genius put them together with every sort of contingency you could possibly think of taken into consideration. He designed that mosaic pattern around the pool personally and stood watch as it was being put down."

Kidd spent the next minutes checking the circuits, making sure everything would be working when Charon II passed south of them. Finally he relaxed. "How is Androssy communicating with his chums in Minorca?"

"Using Mark's radio."

"He's giving all the orders from here?"

"That's what he said. Bragged about it all through dinner," Page replied. "Will he be able to make it work, Alex? Can he really knock out all the Israeli weapons?"

"Most of them, I'm afraid."

"They won't stand a chance."

"They will if we strike first." Alex looked at his watch. "And we strike at one."

"And afterward?" Page asked. "Do we get out or is this what might be termed a suicide mission?"

Alex sighed. "The odds aren't too good."

"Androssy will never let us out alive."

"Maybe we won't have to get out. This room is a fortress in itself. If we can get Judith and Mark down here, we might be able to hold out until help comes. Once in, I'll radio the police or the army, give myself up, so to speak. They'll come running."

"That's a big if," Page Shepard said. "Moving Mark may kill him."

"It's a chance we'll have to take. We both have guns now, and if I recall correctly, you are a pretty good shot. We should be able to keep them off the stairs with two guns blazing up at them while Judith and the doctor get Mark into this room."

A drop of perspiration ran down Page's face. He wiped it away with his handkerchief and then gasped as the spark of survival Alex had just held out to him vanished. "My God, Alex, the fire. It might not get through the Castle walls, but it'll turn this tin room of yours into a frying pan."

Page's logic hit Kidd, but his optimism kept him from abandoning the only escape route open to them. "Not if we work fast. Here we go, Page, get ready to say good-bye to Charon Two. Then up we go for Judith and Mark."

He flicked the antenna switch. "It'll take me only a minute to raise the dish and aim it south. Let's hope none of Androssy's killers are in the tower."

Page moved closer to look over Alex's shoulder as he sat at the console. "What's that blinking red light?"

"Shit," Alexander Kidd muttered. He reached over the panel and moved the antenna switch back and forth. The light still flickered. Moving quickly across the room, he checked the auxiliary power and then returned to the panel.

"What's the matter?" Page demanded.

"Something's wrong with the doors over the dish in the tower. They're not opening. Judith unlocked them this afternoon and unless I get that dish up . . ." He moved to another piece of equipment and flicked several switches.

"It's still blinking, Alex." Panic sounded in Page's voice.

"Fucking damn," Kidd swore. "We'll have to open them manually."

The two men stared at each other, realizing the danger. Page was the first to speak, his panic dissolving as resolution set in. "Not we, Alex. Me. I'll do it, just tell me how."

"Page you don't—"

"How, Alex, just show me how," he said firmly and evenly. "You're the only one who can blow up that damn satellite. I helped get us into this mess, let me help get us out." He stared down at his friend. "I can move around up there at will; they'll shoot *you* on sight. Besides, you can hardly walk on that leg."

Kidd reluctantly drew a rough diagram of the doors and

the hidden wrench that Page would have to use to raise them. And he gave Page the combination to the transmitter room door. "As soon as you get them open, move your tail out. When the light goes off down here, I'll raise the dish, aim it, and send off the self-destruct code. The actual transmission shouldn't take longer than a few seconds."

"Androssy's men will see it."

"By the time they do, it will be too late. On the way, tell Judith what's happening and to get Mark ready to move when the pandemonium breaks loose up there. I'll come up and, with luck, meet you to cover the retreat."

Page frowned skeptically.

"I know it's a long shot, buddy. If we buy it, at least we've put Charon Two to bed and fucked up Androssy and his Russian pals." Alex put both hands on his friend's shoulders. "And Page," he smiled, "thanks for the years together. Where you go, so go I."

Page Shepard embraced his friend briefly and then turned to walk to the steel door. Alex followed, switching off the light as the other carefully opened it and, seeing no light through the cracks in the wine rack, swung it open.

"If something goes wrong, come back here," Alex whispered. "Use the combination. We'll figure something out."

"Right," Page answered, switching on the flashlight.

Alex watched the light disappear in the maze of old cellblocks and then retreated, pulling the wine rack back into position and closing the steel inner door. He walked slowly back down the steps to the radio console and sat heavily in the chair before it. His eyes moved between the blinking red light and the code on the paper in his hand. If he beamed it up to Charon II in a clockwise order, he would turn on the transmission that would immobilize the Cerberus chips. In its current counterclockwise order, the code would cause the satellite to self-destruct. He had directed Page to write it down in reverse order just in case it were to fall into Androssy's terrorists' hands. Tisiphone, the late Simon Felton, had thought of everything.

* * *

Miklos Androssy frowned as he walked out into the courtyard from the younger Kidd's radio room. His base in Minorca reported everything going according to plan, but he felt trapped here in the Castle. The baron could not afford to leave the radio until he knew of the success of the Charon II operation, and he had to remain to intercept Kidd before he got his hands on the code; Androssy knew Kidd would come sooner or later—he had to. And to add to his discomfort, the flames from the Casbah were getting too close for safety. The air was choked with smoke, and burning cinders rained over the place. Already his PLO men had had to remove the outdoor furniture and tear down a canvas awning that flared up. The police had visited twice, ordering the occupants of the Castle to leave, but the terrified maids, PLO guns to their heads, had fended off their orders to evacuate. Where was Frankel? He had been gone for hours. Androssy needed him; he did not trust the PLO peasants. Frankel would have to kill Shepard, the woman, and the Kidd boy and his doctor.

He looked up through the smoke-filled air. What was that? Someone crossing the roof toward the tower? It was too dark on this side of the tower to tell, the contrast between the light from the blazing Casbah was too great. He looked about him for one of the Arab guards.

Breathing heavily, Page knelt to check the latches; both had been released. So it *was* a mechanical fault, he thought. Moving to the southwest corner of the tower, he pulled at the built-in, three-foot wooden cube that served as a corner table. It took nearly a minute before he could wrench it free. As Alex had described, beneath it he found the gearbox and hand wrench that would crank up the doors covering the dish.

A wave of thick smoke swirled around him, nearly obscuring the gears. He stifled a fit of coughing. Tears streamed from his smarting eyes. Shepard pulled at the wrench. Frozen with rust, the gears refused to turn.

Swearing under his breath, Page reached over to pick up the heavy wooden cube and struggled to lift it above his head. The shouts and crashing walls from the conflagration below covered the sound when he brought the cube down upon the unyielding wrench. It moved an inch or two. Again he raised the cube and brought it down. The gears freed themselves. Putting aside the cube, Page grasped the wrench and with great effort began to turn it. Slowly, ever so slowly, a crack began to appear across the center of the tower floor as the doors began to raise.

Holding a wet handkerchief over his nose, the Arab climbed the steps to the tower. Although grumbling at the apparent uselessness of his uncomfortable errand, he moved cautiously, his gun ready. He would have liked to turn his weapon against that bastard foreign baron who ordered them around as if they were pigs. The time will come, he thought.

The doors were half up when some instinct made Page stop. Crouching, he turned toward the opening in the parapet at the top of the stone staircase and pressed back against the banquette. He saw the dark head and then the body slowly rising through the smoke. Page thought of his gun, but it lay far below with Judith. He prepared to spring. Low as he was, the American was not at first visible to the PLO terrorist. The man took several steps forward, expecting to walk on a flat surface. Instead the forty-five-degree angle of the half-raised door before him caught him by surprise. He stumbled forward, falling sideways against the door, and slipped down, his gun spinning from his hand. At that instant, Page leaped upon him, his fist slamming into the Arab's face.

Taken completely off guard, the startled terrorist took a second blow to his throat before recovering his senses enough to grapple with his attacker. Page's hands clenched around his windpipe, choking off the air. But younger and more muscular than his American opponent, the man fought back, digging his fingers into Page's face, forcing it backward and away. They rolled over and over in the confined area, the Arab slowly gaining the upper hand. Page found himself pressed back on the half-raised door in a semistanding position as the other slammed an agonizing blow deep in his stomach that doubled him over. Smiling grimly, the terrorist brought his knee up under Page's face, smashing him back against the door. He did not need help; he would finish off the American dog himself with his bare hands and the knife the way his fathers used to fight. The blade glinted only briefly in a burst of flames from the Casbah that exploded through the smoke surrounding the tower. Seeing it, Page rolled to the left and dropped to the floor of the tower as it bit deep into the wood of the door beside him. He grabbed the wrench from the gearbox. The Arab yanked his knife free. "Die," he muttered as he lunged forward at the same time Page lashed out with the heavy tool. The two collided, the terrorist's knife plunging deep into Page's abdomen as the American's wrench crashed into his temple. The Arab fell lifeless across his fainting victim.

Far below, Alex sat sweating before the console as he stared at the blinking red light. The tension he felt was far greater than any he had ever experienced. He looked at his watch. An hour had passed. Something had happened to Page. He would just have to go it alone.

Judith and the doctor hovered over Mark, doing their best to restrain his delirious movements. "We are approaching a time of crisis," Dr. Evans told her. Withdrawing a syringe and glass vial from his black bag, he punctured the rubber seal of the vial with the needle and held it up to the light to measure the flow of pale liquid. Satisfied, he returned to mark and injected it into the artery of his left arm. "This should calm him."

"How much longer do we have?" she asked.

He shook his head. "Not much. We must get him to the hospital."

"We can't; our only hope is to get him down below."

Where were Page and Alex? They should have been there by now. Judith felt in her jacket pocket for the reassurance of the gun Page had given her.

Switching on other equipment in the sophisticated transmitter room, Alex worked feverishly to record the self-destruct code onto tape and loop it so his message could be played continuously over and over again without his being at the console. Next he hooked the tape recorder into the radio ready for transmission. He then set about programming a computer to the course that Page had said Charon II was following so that as soon as the radio dish in the tower was raised, the computer would automatically turn it to the exact point in the heavens where the satellite was at the time. Alex looked at his watch for the hundredth time. Two thirty-three. He had only twenty-seven minutes left before Charon II reached its destination and the holocaust began.

A fast, final check and he switched on the radio, starting the automatic transmission. Even though useless now, as soon as he managed to raise the antenna, his self-destruct code would reach Charon II's computers within seconds.

Kidd quickly stripped off his clothes and exchanged them for those of the dead Arab terrorist. "Damn," he cursed, remembering his blond hair; it would be a beacon to his enemies above. Reaching down, he snatched up the striped workman's shirt he had been wearing and tore off its back to fashion a primitive kafiyeh for his head. He had noticed several of the Castle's PLO invaders wore then.

Alex took a last look around the room as he jammed his gun into his belt. Leaving the now super-heated transmitter shack, he locked the steel door and took care to push the covering wine rack back into place. No one must find what lay hidden behind it.

Not daring to risk a light, Kidd felt his way through the maze of cells in the old prison cellar. The air was thick with acrid smoke, but cooler than that in the radio shack. He stifled a cough as he moved to the foot of the stairway leading up through the west wall. Cautiously edging his way up one step after another, Alex held his gun alert. No guard interrupted his climb. He passed the courtyard and heard the shouts of the Arab invaders as they prepared to flee the place. Like rats deserting a sinking ship, he thought. Kidd continued on up toward the roof.

A terrorist suddenly appeared before him from a room to the right. Alex froze, his finger tight on the trigger. The other barely glanced at him as he passed, his attention directed solely on the heavy suitcase he carried, bulging with whatever valuables he had found in the guest rooms.

The door at the top of the steps stood open. Encouraged by the lack of interest shown him by the guard and the confusion going on below in the courtyard, Kidd decided on boldness rather than stealth. He limped out onto the roof and strode as best he could across it toward the tower.

The sky seemed to undulate like some great volcanic eruption of swirling flame and smoke above him. The situation was far worse than he had imagined. Alex realized the Castle could not survive the wave of fire sweeping toward and around it. The radio shack would be no sanctuary for him and his family.

"You."

Was the voice calling out to him? Pretending not to hear, Kidd lowered his head and looked straight ahead. The tower steps were nearly within his reach. He glanced up briefly. He saw no one above. What *had* happened to Page? He prayed to God that the door mechanism still worked after all these years. Reaching the bottom step, Alex started up.

A firm hand grasped his shoulder.

He whirled around to stare into the muzzle of a gun pressed close to his face. Zaki Osman spoke. "Make not one move or you will have no head." Despite the heat, Alex felt like ice. "That is right. Now drop the gun and slowly raise your hands." Neither man's eyes moved from the other's as Alex let his gun fall and lifted his hands above his head. Osman relaxed, a smile spreading across his face. "You are Alexander Kidd, no?" He pulled off the kafiyeh.

There was no point in denying the obvious. Alex nodded.

"The Baron Androssy has been waiting a long time for

you." He quickly scooped up Alex's gun while keeping his gun aimed at the American's face. "Now maybe we can leave this hellhole. Come."

Prodded from behind, Alex walked carefully back across the roof.

"Ah, Mr. Kidd," Androssy said, looking from the radio as Zaki Osman herded his prisoner into the room, "what a not so unexpected surprise. You did not disappoint me."

Osman pushed Kidd back against the wall and tossed the American's gun onto a table beside the baron. "I found him on the roof."

"Come to do mischief, Mr. Kidd?" Androssy smiled and turned to the Arab who sat at Mark Kidd's radio transmitter. "Bring in the woman. I think our friend will be less likely to give us trouble if his wife suffers the consequences of any rash act he might make."

The terrorist rose and unlocked the door beside Alex. Passing through, he roughly pulled Judith up from her son's side and, without a word, dragged her back into the radio room.

"Alex," she gasped.

Shaking his head to cut off any incriminating statement she might make, he asked Androssy, "May I lower my hands now?"

The baron nodded. "But be careful."

The Arab released Judith. She moved to her husband's side. Alex put his arm around her without looking, his attention focused on Androssy.

"Tell me, Kidd, what do you know of my man, Frankel?"

"The little weasel?"

"Frankel," the baron repeated firmly.

"I'm not sure, but I think he got burned up out there." Alex nodded in the direction of the flaming Casbah. "And we may do the same if we don't get out of here. Hot, isn't it?"

"Bearable," Androssy replied. Frankel's death came as no surprise to him. Now Zaki or one of his men would have to carry out the executions of the Kidd family. "Where have you hidden the code?"

"It's right out there in plain sight where everyone can see it." Alex smiled. "Come on, I'll show it to you," he said, pausing, "and to all your PLO friends here. I'm sure they'd be very interested—"

"There is no need," Androssy interrupted. "Now that I know it *is* here, I will let the fire take care of its destruction." Androssy studied his watch.

"Your satellite should be just about at thirty degrees latitude by now," Alex said. "Shame you can't do it yourself. I should imagine it would be quite a thrill to knock out an entire country with just the push of a few buttons."

"A thrill that would not be new to me," the baron replied, smiling.

"Ah." Alex understood the other's meaning. "Then it was you who brought down the Tomcats and charter jet over the Mediterranean?"

"Precisely."

"Well, once is enough, I guess. Your monkeys in Minorca have the codes?"

Androssy nodded. "One trusted associate. Only he and I"—he smiled—"and you, Mr. Kidd. But soon there will be only two again."

Alex frowned. "At least let my family go. Neither Mark nor Judith know the code."

"You said 'in plain sight.' Surely they must have seen it."

"Only if you know what you're looking for."

"Sorry, too dangerous."

"My wife knows nothing," Kidd insisted, tightening his arm about Judith.

"Too dangerous," the baron repeated, shaking his head. "Contact Minorca," he ordered, turning to the terrorist who had resumed his post at the radio. The link established, Androssy took the microphone and asked, "What news from the east?"

"All on schedule," a flat, heavily accented voice responded.

Between clouds of billowing black smoke, the sky over the Castle glowed red. The roof of one of the buildings across the square suddenly flared up and flames gushed out from under its eves. The wind through the Strait of Gibraltar strengthened and the conflagration poised to sweep up over the entire hill, taking slum dwelling and luxury home alike. A glass window in the tower shattered. The heat moving toward them was intense.

"Scared?" Alex asked softly.

Judith nodded, her head pressed against his shoulder.

"Me too," he said, "but just a bit. Don't give up."

Her eyes followed his to the gun lying on the table halfway across the room. "No," she whispered. "In my pocket. Page's gun." Judith felt his hand touch her side.

Farther to the east the sky just above the horizon also glowed. It glowed not with flames, but with the beginnings of sunrise. In Libya four squadrons of jets readied themselves for takeoff. Patriotic anthems played over loudspeakers, and the early morning breeze fluttered the silk scarfs of that country's elite young pilots as they walked confidently to their planes. Across the Mediterranean, bombs were carefully being loaded into Russian-made planes based in Syria. Tanks rumbled across the sands of Jordan toward the Israeli frontier. Arabs in the Gaza Strip and the West Bank waited impatiently for the first strike. They fingered their recently unearthed weapons nervously.

The Israelis were not asleep. Alerted by their intelligence, a general mobilization was in force. Soldiers and pilots raced to their bases to man tanks and fighter planes that would soon fall from the sky. Behind them, mothers and children waited anxiously.

Sweat poured down the bodies of the four men and the woman standing in the radio room of the Castle in Tangier.

Alex tore off his shirt and wiped his face and chest with it. Zaki Osman stood irritable but vigilant, his eyes moving between the American captives and the radio where his lieutenant sat under the eager gaze of Baron Miklos Androssy.

"We have set the satellite in its new orbit at thirty degrees east," the voice from Minorca stated in a dull, monotonous tone. "We start transmission in five minutes."

Androssy turned to Alex. "Thank you for making all this possible, Mr. Kidd."

The Libyan jets took flight one after the other, circled while taking information, and then streaked off to the east. General Ivan Ivanovich Guryanov raised his binoculars as he stood sheltered on the Jordanian border. As expected, a flight of Israeli jets swooped low overhead in a reconnaisance mission. He glanced at his watch. "Soon, my Zionist friends, you will be digging your own graves," he muttered. Ali Gemayel, the Syrian adviser, nodded. "Our bombers take off in precisely six minutes."

Page's eyes slowly opened to the searing heat and then closed. He was in the middle of Hades. Flames soared high above him; the burning cushions and wooden benches of the tower formed a square of fire around him. Where was he? What was happening? He felt numb, disassociated from this place. He looked down through half-closed eyes at the weight on his chest. A man. He tried to focus on the face and then the thing in his hand. It was a wrench. He looked over at the half-open doors and then back to the gearbox. A fit of coughing wracked his body. He tasted blood.

The doors. For some reason he had to open them with that wrench. Everything was in a haze. Page pushed the dead terrorist off his chest. Nothing—he felt nothing below his waist. Using his arms, he slowly inched his useless body to the gearbox. A wave of dizziness swept over him. Fitting the wrench, he struggled to lift himself over it, using his weight to turn it down. The doors opened a further inch.

The seat above burned, yet he felt strangely calm. Moving like an automaton, Page refitted the wrench and again lifted his body over it. The splinter of burning wood that fell on his arm went unnoticed. His eyes glazed as he pressed down on the wrench. He saw Fishers Island, the boys, and Mary. He could feel the heat of the sun on his back. Page refitted the wrench. Flames crept toward his pants leg.

"Forty-five seconds." The blind Minorcan voice over the loudspeaker droned on.

As all eyes stared at the radio, Alex slowly edged toward the door to Mark's room and, reaching behind his back, relocked it and slipped Judith's gun from her pocket. He might have lost the battle for Charon II, but damn if he would lose his family too.

The Minorcan station continued its countdown. "Ten, nine, eight . . ."

Androssy was smiling.

Kidd looked beyond him through the archway as a movement atop the tower caught his attention. His eyes widened. Reflecting the flames around it, the great shining dish rotated to the right and tipped upward toward space.

"Four, three . . ."

The baron's grip tightened on the microphone in his hand.

Twenty-one thousand miles above the earth, the micro-computer aboard the Charon II picked up a signal and began to feed it through its intricate circuitry. The radio transmitter from which it would beam down the Cerberus immobilization signal clicked on just as it had done once before on the morning of August 31.

A flight of Syrian jets took off. The Libyan planes crossed the Nile and swooped low over the Sinai Peninsula. "They're coming in from all sides," an Israeli radar captain shouted. Within seconds, the planes of Israel rose into the air to intercept.

The Charon II computer hesitated only for a fraction of a second. Another set of circuits clicked into action.

On order, the Libyan planes swerved north over the Mediterranean to buy time. The Israeli jets closed in.

The Charon computer rechecked. The transmission was being received in reverse sequence.

"Two, one. Starting transmission," the voice from Minorca stated.

The silence in the room was broken only by the roar of the conflagration around the Castle. Its five inhabitants stood holding their breath, their various expressions frozen on their faces. They waited.

"Satellite radio not functioning," Minorca reported flatly.

Androssy looked across the room at Kidd, confusion in his eyes.

Zaki Osman started to say something, but held his tongue as he stared at the baron. Something was going wrong, and he did not know what to do.

Up in space the brain in the Charon II computer committed itself.

"Israeli planes engaged in full combat," the voice from Minorca stated.

The PLO leader was beside himself. "It's going wrong," Zaki shouted. "Do something."

"Shut up, swine," Androssy shouted back.

Twenty-two thousand miles above the earth, millions of tiny pieces of metal, plastic, and insulation exploded in all directions, some to burn up on their way down through the atmosphere, others to float like cosmic dust for eternity through the universe. The blinking light of Charon II suddenly vanished from the monitor in the transmission room in Minorca.

The voice from Minorca filled the room. "Our scanners cannot pick up the satellite Charon Two. All contact has been lost."

Androssy and the Arabs stared stunned at the radio before them. There was a long silent pause before it spoke again.

"Fierce air battle over Haifa. Libyan planes disengaging.

Syrian tanks suffering losses. The operation has been
aborted. Repeat. The operation has been aborted."

Alex braced himself. The time had come to make his
move.

Androssy slowly turned to him. His ears refused to accept
what the voice was saying. Seven years of work and dreams
had suddenly vanished along with that bleep on the
Minorcan monitor. He was a dead man; the KGB would see
to that. Somehow Kidd had tricked him. His voice was cold
and decisive. "Kill them. All of them."

"Down," Alex shouted to Judith as he fired at Zaki
Osman while flinging his shirt in the face of the radioman
and diving to the floor. Carried off his feet by the impact of
Alex's bullet, Osman fell dead against the wall, legs spread
wide in front of him. Taken by surprise, the other terrorist
fired as he tried to untangle himself from the shirt. His first
bullets missed, but the next found Kidd's already injured
leg. Alex caught the man in the cheek with his next salvo.

In one swift movement, Androssy swept up the gun from
the table and ran to the door, turning to fire wildly at Kidd as
he ran into the courtyard and vanished into the wave of
black smoke that engulfed him. Screaming from the pain in
his leg, Kidd flung himself at the door to seal them off from
attack.

Judith ran to him. "They hit you."

"In the same fucking leg," he gasped, handing her the
key. "Quick, get Mark and Evans in here. That madman is
out for blood." She ran to the door. "And bring the
blankets."

Judith looked back to him in surprise.

"The whole place is going up. The pool's our only
hope."

"But Androssy's out there, he'll—"

The room shuddered violently, cutting her off as a part of
the Castle collapsed.

"Does that answer your problem?" Alex asked quickly.
"It's take a chance on Androssy and whatever of his men
are brave enough to be hanging around, or bake to death.

We'll try for the pool." His gun ready, Kidd reached up and slowly pulled open the door to the courtyard.

Judith and Dr. Evans gently carried Mark Kidd into the radio room as his father tried to probe the smoke-filled courtyard for his enemy.

Again the Castle shook as the roof over the living room fell in, opening up a large vertical rent in the north wall. The ensuing gush of hot air and flame swept up from the cellars through the winding staircases of the west wall. The tinder-dry beams supporting the ceilings overhead burst into flame. Fire erupted in the rooms on either side, lapping out around their door frames and windows.

His face a mask of contorted rage, Miklos Androssy stood firm behind an arch on the other side of the courtyard. A handkerchief pressed to his nose, the gun he clutched was aimed at the entrance to Mark Kidd's radio room. Around and above him the wooden beams of the Castle flamed, and the shattered windows of the tower gushed fire to form a single tall torch visible in the night from every part of Tangier. Revenge was the only emotion Androssy felt at that moment, revenge and hate. He would not be satisfied until Kidd was dead either by the flames or the gun in his hand.

"Where is Zaki?" the only PLO terrorist remaining in the burning Castle demanded. He crouched low at the baron's side.

"Dead," Androssy answered, not looking at the man but at the doorway. "The American shot him."

"Pig," the terrorist hissed. The wall of sliding glass doors in the dining room at the south end of the reflecting pool exploded outward, showering the entire place with shards of blackened glass. A gust of flame swept out behind them. "We must leave," the Arab insisted. "The whole place will soon come down on our heads. The firemen have abandoned this side of the square." He started to rise.

"No," Androssy ordered. "Not until Kidd is dead."

"Let him roast alone. I am going."

The baron turned and pointed his gun at the Arab. "You are staying until this is over."

The terrorist was not intimidated. "Fuck you, Russian slime." Misjudging the look in Androssy's eyes, he turned and started for the south gate as the shot rang out. Whirled around by the force of the bullet in his back, he staggered to one side, his eyes staring wide in surprise. The man tried to raise his own gun, but slumped dead to the tiles. Androssy turned back to the doorway.

The sound of the shot alerted Alex to the baron's position. He peered around the door frame. A bullet shattered the wood just above his head. He pulled back. "I don't know how many of them are left out there, but we sure as hell can't stay in here." Again he moved forward, taking a cautious look out, and then sat back. "They're behind the arches on the other side. The whole roof over them is burning, I don't know how long they can last there."

"Or we here," the doctor countered, looking up at the smoke oozing down through the cracks around the ceiling beams. Fire crackled above them.

Judith looked at the dirty, soot-covered pool only feet away. It looked like Eden to her. Alex forced himself into a crouching position.

"What are you doing?" she asked warily.

"Going to make a dash over there for a better shot. You two get Mark ready. When I go, run for the pool—and bring those blankets."

"In other words, you're going to draw their fire away from us." Judith picked up the fallen terrorist's gun. "Two diversions are better than one."

"Don't argue, damn it."

"Alex, your leg."

"Get ready," he ordered, brushing aside her protest. Bracing himself, Alexander Kidd was about to launch himself forward into a desperate, limping run when the entire Castle shook as if an earthquake had hit it. He fell face down into the courtyard. Across the way, Androssy raised his gun to fire but lost his balance, staggering backward. With a great, rending rumble, the entire tower slowly pulled itself away from the corner of the old fortress,

crashing in upon itself in a spectacular explosion of flame
and sparks that washed through the courtyard, carrying with
it the body of Page Shepard as it crushed the transmitter
shack below and swept it off the cliff in an avalanche of
stone and flaming wood to the waves below. Looking up
through the searing firestorm, Androssy watched the flaming beams snapping overhead as the entire ceiling began to
crumble in horrifying slow motion around him. Grabbing
Mark, Alex pulled him up and out as pieces of the west wall
tore loose and began to topple over the cliff, the rooms
behind collapsing one on top of the other like dominoes.
Staggering to his feet, Miklos Androssy ran unsteadily
toward the south gate. Almost there, he looked up. His cry
mixed with the sounds of the stone ceiling and flaming
rubble that screamed down upon him. With Mark in his
arms, Alex plunged into the black water of the pool. Below
in the city, watchers crossed themselves as the centuries-old
landmark atop the flaming hill disintegrated, sending a
column of fire and white-hot sparks shooting high into the
glowing sky.

"Almost like an atom bomb," a young intern said to the
nurse beside him as the two stared out of the hospital
window in fascination at the sight. The floor of the corridor
behind was filled with the weeping victims of the fire. "I
wonder," the intern mused, "if anyone up there got hurt."

"Oh, I doubt it," the nurse replied. "Only a fool
wouldn't have seen it coming."

CHAPTER 29

"I can't breathe."

"Judith, you *must* be able to breathe," Alex countered, "or else you wouldn't be talking." The two crouched in the shallow end of the reflecting pool holding Mark's head above the inky water. The blankets formed a wet tent over them. "How's he doing?" Kidd asked Dr. Evans.

"Not good. Still burning?"

Alex cautiously lifted a section of the cloth and peered out. "I think we're safe now." He sat back with a sigh of relief.

"Thank God. How long have we been under this thing?" Judith threw off their covering. "Oh, Alex," she gasped as she looked about her at the still-burning rubble of the place she did not recognize but knew had been her home.

"Steady." He pulled her closer.

She looked down and stroked her unconscious son's hair. Alex held her even closer, but she turned from him, her voice choked with tears. "They've killed him."

He reached for her chin and pulled it back toward him. "No one can hurt a Kidd," he said softly, intimately, "only another stupid, son-of-a-bitch, bastard Kidd."

"I love you, Alex," Judith said, looking directly into the blue eyes in the blackened face before her. "I always have, I always will."

Alex kissed her gently. "And I love you."

CHAPTER 30

The white hotel shimmered in the Moroccan sun, its surrounding gardens blooming in garish reds and yellows, a Technicolor contrast to the cool green lawns and trees surrounding the old structure of the colonial empire. A man and a woman walked across the outdoor terrace, he with a cane, she pushing a wheelchair. Settling at their shaded table, Alexander Kidd looked across the sparkling water of the Mediterranean, inhaling the warm salt air.

"You're really going to rebuild the Castle?" Mark asked, his voice frail but filled with enthusiasm.

"No," Alex replied, "you are."

His son looked at him uncertainly.

"Look, I'm the capitalist around here, remember? You're the punk kid artist," Alex said, a smile playing about his mouth. "I'll supply the cash, that's what I'm good at. You supply the talent. Isn't that what you said life was all about? Different ideas, different philosophies? I'm the Yankee Doodle Dandy, you're the thinking conscience." As he looked at his son, so much love welled up through him that Alexander Kidd had to blink back the tears. "That, my friend, is why we're going to make such a good team."

Judith looked away from father and son, quickly wiping both eyes with the back of her hand.

"You're plotting something," Mark Kidd said.

"No plot at all. It's just that if you're interested, there's a spot open for some cultured, Sorbonne-trained gent to put back together the pieces of a KWEN culture channel." Alex smiled. "From what I'm told, I don't have the patience or artistic temperament for it."

"KWEN? I thought you were out?"

"In the absence of a behind-the-scenes, titled puppeteer and the loss of a satellite, our dear ex-friends have come crawling back to your good old, reckless, run-off-at-the-mouth dad to pull their fat out of the fire. Interested in that job?"

"Before or after the Castle?" Mark asked.

"During. I don't want some lazy fuckhead on my staff."

"Does he ever let up?" the younger Kidd asked his mother.

"Never. You better make sure you know what you're getting into." Her voice lost its lightness. "Look," Judith pointed at the international *Herald-Tribune* on the table, "Baron Androssy failed to show up at the opening ceremonies of the World Banking Conference in London yesterday." She picked up the paper and read on: " '. . . and his sudden disappearance still remains a mystery to his associates and family.' "

"Let me see." Alex took the *Herald-Tribune* from her and studied the distinguished photograph of Baron Miklos Androssy. Then his eyes caught another headline farther down the page:

> RUSSIA REJOINS
> ARMS LIMITATION
> TALKS WITH U.S.

He showed it to them. "I can't imagine why," Kidd said with bitter sarcasm, looking up into the cloudless sky where Charon II had floated not so long ago. He sighed. "A lot of good people died to make it happen."

"How *did* you get out of Sandra's murder?" his son asked. "And General Carmody's? I thought all of Interpol and the FBI were after you."

"Thank your mother. Based on the information Androssy dropped at dinner the last night, they were able to grab

Page's friend, Helmut. He's asked for political asylum. It's all out in the open."

"Open?" Judith asked.

Alex nodded. "Perhaps it's better to say it's all back in the closet. Charon Two's magical powers, Acheron, poor Megaera and Tisiphone, they never existed."

"And Alecto?" she pressed.

"Oh, that bastard," Alex smiled. "Well, fortunately he's still around." He looked deep into Judith's eyes. "And he's going to stay around for a long time."

ALLEN DRURY

"Drury is a slick writer and knows the ingredients that go into the making of a bestseller."
—*West Coast Review of Books*

LEWIS PERDUE

THE TESLA BEQUEST
A secret society of powerful men have stolen the late Nikola
Tesla's plans for a doomsday weapon; they are just one step away
from ruling the world.
☐ 42027-7 THE TESLA BEQUEST $3.50

THE DELPHI BETRAYAL
From the depths of a small, windowless room in the bowels of
the White House, an awesome conspiracy to create economic
chaos and bring the entire world to its knees is unleashed.
☐ 41728-4 THE DELPHI BETRAYAL $2.95

QUEENS GATE RECKONING
A wounded CIA operative and a defecting Soviet ballerina hurtle
toward the hour of reckoning as they race the clock to circum-
vent twin assassinations that will explode the balance of power.
☐ 41436-6 QUEENS GATE RECKONING $3.50

THE DA VINCI LEGACY
A famous Da Vinci whiz, Curtis Davis, tries to uncover the truth
behind the missing pages of an ancient manuscript which could
tip the balance of world power toward whoever possesses it.
☐ 41762-4 THE DA VINCI LEGACY $3.50

CROSSFIRE

*The explosive action/adventure
imprint from Pinnacle Books...
the leader in
espionage and intrigue*